hand over fist

by

henry h. noyes

---

south end press   boston mass

Copyright © 1980 by Henry H. Noyes

Copyrights are still required for book production in the United States. However, in our case it is a disliked necessity Thus, any properly footnoted quotation of up to 500 sequential words may be used without permission, so long as the total number of words quoted does not exceed 2,000. For longer quotations or for greater volume of total words, authors should write for permission to South End Press.

Library of Congress No: 80-51041
ISBN:0-89608-025-0 paper
ISBN:0-89608-026-9 cloth

cover design by Peggy Lipschutz

Typeset by David Garrett, Greenfield, Mass.
Printed at Maple Press Co., York, Penn.
Publishing and production at South End Press, Boston

PART ONE

#1

In the afternoon the snow stopped and the sun came out over the city like a congealed yellow cloud. The temperature went down and down.

With a black shawl bound around her forehead and chin, a little old woman with glasses stumbled up the church steps in a great hurry to get out of the north wind. Her hands balled themselves energetically around the handle of the door. From its weight of wood and wrought iron, she was afraid for a moment she would not be able to open it, but slowly, all too slowly, the door began to move. She squeezed through the narrow opening.

In the huge darkness inside St. Joseph's, only the holy water fount glimmered. She plunged her fingers into the marble basin. What agony! It was freezing cold and the edge was rimmed with ice.

Was it this cold in Korea, she wondered. Or even colder?

"Oh Lord, spare my son!" She crossed herself and hastened up the aisle toward the altar.

The light from the high windows scarcely penetrated the darkness below. Only through the stained glass window, through the Savior on the cross, the last sun tumbled down in many colors on the gold of the altar cloth. The head of Jesus, the Son of Mary, was crowned with thorns. And pierced with golden nails, the hands of Jesus, the carpenter's son, were bleeding away the life blood of man.

As Kathryn Bianchi gazed up at the face in the stained glass, her eyes floated on a mist. She saw the face of her youngest son, twisted in pain, and his brown eyes wide and pleading. "Ma—" she could even imagine she heard the sound of his voice.

She bowed her head and knelt down on the altar step to pray, "Sancta Maria, it's terrible, the war." Even if every other mother's son came back home alive from the Yalu River, something would happen to her Luigi.

The bells in the tower startled Kathryn as they gave out the four o'clock hour with four solemn dongs of the big bell and a flutter of excitement among the small bells like a flock of doves passing through the belfry. The bells reverberated deep within her heart of fear. For two months of endless days and nights, no word had come from her son. Luigi was full of life when she had last seen him, but in her fear she could only think of him coming home in a flag draped casket—or worse, alive in a basket.

As the last reverberation trembled away through the twilight, the caretaker came out of the vestry to light the candles near the altar. It seemed darker to Kathryn than before. And the intense little lights of the candles, burning like stars in a bed of artificial roses and foliage, made tears swell in her eyes.

In the midst of the holy garden sat Mary cradling her child in her arms. Sheep lay peacefully watching them. "Oh Holy Mother of God!" Mary would understand what it was to have a son in that frozen waste around the other side of the world. "You gotta bring him back home to me alive," Kathryn pleaded. "He's done some crazy things, I know. But he's a good boy." Kathryn's eyes were so filled with tears, she did not see the young priest come out of the vestry and bow his head in her direction. She could only see her son sprawled in a great white plain with his limbs awkwardly stiff from the cold. "Twenty-five is too young to die," she prayed. "Save him, Mother. I got plans for him. You must do this for me!" she spoke out hysterically.

"Mother Bianchi—" The priest's voice quieted her. It was a voice from an eastern seminary, cultured and pitched to lift her from a mood of anguish, a young voice. "We must have more confidence." He raised her from the cold altar steps.

Father Antonelli was half Kathryn's age, only a few years older than Luigi himself. It seemed strange to be calling him

Father. He had a round full face with pale olive complexion, penetrating but detached eyes, a large forehead, and shining black hair. He had only come to the parish two months before and he was already so popular that people were whispering: One day Father Antonelli will be a bishop, perhaps even a cardinal.

Kathryn drew her shawl back on her head, brushed away her tears and freshened her eyes with her handkerchief. She didn't want to give the young priest the impression that she was an hysterical old woman. Nonetheless, she looked ghost-like with prominent cheek and jaw bones, and a thin face surrounded by a shroud of iron grey hair streaked with white. "But Father," she complained, "we haven't heard from Luigi for two whole months. Before the bad news about retreat."

"Is it strange in such circumstances that you haven't heard?" His tone dulled the sharp edge of her fear. "There are many security regulations."

Father Antonelli put his hand graciously on her shoulder. "Mother, we must have more faith." It was a criticism. "We must overcome our pride and ambition even for our children. In moderation, good. But in excess, even fear for their safety—" He shrugged very slightly as if debating with himself. "These are temptations, set in a mother's path. We must believe—"

"But Luigi's my favorite son, Father." Kathryn had to make him understand. "Carlo, my oldest, he's a disappointment. Georgi, he's moved to San Francisco," she sighed. "And Della's married. I have only my Luigi left—in my old age."

"You love him very deeply?" The priest's eyes were trying to penetrate the depth of her feeling.

"How can you ask? He's a good boy, Father, generous. Everybody thinks he's OK. Maybe he's done some crazy things—" She stopped because there was no need to defend Luigi.

"Yes, I've heard about your son," said Father Antonelli with his little smile of irony.

Kathryn was full of anxiety. What had he heard? Only two months ago the young priest had come from the east, and already he seemed to know everything. No doubt he'd heard about the parade St. Joseph's day, the time Lou and the Angelino boys stripped the contributions from the statue of the saint in the fieldhouse before returning him to his niche in the church. Or the night Luigi brought two colored kids to the bingo game in the church basement—one of them a girl. Or the time Luigi and his gang got mixed up with the law and had to go to juvenile court. There was no end of stories Father Guidarello must have told him by this time. What hadn't he heard about Luigi? The boy never came to confession and only once in a great while to mass.

"You must talk to Luigi when he comes back home," Kathryn urged. "Father Guidarello is an old saint already. How can he understand? But if you tell Luigi to come to mass, he will listen to somebody near his own age."

Father Antonelli brushed off her criticism of his senior with a slight frown, but his eyes were amused. "I will talk to your son when he comes home."

"I hope—" Kathryn began.

But the father interrupted with a glance at his wristwatch. "You want a special novena to preserve your son in life and health?"

"Yes, Father, that's good." Kathryn reached into her purse and drew out a folded ten dollar bill. It still seemed a lot of money. Maybe five would have been enough. But why should she short change the chances of her favorite son?

"We are poor folks—" she said shrewdly with a side glance at the priest. "But we give what we can."

Father Antonelli accepted the contribution and mounted the altar steps while Kathryn retired to the first pew. As she listened to him intone the Latin words of the prayer, she could believe that Luigi would come back alive from Korea. Father Antonelli had raised her up from despair itself. She could listen all night to his sonorous inflections.

But as hope filled her heart, an old anger began to pound again. She had planned for Luigi to be a priest. He was full of energy and spirit, the smartest of all her children. He had some brains, Luigi. He was stubborn, too. Once he set his mind to a thing, it got done. But he never would set his mind to his school work. How many thousand times had she tried to call him away from a ball game in the little park across from their house to do his homework? And, in the end, what good was all the scolding? He ran with the gangs. He organized baseball leagues, basketball, football—it made her dizzy to remember what all—for the church or park district, it didn't seem to matter to Luigi, as long as he was getting the boys together. And it didn't seem to matter much to him if they were good Catholic boys or the others, even colored. After all her scolding, he never did learn more than *amo, amas, amat* in Latin.

It was a misery for Kathryn to think about these things, how his grades got worse and worse in high school until he dropped out and went to work with his dad in the factory. Lying, too, that he was eighteen when he was only sixteen, so that he could get a job. And his pa had covered up for him—shamelessly. After all her plans for him, Luigi had become a machinist, slaving with his hands week in and week out in a factory, talking about the men and the union in big words and coming home with a nickel raise in his pocket once a year. That was what his father wanted for him as if he'd learned nothing himself in sixty-five years.

Luigi was stubborn like Pete. It could be him up there saying the mass, Kathryn reflected bitterly. In an eastern seminary her Luigi, too, could have learned to intone the Latin like Father Antonelli. And important people in the community would be whispering about her son: One day he'll be a bishop, maybe even a cardinal. And Luigi never would have been drafted to serve in a war so far around the other side of the world it was day over there when it was night in Chicago.

Kathryn was so full of ambition for her son, that even to think about his stubbornness was enough to make her heart beat fast. "Oh God, change my Luigi. Take the stubbornness out of him. Make him—" She stopped. It was perhaps blasphemy to speak to the Lord the way she was doing, half in entreaty, half in command. She became aware that Father Antonelli had finished praying and was moving down the steps toward her. He paused to kneel in front of Mary and her child. "A brave mother—" was all Kathryn could hear him say. Suddenly, she felt very proud and happy. And as the young priest took her arm firmly and guided her down the church aisle, she was no longer afraid for her son's life.

"Father, when my boy comes home you must help me. I have plans for him. No more slave in the factory with his hands all day like his father."

"Plans?"

Answering his question would lead Kathryn on to saying things she didn't want to admit to the father. He would think she was rich. She had worn a scarf and her old cloth coat on purpose, leaving her new hat and persian lamb coat hanging in her bedroom closet. So she nodded in answer and kept quiet.

The priest's hand closed on the great knob as he opened the door. A sweep of wind blew in and the nearby street lamp flecked a cold light on his face. Kathryn pulled her shawl around her head and chin, anxious to rush off home. But Father Antonelli, standing bareheaded in the blast of wind, still held her arm.

"You are a practical woman, Mother Bianchi." He spoke with an urgency that made Kathryn instantly reserved. "I hear you made six thousand dollars last year on that tenement in Pioneer Street you rent to colored people."

"That much, on that old building?" she countered. "Father, somebody has been telling you stories."

"The amount isn't the important thing, but the need. We are proceeding with plans for a new school so that the children and grandchildren will have a Christian education. And we must think of the newcomers, too—how to influence them to find the right path."

"Maybe it's good money wasted on colored," she complained. She knew he was talking about the Negro families moving into the community as family after family of her own people sold their houses and moved into other parishes.

"We have to face the reality, mother. Three quarters of the world's people are colored. Soon it may be the same in our own community. Should we abandon the holy mission of the church, or should we learn that the soul of a man is more important than the color of his skin?" The young priest spoke to Kathryn with an earnestness that made her feel ashamed, for a moment.

Slowly she reached into her purse again, protecting its contents from the wind. "Public school was good enough for my children," she couldn't help complaining as she handed him a ten dollar bill.

As she hurried down the steps into the street, she barely heard Father Antonelli calling after her, "May God bless you, Mother Bianchi, and bring your son home safe—and soon!"

#2

Kathryn gathered her great black shawl about her head, leaving a slit for her eyes, as she headed into the north wind. It was a sin to be angry with Father Antonelli, especially since he had said the mass to save her son's life. Next time, all the same, she would bring only one ten dollar bill in her purse.

The thought of money reminded her that the Robertses who occupied a basement flat in her tenement in Pioneer Street owed her two weeks back rent, forty dollars, twice over what she'd given to Father Antonelli. They were the ones to be angry with. Geneva Roberts had put her off with the excuse that her husband was hurt in an accident at the steel mill. Maybe it was true, but more than likely he had blown the money at the tavern.

At every step Kathryn's resentment grew. That sister who lived with the Robertses was able to pay if she wanted. But Anna Mae Green had an insolent manner. Because she was a practical nurse and wore a uniform, she thought she was somebody important. It was a shame, when all the other tenants paid their rent and seemed grateful to have a place to live.

The wind clutched down at Kathryn from a bitter sky. A green zero light in the west was all that was left of the day. People who passed her on the way home from work were hunched over to protect themselves, their eyes fixed on the frozen, treacherous surfaces of the walks. Most of the faces she passed were black or brown. Only a few whites still lived in that block.

With the light in the sky and the darkness in the street and the light in the windows, the decay of the slum was blotted out. The snow blanketed the roofs, loaded down the rotting windowsills and held every pane of glass in a white frame. The garbage cans looked like snowmen bunched together.

Above the two-story frame houses, old derelicts with new faces of shingle, red brick tenements shouldered up three stories into the sky. They all seemed to have been built from the same plan, with bay windows and high gabled roofs overhanging the sidewalk. The stone work under the windows was constructed to last for generations, but the bricks were already crumbling.

From a block away, Kathryn could already distinguish her building because it had a diagonal crack across its face patched up with white mortar. It was a sight to make her heart leap with pleasure, a gold mine producing two hundred forty dollars in rent every Friday—when all the tenants paid up. And the Robertses would have to pay or move, that was definite. Maybe it would be better if they moved. That Anna Mae Green was a troublemaker.

Kathryn stepped forward aggressively into the alley, slowed down by the side entrance to her building, cautiously turned the door handle. Going down the basement steps in the dark appealed to her less and less. On the brightest days, she felt like a stranger when she went inside, even though it was her property. All her tenants were Negroes. Behind their surface politeness, she never knew what they were thinking. They were a different kind of people, that was all. But at night, it was a thousand times worse. Every step down to the basement creaked under Kathryn's slight weight as if in pain. It was dark beyond belief and the darkness seemed to be filled with drawn knives. She groped her way back along the corridor till she saw the light under the Roberts' door. A clothes rope almost strangled her like fingers reaching around her throat.

She knocked feebly, gasping for breath. The opening door flooded light out into the basement and made Kathryn blink and step back. "What is it you want, ma'am?"

Kathryn marvelled at the poise of Mrs. Roberts. "What is it I want?" Kathryn herself was afraid, mad, and out of breath, while Geneva Roberts stared at her with polite indifference. For a woman in a crowded basement room with four children and somebody sleeping in a bed, she had remarkable self-possession. If she'd had a white skin, she would have looked like one of the Madonnas in the church. With her curly headed kid at her breast, she made Kathryn think for a moment of Mary with her child and the sheep crouched around. Was it true, what the priest said, that the soul of a person was more important than the color of her skin? It was truer, in any case, what her son-in-law kept telling her, that she couldn't make money and friends out of the same people.

"You know what I want, Mrs. Roberts. And I'm gonna tell you for the last time. Forty bucks!" She spoke more sharply than she intended. But the words were out and she'd have to stand by what she said. "Forty dollars, please," she repeated in a softer voice.

The little boy was pushing his train in the space between the bed and the stove, and the baby went on holding and nudging his mother's breast as if everything was the way it should be. But the two girls were old enough to stand staring at Kathryn with eyes full of fear and resentment because she was talking to their mother in a tone only white people used.

Geneva glanced over at the bed. "We been waitin' on Mr. Roberts' accident insurance. They promised they was gonna send it out this week. Like I said, he was hurt real bad."

It was impossible for Kathryn to tell who was lying there, Mr. Roberts or some one else. When people didn't pay the rent, somebody was always hurt bad or somebody's mother was dead down south. How did she know he really was hurt at the steel mill? Maybe that was him lying there drunk.

"You said your sister gets paid today," Kathryn's tone of reminder cut like a knife.

"Anna Mae's late home tonight." Geneva spoke wearily as if she hoped Kathryn would have the good sense to go along home.

"Well, if you folks think you can live rent free, you're gonna do it in somebody else's building. That ain't the way I'm running things around here, Geneva Roberts. And you can tell Anna Mae that, too." There was something defiant in the way Geneva stared back that made Kathryn raise her voice. "And you tell your sister to stop making trouble, understand? She's been telling Mrs. Osborne the rent's too high and who all I don't know. I only charge like everybody else."

"My sister don't make nobody trouble." Geneva's tone was a warning to Kathryn that she could run her mouth against anybody else she wanted, but not against Anna Mae.

Was that any way for a black woman to talk? Kathryn was owner here, not Geneva Roberts or Anna Mae Green. "You must be crazy!" she shouted.

Geneva made no attempt to defend herself, but she stood staring at Kathryn as if she must be the crazy one. In the silence they both could hear the basement steps creak under rapid feet. "Auntie Mae!" said the oldest girl. The blankness went out of the children's faces. "Auntie Mae!" the younger girl whispered with a new hope. The little boy stopped running his train and smiled. The oldest girl darted past Kathryn to open the door.

"Who's crazy?" Anna Mae stopped in the doorway. "Oh, it's you, Mrs. Biomchi!" She pretended surprise and winked at the two girls to tell them no landlady was going to frighten them or her, it didn't matter what she shouted or how loud.

"Don't even get my name straight," Kathryn muttered. "Now look here, Mae Green, if you think the rent's too high like you told your sister—"

Anna Mae was wearing white shoes and stockings which looked ghostly against the darkness. But it was the smile shaping up in her eyes that made Kathryn stop in the middle of what she was saying. It was an insolent smile and she stood deliberately blocking off the doorway. She was a short woman with big rough looking hands, a bold face spotted with freckles, large lips and a sharp confident voice. But it was her eyes, even more than her physical strength that made Kathryn afraid.

Most colored people had dark eyes. But Anna Mae's were an amber color, lighter even than Della's, the color of the eyes of a tigress.

As Anna Mae closed the door, Kathryn edged around her until she could grip the knob. Then her confidence seeped back into her throat. "You could get out and get a cheaper place any time you wanted."

Anna Mae held out her hand to the baby long enough to let him grab her little finger. "Ain't no places," she whispered as if even the baby would understand that. She threw her nurse's coat over the foot of the bed, then turned back to tell Kathryn, "You folks know that. You got 'em all bought up."

Kathryn had to strain her ears to understand what Anna Mae was saying. She was cunning, Anna Mae, but still only an ignorant peasant woman from Mississippi. Let her throw her weight around and pretend she was somebody, when all the time she was only a practical nurse. She didn't even need to know reading and writing to handle a bedpan. Kathryn's fear of her melted away. "If it's the same rent everywhere, what you got to be so crabby about?"

"We done crabbing." Anna Mae's expression toughened. "Now we gonna get back all what you overcharged since we been livin' down in this old piece of rat hole."

It was an empty threat, maybe, but what she said stirred a fear at the back of Kathryn's memory. When she first bought the house, her son-in-law who handled the deal, Anselmo, had told her there was an old law on the books about overcharging. At the same time he'd said there was nothing to worry about because the law was hardly ever enforced. But what if Anna Mae had found out about it?

"I know you got paid today." Because of her own uncertainty Kathryn spoke in a loud voice. "You gonna pay the forty bucks you owe?"

But Anna Mae didn't intimidate. "When I get my check cashed round at the store." She let Kathryn know with a smile that it was one of those things she would get around to doing when she was good and ready.

"You better make it soon!" Kathryn slammed the door, but she couldn't shut out her fears. What was it Anselmo had said about overcharging?

She was no longer aware of the bitter cold. As she gripped the rail to climb the basement stairs, the sweat came out on the palm of her hands.

#3

Kathryn had only one thought in mind as she hurried across the little park: to unburden her worries on Anselmo the moment she could reach her telephone. When she entered her own street, however, she began to calm down. Why should she let an ignorant peasant woman knock the bottom out of her confidence?

In Hemlock Street the faces were familiar to Kathryn. It was a relief to exchange good evening in Italian and feel she was a woman of importance among her own people.

"Evening, Katerina," Maria Ferrucini called out in her hearty way. Hatless and coatless, she stood at the front door of 758 peering down in the direction of Pagliani's tavern. Under the neon light they could both see a man weaving his way home and they both knew it was Tony Ferrucini.

"Tony!" Maria shouted in a voice that rose skyhigh like a fire engine siren. "Wino," she complained to Kathryn. "Some day he drink himself to death." She made a gesture with her fingers as if she could wring his neck. "See if I care."

"What can you do?" Kathryn shook her head as if her problems were the same as Maria's. "All down the drain."

"But you buy your house," said Maria with a bitter shrug. The old tenement she'd lived in for thirty-five years towered above her in the dark. She'd raised her family here, seven sons and two daughters, and now all she had to show for her life was a drunken husband staggering home at the day's end. "All down the sewer, you said it. Now they send Mario out to Korea, that's finish."

"What can you do?" Kathryn repeated, all the time thanking God under her breath that her Pete was not like Tony. For years, he had passed the tavern, even on payday, without boozing away a cent so that they could pay off the mortgage. Under the street light, the Bianchi house looked clean and neat with its brown shingle rippling to the gabled roof. It was the smartest house on the street, and anybody could see from the brass knocker on the door and the brown and green striped porch that it was owned, not rented.

Impulsively, Kathryn put her arms around Maria, her oldest friend in America. "One day, maybe—" But what she was going to say was suddenly forgotten. "My God!" she yelled. "Where we're standing! It's unlucky. It's where they shot Anselmo's father!"

Maria shrugged as if it made no difference to her, but Kathryn rushed on into her own house. It was bad luck. Back in prohibition days, Anselmo's father was machine-gunned from a car on the very spot where she and Maria were standing, on one of those warm summer nights when the kids were roller-skating in the street and the young fellows were playing poker on a box under the street lights. Anselmo Senior used to come and go at nights, glancing up and down the street with eyes that ferreted into every corner and behind every post and tree. All the same, they mowed him down.

Nervously, Kathryn jabbed her fingers in the dial holes and waited for Anselmo to come to the phone. She was still remembering how she'd taken Lou and Della, who were only babies, into the house when the shooting began. But Carlo and Georgi ran out again. When the ambulance men finally came, they counted eighteen slug holes.

It was a frightening memory for Kathryn. She was glad to forget about it when she heard her daughter's voice on the phone. Della sounded affectionate until she found out what her mother wanted. "Ma, I told you never to call Gene at home on business," she said in the cold and formal tone she used with strangers. "Call him at the office tomorrow, please!"

"But it's something I have to talk to him about tonight. It's an emergency."

"OK, then," said Della as if her mother could be making a fool of them both. "But it had better be pretty important—"

Kathryn began to wait with a bitter feeling at heart. Now that Della was married to Anselmo and lived on Lake Shore Drive in a ten-room penthouse apartment, she treated her mother like a servant, with all the borrowed airs and manners of a society woman.

It was winning a beauty contest sponsored by the Italian Hour that had changed Della's whole life. Before that she was a nobody, a stenographer working in Anselmo's front office. The office manager who was twenty years her senior always ran her down to Anselmo. But he suddenly began to take an interest in Della when her picture appeared in all the papers.

By nature Della was reserved. Her mother's voluble temper had driven her to consult her own thoughts and say very little around home. In the past few years before her marriage, she had lived in the Bianchi house like a boarder. Only when Kathryn manoeuvered her into Anselmo's office did mother and daughter begin to plan a campaign together. The winning of the beauty contest led to victory.

As soon as Anselmo began to date her, she quit her job in his office. Her appearance on a national TV hook-up to receive the thousand dollar prize built up her prestige tremendously in the Italian American communities. Everybody knew the name of Della Bianchi. And when she went the rounds of the night clubs with Anselmo, fans crowded their table to admire her beauty and slap Anselmo on the back.

With Anselmo, Della didn't have to play hard to get. She was that way by nature. She refused to go to his apartment alone with him and on one occasion used her elbow against him when he tried to get too possessive. Step by step mother and daughter discussed the moves and countermoves which finally led to the engagement party and two months later to the exchange of rings at the altar steps in the cathedral.

Since her marriage two years previously, Della had become little more than a voice on the telephone to her mother. Kathryn hadn't seen her or Anselmo for more than two months, nor had she been up to their apartment more than a couple of times, and then only in the morning when Anselmo was down at the office.

Kathryn waited anxiously for her son-in-law to come to the phone. He had a way of keeping her waiting. She knew he did it on purpose to show her what a big shot he was. Still, she was lucky to have him for a son-in-law. He knew everything about the rent business and he made money out of anything he touched. After his father's death, he had finished up at law school and gone into partnership with an old lawyer who died a few years later and left him his practice. During the second World War, he wangled a commission as major in the Real Estate Division of the Corps of Engineers and was able privately to branch out into real estate. Since then, his business had mushroomed. How many buildings he owned or managed even Della probably didn't know—or at least wouldn't tell her mother.

"Emergency, mama?" When Anselmo finally came to the phone, his tone was cheerful but crisp. Before Kathryn had half-finished pouring out her fears, he cut her off. "I explained the risk to you before you bought that building, remember? How if we charged the tenants rent ceiling prices we'd go bankrupt," he explained in a clear cut business tone. "You figure that basement apartment would be listed at say six or eight bucks down at the rent control office, and you're charging—?"

"Twenty," Kathryn whispered tensely.

"OK, then. Supposing this Green woman gets a lawyer to look up the rent ceiling and enter a triple damage suit against you—"

"Then I'm ruined? Oh, Anselmo, what can I do?"

"Mama mia," Anselmo laughed. "Let a little grass grow. We're just supposing. When she actually files suit will be soon enough to worry. By the way, you haven't given her receipts?"

"No, you told me never to sign nothing."

"That's using your head, mama. So what are you afraid of?"

"That Green woman, Anselmo. She looks at me savage, with those eyes—it's dark down there in that basement."

"Don't go down alone, then. Take papa!"

"He don't want no part of it."

Anselmo paused a moment, then said, "Try that Boatman over at Pagliani's. He's an ex-prizefighter. And if there's any problem we'll get you a rod."

"A gun?" Kathryn took fright again.

"Mama mia!" laughed Anselmo. "You worry too much. Everything's gonna be all right." The cheer in his voice was reassuring. "Now I've got something more important to talk to you about. I was going to give you a buzz tomorrow. A sweet little deal right in your own street—number 758."

"But that's Ferrucinis!" Already Kathryn could hear Maria's siren of a voice rising against her the morning the mailman delivered the notice to vacate. "You mean we should move out Ferrucini's?"

"Then we can remodel." Anselmo had no time for objections. "Instead of six families at fifteen dollars a month, we can put in twenty at twenty dollars a week. And we can get around the triple damage business. Once we remodel, understand, the rent ceiling goes off. That's what we should have done at 1250. Then this Green woman wouldn't be able to cause us any trouble."

"But Trombatores, Lapiaglis—" Kathryn began to worry out

loud. Their children and grandchildren had been born in that building. "Thirty-five years—"

"So what?" Anselmo cut her off. "It's time they all moved anyway; you and papa, too. That neighborhood's running down at the heels. Leave it for the niggers."

Anselmo's proposition didn't sound so bad after Kathryn had a moment to think about it. It was time they moved, that was for certain. With twenty Negro families at twenty bucks a week, Bianchi's could live up by Lincoln Park like the Anselmos. "You wanta talk about it," said Kathryn with sudden enthusiasm, "come and bring Della for supper tomorrow. How about it?" she urged.

Anselmo hesitated which was a hopeful sign. For two years he'd turned down all her invitations point blank. But his hesitation was brief. "Sorry, mama, I'm busy tomorrow."

"What about day after, then?" Kathryn began to scold him lightly, "You promised me Anselmo, ever since you been married."

"Honest to God, mama, I'm head over heels. Can't you come to the office?"

"Have a heart, Generoso," she said with deepening disappointment.

"Well OK, mama," he yielded with a good deal of charity in his tone. "But I'll have to eat and run. That's life."

"So you go along when you have to and leave Della by me." A conversation with Anselmo left Kathryn feeling excited and frustrated at the same time. He was always the first to put down the receiver and he didn't even ask about Lou. The maddening thing about Anselmo was his perfect friendliness and indifference.

A sudden bar of light yellowed across the front room from the kitchen. Kathryn heard the back door close and jumped up from her desk. She had forgotten all about her husband's supper.

#4

Kathryn couldn't wait for Pete to hang up his jacket and kick his boots into the corner to tell him her wonderful news. "They're coming for supper, Anselmo and Della, day after tomorrow. Ain't that the best ever!"

"And Luigi?" he asked. When she shook her head, he breathed heavily with disappointment, "Sixty-one days we don't hear!"

"What I'm telling you, Pete—" Kathryn was irritated at the way Pete ignored her announcement. "Anselmo is coming for supper. *Capice?* For the first time!"

"Anselmo," Pete muttered. His eyes seemed squeezed upward between his high cheek bones and his heavy white eyebrows from worry and fatigue. There was a time when he used to smile at his wife when he came home from work and she brought the homemade wine out of the pantry. That was before Lou went overseas or Della became engaged to Anselmo. Now all he heard about when he came home worn out from nine hours bending and packing and taking orders from the superintendent was Anselmo and the rent business. Half the time, like this evening, his supper wasn't ready and he had to go to the pantry to pour out his own glass of wine.

Kathryn's irritation with Pete increased as she watched him sit down at her table without even going to the sink to wash up. In her kitchen everything had a mirror surface: the spotless oilcloth matched the red and white checked curtains and a bright linoleum. "Just once, Pete," she scolded, "maybe you wear street clothes to work, leave them old overalls by Farmway."

"OK, OK," he said. It wasn't worth an argument. "Sixty-one days," he muttered to himself. He shook the snow off his newspaper and spread it out on the table.

"We ain't seen them for two months," Kathryn was angry with Pete now. "You don't care!"

"Anselmo wanta see us?" Pete looked up at Kathryn with suspicion that gathered in the lines of his face and collected in the depths of his eyes. He was late home from the union meeting, the supper wasn't ready yet, he was hungry, and all she could do was talk about Anselmo. "What he want this time?"

Kathryn was too angry at Pete to give him an answer. She moved swiftly around the kitchen preparing supper. When she could trust her voice, she complained, "You better quit by Farmway, Pete. You ain't human to live with no more. With rent money coming in steady—"

"When I quit, I'm gonna be dead."

"Did you get that raise you been talking about since Luigi went into the army?" she shot out at him on the offensive.

Pete hesitated to answer. "Maybe yes, maybe no. Maybe it's the boss—maybe it's Washington—maybe it's both in the bed together." Pete twisted around in his chair to find a more comfortable position. His back ached from the day's work. "Dougherty says—"

"That Dougherty, he's a no good," Kathryn interrupted him scornfully. "How many times do I have to tell you? Three bucks a month down the drain. You got a no good union."

What was the use of the same old argument? "When Luigi comes back home, things are gonna be different again," he muttered with some satisfaction. The wine was beginning to lighten the fatigue and Pete's habitual smile came out again as he thought of his son coming home. "When Luigi goes back on the committee, then we gonna see."

"When Luigi comes home, I got plans for him," she countered. "No more slave with his hands all day." It was another familiar argument. Pete didn't even raise his head until she went on to say, "Anselmos got a new deal for us. Right in our own block."

So that was it. Pete knew Anselmo wouldn't be coming out of love for his father- and mother-in-law. "Hemlock Street?" he asked.

"758," she answered him sharply.

"By Tony's?" Pete shook his head. Anselmo would advise her to clear out the whole building and put in Negro tenants. All his old friends would have to move. "Tell him it's no go. Ferrucinis lived there thirty-five years like us here. Fiuccis, Dombardos—"

When Anselmo had told Kathryn about 758, her reaction was the same as Pete's. But now it made her angry to be reminded of her own fears. "Time they moved. Time we all moved out of this slum," she snapped. "Rent it to the niggers."

"That's what Anselmo tells you?" Pete asked. When Kathryn didn't choose to answer, Pete went back to reading his newspaper with a frown of disgust.

It was quiet in the kitchen for a few minutes. On the shelf above the table, the old Italian clock ticked out the seconds. It was an heirloom, the only object of value Kathryn had brought over from the old country. Why was Pete so opposed to everything she wanted? It was terrible. In the old days they had wanted everything together. They had saved every penny to buy the house on Hemlock Street and only three years ago they'd had a big party to celebrate the burning of the mortgage. Pete had grumbled about borrowing money to buy 1250, but he'd gone along and even signed the papers. And he and Lou had done minor repairs on the building before the boy went overseas. But since then he had grumbled about everything.

If only Lou would come back home, things would be all right again. Then Pete would be like before, the way he was when she first knew him.

The ticking of the old zodiac clock took her back in memory to her father's store in Valone. When she was a girl, the clock used to stand on her father's desk in the alcove where she would sit making entries in his account book with a round school girl hand. How the pendulum, shaped like a half-moon cupping a star, reminded her of the afternoons lengthening out until Pete would finally stick his head through the window. He was a ruddy faced lad then from working all day in the fields. Kathryn sighed as she remembered how dark and curly his hair was and how his brown eyes dared her to come out under the trees. And sometimes, when the sun was going down, they would climb up the hill above the village to gaze down the valley toward Palermo and the west.

In Sicily a peasant was always a peasant. His children slept like pigs on the straw in the corner. But in America—?

They began to save money. Her father was sometimes drunk and generous . . . .

"Pete," Kathryn said in a tone of affection, "when the boy comes home, things will be different, eh?"

While Pete was eating, she hopped around her kitchen like a bird in a familiar cage. Her dark eyes moved like beads behind her glass prisms as she attended to his needs.

With the years she had grown angular, unlike many Sicilian women who grew stout and filled the doorways on Hemlock Street. But with Kathryn there was not a spare ounce of flesh on her anywhere. Her skin was drawn tautly over her cheek bones. Her grey hair was streaked with white and already thin over the forehead. She wore it clipped and curled.

"Pete, when Luigi comes home, ain't he gonna be surprised how we fixed up everything? Paint his room like Anselmo's office—green and brown, eh? What you think?"

Kathryn was just sitting down to begin her own supper, when there was a sound at the door more timid than a knock. The door handle rattled as if a cat was trying to paw it open.

Kathryn opened up cautiously and found herself blinking at the lights of the house in the next street. When she looked down she saw the eyes of two Negro children staring up at her. "Mama said—" the taller child began to blurt out, then stopped. The other merely stared into the kitchen at Pete eating his supper.

"Come on in and stop freezing the house," Kathryn yelled. "Nobody's gonna eat you." She was annoyed at the Roberts kids for coming just as she was sitting down to enjoy her supper. She took a sealed letter which the older girl handed to her. As she tore open the envelope, she noticed that Pete was handing out slices of pizza to the two girls. The elder took a piece and wolfed it, but the younger one kept her hands behind her back.

"Honeys," Pete was saying playfully, "ain't you the bad girls to come out without your coats. Your mama will whip you."

The older sister, Charlene, had a woman's shawl wrapped around her shoulders. Randy, the younger, was wearing a thread-bare sweater a few sizes too small. Her lips were white with cold and she was shivering.

"Ain't got no coats," said Charlene. That ought to be plain to white folks, her tone said. Her braids stood out at a stubborn angle. She wasn't afraid of Pete. When she'd finished her slice of pizza, her eyes went hunting in the pantry where the colored labels of a hundred cans shone down at her from the shelves. There were also dozens of spice shakers and cartons of spaghetti—food-a-plenty.

Pete handed her the pizza which Randy had refused. "Ain't got no coats?" he asked in surprise. Upstairs in the cedar chest in Luigi's room were plenty of coats, boys' coats, of course, but what did that matter when the temperature was down to zero?

Kathryn saw Pete go up the backstairs and heard the floor boards creak as he went into the front room. What's he up to, she wondered as she put two ten dollar bills back into the envelope folded it across and then, doubling it securely, handed it back to Charlene. "Take this back to your mama. Tell her it's forty she owes, not twenty, and she knows it."

Charlene stood holding the envelope at arm's length. "My Auntie Mae said you had to give us a receipt."

"A receipt?" Kathryn's voice went skyhigh as she remembered what Anselmo had said about receipts and triple damage suits. "You tell your Auntie Mae," said Kathryn icily controlling her anger, "since she don't want to pay the rent, she'd best find another place to live before I put you all out on the street."

The younger child burst into tears and ran out the door. but Charlene stared at Kathryn angrily before following her sister.

When Pete came down the stairs, he was surprised to find the kids gone already.

"Imagine, they want receipts now!" Kathryn exploded. "How do you like that? They wanta live rent free. He's drunk all the time, that's why he can't get out of bed and go to work like any decent person." She paused as her eyes caught the bundle under Pete's arm. From the navy blue, the brass buttons, and the red lining, she recognized one of the coats that Luigi wore when he was a kid. "What you got there, Pete?"

"The girls don't have no coats," he answered. "Son-of-a-bitch, cold," he muttered as he shuffled across the kitchen to put on his cap and jacket.

"But Pete, you don't understand. That Geneva and Anna Mae, they're trying to ruin us. They want to be boss down there. I can't have it. Understand, it's them or me." She was ready to cry from exasperation. "And you want to give them Luigi's coats!"

"Get a night cap by Pagliani's," said Pete quietly heading for the door with the coats pressed under his arm.

"Give 'em to anybody, Holy Mother of God, Pete, but not *them*. Anselmo said—"

Pete's eyes narrowed at the mention of Anselmo. "Luigi would give them the coats," he interrupted. "The boy has a heart."

Pete opened the door and went out while Kathryn shouted in the empty room, "Paisan! I ain't got a heart, too?"

#5

When the two children fled from the Bianchi kitchen, the wind at their backs whipped them across the little park. They ran so fast they were out of breath, panting hot and cold at the same time.

"I'm froze," sobbed Randy who could run no more. "Charlene, will she put us right out in the snow?"

"Didn't she say?" Charlene scolded as if Randy needn't be a big cry baby and make things worse. She took her by the arm and rushed her down the last block. "Our ma will be mad, you wait."

"And what about Auntie Mae?"

They turned into the cramped little alley, slipped through the door that never completely closed, and clattered down the basement steps.

"Now you hush, Randy. If you wake papa, you'll get a bad whippin'!"

Charlene turned the knob cautiously and tiptoed into their room. She handed the folded envelope to her mother and whispered, "If we can't paid it all, she don't want none." Then she said in a louder voice to her Aunt Mae, "She wouldn't give me no receipt. And you know what, Auntie, she's gonna put us out on the street we don't move—right out in the snow."

Randy, standing timidly by the door, nodded. Her eyes were large and brilliant and full of fear. Her voice was like a kitten's. "That's what she say."

Geneva unfolded the envelope and handed the two ten dollar bills to Mae. "What's wrong with that old grab bag?" Mae asked in a rising voice. Her brother-in-law turned over heavily. His arm flung out across the blanket and sagged over the edge of the bed to the floor.

For a moment there was silence except for the hissing of the burners on the stove. The walls sweated from the damp heat. The flicker of blue light danced on the ceiling and threw a shadowed haze over the room. The baby slept on a blanket at his father's feet. The little brother, his head sagging backwards, had fallen asleep in Mae's arm.

She slipped him under the blanket. "You ready for bed, too, Randy?"

"We want our supper," Charlene answered for her.

Mae looked at the two ten dollar bills balled up in Geneva's hand, then smiled. "You want some smelts, baby?" she asked Charlene. She put on her coat over her nurse's dress. She was still wearing white stockings and shoes.

"You promised you'd fry us an ol' chicken some day. Ain't that enough money?"

"Smelts," Mae repeated. "What you dreamin', child, about chicken! We rich folk?"

While Mae was away at the store, Randy asked her mother, "Will she put us out in the street for real just like she say?"

Geneva took Randy in one arm and Charlene in the other. "Don't ask me what them white folks won't do. But don't let it fear you none, either. The Lord made your pa and me and your Auntie Mae to look after you and little brother and the baby and bring you up to grown folks. And that's what we're gonna do."

Randy looked up into her mother's full large eyes. Her expression was angry and firm and loving at the same time. And with her smooth black hair parted over her forehead and coiled at her neck, she seemed very beautiful and very determined. Randy's fingers reached up to touch, then to stroke her mother's hair.

That old witch, Geneva muttered to herself, angry and hopeless at the same time. She had any woman in her, she wouldn't go fearing the kids. If the landlady had only believed them in the first place about Charles' burn, all this trouble wouldn't have got started. Geneva would have paid her the rent.

But now Anna Mae had gone down to the rent control office, and she would never let go a fight once she started. In the end, right or wrong, they would get the worst of it because the law was a deck of cards stacked against them.

Anna Mae was nobody's fool, but she had a fool's confidence she could beat the rap. Geneva wished she had more of her sister's spirit. But all she could see ahead was themselves and their furniture out in the street with no place to go. In the South where they were raised, Negroes never whipped the whites with the law. It was always the other way around. And in the North, the whites were burning and bombing folks out of their homes. In Cicero, the cops stood by and watched the mobs throw the furniture out the windows, piano and all. Geneva had seen the pictures in the paper. So what made Anna Mae so confident that the law was any different just because she'd been down to the rent office with her friend Ernestine and seen some figures on paper?

The basement steps began to clatter and creak and the door flapped open. Mae was already untwisting her scarf from around her head as she set down a grocery bag on the table. In contrast, to Geneva, she was short and quick in her movements. Her complexion was freckled like a dark pepper and salt fabric, while Geneva's skin was like satin. Mae's lips were worn, chapped, twisted with a smile. She was twenty years older than her sister.

"I been thinking we better find another place," said Geneva.

"When you hear all about it, sister, you gonna cheer up. Old Biomchi be hollerin' like she got the toothache."

"Wish I had all that sass." Geneva couldn't help being infected by Anna Mae's enthusiasm for battle. Anna Mae was the person she loved best in the world. Their mother had died the day Geneva was born. And Anna Mae, the oldest of ten children, had raised the whole family. Her husband, Jack Green, took over the tenant farm when their pa got so crippled up with arthritis in the finger and knee joints he could no longer hobble along behind their mule or hoe a row of cotton. For years he sat in the doorway rocking and looking out over the land he'd worked and watching his boys scatter north to the factory towns—until he passed away sitting in his chair. Anna Mae nursed him all those years. She loved looking after the old folks and the babies. She had the biggest heart of anybody Geneva had ever met up with in the world. And now she was as much a mother to the children as Geneva herself.

"Auntie Mae, what you got in that ol' brown bag?" Charlene was already at the table, probing while Anna Mae was rolling up her sleeves. "Chicken?"

"Charlene, your nose don't lie to you. Just ol' smelts." Mae pushed her away from the table and began to peel potatoes so fast Charlene couldn't see her hands go. The potatoes dropped with a hiss of steam into the boiling pot.

This was too good to miss. On tiptoe Charlene peered over her aunt's shoulder. A cloud of flour dust rose in the air, then a sizzle in the frying pan. What she saw wasn't smelts and there was no fish smell in the air. It was honest-to-God chicken setting up a wonderful frying song like nothing else on earth.

"Chicken," shouted Charlene in delight. Her scream woke her father who was suddenly raising himself up on one elbow and wiping the sleep out of his eyes with the other hand. "Chicken!" he said. "Must be pay day."

His hair curled up into spikes like horns rising from his forehead. He was a handsome man with a thin oval face and deep resenting eyes. The skin on his face and hands was pitted and welted with healed burns like most steel workers.

Mae propped him up against the bedstead and pushed the table over close to the bed. In a moment they were all chewing hungrily at chicken bones as if they hadn't eaten for a week. When the chicken was gone, they finished up the potatoes and gravy. Then Randy and Charlene were ready to turn in, Randy beside her little brother and Charlene at the lower end of the same bed. "Them were sure good smelts, Auntie Mae," Charlene said sleepily.

"Ain't nothing like chicken smelts," said Mae. "One day we all's gonna go back home and grow our own chickabiddies. We gonna feed up till they come flappin' out our ears." Anna Mae made a flying gesture with her thumbs poked into her ears. "But now you babies go on to sleep. Us grown folks have serious business. How you feel, Charles?"

"OK, OK," he said impatiently. "Get on with it Mae, your serious business."

"I'll fix up that old leg later."

"Yeh, let it rest," said Charles sarcastic-like and with a tone of resignation as he settled back against the headboard. His face still had an unhealthy grey pallor. He fixed his eyes on Mae wearily. If she wanted to talk, nothing on God's earth would stop her. For his own part, he'd rather listen to the radio and leave all their problems on the other side of the door.

"How much you reckon old lady Biomchi makes on this here building, brother?" Mae asked.

"Umph, umph," he muttered, pushing his shoulders up in a shrug. "Plenty." His eyes were wide open now.

"You believe it, how much?"

'Mae, go along with you, speak out," said Charles irritated with her long-winded questions. "How much?"

"Twelve grand." Mae waited for the impact to register.

"Na," said Charles.

"Figure it out." She named the families in the basement, then on the first floor.

Charles interrupted her again. "You're driving me nuts, sister Anna Mae. So how much rent we all pay a week without all that 'rithmatic?"

"Two hundred forty bucks," she said impressively, "every week in the year."

"That's a lot of money," Geneva sighed. The baby was beginning his hungry cat calls and clutching his red mad little hands together for his supper. She took him to her breast.

"That ain't money," said Charles. "That's sweat and blood. Two hundred forty bucks! Takes me three weeks to earn that kind of dough while she's just sittin' on her fat ass. What you been up to, sister Mae?" asked Charles with sudden suspicion that Anna Mae was starting trouble again. "Now come out with it."

"She was right, that Ernestine I work with at the hospital," said Mae. "There's a law against it. She got no right making all that gravy."

"Yeh?" asked Charles skeptically. "Sister Anna Mae gonna stop her? Or get throwed out in the snow?"

"You read what it says, you know everything." Mae handed him a newspaper article, much folded and unfolded and soiled.

Charles began to read with his finger scanning the print line by line. "Triple damage suit," he read out loud. "Baby, get me a suit like that," he laughed. "Four hundred bucks overcharge. Twelve hundred bucks they got back."

"That's the kind of trouble old lady Biomchi gonna get." Mae's lips were bunched together in a grim smile. "And plenty more."

"What you and Ernestine find out down at that rent office?" Geneva asked dubiously.

"You know what the law say?" Six bucks for this ol' piece of rat hole, 'stead of twenty." Mae's fists were doubled as she pounded the table. "Biomchi gonna have to pay us back fourteen dollars three times over for every week in the year we paid her rent."

"You seen that in the books?" Charles couldn't believe it.

"Me and Ernestine," said Mae proudly. "They carry on like it's a sin to bring out the book. And they wouldn't of, either, only Ernestine says we'll sit here till you do. That's what the lawyer told her to say. I seen Osborne's, too. Ceiling on her flat is ten bucks, and she pays twenty-five. There's just one trouble—we gotta show receipts from the landlady or them stubs on the money order and we gotta be paid right up."

"But we ain't got the receipts," said Geneva depressed, "and white folks got the law on their side." It was like knowing the promised land was in the next valley without having what it takes to get over the hill.

"You go upstairs and talk to Mrs. Osborne, Genny. Tell her she don't have to pay more'n ten bucks rent money. That's what the law say. Get her mad at old Biomchi."

"You go, Mae."

"No, you. I got your old man's leg to dress up before he starts kickin' the bucket. You take the baby up with you. Osborne won't say no when she hears him holler. Then we can send old Biomchi a money order and we got the receipt. Remember,

Genny, it's forty bucks we need now we done ate the chicken."

"I ain't got my heart in it, sister." While Anna Mae was talking about rent control offices and triple damages, Geneva could only remember the things that had happened before. "You think we gonna win over against her? Remember old man Williams? When we thought we had him whipped—"

"We had him whipped good," Anna Mae cut in fiercely.

"And six months later, they run Jack off the road—" Geneva and Anna Mae stared at each other with the memory of the day they dragged Jack's body out of his wrecked car right at the foot of their lane.

Since Jack's death, Anna Mae had never met another man she could love. They were both young when they got married. Jack had just come home to Mississippi after serving overseas in the first World War. In France, the color of a man's skin didn't make so much difference. But back home things hadn't changed. Jack nursed his bitterness year by year with his back bent over a hoe, ploughing the black soil behind his mule, pulling cotton in the blistering sun. And most of the time Anna Mae worked along side him. She could hoe as long a row and pull as many bags of cotton as Jack any day in the year. But depression times were hard. No matter how hard they worked, they always owed a year's back money to the store. And Fred Williams who owned the store also owned the land they rented and took and weighed their cotton on his own scales.

The trouble started when an evangelist preacher came from Arkansas and stayed on the Green's farm. At nighttime from the doorway, he preached about Daniel and Moses while all the folks from the neighboring tenant farms gathered in the yard. It wasn't the preaching and spiritual singing that worried their landlord. It was the preacher explaining why there were always cut places in the papers they got from the post office. He showed them his own papers which hadn't been tampered with and read out how tenants all over the country were getting money back from the government not to grow so much cotton. It sounded crazy at first, but when he explained how their landlord was pocketing all that money from his fifty tenant farmers, they suddenly got the hang of it. And they all knew who was cutting their papers because old man Williams' nephew was postmaster.

In two or three days, the landlord got wind of the kind of evangelism preached on the doorstep of Green's farm. So his hired man came riding over to tell Jack the preacher should be on his way back to Arkansas before the sun went down. Jack didn't say one way or the other. But the sun went down and the preacher preached again. And that night a few dozen new voices joined in the spirituals.

In the morning the landlord himself came cantering across country. Jack slipped around to the next farm to call over the women. That was Anna Mae's idea, to give old man Williams a welcome when he came cantering up their lane with a pistol on his hip and cracking a bullwhip over his head.

"Where's that Moses?" he shouted.

The preacher who had no fear in him came out to confront the whip with a text from the gospels. One thing and another was said and shouted. From the neighboring farms the women started to flock over to join Anna Mae's welcoming committee. When the landlord started lashing out at the preacher's face and neck, he found himself surrounded by a wall of women on every side. And Anna Mae Green was hacking away at him with a hoe. He grabbed the reins to veer from the attack and the hoe sank into his horse's flank. The horse reared straight up, threw him to the ground, and went galloping home across the cotton fields, while its rider picked himself up in the midst of a threatening silence. "You must be crazy," he shouted at Anna Mae with his hand on his pistol. But he hobbled off down the lane not daring to use it.

That night he came back up the road with a posse and three cars. The moon was out glinting on fifty guns that were waiting in the Green's lane. For three nights in a row the sheriff's cars drove back and forth up the road but never came up the lane. Then the preacher went home and the trouble seemed to die down. The checks came through and there were no more cut places in the newspapers about the AAA payments. That was the best time of their lives—till, six months later, Jack was run off the road in his car and ended up against a tree with six bullet holes riddling his body.

"All the same, folks got their money back," Anna Mae said fiercely to Geneva. "Ain't gonna never win you don't fight. And my Jack's a saint up in Heaven. But where you gonna find old man Williams?"

When Geneva finally went to borrow the forty dollars, Anna Mae turned to Charles with a fierce look. "Now we gonna dress that leg."

Charles tightened the covers around his neck. "You leave my leg rest for tonight," he ordered. Anna Mae always got angry and rough when she thought about that Jack of hers. After ten years it was time she forgot him and married somebody else.

"I'll leave it rest for one minute." She was glad to have something to do to take her mind off the past. She dashed out into the little cubicle next door where she had her bed. In spite of the beaverboard, the room still looked like a coal cellar and felt like a refrigerator. Its only opening on the wall side was a coal hole bolted down with a heavy iron door. Mae's dressing table was a large packing case covered by a cotton towel. She seized scissors and ointment and bandages and rushed back to the bedside.

She grabbed the blanket which Charles was holding around his shoulders. For an instant he struggled. Then he closed his eyes from the pain which seemed to drill through the bone into the inner marrow. He gradually released his hold on the covers. He opened his eyes to see her scissors flash and pleaded, "Anna Mae!" when the pain became too great to bear.

"You got an awful leg here, brother Charles. You sure let them burn you up at that old mill. It looks like eggplant fried in a deep skillet."

"Oooh—" he whistled softly. Every quiver in the old house started pains jabbing into his leg. The basement steps began to rattle and squeak, the partition quivered. Always somebody came down at the worst moment. As somebody knocked and the door rattled, Charles muttered, "Tell 'em to go to hell."

"Come in," yelled Mae over her shoulder.

It was the last person in the world Charles expected, Pete Bianchi. He closed the door behind him and stood awkwardly with a cap in hand and a bundle of coats under his arm. To Charles, his face seemed round and well fed, with a healthy reddening up from the cold. Pete's forced smile turned to a look of pain as he recognized the seriousness of Charles' burns.

"That's a bad leg," said Mae. It was too late to close the door in old Bianchi's face, so she said sarcastically, "Step right up and take a good look."

"Jesus Christ!" Pete drew back again. The burn was all shades of yellow, white, purple and brown.

As Mae smeared on ointment and lightly bound gauze around his leg, she said, "They tried to roast him up."

"Rest yourself," said Charles with an expression of courtesy covering up his surprise at the visit.

"That's bad," said Pete.

"Bad!" Mae was scornful. He's lucky to be lyin' there and not a burnt up cinder under the ground."

"What happen?" Pete asked. He was ashamed to remember how Kathryn had said Roberts was drunk all the time.

"You work in steel?" Charles propped himself on his elbow so that he could look straight into Pete's eyes.

"In a mine out by Colorado I seen an explosion," said Pete. "Joe, my cousin from the old country, got his hand burned up bad. Steam. I seen it—"

"Smart guy—" said Charles.

For a moment Pete wondered if Charles was talking about him.

"—wouldn't build them two rows of brick like I said. You can't tell nothing to some guys, you shout your guts out. They got to beat the rate." Charles' face was bloodless, his cheeks sucked in. "He tried hidin' back of his shovel when the hot stuff came over the bricks." Charles was still holding in the pain. He wanted to cry out. "You seen the way acetylene burn?" he asked harshly. "There wasn't nothing left of that guy to look at."

Mae brought a glass of cold water and put it to his mouth. "Hush, now," she said. "Why you wanta go through it all over? Can't you be done with it?"

But Charles made as if he didn't hear her. "That guy was burnt up so bad, Mr. Bianchi, you couldn't any more tell than me what he was, black or white."

"Same everywhere." Pete was thinking of Luigi. Somewhere, maybe, his own son was suffering like Charles Roberts. He put his bundle of coats down on the table. "I brought the kids some coats. Keep them warm."

"Thanks," said Mae scornfully. "Bring them a new place to live in, that's what they need. Bring their old man a new job, 'cause he can't go back to work in no steel mill."

"Mae!" said Charles sharply. But there was no stopping her.

"They'll need more'n coats when your old lady throws them out in the snow."

There was nothing for Pete to say. But as he turned to go, Charles called through the door, "Thanks, Mr. Bianchi. Don't pay no mind to my sister."

#6

The stars pressed close down over Pete's head. The wind blew tears into his eyes and froze the breath in his nostrils.

Cold in his bones always reminded him of the nights long ago on the hills above Palermo when he watched the sheep through wind and storm. He never had enough clothes himself in those days. He used to crouch down among his flock and watch the eastern sky for the first promise of day. He was glad now he'd taken the kids the coats. But he was also glad to be out of the range of Anna Mae Green's tongue. She had a sharp one, that woman.

All the same, he couldn't blame her for standing up for her own folks. And Charles Roberts was hurt bad, not drunk.

Pete wondered how his wife could ever forget the first winter in Chicago when the Bianchis, too, had lived in a basement flat. Rats ran in the walls and through the rooms and Kathryn was terrified because her eldest son, Carlo, was only a baby then. If Pete had been hurt on the job, they wouldn't have been able to pay the rent any more than the Robertses. It was two years before he earned enough to move his family into an upstairs flat and five more before they could make the down payment on their house. In those first winters in America, Kathryn would have given her own coat to anybody who needed it worse than she did.

Across the park, Pete could see no glimmer of light in his own house. He wondered if his wife was sitting alone in the kitchen nursing her anger against him. Pete had no stomach for more arguments. Before Anselmo stepped into the picture, he and Kathryn could shout at each other at the tops of their voices and make up when all the excitement was over. But now their disagreements seemed to swell and grow like fungus in the dark feeding on their love and eating out their respect for each other. If it wasn't the coats, it would have been something else: always the conflict without the reconciliation any more.

So Pete took the diagonal path across the park, encouraged by the neon sign of Club Pagliani and its promise of red wine and a game of cards with his old friends. There was always talk and excitement in their company and sometimes the cards lay on the table face down when the arguments started with the young fellows. The second generation thought they knew everything. Easy come easy go in America. But the old guys never let them forget that a man was born a man, not a lizard or a ward heeler.

The lights in Pagliani's were low. A moon of neon light around a semicircular bar threw a paleness outward toward tables and booths which retreated into shadow. Pagliani, himself, a man of tremendous proportions, was talking quietly to two men who looked like pygmies as they faced him. He glanced up only an instant to smile in an absentminded way as Pete came in. With a bookie joint in the back room and greenbacks to pass around on election day for Anselmo, Pagliani always had business to settle in hush-hush huddles at the cashier's end of the bar.

Pagliani's was a social center for two generations of Italian Americans. The younger men were members of a bowling team which they named after their patron, Pagliani himself, who supplied shirts annually and paid the fee to enter them in the city league. Gathered around Vico Angelino at the lower end of the bar Pete recognized Vico's usual buddies: young Philippe who managed the cleaners around the corner for his father who was bedridden with arthritis, also the younger Gagliano from the grocery store, one of the Fiucci boys who lived in the same building as Tony Ferrucini, and Tony's youngest son Mario. These were the boys who had grown up with Lou in the same gang.

The older generation were sitting around a table in the corner playing blackjack: Sam Vincenti and William Santiani, Joe Angelino and Toni Ferrucini. They were all members of St. Joseph's which they had founded as a secret protective society in honor of the patron saint of their home village when they first moved to Chicago. Sam Vincenti had always been president. He was the first Sicilian to settle on Hemlock Street and battle the prejudice of German and Swedish immigrants who had arrived a few years earlier. Sam himself was a warehouse worker, the Germans and the Swedes had been carpenters and machinists. As they began to move out of the neighborhood, Italians moved in: dockworkers from Palermo, peasants from the villages back on the hills, and finally a few industrial workers from the north of Italy, Milan and Turin, all coming to America to escape the land draft, conscription into the army, and abject poverty back home. They brought muscle and hope and sweated out their lives in the factories, on the construction gangs, in the warehouses, breaking their backs to give their children advantages they never had themselves, at the very least Sunday clothes and meat with their bread.

The old guys at the card table were too busy playing out their hand of blackjack to notice Pete come in. Every time Tony Ferrucini banged a card down with the flat of his hand, the glasses and money jumped and tinkled. In the end, Tony swept cards and money in Sam's direction with an angry swipe of his arm, then started waving his index finger at Vico Angelino as if the game had interrupted an argument between them. "You call that, job for a man?"

Automatically, Sam and William reached out a hand to keep Tony in his seat. But Tony shook them off and pushed himself up to a standing position. Though in his sixties, Tony had fierce black hair without a touch of grey. His voice was throaty and hoarse like a bull's. "I tell you, Anselmo-boy—" He spat on the floor.

At this the young fellows laughed, but Pagliani looked up with a sharpness when he heard Anselmo's name taken in vain.

"Just because you ain't got the brains, you old goat—" Vico took time off to run his eyes casually over Tony's clothes from the mudstained jacket to the muddy boots.

Pete could have taken his belt off and lathered Vico for that kind of talk, as if his own father, old Joe Angelino, hadn't been a laborer all his life. Now Vico worked for Anselmo, he had big ideas.

In the old days, Vico was a brown-eyed kid like Lou. They went to school together. They talked with the same Chicago accent, different from the older generation with the carry-over from back home. Lou and Vico were best buddies as they grew up together in the neighborhood. They played on the same teams and went to high school together. Together they tinkered night after night on "Holy Jeepers" and banged themselves up in the hotrod races. Finally, they were nabbed together by the police for running hot auto parts. That was the time Kathryn first went to Anselmo in the LaSalle Street office. She begged him to keep her boy out of jail. And Anselmo had gone to juvenile and got the boys off on a suspended sentence.

Lou was sixteen when he went to work at Farmway. In a few weeks he had enough money to make the down payment on a car, to take girls out to dances, and to pay his mother room and board. That was the best, Pete figured, if a boy had a job and some money to spend he would go straight. But Vico was a different type. He began to mix with a fast nightclub gang and made his money after midnight. As he grew older, he joined up with the local precinct captains and was their boy on election day. Finally, he signed up with Anselmo as one of his junior lieutenants in the rent business.

Vico could talk about dirty clothes, thought Pete bitterly. He never soiled his own, working for a living, that was sure. Let him talk like Anselmo, like he was boss in the ward. All the same, old Joe was a better man than Vico, and Tony was worth ten of him.

All his life Tony had worked on construction gangs, for years repairing street car tracks, many times working through the night in the glare of the welding torch and the hammer of the pneumatic drills. Now that busses had replaced street cars on most routes, he had been transferred to the Department of Streets to dig sewers. His hands and clothes were always clotted with mud.

Vico's smile like that of a tough young matador inflamed Tony to attack. "Turn off water, gas, that's job for man, eh? Freeze everybody takes brains." Tony's fists were shaking out of control as he yelled, "Boy, I promise you, at 758 you come once—bang! After that, no more." Tony's voice shrilled up in a scream, "never we move from Hemlock Street."

"What's all the bust-up?" Pete asked Joe in a whisper. If Vico had told Tony that Kathryn was planning to buy 758, then the good times they'd had together for thirty-five years were finished. In a moment Tony would turn to wave his fist at Pete.

"The boy says we should all move away." In anger Joe Angelino stared at his son. "Anselmo gets us better place up north." Joe clutched and unclutched his right hand which was scarred and blistered. It reminded Pete of Charles Roberts' leg and all the suffering and misery of the world; also, of the day the steam pipe bust in the mine and withered Joe's hand. That was a year when jobs were hard to find in Chicago and Joe and Pete had gone out to Colorado to work in a copper mine. He was happy to hear Joe saying, "Anselmo, he try to change everything. Why we wanta move, Vico, when we got nice place where you were born?"

Vico smiled cynically and went on attacking Tony. "You want everybody wear mud on their pants? Hey, Tony, tell me. You ever took a bath in a real bathtub?"

With eyes hopping in his face from anger Tony appealed to his son for support. Mario was leaning over the bar sipping at his glass of beer, concerned mainly with his own problems. He was to be transferred to San Antonio the next week and suspected it would be his bad luck to be assigned to Korea. "For Chrisake, Vico," he complained, "why the hell don't you shove off?"

With his son's indirect support, Tony raised his voice even higher. "You big shot, that's what you think." He squeezed his voice out in a high whisper. "I tell you, boy, when Anselmo wants—" Tony twisted his wrists in a strangling gesture "—then that's finish!"

"Play cards or go home," Pagliani commanded. Even in the midst of confidential business, his ears were still watchdogs for any criticism of Anselmo.

"Big shots," muttered Tony enlarging his eyes at Pagliani. "Make all the money."

"What you expect?" William Santiani growled. "Kick you in the face. Same difference, all the bosses."

"If you had brains like Anselmo," Vico countered, "you assholes would be running this town, instead of digging the ditches."

"You talk!" Tony snapped his fingers. "You ain't never done a day's work. Easy money from the women." Tony's eyes went soft and sentimental. "Lover-boy!"

The young fellows around Vico began to laugh. "Look who's talking!" he lashed back. "Maria don't knock the shit out of you every night? Don't tell me. I hear you hollering half a block down the street." The sport of baiting Tony was wearing thin with Vico. It was time to get to the bowling alley. "Come on, guys, I'm gonna make that three hundred tonight. We ain't brought home the trophy to Papa Pagliani for a dog's age."

"Never brought it home yet," Pagliani complained. "Shirts, league fee, what the hell, you guys no damn good. What I waste my money for?"

Vico winked at Pagliani as he delivered his final thrust at Tony. "When we all move out of Hemlock Street, we leave Tony. It's OK with me he wants to live with the niggers."

The storm door banged open in Vico's face. In a blast of wind Nina Pagliani blew in. She threw her scarf back from her head and her hair came free in a tumble of flame-red. Snow had whitened her brows but her eyes were brown with a natural liveliness. She pressed the back of her cold hands against Vico's cheeks, but when he tried to catch her wrists she dodged free and ran behind the bar.

In a silence that seemed deadly to Pete after all the shouting, everybody in the room stared at Nina and Vico. Pete was wishing she hadn't put her hands on Vico's face, though her act might have been meaningless like the impetuous gesture of a younger sister. All the same, she was Lou's best girl before he went overseas.

"You work late tonight?" Pagliani asked. Nina rarely came

into the tavern and he glanced at her in surprise.

"Car couldn't start. If one of you gentlemen," she appealed to the younger crowd, holding her car key out in the palm of her hand "—it's down at that Madison Street garage now." Snow was melting on her forehead, but fine crystals still glistened on her hair.

She was beautiful, Nina. Still, Pete was thinking, she should have kept her hands off Vico. Why should she give anybody a reason for believing the rumors that were circulating around the neighborhood? Nina was no longer a teenager. She had grown up since Lou was shipped out to Korea. She had bought a car. She had graduated from business college and taken a job in a legal office downtown. All the same, Pete couldn't help thinking of her as the kid in blue jeans—with the natural brown hair and the liveliest brown eyes in the world—riding behind Lou on his motorcycle and making out with him on the front porch all through the summer nights.

Pete's memories died in him as Vico, with a pounce like a great cat, seized Nina's hand and the key with it and closed them both in his fist. "What's my reward?"

She struggled to get her hand away. "You're hurting, you fool," she scolded him. She glanced at Pete almost as if appealing to him for help.

But Vico wouldn't let her go. He leaned his head over the counter close to hers, kissed her on the forehead, and whispered something that made her look over in Pete's direction, then wrench herself free. "Leave me alone," she ordered in a whisper fiercely. She leaned against the shelves of bottles with her hands behind her back, breathing heavily.

Vico tossed her car key in the air with a victory smile, "I was only doing you a favor, kiddo. You asked me, didn't you?"

The way Vico looked at Nina as if he owned her body and soul made Pete feel cold all over. "OK, so we'll play it your way," Vico said with a wink at Nina. "See you later."

"One of these days." Her words tumbled over each other.

"You want your car key back don't you?" He threw the key to the ceiling, then caught it behind his back with his hand twisted upward. Nina's room was above the tavern. She lowered her eyes from Vico as she said, "If you can get her started, leave her in front. She wouldn't even turn over, like she was frozen solid."

"I'll melt her down," he said with a winning smile. "I got what it takes."

As Vico led his gang out, Tony shouted after him, "Sure I stay in Hemlock Street. Dynamite. Atom bomb. I stay!"

"You don't bother your head, Tony," Vico shouted back. "When Anselmo gets good and ready to buy 758, he'll kick you out. Don't worry."

When the door closed behind Vico, his father, old Joe Angelino, sucked his mouth down in a fatalistic way. "What can you do? Anselmo got police, bailiff—" Joe clutched and unclutched his withered hand. "You gonna stop him from making all the money?"

But Tony didn't seem to hear what Joe was saying. He was watching his youngest son in uniform follow Vico into the street. "Take my last boy away. Now who pays all the rent? What the hell we want Korea?"

Pete put his hand on Tony's shoulder with a grip to pull him up to his feet. "We go home now." He reached for his cap and jacket. Sooner or later he had to go home to Kathryn. Maybe she was asleep already. That would be the best.

Pete heard a flutter of steps behind him. "Pop, you look so sad tonight—" Nina had run across the room to fling her arm around his shoulder, then help him put on his jacket. "That bully, Vico, I'm gonna fix him next time but good." She laughed like she was talking about a brother. "You wait and see, I promise you. So pop, you gotta cheer up." When Pete didn't say anything, she went on anxiously, "It's no bad news from Lou?"

Pete was glad to shake his head. "We don't hear all the same." After all, he couldn't blame her for the way Vico behaved.

"Me neither," Nina sighed, "It seems like a million years!"

"She gets tired waiting for that bambino," Pagliani grunted. "A bird in the hand—"

Nina's eyes stormed at her father, but she didn't say anything.

"Your papa wants you to marry a big shot," said Pete with a sour smile, "like Anselmo—"

"Or Vico," Pagliani interrupted.

"So one day Lou will be a bigshot," Nina snapped at her

father, "and fool you."

"Big shots!" Pete shook his head. "Better you marry a man who works for his money," he said with a scrutiny that made Nina bring her head close to his.

"I love him best in the world, our Lou-boy," she whispered.

"And Vico?" Pete insisted. What Pagliani said had made him wonder if Nina was as innocent as she made out. Why did she want to dye her hair and have it plucked like a nightclub singer?

"Vico loves only himself," said Nina with a seriousness. "Pop, you gotta believe me." In a rush she added, "And we gotta cheer up about Lou. Maybe a telegram tonight. Or tomorrow—" She gave Pete a kiss on both cheeks and ran out the back door.

He could hear her step on the stairs, then in the room overhead. And he could hear again the clink of a car key as it hit the ceiling and see Vico's upward look. Tonight, it seemed to say, not just one of these day.

The thought of Nina in Vico's arms was enough to make the red wine sour in Pete's stomach. But maybe Lou would never come home. So why should he worry so much about Nina? The man who married her would sleep on a bed of thorns before he was through, anyway. With all that beauty and ambition— Kathryn was like that once.

"Tony!" From the street Maria Ferrucini's voice cut into Pete's bitter reflections. With the scream of a fire engine siren, she was calling her husband home from the tavern. Already in his mind's ear, Pete was listening to Kathryn's voice rising in a dark house. His heart sank down and still further down. He grabbed Tony by the arm. "We go home."

Together they stumbled out into the street. Snow had stopped falling and the wind smacked their faces with subzero cold. Tony staggered and fell into a drift and roared with pain.

Pete began to curse as he thought of his son in battle around the other side of the world. A man could fall down and freeze to death on a night like this with the stars pointing their cold flames at him.

"They take my boy, Mario," Tony moaned as Pete helped him stand up on the icy walk. "What we want with Korea?" he bellowed at the stars.

#7

An icy truce was maintained between Kathryn and Pete next morning while he ate his breakfast. Then he pushed his plate aside and rushed out as if he was late for work. No smile that made it worth Kathryn's while cooking for him. He didn't even give her the usual good-bye kiss. Kathryn was almost pleased to see he had forgotten his lunchbox. "Serve him right!" But Pete came back, thrust the lunchbox under his arm, angry at her and himself at the same time, and banged the kitchen door on his way out.

"Serve him right to slave with his hands all his life!" she muttered to herself. What a stubborn donkey she had for a husband! Why did she put up with him and his dirty clothes all these years? And dishes? Wash, scrub? Holy Mother! She'd know better next time.

There was no use asking Pete any more to help collect the rents or even do repairs. Anselmo was right. She needed protection. But carry a gun? That was frightening.

The house was empty and dead silent. "Come on little cheerful, sing to me," she commanded her canary as she freshened its water. "Mama needs to cheer up." Kathryn had to wash and dry every dish, knife, fork and spoon till they sparkled. soap off the linoleum-topped table, and leave the sink shining like the day it was installed, before she felt ready to trot off to Club Pagliani.

She hated Pagliani for the way he had treated his wife—like a servant. Constancia had been Kathryn's good friend back in Palermo even before coming to America and they had been the closest of friends until her death fifteen years back. Kathryn was sure Constancia had died because of a savage beating Pagliani had given her. So Kathryn had misgivings about seeing Pagliani, wondering if she could control her anger. But she'd have to. This was business, Anselmos's orders.

As she hurried down the street, memories of prohibition days, unwanted but impossible to dismiss, thrust themselves upon her. Her eldest son Carlo used to drive a truck for Pagliani, the first job Carlo ever had. Only seventeen at the time, he had talked about the Capone brothers like the holy saints. It was all shoot-out in those days. Anselmo wanted her to carry a gun. It was frightening like those days were coming back.

Club Pagliani had been a restaurant back then, but wine and liquor were sold in the basement. For Pagliani, the restaurant business had not only been a useful blind, but a profitable one, too. Many a night Kathryn had come over to help Constancia cook and bake and wash dishes. Constancia's life was worse than a servant's. She often had to work till two in the morning and get up at five to fill the ovens while her husband snored in bed, growing fatter each year till he was no longer able to climb the stairs and had to sleep in the back room behind the kitchen. When anything went wrong, he beat her. She kept grim mouth and eyes and talked only to her best friends like Kathryn about her troubles. When Nina was born, she brought her older sister, Maria, over from Sicily to raise the girl. Constancia had no time for children. Her three boys, as soon as they were old enough to drive, went into the liquor business with their father. When Constancia protested, he beat her. The youngest son was shot the same night as Anselmo's father and died in the room above the tavern which was now Nina's room. Constancia knew who killed her boy, but her mouth was clamped shut when the police came round.

The sight of Club Pagliani brought back the terror of those days to Kathryn. It was a judgment that Pagliani's wife was dead. What a shame for Nina to have such a father! If only Constancia had lived, Nina herself would have been different.

With a nervous twist of the handle, Kathryn let herself in through the storm door. The chairs stood upside down on the tables and the linoleum was glistening with soap and water. While Boatman mopped the floor, Pagliani supervised, his chin resting comfortably on the backs of his hands and his elbows propped on the bar. It was the same floor, Kathryn remembered, Constancia used to scrub every morning while Pagliani had watched her from behind the counter without ever lifting a mop to help her. The old resentment flashed through Kathryn in a heat. Constancia was better off dead. If Pete had treated

Kathryn that way, she never would have put up with it, not for five minutes, beatings and the rest.

Pagliani's eyes rose to measure her with a coolness and distrust dating back many years, then exploded with surprise. "Katerina Bianchi!" he exclaimed, "long, long time—" He smiled with an effort that seemed to cause him pain. And Kathryn had to return his smile because she had come to ask a favor. "Since Anselmo and Della—" Pagliani reminded her of the last time he and Kathryn had had anything to say to each other—at the cathedral after the marriage ceremony. Since then Kathryn had only seen him, in passing, through the plate glass window like an enormous blur in an aquarium. "Anselmo—" Pagliani repeated with a smile of deference as if he was talking not with Kathryn Bianchi, but with Anselmo's mother-in-law.

Angry and impatient, feeling she was betraying her friend's memory to smile at Pagliani, Kathryn began to explain her business. She turned her face away from him as she talked to watch Boatman mop a great semi-circle across the floor. His movements were slow and deliberate, calculated to reserve energy for a long day and night ahead. He had too heavy-set a face for her liking and she wondered if he'd got the scar across his cheek in some tavern fight. If he'd come to her door to ask about a flat, she would have said automatically, "No vacancy." But when Pagliani called him over, Boatman said "Ma'am" with a flattering kind of politeness. He watched Pagliani closely as Kathryn offered him ten dollars a week to go the rounds with her every Friday while she collected the rents. There were a few other duties she would explain to him as necessary. Later, when the Robertses moved out, she wanted him to live on the premises as caretaker. Then, instead of paying him ten dollars a week, she would let him live rent free at 1250.

Boatman waited for Pagliani's nod before he said, "OK, ma'am, when you want me to start out?"

"Friday this week. Come at six o'clock."

It was a deal. Pagliani signaled Boatman to go back to his mopping.

Boatman had a massive back and pair of shoulders. His head pressed heavily down on the circles of flesh around his neck. Kathryn was still fearful. "You don't have a thing to worry.

That's a good boy." From the loudness of Pagliani's whisper, Kathryn understood that he intended Boatman to hear. "The law wants him down in South Carolina." Pagliani shrugged. "Rape. You know how it is. A colored boy don't stand a chance. They can hang him for less than that down south. So why would Boatman wanta go back home? He got good job by me." Pagliani raised his voice. "What you say, boy, you wanta go back home?"

"No—" It was a long time before Boatman added, "—sir." Pagliani turned to Kathryn with a wink of assurance, at the same time pressing his thumb and middle finger together in a circle to indicate the deal was closed. Then he clasped his hands on the bar, leaned forward to ask confidentially, "Make lots of money, eh?" He bunched his lower jaw with an up and down motion of his head.

"For Luigi," she answered with a sigh, "and Nina." Grief welled up in her throat. "Everything—" she choked.

Pagliani stared with a monstrous lack of expression. Then he put a hand on Kathryn's arm and said almost tenderly, "I tell you about Nina. She wanta go places. Drive around, Lincoln sports model. Put on the dresses. Ooh!" Pagliani raised and lowered his head with a squeezing together of face till his eyes were smaller than pig's eyes. He knew what women wanted. "Be big shot queen like Della. Luigi, he's got the big smile for everybody. Plays ball with the nigger kids. Nice boy. Talk big mouth about the union, what he's gonna do. But make money?" Pagliani tapped his head as it moved back and forth on his shoulders, shaking from a vast upheaval of amusement.

Kathryn pulled her arm out from under his hand. "You no like Luigi." She boiled with the old anger she'd always felt for Pagliani in the days Constancia used to slave for him. "Blame him for the fire."

"Now we talk serious—" Pagliani waved the past out of existence. But it was true what Kathryn said. He had always had it in for Lou from the time the neighborhood kids were firing Roman candles one fourth of July in the alley behind the tavern from milk bottles. One of the bottles blew over on its side and the rocket sizzled through the basement window. The fire was put out soon enough, but the firemen went out the back way with pockets bulging and Pagliani's inventory on gin and whiskey hit bottom low. But it was more than the loss that accounted for Pagliani's prejudice against Lou. He preferred Vico for son-in-law. "Luigi nice boy," he repeated in his friendliest manner. "He write you letter he's OK?" Kathryn shook her head. To prove there was no hard feeling for Anselmo's mother-in-law, Pagliani reached up to his top wineshelf for a bottle of Marsala to pour Kathryn a glass. "Vico got job with Anselmo. Cadillac sports—"

"Luigi gets job with Anselmo, you wait see." Incensed almost out of speech, Kathryn snapped her fingers in Pagliani's face. "You think my boy won't drive the big car? And who you think Nina wants? Luigi. She's his girl." A cunning smile flushed away her anger as she taunted him, "What you know about love? Beat your own wife. You talk!"

"Love?" Pagliani mused at the idea. His eyes wandered from Kathryn to stare out the window as if love was something outside his present world, but something he'd known about a long time ago. "All the same," he said with a ponderous nod, "she will marry Vico."

"Luigi!"

"Vico!"

"Oh," said Kathryn with a rasping voice, "you force her?"

"Force? Nina?" Pagliani's cheeks sagged with a laugh that went down into his belly and rippled back into his face. "That's one bambina makes her own bed."

"She loves Luigi, I know," Kathryn had to shout. "She told me a thousand times already."

"Go dancing, that's love? Senior prom, like the kids say? Sit on the front porch all night, blue jeans? Maybe—" he shrugged as if it wasn't a matter of basic importance whether Lou had ever got into Nina's bed. "Bambini, Katerina! Now she been to night school, learned the typing and the short hand, got good job by lawyers' office downtown—who gets her that job? Luigi? No, Vico. Buys new car. She's no baby no more—" Pagliani cupped his chest with tremendous hands to show how Nina had matured. "What she want? Wash blue jeans for Luigi in the basement?"

"I tell you, Luigi get the job with Anselmo. Della talks to him." Kathryn leaned forward across the bar to shout in his face. "When the boy comes home, I got two houses, *capice*? Rent money coming in. You gonna see."

Pagliani drew back with a sneer. "We gonna see. Maybe he come home like the Terrazino boy, eh, with Japanese woman?" Pagliani hugged himself while his eyes went up piously to the ceiling. "That's nice love, eh? The boys get lonely out there. Or maybe, mama mia—" His eyebrows folded and his voice went way down, "—like Paul Gagliano." Rocking, rocking at the window of the house in the next street with brain and half his body gone. Pagliani's head swayed back and forth in sympathy. "That's gonna be a man for Nina?"

Kathryn's fingers tingled to slap the cheeks that bulged almost into her face again. She turned in disgust, gathering her shawl around her head and shoulders. Boatman was still circling the floor with his mop. "You don't forget. Come six o'clock," she ordered. "Friday."

The back door creaked open to admit Pagliani's eldest son, Nicolas. In the peculiar silence, he hesitated a moment to stare at Kathryn before he came up to the bar and laid a scratch sheet down in front of his father. Nicolas began to mutter the names of favorites and make pencil checks in the margin.

"We gonna see!" Kathryn shouted back over her shoulder at Pagliani.

'Why not?" Pagliani shrugged as if he had already forgotten what they were talking about and it was no use arguing with a woman anyway. He grabbed the scratch sheet from his son and began to concentrate with the wrinkled brow of a man who knew how to pick a winner.

Kathryn was too furious to speak. It was the old Pagliani with the devil in him playing cat and mouse the way he used to with Constancia. She reached out for the storm door with the urge to slam something in his face. His voice pursued her, "That's gonna be a good boy, Boatman. He don't wanta go back south." Then Pagliani began to mutter, "Gold Flakes, Silky Susan, Royal Girl—" as Kathryn went out.

She was shaken by what Pagliani had said even more than she wanted to admit to herself. What if Nina didn't love Lou any more? Vico? How could she? That gigolo! Instead of going home, Kathryn made a U-turn into the side alley. There was one person who could put her out of doubt, Nina's aunt. "Maria," she called up the stairs, "It's me, Kathryn." She could hardly wait for the rattle of an old woman's voice inviting her to come up.

Maria's room was an attic above Club Pagliani, with one wall sloping away under the roof and the two windows arched and leaded in convent style. The walls were completely bare except for the cross above the severe iron bedstead and a picture of the Madonna and Child. A wheelchair, a bureau and a night cabinet large enough for a bedpan were the only other articles in that bare room. Even the light coming from the north window was cold and severe as it settled on Maria's old face like a grey frost. She lay, a ghost of a woman, propped against white pillows. For two years now a broken hip had confined her to her room. She couldn't read to pass the time. She had never learned how. What memories she had were worn smoother than stones on a beach from constant turning over.

Once a week, Kathryn paid her a visit to talk about the past they had in common, about Constancia and Nina as a child. But whenever she brought the talk around to the present, Maria listened with patience in silence. However much Kathryn probed, Maria appeared to know nothing about Nina's comings and goings. But her eyes went up steeply as if she was praying for the girl's salvation.

Now, infuriated by Pagliani, Kathryn was determined to find out what was going on between Nina and Vico. "I am so angry, Maria," she let fly as soon as she came into Maria's room. "What I hear Pagliani say. Nina, she's Luigi's girl, not Vico's, understand?"

Maria's eyes were startled out of prayer. She stirred uneasily in bed.

"I beg you, Maria. You must help me, help Nina. Remember, I promised Constancia. I would be like Nina's own mother." Genuine tears of anger came to Kathryn's eyes. "How she smiled at us, Maria? Put her hand in your hand, in my hand. That was the end. Can we forget?"

"She wanted, Constancia, her girl be holy sister," said Maria harshly, "no man to beat her."

What Maria said last was true, Kathryn knew, but the rest was an invention. Constancia had never said she wanted Nina to be a nun, but after her death Maria had filled Nina's room when she was still a child with crosses and holy heads and groupings of the Madonna and Child which she modelled out of dough. She gathered timothy heads from the corner of the park where the grass grew tall and made miniature harvest shrines in the fall like the ones she remembered in her home village in Sicily.

"But Maria," Kathryn objected, "Luigi—"

"I raise Nina to be a holy child," Maria interrupted. "Every night I burn a candle. I pray all night long. Holy Mother, I pray, make Nina like she was at confirmation. Like a lamb again, Mother." Maria was crying now, a dry rasping cry without tears as if her whole life was a failure. "Remember, Kathryn, the white dress—"

"I remember," said Kathryn quietly.

"The little gold cross around her neck—"

"Maria, we must ask ourselves what the Holy Father wants. I decided my Luigi should be a priest." She rested her hand on Maria's arm to comfort her. It was an arm of bone only that made Kathryn withdraw her hand with the fear one day she would have so little flesh herself. "But my boy could never learn the Latin. You want Nina for a sister, but why did the Holy Father make her face so beautiful, her flesh warm, Maria? I know, I know!" Kathryn insisted, beating with the flat of her hand on her chest. "He wants Luigi and Nina should love each other, get married, have children. If there are no children, who will be priests and sisters? His plans—?" Kathryn held her hands upward and outward as if it was sinful for Maria to lie in judgment. "Maria, He did not make Nina to cut her hair and spend nights on her knees with the holy beads."

"I have prayed, Kathryn—" Maria began with a kind of terror that seized and blocked off her throat.

"But that is not enough. It's a sin the way she lives, you must help me. You must tell me, Maria. Or the sin is on you. You understand?" Kathryn gripped her arm and held it tight. "I know you are afraid, if you talk, what Pagliani will do. What Nina will say. I will never tell them. So the Holy Mother is my witness, I promise."

Maria's eyes filled with terror, then went up to the ceiling in prayer. For a long time her lips moved, but no sound issued. Finally Kathryn heard her say, "Holy Mother, every night I beg her.

All the same she shuts my door. I hear steps coming up the stairs, boots. I know she gave him the key because he opens the downstairs door. I call out Nina, Nina, are you all right? Who is it? And she laughs, 'Don't worry about me, Auntie. I can look after myself'—"

"Who is it?" Kathryn demanded. "Vico?"

"I didn't tell you," she pleaded. "I didn't tell you." Maria's eyes blinked at Kathryn as if there was no one left in the world she could trust, eyes like dried up pools, a last glitter of blue at their center.

"No, you didn't tell me." Kathryn turned away to hide her anger from Maria. "All the same, I know."

With a sudden determination, she stepped across the hall into Nina's room. She would have it out with her. The girl would be at work, but Kathryn would leave a note. Come and see me, that would be all. Kathryn looked for a pencil on the desk. But there was only Nina's typewriter. Not to know how to use the machine gave her the feeling she was an intruder. She stood looking around the room, forgetting her purpose. Nina had long dispensed with the holy dough figures Maria had modelled. Her room was now like a place in a foreign country with an oriental luxury in its furnishings. The floors were lacquered black. The walls were grey as twilight. The bed was a black rectangle with a square of orange yellow leaping out of the gloom. On the floor lay an oval moon of a rug like a flower floating on a lotus pool at midnight. At the window stood Nina's drawerless desk in teakwood and the chair in front of the typewriter was a corseted piece of furniture in natural wood with a skyblue seat and back.

Through the window the Loop buildings rose in the winter haze like a city on another planet. And paintings opened up the walls of Nina's room into an even more fantastic world that mystified Kathryn with its girders and bars and circles and its colors out of a madman's quilt. She felt not only mystified, but humiliated, as if modern life had no place but a shelf in the cupboard for her generation. A magnet of bitterness drew her eyes back to the bed. She was sure now Nina was sharing it with Vico.

"Remember, I didn't tell you!" Maria's half-crazed voice rattled across the hall. She was like a bird leaning forward for flight, but in danger of falling on the floor.

"I promised you, didn't I?" Kathryn shouted at her. Maria slumped back in bed against her pillows as if the anger in Kathryn's voice had hit her a blow. Her frame of bones and skin trembled to draw a breath.

It was easy enough for Kathryn to shout at Maria and at the same time make promises, but what was she going to say to Nina? To make her give up Vico, what did she have to offer? A son who was dead? A cripple who would come home in a basket without power to satisfy a woman's love? A man married already, bringing home a flat-breasted wife?

Goddam that Pagliani, Kathryn cursed as she slammed Nina's door. She hoped a special place at the bottom of hell would be reserved for him. And Vico.

#8

The hour hand on the old zodiac clock took an unbelievable time to move from two to three as Kathryn listened for the step of the mailman in the alley. And there was an added strain because the snow lay thick in the street, the frost had glazed over the window panes, and all sounds were deadened. Except for the whirr of a motor and the spinning of tires in the ruts, the whole city around her seemed to lie under a blanket of silence.

As Kathryn worked at the kitchen table her hands flew with the roller. She was making Lou's favorite *crostate di fichi* to send out to Korea. At the same time she was planning and preparing an old-country style meal for Anselmo. That's what Della said he would like best. First, though, she would serve him with his favorite whiskey and antipasto as soon as he arrived. Then at table, *fortella* of artichokes, homemade noodles with a rich tomato sauce, meatballs Sicilian style, stuffed eggplant, and a chocolate *tortone* with coffee. She had chosen a bottle of *villa grande,* a Sicilian red wine, to go with the meal. After Anselmo left to go to his fraternity meeting, she would surprise Della with a glass of sweet *Marsala* and *biscotti.*

With all the preparations in mind, Kathryn still listened intently and watched the minute hand like a cat. The half moon cupping the star on the pendulum swung back and forth and it seemed to her as she listened to the slow tick-tock that the letter she yearned for would never arrive.

At last, when the clock chime rang the quarter before three, she heard the crunch of boots on the front steps. With her hands covered with flour, she flew up the hall. She expected the letter box to clank and the letter from Lou to fall on the carpet in the front room. But instead, the doorbell rang.

"Registered letter. Please sign here." The mailman handed her a pen which trembled in her fingers. Her signature was a scrawl she wouldn't have recognized herself. She seized the letter and slammed the door in her excitement. "Holy Mother of God," she sighed and sat down in the chair.

Her heart was beating up somewhere in her brain. The whole back of her head and neck were throbbing. Was it his writing? The address ran together like water and she could not even read the postmark. Was there a return address? Was it really Luigi's writing?

Finally, her hands were steady enough to open the envelope. Inside was a money order for forty dollars. It was signed by Geneva Roberts. Kathryn read the brief message, "Please send receipt for two weeks rent and oblige."

Don't sign anything. Don't sign anything. Anselmo's words clutched at her brain. "Holy Mother!" she roared out in misery. "What have I done?"

Like a mad woman she rushed to the door. The mailman had disappeared around the corner. "I'll make him take it back. It's a mistake. It wasn't from Luigi." But she stood at the door without taking the first step. She had signed it.

Why was God punishing her? Would she ever hear from her son now? She shook her head hopelessly and closed the door.

Everything was against her and everybody, even her own husband. She and Pete had hardly spoken a word to each other since the night before last when he took the coats down to the Roberts children. That stubbornness! It wasn't the kids or the coats, hadn't she tried to explain? It was Anna Mae Green, a tigress of a woman, menacing her authority and raising fears in her heart that were unreasonable but all the more terrifying. What if all the tenants should join with her in triple damages? Three times—three times—Kathryn's head swirled to think of how many thousand dollars that would add up to; more than all the money she had in the world, the house in Pioneer Street, their own house, and their life savings in the bank. There would be nothing for Lou if he should come home a cripple for life. Maybe if she explained it that way to Pete, he'd come around to his senses.

Kathryn poked up the canary sleeping in his cage. "Come on, little cheerful, sing for mama." But the bird only blinked at her. She went back to the kitchen to finish Lou's cookies and prepare dinner for Della and Anselmo.

While the cookie tins grated and scraped into the oven, her heart sagged in her breast like a lump of dough. "I signed it. I signed it. I signed it," she muttered. "I could kill that Anna Mae Green."

Late in the afternoon, Kathryn spread out her best linen cloth on the mahogany table in the front room. She unlocked her glass cabinet and took out her most precious plates and goblets. The glow from amber cruet and vase and the sly sparkle of silverware began at last to warm her heart.

The central chandelier hugged the table with its colored glass and embroidery and threw a reserved light out into the rest of the room. A worn crimson carpet and curtains to match, a couch and chair with heavily carved lion's paws and a radio cabinet completed the furnishing of the front room, except for a few round backed plush chairs. It was like a sitting room in an old fashioned hotel where the furniture had lasted as long as the building. Kathryn was pleased with the effect of the brilliant table and glad the rest of the room withdrew into shadow.

A glance at the mirror told her it was time to bathe and make herself up. Her face was scrawny and pale. The purple veins stood out in her arms. And her hair with its streaks of white that needed tinting made her look like an old woman.

An hour later she stood in front of her mirror again to admire her new olive colored dress, sweeping almost to the floor and long in the sleeves. Della had shown her how to make up her face to minimize her wrinkles and give artificial life to lips and cheeks. She had also taught her how to tint her hair with a bluegrey preparation that misted out the white streaks and made her look a generation younger. Not bad for an old lady of sixty, she smiled at herself.

Then she laid Pete's new suit out for him on the bed, the expensive grey suit he had worn to Della's wedding. "Hurry, Pete," she ordered when she heard the kitchen door open. She made an attempt to sound cheerful.

Pete's face was pale, a little gaunt and green around the eyes from the day's work. "No letter from Luigi?" he asked. All day he had been hoping. When Kathryn's eyes said no, he muttered, "Sixty-three days."

"It's terrible," she stopped long enough to say quietly before she raised her voice again to remind him that Anselmo and Della would come at six. "We ain't got time to talk now."

"OK, OK, OK," he grumbled. He stared at the table and sighed to himself, but loud enough for his wife to hear, "For Anselmo she does everything."

When Pete saw his new suit laid out on the bed, he hung it back in the closet. Anselmo or no Anselmo, he was going to be comfortable in his own house. Besides, Anselmo knew Pete was an ordinary packer at Farmway, and before that in the old country a peasant boy raised in the hills behind Palermo. So what was the need for a lot of hypocrisy just because Anselmo had gone to college and learned how to pull strings around City Hall? Pete lumped all lawyers together as sharpies who knew how to use the law to their own advantage—Anselmo even more than the rest. How else could he get all those houses and grow rich on the work and misery of other people? But what Pete held most against his son-in-law was the way he gave Kathryn big shot notions. She wanted to sell the house they'd taken twenty years to buy and move to a strange neighborhood.

Anselmo was changing everything at Bianchi's and in the neighborhood—and making money out of people coming and going. He thought he was boss of the whole show. And Kathryn was getting more and more difficult to live with. The only thing they had left in common, Pete reflected bitterly, was their love and fear for their youngest son. Pete wished Della had never gone to work in Anselmo's office. That's what started the whole business. With a certain grim satisfaction he took out his old blue suit from the closet and laid it on the chair in the bathroom. It was faded and out of press, but he would wear it whatever she said.

In the kitchen, Kathryn was making final preparations for the meal she had spent the whole day planning and cooking. She stirred up the meat sauce with a wooden spoon. She mixed the salad in her precious Florentine bowl. Then she rushed up to the front room to set a salad fork at each place. She put iced beer and a bottle of old wine on a tray. She unlocked the bottom compartment of her desk and drew out a fifth of imported whiskey, the brand Della told her was Anselmo's favorite. She set the tray on the low table in front of the sofa. At last everything was ready.

At six o'clock, prompt as she expected, the bell rang. In a moment mother and daughter were in each other's arms.

Della was daughter to be proud of, a beauty with her long oval face and amber eyes and hair parted and groomed and square shoulders held with the grace and perfection of a model in one of the Michigan Avenue stores. With an overflowing love and admiration Kathryn hugged Della a second time. Her mink coat felt warm and soft to Kathryn's rough hands. But why no grandchild on the way?

"How lovely, mama!" Della exclaimed as she examined the table. "All that bother for just us!" She was pleased that her mother had put her whole heart and soul into giving Anselmo the kind of spread he was used to. It wouldn't be like pulling teeth another time to get him to come.

Anselmo stood in the background for a moment until he could seize the center of attention. He was wearing a heavy-pile cashmere coat which bulked around him like an enormous bear fur. "Hi, mama, how's your health?" There was a great cheer in Anselmo's voice but little warmth. He had immaculately brushed hair which shone like a mirror. His face was heavyset on a heavyset pair of shoulders. He had a blunt, clumsy nose and a pitted complexion. From his father in prohibition days he had learned to study everything and everybody in a room at a glance. His eyes had no reticence. They pried, they stared, they roved, they glittered—and through all they never missed the shadow of an expression on anybody's face. The world of men and women was his book which he read and re-read at a glance and whatever he read he turned to his advantage sooner or later.

Before Kathryn could answer his question, he was already asking another, "But, mama, what's on your mind? Troubles at 1250?"

Kathryn had intended to tell him her bad news after dinner, but Anselmo was clever. He had guessed the worst already. "Holy Mother, I signed it," she blurted, "after all you told me!"

Anselmo's stillness was enough to frighten Kathryn. His eyes grilled her now without the cheer.

"It was a registered letter. I signed the receipt. Oh Anselmo," she almost cried, "I thought it was from Luigi."

"Christ Almighty, mama, how stupid can we get?"

Kathryn had already run over to her desk, lifted the blotter, and was bringing back the registered letter for Anselmo to see. Her hand wobbled as if she were handing him a loaded gun. At the same time she poured out the whole story about the Robertses.

"It's bad, Kathryn, bad," he said with a frown as he examined the letter and money order. "They have evidence of payment, now. The exact amount."

Kathryn shook her head in confusion. "It was terrible," she moaned. "When I tried to catch the mailman, he was gone." She was ready to break into tears.

Della twisted her shoulders nervously. "Later, Gene, with the business. I see mama's got a wonderful dinner ready. Let's not spoil it with evictions and triple damages."

"She's sharp tonight, eh?" said Anselmo caressing Della with a sudden baby expression in his eyes as if he'd already forgotten the special delivery letter. He threw his coat over the sofa and sat down to pour himself a drink. His hand settled lovingly around the neck of the whisky bottle. "My favorite, mama," he said with a wink at Della, "how did you guess?"

He downed his first two ounce glass and filled up again. "By the way, heard from brother Lou yet?" Anselmo's face was flushed a deep redwood color from lifting the bottle all afternoon.

Kathryn shook her head. "It's two months—" she hardly had control of her voice.

"Cheer up, mama," Anselmo interrupted her. "We'll be back up at the Yalu one of these days. Things aren't so bad out there as the papers make out." Flushed with thoughts of eventual victory in Korea, he raised his glass. "To our hero-boy!"

While Kathryn and Della were hanging up the coats in the kitchen by the stove, Anselmo went on thinking about Lou, "He should have played it smart. I told him I could get him a commission—the night Della and I announced our engagement. He should have grabbed himself a safe foxhole at home. He was soft in the head to wait for the draft. Still, Lou's a solid guy, stubborn, but the stubborn ones go furthest. Maybe I can use him in the business when he comes back with the battle stars."

Anselmo poured himself another drink as he caught sight of Pete coming out of the bedroom, "Papa," he said, examining Pete's old faded suit, his slow moving feet in slippers, his tie hanging loose around his neck, and the top button of his shirt left undone on purpose, "you look like you need a pick-me-up."

Pete's hand was shaking from nervousness as he drank the shot his son-in-law handed to him. Even in his old suit he felt stiff and crated up in Anselmo's presence. Such boundless self-confidence made him shrivel into himself. He couldn't help simpering instead of smiling.

"Pop, why don't you quit that job at Farmway? With this new deal I've been telling mama bout, you can both live on easy street the rest of your lives. Christ, man, you have the right at your age."

It made Pete angry the way Anselmo planned his life for him and put all these ideas he'd heard a thousand times into Kathryn's head. Anselmo had made a parrot out of her in a couple of years. And, she wanted fancy things so bad.

"Everything OK by you?" Pete finally asked trying to think of something to say that wouldn't start an argument. As he sat down beside Anselmo on the sofa, he watched his pink manicured hands fondle the neck of the whiskey bottle. Pete put his own hands out of sight under his knees to hide his jagged nails and his rough stained skin.

"OK, pop," Anselmo answered absentmindedly. "About the same." He was already studying a document which he had drawn casually out of his pocket. "This is the new deal I'm talking about," he explained to Pete. "758 down the street."

"She told me," said Pete.

When Kathryn began to set a casserole and other steaming dishes on the table, Anselmo turned to her. "Mama, this is all hunky-dory soon as we get the sister out in Portland to sign up."

After giving her father a quick hug and duty kiss, Della came up to Anselmo playfully to sit on his knee and put the legal paper back into his pocket. "What did I tell you, Gene?" she scolded him lightly. "After dinner, business."

"That's right," said Kathryn. "First we eat what I cooked for you." She had recovered from her burst of anger and humiliation. And now, above all things, she wanted Anselmo to enjoy himself so that he would feel like coming more often. If she could only persuade Pete to move up by Lincoln Park, then she was sure Anselmo and Della would make it a weekly event—family night.

But Pete wasn't in a mood to drop business so easily. "Number 758, that's Ferrucinis—"

"I said eat first." Kathryn's voice fairly lashed out at her husband. Then she noticed with horror that he was wearing his old blue suit with the threadbare cuffs. The worry about the registered letter came back to nag away at what was left of her appetite.

"Mama, a feast!" said Anselmo as he sat Della down beside him at the table. There was nothing wrong with his appetite. He drank and ate heartily, praising every dish as he polished it off.

"The antipasto was splendid, mama. A knockout this *fortella*. A miracle these homemade noodles with what a sauce! And *caponatina di melanzane* with *villa grande,* mama, you ought to go into the restaurant business! Why keep such talent hidden away in Hemlock Street?" Kathryn warmed to Anselmo's compliments and began to smile with pride, almost forgetting the registered letter. "New York, London, Paris—Palermo, ah!—where can you find such eatments?" And all the time he talked and ate, he feasted his eyes on Della. And Della, while eating a cautious little of everything, followed Anselmo's every move and expression. It was like the moon constantly turning her face to the sun.

"Remember when Carlo and I ran the lizzy through the back of Gagliano's garage?" Anselmo laughed more heartily than anybody else. "You were just a bitty kid then, Della, with pigtails."

"Gene, I never wore pigtails," she contradicted him with a smile of devotion. "Maybe braids."

"And remember, Generoso—" Pete deliberately used the first name Anselmo hated and had tried to bury "—when you threw the cat through our kitchen window, glass and everything? Bang, crash, meow!"

There was an awkward pause before Anselmo began to laugh with great explosions. But Della spoke sharply to her father. "Why remind us?" And Kathryn could only glare at Pete.

OK then, Pete thought, do all the talking. He couldn't stand the way his wife and daughter hung on Anselmo's words as if they had no minds of their own. And he had to sit and watch Anselmo consume almost the whole casserole of stuffed eggp- plant as the meal lengthened out endlessly.

"Bet the boys out there'd give their bottom dollar for a spread like this," Anselmo broke the uncomfortable silence. "Poor old Lou, bet he's feasting on C-Rations tonight."

After that Pete laid his fork and knife down on his plate and sat on his hands. Maybe Anselmo's a big shot, but he ain't got a heart, Pete was thinking, to talk that way about Luigi. Even Kathryn glanced at Pete with a look of worry for an instant, instead of the glare which had silenced him.

But Anselmo went on blithely eating and making love to Della until finally after dessert, he raised a glass of villa grande to the chandelier to let the light sparkle through. "And now business, eh mama?" he said in a tone of infectious cheer. "I'm due right now at my fraternity meeting, being the treasurer. But the boys will have to wait a few minutes for the financial report. That's life!" He pulled the legal paper out of his pocket again and pushing aside glasses and plates set it down in front of Kathryn.

"It's a good deal as deals go." No matter how much he drank, Anselmo still had a steady hand for a document.

What was good about it, Pete wondered, as he heard Anselmo explain the details. It was the same kind of deal as 1250 Pioneer Street. It meant clearing out their own folks first, then crowding in Negro tenants. "758, Anselmo, that's where Tony and Maria Ferrucini live for thirty-five years, our oldest friends in America—" Pete began to protest. "And Fiuccis, Dombardos, Trombatores—we started St. Joseph's Club together—when you were a knee-high boy, Generoso. Remember, Kathryn, long before depression?"

Anselmo turned on Pete with a snap of impatience, because he could see Kathryn was still worried. "Old water under the bridge," he laughed.

"It's gonna make hard feeling with all our friends," Pete went on. "Cause us lot of trouble."

Anselmo controlled his impatience by reaching across the table to give Pete's shoulder a friendly massaging. "You got it back side to front, Pop. You mean it's time they all lived in a decent place with a bath tub. Get out of that old fire trap. And I'll fix them up, don't worry, so they'll wonder why they didn't move years before." Pete had put his finger squarely on the reason Anselmo was anxious to dump 758 on Kathryn and not buy the place himself. Once Bianchis had opened up the street to Negroes and drawn off the wrath of his people, Anselmo would move into the situation to buy up right and left and make a fabulous profit out of people moving out and moving in. "Another thing, mama—" he went on quickly to develop the advantages of the building, afraid Kathryn might catch on. She was sharp, the mother-in-law. And finally he wound up, "And, mama, like I explained to you on the phone, when we remodel the rent ceiling on that building goes off. No danger of triple damage suits."

The mention of triple damages was enough to heat up Kathryn's kettle of worries. "But Anselmo, if I'm ruined—if that Anna Mae gets all the tenants—three times all the rent we collected—that would be three times twelve grand—" The enormous amount made her stop what she was saying. Her eyes fell at random on Pete. "Holy Mother of God!" she screamed, forgetting Della and Anselmo were in the room, "and you take coats to those Roberts kids when they're trying to ruin us!"

Before Pete could answer her back, Anselmo intervened. "Not three times twelve grand, mama. Only three times the overcharge."

Della's eyes were down. She was thoroughly ashamed of her parents after all Anselmo had tried to do for them. Her father was a paisan, that was all there was to it. And her mother should learn to control her hysterics in front of Anselmo. It wasn't respectable behavior. "Why don't you leave it to Gene, ma?" She got up from the table to dissociate herself from her folks, sat apart on the sofa and leafed through a magazine.

"Can't we get them out, Anselmo?" Kathryn almost pleaded. "Send them a notice tomorrow?"

"It's not that simple. Those five day notices don't mean a thing if they're getting advice from a lawyer. I'll send them one, of course, but he'll tell them to disregard it. They've got four kids. If we take them to court, the judge won't evict during this war emergency situation. No, we've got to persuade them to move. We've got to turn off the gas, the light, let the plumbing freeze—in a week or two they'll be glad to move."

"But the babies!" said Kathryn involuntarily. She remembered how the little boy pushed his train in the narrow space between the bed and the stove and the baby clutched at his mother's breast.

"OK, mama, that's their responsibility. They started trouble, so now they're going to take the consequences. If we don't put them in their place—" Anselmo showed with a shrug that it wouldn't be the end of the world. Then he glanced dubiously at Pete.

"Turn off the heat?" Pete's answer was in the stubborn closing of his lips as he stared back at Anselmo.

Ignoring Pete, Anselmo pushed the contract to purchase 758 back in front of Kathryn. "What do you want to do? Sign and get it over with?"

Kathryn took up the pen he handed her. For a moment, she hesitated. Pete was frowning at her in a way she couldn't bear. But Della was nodding at her from the sofa. "Surely, mama, after all—" But Della didn't need to finish. Hardly knowing what she was doing, Kathryn was already scratching her name down on the line, while Anselmo was saying, "We can make the same arrangement for a loan as on 1250 with the same company. You know, same interest. Five years to pay, OK?"

When Kathryn handed him back his pen, Anselmo pushed the contract in front of Pete. "Better both sign."

"It ain't none of my business no more." Pete pushed the document back at Anselmo.

"But you signed the 1250 contract—" Anselmo studied Pete to fathom his resentment. "Somebody else will buy 758 and make all the gravy if you folks don't. And soon it's going to be a colored neighborhood anyway. Things change, papa. That's life."

"It's you wanta change everything round here," said Pete standing up abruptly.

"Dad!" Della cautioned. Her magazine flopped on the floor.

"OK, OK," said Pete. There was no use telling Anselmo what he thought of him and breaking up the family. "I ain't feeling so good." He groped down the corridor and the kitchen door swung to behind him.

"It's the worry about Luigi," Kathryn explained.

"Talk it over with him, mama," said Anselmo as if there was all the time in the world to worry about Pete now that Kathryn herself had signed. "So, bring it down to the office Saturday and we'll clinch it."

"But Pete won't sign," said Kathryn with certainty.

Anselmo drained his glass for the last time and bent to pick up his brief case. "Why did he give the kids the coats?" he asked. "It wasn't the first time those kids were cold, eh?"

"I don't know," said Kathryn desperately. "He don't want to make repairs down at 1250 no more. Before, everything we did together—but now, it's different. Maybe it's his age. He's getting soft in the head—"

"Or the heart. It's the same thing," laughed Anselmo. "Papa has a big ticker. But with you and me it's different. Keep the head cool, eh?" He pointed his finger humorously at his temple and agitated his thumb as though pulling a trigger.

"Papa's only a paisan," said Della ashamed of her father's behavior.

"I like to see you stirred up a little, beautiful," said Anselmo throwing a great hug around her. "You got spirit, you know?" He fondled her for a moment as part of his preparations for leaving. "I'll be home early, hon. And say good night to pop for us both."

With brief case in hand, he gave Kathryn a duty kiss. "What a feast, mama!" As he was rushing out the door, he suddenly turned back to wave his index finger at her. "And don't forget, we can't make money out of people and friends at the same time."

#9

When Anselmo was gone, Della started to tell her mother about a recent trip to New York, while all Kathryn could think of was what she would say to Pete later.

"Why did he do it?" she finally burst out. "He wants to spoil everything for me. Anselmo will never come again."

"Mama, you won't make Gene's mind up for him. He'll do what he wants when he wants. And don't forget, he's known pop since he was a kid. He makes allowances."

"But the cat—?"

"OK, ma, so Gene was a kid once like everybody else."

Kathryn was tremendously relieved. "You love him very much?" she asked.

"I adore him," said Della with a warmth that was unusual for her.

"Then why you have no children? You been married two years—"

"Mama, you'll have to leave that to Gene and me," Della answered with a kind of patient annoyance, as if Kathryn had asked her this question a thousand times already, and went on to praise Anselmo. "I think he's a genius."

Kathryn was glad that Della was happy—and a success. But for herself, she could see nothing ahead but problems. "That Pete," she grumbled. "Maybe I should give up the rent business."

"After all Gene has done for you? Mama, you can't be serious?"

"I guess I didn't really mean it, Della. You won't tell it to him, what I said?"

"Of course not." For an hour Della poured out praises of her husband and her new life on Lake Shore Drive. There was no trace in her talk of the life she used to live with her father and mother. And though Kathryn was proud of her till her heart overflowed, at the same time Della was no longer *her* daughter. She was Anselmo's wife.

In a year, Della's face and gestures had changed. She had abandoned an old self in favor of a more sophisticated new personality. Her smile was different, more studied. Her face was slimmer, more oval perfect. Her hair was groomed madonnalike to accent the beauty of her high forehead. Her complexion was smoother, more tended than before. Her hands moved with more grace and self-confidence. She sat casually on the sofa with one knee drawn up under her skirt and the other leg stretched out easefully as if this was the informal attitude recommended by her etiquette book for a tete-a-tete with mama.

After an hour, she fixed her attention on the watch Anselmo had given her as an engagement present as if it was already time to go back to him.

Kathryn followed Della out to the kitchen to get her coat. In front of her, Della's shoulders rose square and graceful and her casual jacket seemed to float on air. A magnificent woman at the height of her beauty, a daughter to be proud of! And what a perfume! Fifty dollars a bottle at the least!

But Kathryn's pride was gone the instant she saw Pete slumped forward on the kitchen table. His hands were rough and his nails black against the oilcloth. "He wore his old suit," she choked out, "and I put the new one out for him, the grey suit, remember, when you were married at the cathedral?" The memory of that day made Kathryn even more ashamed of Pete.

He had thrown his old blue coat on the chair and torn open his shirt collar. He was snoring.

"Don't wake papa," said Della. As the clock ticked, the past of the family lived again for her—the grease on denim shirts and pants from the factory, the washing at the sink, the desperate poverty when her ma and pa were saving every cent to pay for the house. She was glad those days were finished for her. "You'll be happier, ma, when you've moved out of this horrible slum. That's the trouble."

"But your father don't wanta move. Sometimes he's a donkey like tonight. Whatever gets into him?"

"Don't work yourself up again, ma. It's bad for you. Pa's behaving like a child, but he'll come around when Gene talks to him again." Della slipped into her mink coat and bent to kiss her father on the forehead. It was a kiss of regret as if her father had never known what it was to live—and was too old to learn now.

Pete stirred uneasily and brushed his head with the back of his hand. The scent of Della's perfume still permeated the kitchen an hour later when he woke up. It was hard for him to remember at first what had happened until he heard Kathryn calling him to come to bed.

"She's gone, Della?" he asked.

"She's gone." The house seemed empty to Kathryn, a ghost place. "Pete," she coaxed, "we move up by Lincoln Park. You take it easy, feed the bread to the ducks. We ain't happy here no more."

Pete shook himself free of her arm and stood up. "We go to bed—"

"Pete," she pleaded, "everything we did together. Remember Valone—my papa's shop—when night comes—how you put your head through the window?" She was no longer angry at him or ashamed as she remembered the days they were young together. "How you say 'Katerina' and we go under the trees?" She linked her arm in his. For a moment she had the look of a young girl in love. "How we go to the church with the bells—and then with one bambino, we get on the boat and the moon shines on Palermo and we're coming to America! All our life, Pete, we work our hands to the bone. But now after everything—heartbreak, sweat, dishes, diapers—it's easy street, what you think?"

Pete was thinking about the old country. Maybe one day they would go back home without Anselmo bossing the whole show. Then things would be different.

"In Valone it was flies and rats and holes in socks for always. Here, it's money in the bank. Everybody for himself and his own people. We get up on top. Thank God, Pete, we come on the boat." Kathryn didn't want to go back home, ever again. For her, Valone was a peasant village where the kids slept on straw like pigs in the corner. "Pete, I beg you sign the new contract!"

But Pete made his way out of the kitchen alone. "Our whole life we did everything together," she called after him desperately. "It's for our boy when he comes back home. Maybe he gets hurt, can't work no more." She followed Pete down the hall. It was maddening to watch him get into bed and roll over to the wall with his back to her.

When she turned the light out, he began to mutter, "I ain't gonna sign no more papers."

"Pete!"

But he went on as if talking to himself, "I ain't gonna sign, I ain't gonna sign."

After all the terrible frustrations of that evening, Kathryn couldn't trust herself to say anything more. "Santa Maria," she began to pray silently, "take the stubborn donkey out of my Pete. Make him see things my way! Make us happy again like the old days when we all lived under this roof, Carlo and Della, Georgi and Luigi, all together!"

The sharp, cold ring of the telephone interrupted Kathryn's prayer. "Pete," she ordered, "go answer." She shook her husband by the shoulder, but he brushed her off.

"So go yourself," he muttered. "You're the closest one."

Angrily she stuffed her feet into her slippers and stumbled to the phone. "Hello," she shouted. "Yes, this is her. Why you call so late?"

There was a long, long pause as Kathryn waited on the line. Her heart began to pound with a hope that grew more and more painful. Then she heard the operator saying, "I have Mrs. Bianchi for you. Go ahead, San Antonio."

"Mrs. Bianchi?" a strange but pleasant voice was asking. "Get ready for the happiest surprise of your life. Can you guess what it is?"

In a moment, Kathryn heard her son's voice. "It's me all right, ma. I'm back home."

"Holy Mother of God," she shouted with a joy that was too intense to bear. Luigi was alive!

"Ma, I want you to know they got me out in the repair shop in San Antonio for a few months. But I'll be OK."

Kathryn began to yell and laugh and cry all at once. "Pete! Pete! It's Luigi! He's back home!"

#10

The call from Lou was a release for Kathryn from a prison of fear and hatred. She hugged Pete with happiness that at first had no limits. It was only later she could complain, "Broken pelvis, shell splinters, that's bad." She remembered how weak his voice had sounded. "Operation, maybe two. Six months, maybe more, on his back, Pete. He couldn't lay down for six minutes when he had the measles. What you think?"

"The boy's gonna be OK." Pete could go to sleep now without worrying about Lou for the first time in months. Sleep settled like a drift of snow, softly and insistently taking the fatigue out of his life.

But for Kathryn no sleep was possible. The sorrow that had drenched her whole body evaporated and her heart leaped with a new delight in life. She could plan now for a future. The rosary between her fingers grew warm as she thanked the Holy Mother. From prayer her thought danced on excitedly to what lay ahead, then soberly, then with anxiety. Six months, maybe more, was a long time, hopelessly long to drag out before she could hug her son in the flesh and know he was all right, not only that he said the words to calm her fears. What if his wounds were worse than he said, his pelvis didn't mend right, or there were things he hid back from her? "Oh Mother of God, bring him home to us so he can walk on his two legs again without crtuches. All my life, Mother, I worked with these hands for you. Now for me, please, I beg you—so he can marry, have children—"

It was hard for Kathryn not to be bitter even in prayer. Lou had called Nina first, even before his own mother. He still loved Nina, there could be no doubt from the way he talked. But did she still love him? "Holy Mother," Kathryn implored, "make her heart pure again like on confirmation day." The vision of a child in a white dress with a gold cross shining between her breasts made Kathryn add, "Help me to forgive her." As she thought about Nina, she remembered the way she was before Lou went overseas, full of love for him. The moment he came home from work, they were inseparable, the two of them. Summer nights, Kathryn could still hear them talking on the front steps when the grey was already squaring her bedroom window. And she would doze again from the sound of their voices and dream of the nights when she was young herself and Pete would take her into his arms.

Like his father, Lou was handsome, generous, with an easy smile. With a temper, too, like her own. Kathryn remembered the arguments between Lou and Nina when they snapped and growled at each other. Those things happened between them, she was sure, because the Holy Father wanted to test out a man and woman before they bound themselves to each other for the length of life. A time came when Kathryn no longer heard their voices at night on the front porch. Then she knew puppy love was finished and wondered if they were sleeping together in Nina's room like man and wife.

The last night of all before Lou went into the army was fiesta time. Firecrackers blew up the roof of silence night had built over the city. Triangle flags rustled like the leaves of an immense tree of joy over all the streets in the neighborhood. It was late morning already, when Kathryn heard Lou's boots on the front steps. He came plunging into her room, his eyes still full of night lights and the bursting of candles and baskets of fire. "Come hell or high water, ma, Nina's gonna be my one-and-only." He was drunk with love of her, warm from the pressure of her arms and lips and forgetful of separation ahead.

The month after Lou was shipped overseas, Nina was riding around with Vico in his Cadillac de luxe sports model!

She would have have to give him up. Absolutely give up Vico! In the morning Kathryn would see her. Maybe no ultimatum would be necessary. Maybe the sound of Lou's voice on the phone had already brought her back to her senses. Maybe she would be faithful to him from now on and build a new reputation so the past would die away between them when he came home.

The more Kathryn thought about Nina, the more she was prepared to be forgiving. Nina's father was a tyrant and neglected her, her favorite brother was wiped out in the gang war, and her Aunt Maria was too much of a holy saint to understand her. It wasn't Nina's fault that her mother died when she was only five and left her in the care of an aunt whose only concern was to make a nun out of her. Nina had much too passionate a nature for that. In a convent she would give the mother superior no end of trouble.

No, if Nina had made some mistakes, she would learn from them. Kathryn remembered the days when she was Nina's age. It was easy to fall in love at nineteen or twenty. But once she married Pete, that was it. With Nina she was sure it would be the same way. Better she should live it out while Lou was overseas. She would make all the steadier wife for him when he came home.

Besides, Lou needed a wife like Nina. Unless he had changed a lot in a couple of years, he needed somebody to keep pushing him. He was too easy going on his own, not lazy like Carlo, but just good natured. Nina was ambitious. She would give shape to his life. She would never be satisfied with his going back to the old job, whatever Lou's father wanted. She would light a fire under him, which would raise them both like a rocket into Anselmo's world. Maybe Lou would be inspired to go to night school and become a lawyer. All the things Kathryn could never be herself because she was born a shopkeeper's daughter in Valone and still spoke with an old-country accent, her son and daughter-in-law would be. They would live like king and queen on top of the world like Della and Anselmo.

When the three little bells at St. Joseph's announced the four solemn dongs of the big bell, Kathryn was too worried and excited and happy to stay in bed. She rushed into the kitchen. The switching on of the light was enough to drive away her night fears. The familiar clock ticked and the face of Saint Joseph smiled down at her from his place on the wall. He would be happy, the old saint, that her boy was alive. The future opened up with light again and space and room for happiness. Kathryn felt an immense surge of returning will power.

She reached impulsively for the flour. When she called Pete for breakfast, *biscotti* crisp out of the oven and beaded with a million crystals glistened on the kitchen table. "For Luigi and the boys at San Antonio," she said proudly and hugged Pete as if they should never say angry words to each other again.

She laughed with a young wife's joy as she watched him set out to work. Pete's step was like a youngster's as he swung his lunch pail in a vigorous arc. She stood on the porch to watch him go down the street the way she used to when they first came to America. She held the front door open, forgetting the cold. And Pete, as he used to many years before, turned at the corner by Pagliani's to wave back at her.

Now Kathryn was sure he would sign for 758 and do the repairs again at 1250. They could go back and pick up their life together where separation began.

#11

For the twentieth time Nina flicked the paper out of the typewriter, balled it in her hand, and threw it on the floor. "Dear Lou," she began again. For an instant her fingers moved like spokes in a wheel. "I've got to tell you, even if it hurts. What I said last night was true. I love you more than I can say. But Lou-boy, I didn't keep my promise to you—"

"You're the only guy I love." Nina laughed nervously. "But you didn't expect me to act like a stone saint in the church—"

"Save it for me, kid," he interrupted. "Promise?"

"I told you I loved you—" Vico had come into the room and was standing behind Nina, his head bent over hers, his breath warm in her hair.

"The doc says I'm gonna be a hundred percent," Lou went on in a tone to reassure her if she had any doubts about his love. "Don't get any wrong ideas. I'm still all there. I'll prove it one of these days."

"I'll be counting them." Nina could feel Vico's chest at her back. She twisted her shoulders to open space between them.

"Just once more I want you to tell me—"

"I love you. Always have. Always will," she finished in a whisper, as she put down the receiver and shut out the sound of Lou's good night kiss. Her whole face was a mask which suddenly crumbled. Her voice broke into hysterical sobs.

"So Lou got the breaks after all." Vico's comment was low-pitched. He had never seen Nina so upset.

"You care!" she sobbed.

"What you mean? He was my best buddy." Vico's fingers slipped around the neck of the flask in his back pocket. "Here, kid. You need a pick-me-up. Drink the boy's health. We gotta celebrate the good news." He passed the flat of his hand over the bottle mouth, handed it to her with a cautious movement. His shadow from the night light engulfed Nina.

With an angry sweep of her arm, she dashed away his flask. He held it away from her and raised it to his own lips. "I didn't know you still felt that way about Lou." He slipped the flask back into his pocket. "You were just a kid then." He put his hands on her shoulder, rolling and kneading her flesh possessively.

"I hate you," she muttered and pulled away from him. "You think only about yourself."

"For Chrisake, sweetheart, let's not go off the deep end. You wanta know something, you're the only one ever made a dent with me." He grabbed her up in his arms with a strength she couldn't break away from. "If you think I'm gonna let you go now—" His arms forced her to the shape of his own body. When she pounded on his chest with her fists, he seized and crushed them in his own hands and laughed with assertion of power. "You gotta understand, Nina, I love you. I want you. I'm here now—with all it takes—"

She was breathing with a surging body motion, gasping for breath. She could only cry out in pain and desire, "Let me go. I love him. I promised him—" She clutched at Vico's shoulders to push away his muscle that surrounded and compelled her. If she gave in to him now while Lou's voice was still warm as a kiss in her ear, she would never be able to break with him. "You don't love me, Vico," she said with a coldness she didn't feel. "You only want me. When you're through with a girl—"

"Goddam it, Nina, I'll marry you if that's what you want. You belong to me. You're my style, see?"

"Marry me?" She dropped her head back as far as she could reach to stare at him without the blur of his face in hers. "You? Marry?"

"You think Lou can give you the things you need?" Full of a power only half controlled, his eyes craved her with a hunger that went beyond the present and a jealousy. "Look, Nina, we ain't babies no more. You got what it takes. And me, I got what you want and need and plenty. You and me can go places—like Della and Gene." The urgency slacked out of Vico's arms. He spoke as if it was her whole life he wanted now, and not only her body. He broke his clinch, thrust her back at arm's length to admire. "You got the face of queen." He raised her chin with his fist doubled sideways and she let him handle her like a show piece. "On two dollars an hour, you're gonna wash clothes, dishes, like your ma, get kicked around all your life, have a dozen kids? If that's what you want, Lou's your boy. Solid guy. Factory worker. Go to bed at eight. Sleep tight. Is that what you want? Christ, you'll be shouting at each other in five minutes—like Kathryn and Pete. I can hear them next door through two brick walls. Get up at five every morning? With that build on you? Nina, who you kidding?"

Vico pushed her away from him and began to walk up and down the room as if he was making a speech at ward headquarters. He talked about the houses he owned on Ohio Street and his job with Anselmo. He circled his fists in front of her face with a motion to show he could turn the whole world upside down for her. "Partners in Les Femmes on Clark Street," he went on

The early light caught the frost on Nina's window in a golden cross fire. It made the crucifix around her neck burn like a star. In the midst of all Lou's letters, the light glittered on her brass house key. Nina stared at it, then at Lou's photograph smiling up at her. Hours after his call, she could hear his words coming to her with love and a challenge, "You promised me."

Slowly her fingers came down on the keys again. "Tell me honestly, Lou sweetheart, did you never take another girl into your arms—maybe because you were wanting me, and only me, all the time? I don't know how to say it, but you got me keyed up to loving. Like breathing. I had to be with you to be alive. You know what I mean? You were me. I was you. There was no separation.

"When the army took you, I didn't know who I was any more. The grey days without you—I couldn't stand them! I kept wondering if you'd found somebody else. And the nights! In the cold emptiness of my bed I would reach out for you. I could feel your arm warm under my shoulder and your hand on my breast. But it was only a memory. I could see your face in the moonlight. I would touch your chest lightly while you were sleeping, kiss you with the tips of my lips all over where your heart beat, and rest my head there." Nina caressed the keys for a moment, then attacked them with jabbing fingers. "But what did all the memories stack up to? I was alone and cold, wanting you, and you were the other side of the world—"

She raised her hands to her cheeks. Her head drooped over the letter. "Holy Mother, must I tell him?" She pushed the typewriter back on the desk and rested her head on her arms, shutting out the light. "But I can't. I don't want to lose him."

It was hours since his voice came to her over the phone, "Nina, it's me—Lou." It was his actual voice, weak but unmistakable. She could remember the very caress of his hands in the way he said, "I love you." But his familiar tone, as if nothing had changed between them in two years, made her aware how much she herself had changed. "Tell me you still love me," he insisted. "It's the thing I been wanting to hear all the nights since—"

"Of course I love you, Lou-boy." It was hard for her to say the words he wanted to hear, almost as if she'd lost belief in his ever coming back home. "It's been such a long time. So many things have happened—" Bitterness gripped her throat. If only the army hadn't taken him away from her in the first place. "But it's wonderful, Lou, just wonderful you're back."

"Talk closer to the phone, sweetheart. You sound different. I can't hear you."

"Maybe two years make a difference—"

"Two years or two lifetimes? Remember you and me, that last night together? Flags in the street, the band playing the old chestnuts we heard since we were kids—fiesta time. We watched the fireworks through your window, remember you promised me—"

"It was perfect, Lou. If only they'd never taken you. It's been no picnic for me, these last two years. But what you must have been through—"

"Forget it. I had a lucky break. If it wasn't for a guy by the name of Jesse Williams I'd still be out there in Korea—under the daisies. Heart big as a football, that guy. You're gonna like him, Nina. He's from Chicago, too." Lou's words came to her with a surge rising high in the scale. "They flew us back in the same plane. He's gotta have an operation for kidney stone or some damn thing—"

"And what about yourself?" Nina broke in.

"They got me crated up in a cast. I gotta lie here thinkin' about you for months. Just thinkin'. How do you like that?"

"Months? When can I come to see you?"

"Can't," he grumbled. "It's against regulations. Morale or something. This security business—it's like they're afraid people are gonna know what's happening out there, the kind of beating we took. Anyway, I'm all crocked up for now, so maybe it's for the best. You gonna wait for me like you promised? You love me?"

"You know I do." Her voice went down to a whisper. She heard a key turning in the outside door, then heavy steps on the stairs.

"I can't hear you, Nina. What's wrong? Put your mouth close to the receiver. Maybe I'm going deaf or something."

"You know I love you, I said."

"Sure. I have all your letters. Right here under my pillow. But I want to hear you say it. There's no other guy?"

her off to a gigolo.

Nina stirred as if she was dreaming bad things, maybe that Lou was being killed out there in the war, the way Kathryn had dreamed many times. Her eyelids quivered, then she smiled in her sleep as if the danger was past. She was beautiful, Nina, with the fresh complexion of a child. If only Lou could see her now! Maybe Maria had invented the story about Vico to cause trouble. She didn't want her to marry Lou. She wanted her to be a holy sister. With a guilty feeling for all the thoughts that had run through her brain, Kathryn leaned forward to put her arms around Nina.

But the temptation to read the letter to Lou made her hesitate like a bird hovering. The intimacy of the letter made her catch her breath. That Nina felt those things and could say those things without shame made Kathryn read the words again—"kiss you with the tips of my lips all over where your heart beat." "My God," Kathryn muttered with excitement, "and I worried that she didn't love him any more!" But what a fool Nina was, what a child, to write to Lou like that. There was no mention of Vico, but everything was suggested. She should never finish the letter, Kathryn decided. Instead of hugging Nina, she took hold of the paper between the thumbs and forefingers of both hands and pulled. The letter came free with a rattle of the machine which startled Nina awake.

"Ain't it the best ever," Kathryn exulted while she balled the letter in her fist behind her back. Nina leaped up to throw her arms around Kathryn. They hugged and kissed each other and laughed and cried. "Luigi called you—" Kathryn finally said as Nina gave a quick defensive glance at the crumpled letters on the floor.

"I was writing him a letter—"

"Why you write?" Kathryn interrupted. "Go see him."

"It's against regulations." Nina was staring at the empty typewriter. "Was I dreaming?"

"Why you wanta tell Luigi?" Kathryn held her fist in front of Nina and slowly relaxed her fingers around the crumpled letter. "The boy's sick, Nina—"

"I know, Kathryn, but—" Nina began with a shrillness.

"Don't you tell me about my boy!" Kathryn scolded.

Nina faced Kathryn with a defiance that blazed. There was nothing artificial about her eyes, they were brown Sicilian, full of life and anger. "And when he finds out—?"

"He won't believe. He loves you. You love him. So—"

"But I should tell him—"

"You tell me," Kathryn insisted, "you don't love Vico. You ain't gonna have nothing more—"

"So listen to me a minute before you start running my life. Last night Vico asked me to marry him." Nina picked up the key from her desk, weighed it in her hand as if she was still considering his proposition.

"Vico? Marry? You believe that?"

"He meant it, Kathryn."

"Gigolo," Kathryn snapped. "Same big talk with all the girls."

"Maybe I should marry him." Nina flipped the key in the air and watched it fall in the palm of her hand. "Maybe I don't deserve a guy like Lou. I mean it. Maybe—" she shrugged.

"You love Vico?" Kathryn shouted and grabbed Nina by the arm, digging her nails into her flesh.

"Not that much," said Nina. "But Kathryn, you're hurting—"

"You don't be no fool now." Kathryn forced the letter into Nina's hand. "You write Luigi, I love you. That's all he wanta know."

Nina threw the letter on the floor and stamped on it. "Nobody gives me orders, see? But nobody!"

Kathryn could see all the same that Nina was glad to destroy what she had written. "You ain't got no mother to tell you, Nina. But Constancia told me, 'You look after my girl.' Now you got to listen to me. You wanta know? You ain't the only girl broke promises. You think I never looked at another man except my Pete? But you wanta know, too, when we got married there was no other man for me. Not one time—" Kathryn put her hand on her heart to vow she was telling the truth.

"And you lived happy ever after?" Nina's tone was still cool, but she couldn't help smiling.

"Most times," Kathryn answwered without hesitation, "except when he don't do what I want." The tension was broken between them and Nina could laugh with her.

building himself up. "Every night we'll hop around to a different club. You and me together—see? Like this." His hands closed on the small of her back. "Nina, I'm crazy about you." he used his hands to break down her resistance. "I want what you want. We click."

"If you mean it, Vico, give me back my key."

"Don't be like that, kid," he laughed. He ruffled the back of her head and pulled her face to him with the rough affection she was used to from him. But she didn't respond even to his lips taking hers and the intimacy of his tongue. "You're sweet, Nina. Sweet as all hell!"

"She pulled her mouth away from his. "I want my key, Vico," she insisted. "I want to work things out my way."

When he saw she meant it, his arm muscles grew flabby around her. He could reject her, too. Completely. She'd come around, pleading for him to warm her breasts, and want to put her hands on him in the places he kept for her. He'd made something different out of Nina from the teenager who'd rocked in Lou's arms. He was sure the lockout wouldn't last more than a night or two. He knew her type. Union with him was as necessary to her as food and drink. When Lou actually came home would be the time to worry.

"OK, Nina, so think it over." He handed the key back to her as if it was some child's game they were playing. "But don't keep me waiting too long." He brushed her cheek with his lips, then drummed on his chest with the ends of his fingers. "You make me tick, see? I can't get along without you." He broke away from her after a final kiss, loped down the stairs, and clicked the street door behind him.

"Why did he have to come tonight?" Nina slammed her bedroom door to close him out. But he left her with the feeling she had no right to marry Lou now. She had gone too far too long with Vico. She wondered if she could ever be happy with Lou again. He would be sure to find out that she hadn't been faithful to him. And then what would happen to their love? It was like something she remembered from a dream. Reality was now Vico, his eyes sullen with desire and demanding, the muscular crush of his arms, the way he gripped her mouth and tongue in his mouth's embrace. She knew it was treason to Lou's love for her to think of these things and she hated Vico for his power over her. Yet Vico sounded like he meant what he said. He had never talked marriage before.

She found herself wondering if Lou would go back to work in the factory. She was sure he wouldn't. And yet her fingers pressed the little brass key till the hurt of its sharpness drew sweat and she dropped it on her desk. In confusion she jerked open the drawer where she kept Lou's letters. She read all of them through. She knew them by heart—from Georgia, Japan, Korea. As she read them through, an appetite of heat swelled within her. His love for her was something deep. Vico's was all for himself, on the surface. She couldn't bear to give Lou up. But she would have to write to him and explain everything and let him decide.

Page after page she started only to crumple and hurl to the floor. The last she left unfinished as her hands cupped around her cheeks to hold in her grief. She couldn't tell him the truth. She knew she would lose him. "Holy Mother, must I tell him?" Night was already past and the winter morning sparkled through the pane, the sun invisible behind the frost, as Nina prayed and from prayer finally drifted into sleep.

When Kathryn had climbed the stairs softly so as not to disturb Maria, she found Nina lying asleep with her head on her arm. The crucifix her mother had given her at confirmation lay limp on its gold chain in the midst of all Lou's letters. He wrote so many to her, Kathryn couldn't help being envious, and so few to his mother. And he phoned her first! A sense of her own unimportance made Kathryn feel for an instant that Nina was stealing from her all that she had left to live for. The room itself seemed suddenly hostile with its splash of yellow rug on black floorboards, the strange girders and circles and blocks of color in the pictures on the wall like a city blown to pieces, especially the pillow lying like an orange moon on the bed. It was a reminder of something Kathryn tried not to think about. Nina's hair was an irritation, too. Maybe it was smart, but it was a color Kathryn could never get used to. Did Vico like that particular shade of flame-red, she wondered with a sudden anger. But why should she be so hard on Nina? Her mother died when she needed her most. And all her father cared about was marrying

"You and Luigi, you gonna be happy now, don't you worry your head." Kathryn waved her finger like a fortune teller's wand. "When he comes home, no more work in the factory. Your pop, he gonna see with his own eyes, I promise you—" Kathryn pointed down through the ceiling to where she was sure Pagliani had his chin propped on the back of his hands and was watching Boatman mop the floor. "Della's gonna talk to Anselmo. Give Luigi a job. You wait. I got two houses already. Oh Nina, with Luigi you gonna go places!"

"Maybe things will work out for us," said Nina. "I hope." At the same time she knew they wouldn't if there wasn't honesty between them. The letter she would write to Lou, in spite of Kathryn's advice, was already taking shape in her mind. "Lou, maybe you got to say to me and I got to say to you, 'You haven't been the only one. But from now on'—" With a new enthusiasm she pressed her arms around Lou's mother and her face against hers.

"I promise you," said Kathryn with a wink that meant we all have our secrets, "everything's gonna be OK. Now cheer up, girl." Kathryn gave her a final hug and made for the stairs. She took the time to open Maria's door and shout in, "Don't you worry your head no more about Nina. Luigi's gonna come home soon. The Holy Mother heard my prayers."

Half walking, half running, Kathryn set out for home with her head swimming happily and her heart thumping at top speed. As she passed 758 Hemlock Street, the second Anselmo deal, she smiled up at the old building and gloated over the years of rent ahead. A couple of pigeons eyed her critically from the gable.

Above the roof-tops, the sun was shooting light through fortresses of winter clouds and across the street, the park and the roof of the fieldhouse were white with a new drift of snow. Over the houses on the other side of the park rose the skyline of the city. At the peak was the Board of Trade Building and in the sudden winter brilliance the sun caught the slim statue of Ceres that rose higher than any brick or stone in the whole city. Anselmo's office was up there somewhere at the top of the world. "If he can do it," Kathryn exulted, "Luigi and I can do it—and Nina." Her scarf blew furiously around her face in the wind.

#12

Friday evening Boatman came to the back door. "Ma'am," was all he said as he stood waiting for instructions. The steam of his breath was white. The scar across his face seemed blacker to Kathryn than his face itself. The yellow light from the kitchen threw his great shadow on the wall of the Angelino house across the alley.

Though Kathryn had made the appointment herself, her first impulse was to slam the door in Boatman's face. She knew it was ridiculous to be frightened by her own muscleman. Still, she wished Pete had been husband enough to give her a hand when she needed his help. As she pulled on her old cloth coat and fastened her scarf tight down under her chin with a protective knot, she held her purse close. It was some assurance to feel the bulk of the little gun pressed between her ribs and upper arm. Anselmo had sent the "rod," as he called it, with a Christmas card and a Happy New Year.

Down the alley and across the park and down Pioneer Street, the wind blew at her back. Boatman followed her two or three steps behind. She had a tingling feeling at the base of her neck. Pagliani had told her Boatman was a good boy. All the same, she was glad he walked behind her and she didn't have to see his face, or the size of his shoulders and body. If he'd raped a woman in the south, the thought suddenly struck her, maybe he was only biding his time. She walked faster. Boatman's steps lengthened out to keep pace.

The moment she started to collect the rent, her feeling about Boatman swung to the opposite extreme. Always it demanded an act of courage to knock on doors in a corridor that was badly lighted and the walls of which were dark and scribbled with crayon marks and gaping with ratholes. Now Boatman's company began to give her a confidence she'd never felt before. She motioned him forward to be introduced to her tenants as the new caretaker and the bills accumulating in her purse began to soften the bulky little twenty-two.

Most of the tenants on the third floor accepted Boatman with a neutral stare, but Mrs. Osborne grunted, "Yes, I know Mr. Boatman." Her tone was an indictment of anybody who worked in a tavern—but more than that, a criticism of Kathryn for employing such a person.

Kathryn didn't want to offend Mrs. Osborne in any way because she was a good tenant, paid the rent every week from her pension, and was a strict religious woman. "My boy's alive," she blurted out as if the news would soothe over Mrs. Osborne's ruffled feelings.

"I'm very glad for you," she said, staring solemnly at Kathryn.

Mrs. Osborne was quilting again. The old armchair where she spent most of every day was filled with bright colored squares of cloth. Even with the confusion, she kept as clean and tidy a house as Kathryn with shiny dusted surfaces and fresh curtains. "I must get me one of the spreads for my boy's room," said Kathryn as she took Mrs. Osborne's twenty-five dollars. "They're fancy."

But Mrs. Osborne wasn't in a mood for compliments. "I was gonna ask you a favor, Mrs. Bianchi. My pension don't reach as far as it used, with the prices and all. Since my nephew been drafted to the army—"

"I understand," Kathryn interrupted. She knew Mrs. Osborne was going to ask her to reduce the rent, so she added in a great hurry, "The five rooms are too much for you. Anytime you want to sublet, it's OK by me. And you don't worry, I won't charge you extra."

Mrs. Osborne stared back at Kathryn. Her expression was solemn as an owl, Kathryn was thinking as she hurried down the stairs. "A dear old lady," she said aloud to Boatman.

"Yes, ma'am," he agreed with a deadpan expression.

Since the trouble with Anna Mae, things had changed around 1250. That very morning the Robertses must have received the notice to vacate by special delivery mail. That's the way Anselmo did business. As a result, Kathryn had to admit to herself, Mrs. Osborne's attitude had been noticeably colder. Nor did the Martins on the first floor invite her in as usual. Mrs. Martin, recovering slowly from a broken hip, had always been glad to chat with her. This evening she only nodded and her husband, a withered grasshopper of a man, presented Kathryn with the rent money at the door. He stared at Boatman suspiciously without intending to recognize him though everybody in the neighborhood knew who he was. A retired post office worker, Mr. Martin had a very sociable manner when he wanted to show it, and a wonderful smile. He was a handsome old man, too, with his keen frosty hair and sharp black complexion. But there was no smile for Kathryn when he handed her two ten-dollar bills as if he wished they would stick to the palm of his own hand. Then he closed the door abruptly.

"It's that Anna Mae at the bottom of everything," Kathryn muttered to Boatman. She would be as happy the day she got rid of Anna Mae as the day of all days her son would come home from San Antonio.

"Yes, ma'am," reverberated in the stairwell as Kathryn led the way down to the basement. Anna Mae Green soured the air she breathed. "Leave her alone," Anselmo had cautioned, meaning not to get involved in any personal fights. Nonetheless, Kathryn badly wanted to reassert her authority by introducing Boatman as the new caretaker. She was hoping also that Anna Mae had been frightened by the eviction notice and would want to come to terms.

Kathryn's shoes made scuffling tapping sounds down the basement steps. She was not afraid for the first time in months because she could feel the weight of Boatman behind her bearing down on the stairway. She felt secure in his company by this time as she led him to the two front rooms separated by wall board. A couple of rats slipped out of the garbage can and like a pair of shadows vanished in the dark corridor. "Oh," exclaimed Kathryn, but went on to knock with a hard knuckle on the doors. The two rooms paid off better than any other space in the building—twenty-five dollars apiece. The women who rented them had a different man in their room every Friday Kathryn stopped by for the rent. But that was their business. Several of the tenants had complained that one of the women sold reefers to the kids in the neighborhood. But Kathryn had no definite proof. Besides, Anselmo had told her not to worry her head about it—as long as the rent came in regularly. "Phew," she sighed. The smells of the basement crushed the life out of the air. She screwed up her courage to knock on the Roberts' door.

The sight of Geneva's sullen face and Mae smiling with ill will at her, roughed up a lot of unpleasant memories. At the same time, she saw Randy and Charlene wearing the coats Pete had given them. They were the coats Lou had worn when he was a child yet—with the brass buttons and the red lining. Kathryn tried to keep calm, but her voice wavered. "I don't wish you folks any bad luck. If you wanta pay me Fridays like before and stop all this crazy talk about triple damages, then we'll forget about eviction notices." Kathryn felt she had made a generous offer. But neither of the women staring at her and Boatman in turn seemed to be in a mood to snap it up. "You gonna waste money at the post office?"

"You gonna give us a receipt?" Anna Mae flashed back.

Geneva had more patience than her sister. "We sent it to you already, Mrs. Bianchi, by money order."

"Mailman gonna bring it," Anna Mae added as if she knew she was pressing a thorn a little deeper.

Kathryn tried to bottle down her humiliation. "If that's the way you want it—" she muttered with a shake of her head as if the two women were out of their minds. But Anna Mae had no business using that insolent tone, especially with Boatman standing by. "This is the new caretaker in the building," she went on angrily with her voice cracking like a whip. Boatman would teach Mae and Geneva a lesson they had coming to them.

The children were staring up at Boatman, their toys held suspended, their eyes full of suspicion and melancholy.

"When these folks move out—" Kathryn turned to Boatman as if they were no longer her concern "—you can fix it up any way you like."

As she closed the door, Anna Mae smiled at her in a way she would never be able to forget. Her eyes sharpened like steel points. A savage of a woman, Kathryn thought, ready to spring at her throat. "You can't help some people no matter how hard you try," she complained to Boatman on the way up the basement steps. It was only out in the street she could overcome her sudden fear. Then anger surged into her fingers and made her clutch her fists together.

"Monday their lights go out, understand?" She almost shouted her orders at Boatman over her shoulder as she hurried up the street not waiting for his "Yes, ma'am." "Tuesday, turn the gas off just before supper. Something's broke and it's gonna take a week to repair. Wednesday, the toilet. Don't bust the pipes. That could run into money. But loosen the joints. It should leak all over the floor."

The large, accusing eyes of Geneva haunted Kathryn. And the baby on the bed was laughing while his hands kept on making friends with his toes. Anselmo was right. It wasn't pleasant for either party. But Kathryn would show Mae and Geneva who was the boss at 1250. "Understand?" she turned to prod Boatman who had fallen into silence.

"Yes, ma'am." He was walking two steps behind as they crossed the little park. What was he thinking, she wondered. But what did it matter?

"These were the other duties you was tellin' me—?" Boatman asked as they reached her kitchen door.

"Of course." Was Boatman so dumb he had to ask?

In a voice she could hardly hear, ridiculous for a man of his size, he said, "Good night, ma'am."

Kathryn was glad to close the door on Boatman. But it didn't close out her problems. Anna Mae was a hateful, spiteful, dangerous woman. What would she do when Anselmo's plan was put into action? Would Boatman carry out the orders? Only for Lou's sake was it worth all the worry, the humiliation from the insolence of Anna Mae, and the filth.

Tuesday morning, Boatman showed up on her kitchen doorstep again. His eyes studied hers this time instead of the pattern on the linoleum. "Ma'am, I done what you told me." His voice was deep and yet so slight she could hardly hear him.

"Speak up," she said with the sharpness of fear. There was an insolence in his eyes, she was sure of it, and a rigid bracing of his shoulders which had slumped before. Was the job she'd paid him to do that unpleasant? "Monday their lights go off. Tuesday the gas. Wednesday—" What would Lou think of Anselmo's advice, in the middle of winter, too?

"Ma'am," Boatman raised his voice a little, "they got coal oil lamps now and candles." His head moved back and forth with a warning. "With all them kids—"

"They what?" shouted Kathryn. It would only take one of those Roberts kids to knock over a lamp or candle and burn the whole place down.

"You still want I shet off the gas?"

"What did I tell you?" Though Kathryn blustered at Boatman, she felt like running to the phone and calling Anselmo. Would the insurance cover the loss if the building burned down? Even if it did, she would lose all that income and have to start back down at the bottom. As she thought about it, her tone to Boatman softened. "You do as I say till I tell you different." Then fiercely she stormed, "They're gonna have to learn the hard way who's boss down there."

In the afternoon Boatman came back with a yellow and blue bruise across his cheek. "Ma'am," he said, this time in a powerful voice as if he had come to some decision. "I was shettin' off the gas like you said when somebody comes up behind me—" He rubbed his cheek protestingly.

"That Anna Mae—" Kathryn began with a smile as if now Anna Mae had made her fatal mistake "we'll run her out of there quick."

"Ain't sure it was her," Boatman complained. "Somebody said that Charles Roberts stayed home apurpose today, just layin' for me—"

"We'll call the police!"

"I didn't see nobody, ma'am. It's dark down there since I pulled the wires. They all gonna tell the police, 'No, I didn't see nothin.' " From the growl in Boatman's voice Kathryn was afraid he was on their side. "Over and above that," he went on, "they started hollerin' already 'count of the lights bein' shet off. They gonna get them a lawyer, that's the talk I hear. Go down to City Hall and see—"

"Big talk," Kathryn cut him off. Boatman seemed to take some kind of twisted pleasure in what he was telling her.

Now what should she do? Wednesday, let the plumbing freeze? Anselmo's calendar for discouraging the Roberts plagued her memory. She would have to order Boatman down into that basement again. With that welt across his cheek and the new sound in his voice, she was doubtful if he would go. She remembered the way the clothes rope had caught her around the neck like strangling fingers. Anselmo himself would probably advise her to go easy.

"Maybe we got 'em good and discouraged already," Kathryn bluffed with an artificial laugh. "So just forget about the plumbing. And I'll see you Friday."

When Anselmo heard the whole story over the phone he advised her to turn the lights and gas back on. "They've had their lesson," he said with a lot more confidence than Kathryn herself felt. "And I bet we've scared the other tenants in the building from joining them in any triple damage suit. That's the main thing right now."

"But what am I gonna do?" Kathryn was amazed at the off hand way Anselmo changed tactics. "I gotta get 'em out—before Luigi comes home."

"Leave them alone for a week," he answered her cheerfully. "Then let the toilet freeze. Have Boatman pull their fuse once in a while. Keep reminding them who's running the show, understand?"

"And if they don't move—?"

"We'll take 'em to court after six months. The wheels may grind a little slower than we hoped, mama, but with this war emergency stiuation that's as fast as we can go."

"What if they start takin' me to court first on triple damages?"

"Mama, you cross so many bridges," Anselmo laughed. "Why I bet those Roberts can't shake out enough dough for the lawyer's fee. it takes money, Kathryn, lots of money. What are you so worried about? When Lou comes back, let him handle it."

Kathryn didn't like to say it to Anselmo, but that was exactly what worried her. Lou would be too soft with Anna Mae.

"Did Della talk to you about a job for Luigi?" she asked.

"Ye-es," Anselmo answered thoughtfully. "Maybe I can use him in the business. Have to see how he's shaped up of course. But I think he's got the makings. He won't be a kid any more after all that hell."

"Thank God," Kathryn sighed as she put down the receiver. She knew she should be happy at the news. It was what she wanted most. But her capacity for feeling anything else was boxed in by her hatred for Anna Mae. Fighting her battles through Boatman without knowing for certain he was on her side was an exasperating experience. If she'd met Anna Mae face to face, she would have had at least the satisfaction of blowing off steam. But Anselmo, in his casual way, made her promise to leave Anna Mae alone, as if the woman was in the right all along.

With Kathryn's building in Hemlock Street, things went a little better at first. The title was cleared in January and by the beginning of March all the old tenants had moved except Trombatores and Ferrucinis. As soon as they were out, Kathryn could remodel the building according to plan. Trombatores finally moved on the first of April, but Tony Ferrucini said he would never move. "Dynamite. Atombomb. I stay!" he shouted every time he saw Kathryn. Nobody would throw him out of the house where he'd raised his kids and lived thirty-five years! Anselmo, Kathryn Bianchi, or anybody else!

At Pagliani's and in the corner of the park where the men bowled, Tony caused a lot of trouble for her and Pete both. And Pete, the old fool, went back to his old tricks, siding with Tony instead of his own wife. The truce between Pete and Kathryn, cemented by the return of Lou from Korea, was breaking apart and all the old conflicts coming between them again.

For all that, Ferrucinis would have had to move if Maria's operation for cancer of the breast hadn't gained them the sympathy of the whole neighborhood. When Maria came home at the beginning of May from the hospital, Kathryn couldn't put the heat on her to move the way Anselmo had advised. Maria was her oldest friend in America even if she hadn't spoken to Kathryn since the special delivery man handed her a notice to vacate.

Kathryn could have cried with grief for the old times passed forever as she watched Maria cross the street with a full pail of water only the day after she was back from the hospital. It was a familiar sight at the beginning of May to see her plant geraniums and a border of forget-me-nots around the war memorial in the corner of the park. Only a few years back, everybody who lived on Hemlock Street had shared her grief and Tony's at the death of their oldest boy, Cosimo. Kathryn could remember the day they all heard he was shot down over Strassburg as clearly as any day in her life. Now she couldn't help crying out as she saw her old friend stagger against the curb, "Maria, for God's sake, take it easy!" She rushed across the street to offer help.

But Maria shifted the pail to her other side away from Kathryn and muttered, "Kick the people out!" Then she struggled past her into the park. Kathryn followed at a distance. It was foolish for a woman of Maria's weight to get down on her hands and knees to pull the seedling weeds that had already unsheathed themselves from the soil. Kathryn felt an ache in her own breast as if she herself had had the operation. But what could she do? Maria was no longer on terms with her to accept advice. Kathryn could only lean against the park fence and watch.

It was the growing time of the spring. Overhead, the starlings were croaking in the tree of paradise that rose in the fenced off area of the memorial. There was a red knob at the points of each twig. The clouds were low flying and chesty with a white blue light that caused Kathryn to blink with pain as she watched Maria on her hands and knees making seed trenches with a stick.

"Maria," she called over softly in a last attempt to break through her barrier of stubbornness. "I heard from Luigi. Your Mario, he's out in San Antonio now, too."

"You care!" Maria went on with her planting without even looking over her shoulder.

"OK, you kill yourself." Kathryn felt like Maria had bitten the fingers off her outstretched hand. "See if I care."

There was a sharp click of balls in the opposite corner of the park. On a Saturday morning, the older men in the neighborhood were all gathered to enjoy boche ball and the spring warmth. But for Kathryn there was a feeling of exclusion and guilt. People avoided her. There was no longer the same friendliness. When Lou came home, she was sure things would change back. But in the meantime, there was a tearing at the muscle of her heart, memories of the past sundering from the present. She no longer felt at home in Hemlock Street. She banged her kitchen door to shut out the song of the robins. It was too much to bear.

But Maria's scream penetrated wood and stone. It was a shocking cry of pain that summoned Kathryn beyond possibility of denial and forced aside her injured feelings. "I knew it, I knew it!" Kathryn moaned. But it was something beyond her control, the stubbornness of Maria. She should have stayed in the hospital longer. She should have been in bed, instead of carrying pails of water. Kathryn screamed those things as she rushed down the alley and into the street. The men were already crowded across from the bowling corner around the porch at 758 and it wasn't till Kathryn came up close that she could see Maria lying face down on the walk, a broken pot of geraniums at her side. She had stumbled down the steps with the flowers and a second pail of water and already the wet spaces on the walk were stained with blood. "Leave her alone," Tony was shouting in his angriest voice. But Kathryn bent and with the strength of terror turned Maria over on her back. She tore her blouse off. Blood was welling up through a great torn open gap in her chest wall. There was a cry of pain from the men watching. "For God's sake, get the doctor. Don't stand there. Get the ambulance," Kathryn shouted at Tony and Pete. "Maria, Maria," Kathryn pleaded in a low moan of a voice as she ripped off her own blouse in an attempt to stop the flow of blood. But Maria's breath was gone and her eyes stared up. "Cosimo," she whispered, "where's he gone?"

In a moment Pete and Tony came back with Dr. Thomasello. He knelt for a moment beside Maria. But his head began to nod and a strange fatalistic grimace almost like a smile came over his round face.

"You do something," Tony grabbed the doctor by the arms and shook him. "I tell you—" His voice was a club beating down his fear. In a moment the small fire truck came jangling around from the station because the police couldn't promise an ambulance. And the firemen lifted Maria's body gently and covered it over with a canvas.

The doctor spoke quietly to the driver who was Nic Angelino, one of Vico's older brothers. "Better take her to De Rocco's."

"To the hospital," Tony shouted at Nic.

"Too late," the doctor said.

With a roar of grief, Tony turned and ran into the house and his voice was heard shouting in the empty rooms as the fire truck clanged down Hemlock Street and turned north in the direction of De Rocco's funeral parlor.

For weeks Kathryn could hear Tony roaring at her whenever

he passed her house, shouting like a madman with a deep anger of lungs like a bull's. He would curse her out in all the languages he knew as if she was personally responsible for Maria's death. "One day they gonna take him to Dunning," she said to Pete when the shouting was more than she could bear on a hot June night, "or Manteno. You wait!"

But Pete only muttered, "Your business ain't my business. Change the neighborhood—" He walked out before finishing what he started to say.

In an agony, Kathryn reached for the phone to call Anselmo. She would give up the rent business. How could she evict Tony now and bring down the wrath of the neighborhood on her own head? But Anselmo and Della were out. By the morning, Kathryn was already thinking maybe Lou would persuade Tony to move.

It was the middle of August before the letter came at last with the news she had waited six months to hear. "Ma, I'm coming home in a couple of weeks," Lou wrote, "a hundred per cent OK." Kathryn's eyes flooded with too much joy to finish reading the letter. Her son must have a homecoming that nobody would forget. In fiesta time, too, around Labor Day, when the streets in the whole neighborhood would flutter with pennants and the merry-go-round and ferris wheel and gambling booths and bandstand would be set up in the area yard by St. Joseph's and fireworks would fill the night sky with bubbles and streamers of fire. Saint Joseph would be honored in many other ways, but most of all this year by the homecoming party Kathryn would plan for her son. For the first time in weeks the sight of Maria lying face down on the walk faded out of memory and Anna Mae Green could be forgotten. All problems would be settled at once with an affair so big as to shadow them out of existence. The roof of Kathryn's depression lifted and space opened up again to the horizon.

PART TWO

#1

"For Christ's sake, jump!" The wheels of the truck were spinning in space. Lou was turning around and over in a power dive. There was nothing to hold on to.

"Mama mia!" he yelled. Why couldn't his mother hear? Bayonet peaks thrust up to jab the life out of him while she went calmly about her business, bending at the oven door to take out the pizza.

It was yellow and chunky and crusty and full of little lumps of bacon and tomato.

He pulled on the kitchen door, but the handle came loose. Somebody was grabbing him by the shoulder. Lou turned to strike with the door handle. But it was Jesse, his buddy, smiling at him.

When his mother opened the door at last, she didn't recognize her son, but when she saw Jesse she closed the door in their faces.

The hand was still on Lou's shoulder. "You wanted me to wake you, Mr. Bianchi." The voice sounded familiar to Lou from a long time back, but it was not deep like Jesse's voice. He opened his eyes to see the stewardess bending over him.

"Bad dreams?" she asked with a smile. "You wanted me to wake you when we got to the Mississippi." She pointed over Lou's shoulder at a ribbon of water dividing a continent nineteen thousand feet below. "There she is. And there's your home state. Does that make you feel better?" She leaned against the arm of his seat, looking down over his shoulder.

"I'm OK," Lou laughed. "A fellow can't help dreaming about things."

He leaned forward to watch Illinois roll up out of the sky like an immense harvest field marked with clusters of trees and buildings. He was used to the rough landscape of Korea with its skyline of sharp toothed mountains and its ruined towns and villages folded away in the valleys. But back home in the

Midwest, the land was flat meeting the sky in a perfect circle, and peaceful with the sun dropping away below the horizon. There were no bursts of antiaircraft fire, no roaring dogfights, no planes sinking away in smoke and flame with a doomed crew. On the vast prairies below, there were no faces crusted with napalm burns or towns in rubble or bombed out churches and temples.

"It was rough out there?" Again the voice of the stewardess startled Lou with a familiar ring. It was Nina's, almost exactly the same tone.

"It was no picnic, sister." His smile seemed to come only from the surface of his eyes as he looked up at her. He was brown from the Texas sun, but thin in the face. Deep eyesockets gave him a melancholy expression. He had big worker's hands and a husky pair of shoulders.

"How did you get—?"

"Banged up? It was an accident," he said with a shrug. He stared back down at the darkening land below. Lights were beginning to sparkle on in the towns and villages like clusters of stars.

"Maybe you'd rather not talk about it."

"It don't bother me now," said Lou. "It even seems like it happened to a different guy." He pointed at his insignia. "I was in Quartermaster Service Corps. My outfit was driving down from the Yalu River in the big retreat. Our sergeant was the meanest guy you'd find out there. We called him Snakeface. He always put me and driving mate up front. If anything happened, understand, it was gonna be our skin, not his. There were flares set out along the road which meant take it easy. But sergeant, he kept stickin' that snakeface of his out the cab of his six-by and burning us up. And when it'd be too dark to see, he'd be burping on his horn. It was slow driving account of all the abandoned junk and general conditions, and Snakeface must have been scared they was gonna take him prisoner. That's the kind of superman he was.

"Well, it was snowing and cold. Then it warmed a little and the snow came down like a smokescreen. Visibility was maybe twenty feet. The road was all frozen ruts up and down and round curves. I was doing the driving. My buddy was just beginning to doze off—"

Lou rubbed the back of his hand against his forehead as if he had trouble remembering what happened. The plane was beginning to nose down at a slight angle. In the east, a blur of light grew larger like a rising moon. "Looks like the home town," Lou muttered.

"That's it." The stewardess stood up as if she didn't expect him to finish his story. But Lou went on, "Like I was telling you, on one of those curves, shoulder of the road wasn't there no more." He tried to smile as if it was just one of those things.

"It's all over now."

"For me," Lou said, "but not for the guys still over there."

A moment later, he was startled by the voice of the stewardess coming from up front on the loud speaker. "Chicago —far as we go."

The voice sounded exactly like Nina's, fresh and sharp and full of life. Lou flipped open his billfold to compare the old black and white photo of Nina with the new one in color she had sent him in San Antonio. Why had she dyed her hair red? It would take some getting used to. Nina, secretary in a downtown lawyers' office, driving her own car. Independent.

Mario Ferrucini had told him about Nina's affair with Vico. His best friend before the war! Maybe she was only humoring Lou in their long telephone conversations. Maybe she hadn't given up Vico. He carefully unfolded her letter to read it the thousandth time, the first one she wrote to him in San Antonio. "We've got to be honest with each other, you and me both. Maybe we've both grown up. Maybe we got to say to each other: 'You haven't been the only one. But from now on—I promise!' I do, Lou. Because you do things to me nobody else does. It's like life was a terribly big vacuum till you came to fill it up for me. You loved me like a person, deeply, not like a one night lay. You never left me till I was satisfied as well as you. You know? Nobody else has been like that with me. You *are* the only one I love."

Lou secreted the letter again in a fold of his wallet. Nina loved him as much as he loved her, that was for sure. He had to believe her. But it was difficult. All the fellows back home would know about her affair with Vico. Mario did. What would they think?

But what mattered most? What they thought, or what Nina thought? She was laying down her conditions—if they were to make out together. She was equating her relation with Vico—and others?—with his one-night stands in Japan and Korea. Could he blame her?

Vico's smiling face came up in his mind to taunt him. His best friend! Lou would have to settle scores with him one day up ahead. But with Nina there should be no recriminations.

#2

Things had changed while he was overseas. Lou could tell from Nina's letters and his ma's that things had happened between his parents. His pa never wrote, but his ma had complained in a dozen different ways that he was hard to live with. He wouldn't do the repairs any more on the tenement they owned and he wouldn't sign the contract for the new building she was buying. "It's all for you, Luigi," she kept saying in her letters. They would sell the old place, if she could ever get Pete to agree, and move up by Lincoln Park. The neighborhood around Hemlock Street was changing. Colored were moving in. And maybe when Lou got home, Anselmo would offer him a job. Whatever happened, Lou would never have to go back and work in a factory. With the income from two buildings they could buy a Cadillac like Vico's and live anywhere they pleased. It all sounded like a mother's dream, though Nina wrote, too, about the job with Anselmo as if it was more than a vague possibility.

When Lou thought about his pa and the job he'd left, however, he wasn't sure he wanted to go into the real estate business. Though he had admired Anselmo from a distance, there were a lot of things the brother-in-law did Lou suspected were shady. And after his first skirmish with the law out at juvenile court when Anselmo had got him a suspended sentence, Lou had earned every dime he spent with the work of his own hands. In the plant he had learned his trade as machinist. He was popular with the other workers. They'd elected him committeeman to serve with the shop steward and before he went into the army he had some hopes of becoming a business agent of the union after a few more years in the shop.

If the Anselmo deal looked like a solid proposition, he'd have to consider it, if only to satisfy his ma. But Lou wasn't going to jump into anything new with both feet before he'd made a thorough reconnaissance. Lying in bed in the hospital ward for months had given him plenty of time to think over these things. He was no longer a young punk. In fact he felt a couple of generations older than when he went overseas. Things had happened out in Korea to make him more thoughtful. The last few weeks before his accident, his driving mate in Quartermaster Service Corps was a Negro, Jesse Williams. Their experiences had drawn them very close together until the differences between them meant very little, but the things they had in common became as important as survival itself. Jesse said one time on the last run they made down from the Yalu River in the big retreat, "A guy up in the lines don't ask you, boy, are you black or white? It's OK if you put your hand on his shoulder. Maybe next minute you both gone over the hill." Jesse and Lou had been hurt in the same accident and flown back home in the same ambulance plane. During the months of convalescence, Jesse was Lou's best buddy out in San Antonio. This had caused problems they both had had to deal with.

With Lou's father, Jesse would be no problem. But Lou's mother was different. It was like her—even when he dreamt about her—to close the door in Jesse's face. She had always been prejudiced. When Lou was a kid, she didn't want him to bring Jackson Taylor into the house. And she'd raised a hullaballoo when Lou took him and his sister to the bingo game in the church basement. But Lou was sure his mother would like Jesse when she had a chance to meet him personally. So would Nina, because Jesse was an OK guy.

The plane began to drop down at a steeper angle with heart-compressing persistence. Lou could feel pain again jabbing him in the back reminding him of his first days at San Antonio. He gripped the arm of his seat and stared down at the flatland rising from the east. The lights of Chicago marked out square miles of prairie, seeming to Lou more like an illuminated blueprint than a real city.

And at long last, he could see black beads of cars crossing and weaving in the streets of his home town as the airport circled up to meet him.

#3

After a long, long delay, the announcement of the flight blared out from the waiting room.

Kathryn's heart jumped against the walls of her chest like an animal trying to break out of its cage. She clutched Pete's arm to tell him, "Everything's gonna be OK by us with Luigi back home."

The heartache was finished, the endless waiting and the fears. The war was over for their son and the months on his back in San Antonio. All the worries of their life dissolved as they watched the searchlights marble and streak the clouds.

Pete's face was radiant. A silver plane small as an insect darted across a cone of light. "There!" he pointed up.

Kathryn crossed herself and closed her eyes to pray that no accident would happen to her son now at the very last moment. "Madonna mia—" It was too much happiness for a mother to bear. The grief she had learned how to bear and more than enough. But her heart seemed to melt in liquid fire with the joy.

"That's our boy!" Nina's voice grated on Kathryn's bliss. She would have to share her son even in the first moment with her—because that was the way he wanted it. "Pinch me, Auntie Kathryn, I can't believe he's gonna be home again."

When Nina put her arms around Kathryn, the little edge of resentment dulled away. She hugged Nina with sudden affection. "Ain't it the best ever," she gloated. "Only you and me and Pete like he made me promise in his letter. But he's gonna be surprised with the homecoming party," said Kathryn excitedly. "Anselmo's coming, De Roccos—"

The roar of a plane drowned out what she was saying. With a last swoop and glide a Constellation came bouncing up the runway, then slumped like a sail that loses its wind.

When the first passengers began to pick their way slowly down the ramp, Kathryn could wait no longer. She pushed through the crowd out to the landing space. The floodlights and the baggage wagons confused her. She waited until Pete and Nina caught up. Than at last she saw Lou step out on the platform at the top of the ramp.

Kathryn expected Lou to be different, after all he'd been through. She had told herself maybe he would have to take it easy for a long time. But as she watched him come down the steps and move slowly across the floodlit area, she could hardly recognize her own son. "What have they done to you, Luigi?" she cried out. She covered his face with kisses while he put his arms around her awkwardly. Then her hands pressed up against his face and her fingers rubbed his cheek bones. "He ain't got no flesh on his bones." She turned to Pete with a flash of anger. "They starved him to death."

"What do you think it was out here, ma, a fiesta?" Lou's voice was hoarse and low pitched in the old familar way. He held his hand out to his father. His grip was firm as ever. "Been a century, pop." He looked at his pa and ma with his old time smile.

He was unmistakably their son. "My God—" Kathryn began to cry. Lou stroked her hair to reassure her that he was all right now. He still gripped his father's hand. "Pop, for Chrisake—" It was suddenly a terrible strain. He tried to smile at Nina.

"Never, never," his mother sobbed, "we let you out of sight again. Once was too much already, eh, my Luigi?" With a quick motion she swept the tears out of her eyes. "Two, three weeks, I feed you up. Make you fat as a capon."

"That's one hell of a thing to say, ma," Lou burst out with a deep-chested laugh, "in front of my best girl!" He grabbed Nina in his arms. "Gees, kid, you're a sight for sore eyes." He combed his fingers up through her hair, then laughed again as he held her close. "You gone redhead on us."

"Hear him laugh?" Kathryn gloated. "It's our Luigi."

Nina tried to smile, but his face was so grooved and thin he looked a generation older. "You changed," she whispered. "Oh Lou, you been away so long—"

#4

Everything had changed around home since Lou went out to Korea. He felt like a stranger to come into the kitchen with its new red and white linoleum and curtains and the shelves with little pots of flowers and figurines against wall tiling, a new stove and a new refrigerator. The only survival was the old clock from Valone which still measured out the seconds in the life of the Bianchis with its familiar tic-toc.

Lou's folks had changed, too. His mother had smartened up, cut her hair close and dyed the white streaks. All the same, behind the new color and powder was the gauntness of skin and bones. She had aged in the years he was away. And his father, too. Pete's hair was a frosty white instead of iron grey, and there was a tremble in his hand which had been firm before. Only a couple of years on the calendar—but all the same, a lifetime.

Nina had changed most of all, from the teenager he'd loved for her bluntness and simplicity to a young woman of great beauty. Her moody recklessness had mellowed into the self-confidence of a person who worked for her living. Her feathery flame-red hair was something for Lou to get used to, though he had to admit it suited her. All the same he was glad her eyebrows and lashes were still natural brown like her eyes.

Above all, Lou was glad to see that Nina and his mother had a fundamental respect for each other. "Watch the pizza don't burn—" Kathryn's tone was affectionate and abrupt as if she accepted Nina already as one of the family "—while we show Luigi how we fixed up his room."

As Lou followed his mother upstairs, the house re-echoed with their footsteps. The rooms where Margaret and brother Carlo were still living when Lou went overseas were now empty. It was strange not to hear his nephew's shrill voice. "How's young Fireball?" he asked. But his mother didn't seem to hear the question. With an expansive gesture she opened the door to Lou's room as if to reveal paradise itself.

"Now you take it easy," she commanded with a smile. Inside, everything was new, freshly painted and shining. But with its autumn blonde wall paper and chartreuse woodwork, the room was as strange to Lou as if he'd never seen it before. His pin-up girls were down. In their place hung photos of the family and a hand-touched portrait of Nina with a signature in the corner. There were pictures of Saint Joseph and the Madonna on the wall across and a painting of a sailing boat framed by Greek columns. An expensive mother-of-pearl crucifix glittered between the windows.

"We fixed it up for you, just like Anselmo's office. Same colors," boasted Kathryn. As an afterthought, when she saw Pete had followed them into the room, she went on to say, "Your pa did the paint job."

"It was your ma's idea and Della's." Pete sounded as if he had never approved the colors of Anselmo's office. But his eyes directed Lou's to the new green enamel finish on the tool box which stood on the bureau in a conspicuous position. "That was your old man," Pete said with a wink.

Kathryn distracted Lou's attention by thrusting back a heavy, olive green curtain from the closet doorway. Freshly cleaned and pressed, his civvies hung waiting and his shoes gleamed up at him from the floor.

Lou's parents were like two kids competing for his attention.

"Everything OK?" his ma asked, putting her arm in his to steer him toward the door. When she saw him staring at the many-colored quilt on his bed—a cool combination of yellows, greens, and reds—she explained, "I had it quilted up for you special, Luigi, by an old colored woman, Mrs. Osborne."

The quilt was the only piece of furnishing in the room that had any life to it. And while Lou was staring at it, he asked thoughtfully, "Did Jesse Williams ever show up?"

Pete shook his head, but Kathryn looked at Lou as if she didn't know who he was talking about.

"You remember, ma, the buddy I drove with out there. He left San Antonio a couple of weeks back."

"No, he didn't come around," she said, fussing with the curtain to get his attention back to the room. "How do you like it?"

"Hundred percent," said Lou still thinking about Jesse. "You been slinging the dough around."

As he followed her down into the front room, she went straight to her desk cabinet to bring out a fifth of whiskey. "Now we gonna drink your good health, Luigi, and thank the Holy God." She went on to tell him excitedly how she had redecorated and refurnished the whole room with Della's help so that it would be ready for the homecoming celebration. "I promised the priest if God should spare your life—"

"But, ma, you promised me—"

"Luigi, they all want to welcome you home: Anselmos, De Roccos, Santianis, Fontanas. They think it was wonderful what you did in the war."

Lou could only shake his head. "I wrote you I didn't want the brass band, ma. With all the guys still out there in that mess, ain't nothing to celebrate."

Kathryn studied him with a terrible anxiety. That thinness! Maybe he was still very sick. Maybe in the brain, after all he'd been though. Maybe it was battle fatigue.

"You don't feel good?"

"I'm OK, ma. Hundred per cent." He managed to smile. Suddenly she realized her son had a mind of his own. He was no longer the slaphappy kid who'd gone overseas to win a war. He had grown up. He had broadened out. He seemed taller. His expression was firmer, but somehow—was it with all the pain?—thoughtful, even sad. It must have been terrible out there with all the shooting. In the car coming home from the airport, he'd told them how he hadn't slept in a bed for nearly two years, and then, for six months in the hospital, they hadn't let him get out of bed. He'd had his pelvis broken, three ribs, his lung punctured—it was a miracle he came back alive. No wonder he looked like he'd lost his best friend.

"Ma," he said, "I'm gonna call Jesse before I forget." She watched him put his glass down on her new desk and she bustled over to set it on the blotter.

"Hiya, Jess!" Lou was saying on the phone as if he'd seen his buddy the day before. "Sure, pa's getting out the homemade wine, Bianchi special. Pizza's in the oven. My girl friend Nina's over. How's it with you? Got the kind of job you wanted?"

Kathryn put her hands on Lou's shoulders to convince herself that he was home in the living flesh. She heard Jesse's voice sounding like a deep complaint. Then Lou was saying, "Drop by tomorrow night and I'll let you know what the score is." Kathryn moved her hands back and forth over Lou's shoulders with an impatient caress. Then she filled his glass again. "God Almighty!" Lou was saying in a surprised voice. "That's the way they do things back home? Bad as the goddam army."

When Lou finally put down the receiver, he bust out, "Well how do you like that? Two weeks back home and they're tearing down his building. So he's gotta find a place to move quick."

"If he needs a place to live so bad—" Kathryn pointed up.

"It's OK by me," said Lou. "But you better know first Jesse has three kids."

"I didn't raise you and Della and Georgi and Carlo upstairs?"

Lou smiled at his mother, she was so anxious to please him. "I don't know if he'd wanta live by us."

"Hemlock Street ain't good enough for your buddy?" she asked playfully.

"No, it's not that." Lou studied his mother's face with a curious thoughtfulness. "I'll tell you later."

As soon as she went out to the kitchen to see how the pizza was coming, Lou said to his dad, "I wanta talk to you serious." He lowered his voice. "Pop, are there any colored working at Farmway yet?"

"He's a colored fellow, Jesse?" Pete asked with his usual slant-eyed smile.

"Sure, that's why I'm asking."

"You didn't tell your mother." Pete shook his head with anticipation of troubles up ahead. "She don't like colored. Make lot of money? That's different. Then colored OK, boy." Pete went on to complain about the rent business, how it was causing a lot of hard feeling in the neighborhood. He told Lou Anselmo was going to have the bailiff throw Tony out on the street if he didn't move soon. "My best friend from the old country, Luigi! What can you do?" Pete began to pour out all his troubles.

"It ain't all a bed of roses," said Lou trying to calm his dad down. "I just asked you about Farmway because I promised Jesse I'd try to get him on in the machine shop. What's chances?"

"You know how it is," Pete muttered as if it would be hard getting Jesse a job. "If you come back—" His eyes filled with new possibilities.

From the kitchen Kathryn came rushing in through the swing door to tell them the pizza was ready. When she heard Lou telling his father he would go up to the plant in the morning, she interrupted to tell him not to make any plans because she'd made an appointment for him to see Anselmo. "He's gonna give you a job—when you wanta go back to work," she gloated. "How do you like that? No more slave with your hands." She drew Lou's face down close to hers to whisper, "Ain't it the best ever?"

Pete's eyes narrowed when he heard his son-in-law's name. "Let Luigi decide," he protested.

The tenseness between his mother and father was like something magnetic pulling Lou in two directions at the same time. Affectionately, he dropped one arm around his father's shoulder and the other around his mother's. "In the afternoon, eh pop, I'm gonna come to the plant, see you and the fellows."

Kathryn smiled with the certainty of winning a victory after a long battle. Luigi would see Anselmo first, the way she wanted it. Her ambitions for him and her dreams would be fulfilled. She had never been happier in her whole life as she cried out, "Holy Mother of God, now we gonna go places!"

But Pete only said in a voice that was no more than a whisper, "Better a man works for his money." Then he shrugged fatalistically. "Way you want it, son, is OK by me."

"We'll work out everything together," Lou said with a

firmness to compel his mother and father to bury their differences. "I haven't made up my own mind yet what I wanta do." He tightened his grip on his father's shoulder. "Cheer up, pa. How was the wine this year?"

#5

Over supper, Lou learned what friends and relatives had married, died, or been drafted while he was overseas. Nina told him about her night school and her job in a downtown law office. His mother talked about the homecoming party and the money coming in from the rent business, but most of all about Della and Anselmo. And his father, whenever he got the chance, talked about Lou's buddies at Farmway.

The atmosphere was mellow as the homemade wine which Pete poured into Lou's glass. The wine warmed his heart and reminded him of all the days of his life at home from the time he was a knee-high kid and his father had poured him his first small one. The wine was bitter sweet, nutty in flavor, with a warmth of no other drink on earth.

"Sure hits the spot, pa," said Lou remembering how he used to help his father press the grapes in the basement and set the juice to ferment in the old wooden barrels. "It's home—what a guy dreams about—" The tenseness was gone out of Lou's life. "I remember first time I met up with Jesse, we talked about what we was going to do if we ever made it safe back to home base—"

"Ain't it getting late, son?" His mother seemed anxious to make him forget about the war and the hospital. She began to tell him all about Della's marriage to Anselmo, how they exchanged rings at the altar, and who attended the wedding reception at the Como Inn. But Lou went on thinking about the first time he met Jesse and hardly heard what she was saying.

It was down in the ditch. Out there, a man didn't choose up on his neighbors when he heard the siren. He took a dive for the nearest cover. And Jesse was the guy next to him. They'd both been driving in the same outfit for two weeks, though they hadn't spoken to each other yet. When Lou asked him where he was from, he said, "Same as you, Chicago." He already knew more about Lou than Lou knew about him.

"You figure we gonna get back home by Christmas?" Lou asked.

"Be long time coming, that Christmas." Jesse's tone was deep and sarcastic.

They were quiet listening to a dogfight above the clouds. The racket grew deafening. Then down under the ceiling flared a C 54, growling and spitting like a wounded animal, and nose-ended straight into a mountain across. It dropped like a dead thing into the valley and all they could see was a column of fire and black smoke.

"Maybe they pulling our number next," said Jesse with a grim smile at the clouds. The all clear sounded like a knell for the doomed crew of the transport plane . . .

"Ma, I wanta tell you about Jesse," Lou interrupted her before she had finished her account of the wedding reception. "We was crawling up from Seoul with supplies for one of the advance airstrips. Our six-bys were loaded down and it was pretty rocky driving. You could hear the guns and see the flashes at night. They said China was over behind the mountains. There were mine shafts up there and diggings, but the platforms and equipment was all bombed to hell—or blown up."

It seemed to Lou he was back in the thick of it again up in the Yalu River country. Most of the trees were shot off the hills and only a few stumps stood against the sky. He could see them more clearly than he could see his folks leaning across the table with their faces close to his, as he went on, "You didn't see no people up that way like around Seoul. Maybe an old guy or two with an A-frame carrying firewood. The manure carts were the worst pain in the neck. They use all kinds of manure over there, if you know what I mean. Don't let nothing go to waste. What a goddam poor God-forsaken country! One of those carts was blown off the road up ahead. The smell was enough—sorry, ma, we'll skip it."

Kathryn wanted Lou to go on now, to hear what her son went through. Even if it was late and he was tired from his trip, better he should tell them all about it. Then he could sleep and forget. Most times when a mother's son came back from the wars, he only made jokes—or kept a tight mouth.

"That was my first trip up to the Yalu River country," Lou was saying, "when everybody and his brother was moving up north. The war was over already, way it seemed. Buddy I was driving with, Jimmy Esterhafen, was a hell of a nice guy from Minneapolis." Lou explained how they both got on the sergeant's blacklist the time he found a shovel full of road gravel in his sleeping bag. "It was Jimmy, all right, who done it. He was a genius for getting us both into trouble with all four feet. So after that, sergeant was always chewing our—you know, giving us a hard time.

"Sergeant was about the meanest article a guy ever had to take orders from. He had a long thin face, kind of a cross between a snake and a fox. He'd died in the army already about fifteen years from hatin' his own guts and everybody else's. That was Jimmy's theory about him, anyway. Sergeant was from down south. I met some regular guys from Texas—but not him. We called him Snakeface. But Jesse has a special name for him, String-'em-up."

Lou told them about the first time he met Jesse. As he described how the flaming transport plunged into the side of the mountain, Nina pressed against his arm. "Could have been you," she whispered. Her face was very close to his, her eyes warm and anxious.

Lou brushed his hand against her cheek as if to assure himself that she, too, was warm and living. "Jesus Christ, how I used to think about you out there, Nina. Nights when it rained it was miserable. We generally tucked in under our six-by in our sleeping bag. There was nothing to do except dream about somebody you loved real well—or go nuts. When there was a PX around, a fellow had a chance to get warm and a little slap-happy before turning in. One of those miserable nights after it rained like a son of a gun all day, Jimmy and I was grabbing ourselves a beer at the PX. I had that lucky pair of dice Phil gave me, pop, and a bunch of us including Snakeface was shooting craps. I sure wished I was home with the fellows shooting dice in the shipping room at Farmway and that wasn't the only time neither."

Pete encouraged Lou with his usual smile. He could hear him telling the men at work about Snakeface and the lucky dice. If only he would go back to his old job! Then everything would be the way it used to be.

"Another bunch of fellows was playing poker," Lou went on, "and some other guys were just mooning around going nuts the way they do out there. When in comes Jesse and one of the other colored men—Kurt was the guy's name—and they order up a can of beer."

"Jesse is colored?" Kathryn asked in amazement.

"Sure, ma," said Lou without changing pace. "Sergeant's mad 'cause he's losing. So he slaps the dice down on the floor and stands up to put his big nose right in Jesse's face. 'Colored canteen is down the road, boys,' he says like he's giving them a whipping. 'About five miles,' Jesse answers him without taking a step in that direction you could notice. He ain't gonna walk no five miles in the rain for nobody. He's a big guy, Jesse. Stocky, big face with glasses. Serious type with plenty of brain. Maybe six feet two with an arm on him I couldn't put my two hands around his muscle. And Kurt, his buddy, they said was a golden gloves kid—"

"But Luigi—" Kathryn still looked as if she couldn't believe what he was saying "—why didn't you explain before about your Jesse?"

"Give me a chance, ma." Lou went on to tell how the sergeant started slinging his weight around with his hand on his gun and repeating that Jesse's canteen was down the road. "That kinda burned me up after getting to know Jesse was from Chicago. So I told Snakeface, 'Jesse's an OK guy, see? He's from my home town.'

"Then Jimmy sounds off at him from the other side. 'That's right, and Kurt's from Minneapolis,' he says. 'And that's my home town.'

"Sergeant knew Jimmy was lying because Kurt talked deep south, but he didn't wanta tangle with four guys at the same time. You'll understand, Pop, when you see the size of Jesse. Snakeface looks around for support, but all the guys hate his guts. 'OK, smart guys, if that's the way you want it!' You should've heard the way he sounded, like releasing a safety catch on a gun. Then he took a walk. Jesse and Kurt go on drinking their beer like nothing's happened. In five minutes they're sitting in on the crap game like anybody else—"

"But you didn't explain it!" Kathryn sighed with more discouragement than Lou could begin to understand. "Why didn't you tell me your Jesse was a colored fellow?"

"I'm explaining it now, ma." Lou was irritated enough to add, "They're human like the rest of us."

Kathryn's eyes sank away from her son's.

"Like I was telling you," Lou went on in a quieter tone, "Snakeface fixed us, all right, to his way of thinking. Next morning he puts me to drive with Jesse and Jimmy with Kurt. 'Orders from up top,' he says like he's gonna whip the whole outfit. 'From now on, Bianchi, you will drive with Williams, and Esterhafen with Johnson.'"

"It's getting late," said Kathryn to Nina. "You gotta work tomorrow?"

But Nina said she wanted to hear the rest unless Lou was too tired. "Tired?" He laughed. "I been lying around doing nothing for a dog's age." He went on to tell about his trips with Jesse up and down from Seoul. It turned out Jesse had driven in Redball in the second World War and there wasn't a thing about a six-by he didn't know. When the other teams in the outfit were grunting and moaning halfway into the night repairing their machines, Jesse and Lou were raising their elbows at the PX. "I knocked around with a lot of fellows over there," said Lou, "But I'll say this for Jesse. I never met a guy more one hundred per cent."

It wasn't until their last trip that Jesse really opened up. That time their convoy was ordered to turn back before they had time to unload. Up near the Yalu River, everything was in confusion. The road was lined up like a freight train, tank to tank, gun to gun.

"For two days and a night," Lou continued, "we crawled back south, weaving in and out of so much abandoned junk it wasn't even funny. We took turns driving and trying to sleep. But at first you couldn't sleep in that uproar. It was like the carnival when they let all the firecrackers off at the end. But after a couple of days of that, you get so groggy you can't stay awake no more. I remember it was my turn at the wheel and I told Jesse, 'You'd better keep talking to me, guy, or I'll go bye-bye myself.' So Jesse opened up and told me all about himself. Honest to God, ma, if you think it's tough being called a goddam dago all your life, you oughta hear what this guy had to put up with."

After a moment, Lou went on to finish, "I must have dropped off or something." He put his hands between his fists, leaning on the table and staring down as he remembered. "We went into a tailspin. I got pinned behind the wheel. It took Jesse and Kurt and Jimmy between them to break me loose."

"He save your life," Kathryn sighed. "The Holy God does things in his own way."

"That's about the size of it." Lou raised his head to smile at his mother.

Pete filled the glasses with homemade wine. Lou raised his against the amber light. "It's a good wine this year, pop." He held it to Nina's lips like a loving cup. "A guy's lucky to be alive."

When Lou went out with his arm around Nina to take her home, Kathryn's eyes were too blurred to watch them go. Her son was back alive and safe, but the war had changed him. She had a terrible feeling of loss. Almost he seemed somebody else's son. "Sancta Maria," she whispered in prayer, "if Luigi wants his Jesse to come here, let him come visit. But live upstairs in my house? Never!"

#6

The lights were out in the Angelino house next door when Lou walked out with Nina. The street was deserted and the moon was heading up across the park through a mist.

Lou was happy to be alone with her at last after all the talk. He drew her down to sit beside him on the steps of the front porch—arm in arm the way it used to be before he went overseas. Remembering back to those days was like thinking of the youth of the world. And yet now, with his throat burning with desire for her, all he could think of saying was, awkwardly, "You grew up since I been out there. As you wrote in your first letter to San Antonio—"

But Nina wasn't responsive to his mood. Her chin was raised toward the moon and her eyes were troubled. "You changed a lot yourself," she said in an absent minded way as if she was talking to some older relative. "You're more serious." She reserved herself from him, and the excitement of his body met no response. "You *have* changed!"

"What's on your mind, Nina? You're so—" He seized her cheeks between his hands and brought her eyes around to his "—you're so beautiful."

But she took his hands away from her face. "I don't know why—" she hesitated. "well, I might as well say it, Lou. Wouldn't it have been better if you'd written to your ma about Jesse? It was such a shock to her."

Lou's hands fell listlessly between his thighs. He knew Nina meant it was a shock to her, not only to his mother. "Sure, we've got to be honest," he said moodily. "But I ain't so good writing about that kind of thing and I figured I'd tell her all about it when I got home. What's wrong with that?" he asked as if she was making a lot out of nothing.

"It seems so strange your keeping it all to yourself, that's all." Nina's temper was churning out her thoughts. "Really, I mean, Lou!"

Nina wasn't concerned about him keeping other things to himself, that was plain enough, only about him buddying up with a colored guy. "Nina, I wanta tell you," he said quietly but with a firmness that made her look him in the eyes, "color and those things don't add up to a row of beans out there. Only thing matters, you're a live joe—or a dead one."

"But back here, Lou—" Nina sounded like she wanted to be convinced.

"Back here, too," he said bluntly. "If the world never changed, it would be a doggone poor place to live."

"I dunno, Lou. I hope you're right."

He closed his arm around her to feel the warmth and slenderness of her body. Slowly the tenseness went out of her as she stared at the moon. She began to smile dreamily as if she had forgotten Jesse and Lou's mother. "What were we arguing about?"

"I don't know either," said Lou. The moonlight seemed to radiate from Nina's face and hair. She was something special a man would want to take in his arms, not only for a night, but for always. And yet, he would never be sure he had her for keeps.

"I used to think about you all the time," she said dreamily, wondering if you'd want me—the way you said in your letters."

"Yeh, and I was thinking all the time, she's got a dozen boy friends. She won't think twice again about Lou Bianchi."

"So that's why you wrote me two, three times a week?"

"You mean you didn't look at another guy in three years?" Lou teased. But there was a seriousness back of his question.

"You want me to be like a stone saint in the church?" Nina suddenly froze in mock seriousness.

"God, no. I want you the way you are." Lou tried to draw her head closer to his, but she still resisted.

"If you think I'm any guy's pushover—yours or anybody else's—" She was laughing at him and resisting him with her arm pressed against his chest. But the moon was full and sensual and his hand was afire on her breast.

"Nina, I just wanted you to wait for me," he whispered, "not throw yourself away on one of those tavern bums. That's why I wrote you all the letters. And when I seen you at the airport, honest to God, I thought I ain't seen nothing like this since I been away."

"It was the same with me, Lou. Every night you were gone, it was so empty without you—" Her words trailed off.

"That's over and done with." Lou boxed her cheeks in between his hands and closed her mouth with a kiss. She met him at last with a passion as strong as his.

The moon went behind the mist. A burden of familiar sound began to swell in Lou's ear. It grew louder. A plane, dark against the sky that was already turning grey, came up out of the east. Its lights flashed in competition with the morning star.

"A guy wants a little peace from shooting and killing when he comes back home," Lou whispered. "He wants to live human. He needs somebody like you, Nina. Somebody special. somebody all for himself."

"What does that mean," asked Nina with sudden reserve, "somebody *like* me?"

"You know what it means. I love you."

The roar overhead almost drowned out what Lou was saying. Then the plane flew off to the southwest over factory chimneys and disappeared.

#7

Floating on dreams, Lou slept through the early morning hours. He dreamed of a girl with fiery hair and dark eyes wanting him from a depth of passion as deep and stirring as his own. He wanted her in his arms and he dreamed his arms were around her. And as he half heard the casual familiar sounds in the street, he remembered the full moon and the radiance of Nina's face.

His mother's voice brought him sharply to his daytime senses. "Luigi, we got business!" She came rushing in to hug him and cover his face with kisses. "Get up, lazy bones!" The worries of the night were wiped clean away. In the light of morning, Jesse was like a cloud passing over the horizon.

Kathryn danced over to the window to pull the curtains wide, then beckoned to Lou. The skyscrapers of the Chicago loop rose imposingly above the center of the city. As she pointed to the Board of Trade Building at the end of the La Salle Street canyon, her hand trembled with excitement. "Look, there's Anselmo's office!"

At the top of the Board of Trade Building rising taller than the rest, the statue of Ceres pointed skyward, a golden finger of authority in the morning light. Ceres was the Roman goddess of the harvests, Anselmo had explained, and therefore the patron saint of the wheat pool, the stock market, the insurance companies, and the big banks. "The goddess of take-your-chance and win-the-jackpot," Anselmo had added with a laugh. "She must have been a Sicilian!"

"One day, Luigi," Kathryn gloated, "you gonna have your office up top. Luigi Bianchi in golden letters, just like Anselmo."

"Fine and dandy, ma!" Lou grinned at the idea of his having an office up there. "But let's keep our feet on the ground."

"You got the brains, Luigi," she said proudly. "Go to night school, be a lawyer like Anselmo."

"So it's a lawyer now!" Lou circled his ma's shoulder with a powerful hug. "You always wanted me to go places. First, it was a priest, but I couldn't get the hang of the Latin. For myself, I wanted to pitch for the Cubs. Remember how you used to stand at the door when I was trying to pitch a no-hitter over in the ballpark, and you'd yell, 'Luigi, you got homework!' "

It had never mattered how loud she yelled, though, Lou would go on pitching till the street lights came on, unless his old man came over to get him. And even then, Pete would usually wait for him to pitch out the inning and forget about his homework until it was too dark to play ball any more. In the morning, at the first sounds in the house, Lou used to jump out of bed and wolf his breakfast to get in a few innings before school. It seemed a whole lifetime ago when he was one of the kids in the ballpark yelling, "Safe!" or "Out!" loud enough to drown the clatter of the school bell. Now a new generation of kids had taken over. They sounded just as loud-mouthed about the game as he and Vico when they organized the Beavers in the neighborhood league and Jackson Taylor came around with his Black Bombers —years ago. When the dismal bell rang for the second time and killed their game, the kids groaned with the same kind of anger and frustration. When each one knew secretly he was big league stuff, even if his buddies didn't make the grade, what was the use of a lot of writing and arithmetic?

"Remember, ma, when the teacher caught us kids smoking and made us eat a cigarette in front of the class?"

"She dare!" said Kathryn fiercely remembering how she had rushed over to the school to instruct the teacher she should teach reading and writing, not poison her boy.

"Those were the times," Lou mused as he watched the school door close behind the last of the sandlot champions. "Now you wanta make a lawyer out of me."

Kathryn felt this was too sacred a subject to joke about. "Maybe it was God's will, why he didn't want you for a priest."

"Well, ma," said Lou serious, too, "I been a machinist. I don't know if I can go for this big shot stuff." With an easy humor he went on, "Maybe I don't wanta work for a boss—right in the family."

Kathryn was disturbed enough to answer him sharply, "No, no boss. Partners."

"Me partners with Generoso Anselmo?" Now Lou had to laugh. "Who you trying to kid, ma, me or yourself?"

"You wanta wear greasy pants all your life?" she snapped. Then her tone softened. "Or dress nice? Take Nina to the Como Inn." She hugged Lou again, but in an urging commanding way. "Promise me, Luigi!"

"Look, ma, if Anselmo makes me an offer, I'll promise to consider it," said Lou with a firmness to match his mother's. "Sure, I'd like the dough and all that. Maybe I'd like to get married—"

The phone rang downstairs. Kathryn stopped long enough to finish saying what she had in mind. "Nina, she wants to go places. You're gonna need money, Luigi, to make her happy. Lots of money."

A few sharp words from his mother came up through the ceiling. She sounded disappointed. Lou hoped it was Anselmo cancelling the appointment. He felt lazy and happy as he leaned out the window. It was a baking hot day for September. In a frenzy the flies were buzzing in and out of the neighbor's garbage cans. Burning refuse thickened the heat haze, and smoke and dust hung heavily over the park.

"Hey Lou, you old blockbuster!" Vico called up as he came to a brake-screeching stop in front of Bianchi's. His red and jaunty Cadillac de luxe sports model with all the chrome trimmings was just his style, Lou reacted with bitterness. Here was the guy who stayed home, made love to Nina, and feathered his nest while Lou and Jesse were taking it out there on the chin. Lou didn't invite him up, but Vico came running up the stairs anyway, burst into Lou's room and gave him a hearty bearhug. "All in one piece, buddy. We got you back!"

Vico was still the handsomest kid on the block, now grown and with a layer or two of fat, swinging his new weight around with the confidence of a ward heeler and passing out cigars. "Here, Lou, Havana's best. What you smoke out there? Those gook rope cigars?" What did Nina see in this four-flusher, Lou wondered, and how could Vico ever have been his best friend? Only three years ago! "Christ, the changes around here," Lou was thinking, "or is it me?"

"Things were rough out there?" Vico asked in an easy-going way, the same question they all asked. Then, without waiting for an answer, consoled Lou with "But you got your disability."

"Sure, cracked pelvis. Back plowed up. It wasn't just rough, buddy. It was hell on square wheels."

"I guess we'll beat the shit out of them before it's all over." Vico had an easy jaunty smile he turned on Lou like a male nurse at the hospital using psychology on a patient.

"The hell we will," said Lou. "It's the other way around. Why we don't let them fight it out beats me. It's their country. Let 'em have it." Lou was getting riled up now and for reasons he didn't stop to analyze felt like swinging at Vico, that smiling face of his.

"I know how you feel, buddy. You been through it," Vico said with charity. "But we gotta teach 'em a lesson or they'll swarm over us next."

"Bullshit!" said Lou. "They're seven thousand miles over there. Let's get it straight." Lou could hardly contain himself as he shouted, "You want to whip their ass, why don't *you* enlist?"

"Kidney stones," explained Vico, brushing off the personal question. He could see Lou was getting heated up and his fingers tensing into fists. "No, I can see you had a bad time out there," Vico went on to defuse Lou's anger. "Your eyes—"

"What's wrong with them?"

"Looks like you got a couple of haymakers," Vico said with an easy laugh.

Lou looked at himself in the mirror. His face did look back at him gaunt with deep-set dark eye sockets, one darker than the other. "That was a stateside haymaker with a San Antonio trademark," he explained with a humorless laugh. "Bumped into Mario Ferrucini down there—"

"And he gave you the shiner?" Vico joked. "But honest, what happened?"

"We was just sittin' there chewin' the fat at this bar after a send off drink with my buddy, Jesse. Jesse had already left for the airport and Mario was briefin' me about all the goings on around Hemlock Street—" Lou paused to choose his next words with care "—about the old folks, his ma kickin' the bucket after her operation, about my buddies, you and Nina—" Lou gave him a needling look.

"Hey Lou, lets' can the cat and mouse stuff." Vico's eyes were on Lou's fists with the tenseness increasing between them. "So what did he say about me and Nina? Mario's a goddam liar, you know that as well as me."

"So like I'm tellin' you—" Lou ignored his comment, "this cowboy comes along, wide hat, his gang in boots with him. Seems they didn't like seein' us buddy up with Jesse. But Jesse's a powerhouse they didn't want to tangle with. So they wait till he's gone, then they gang up and this cowboy starts callin' us jagoffs. So OK, then it's nigger-lovers."

"This guy Jesse was black?" Vico sounded like he couldn't believe it.

Lou nodded. "So Mario jumped him. Nobody knew who was hittin' who, things got so messed up. Somebody taps me friendly-like on the shoulder. I'm turnin' around—WHAM! A guy twice my size puts his knuckles into my eye. Next thing I'm seein' stars and bells are ringin'. When I begin to come to, here's Mario dead to the world flat on his ass and, Chrisake, the tavern's full of MPs, army and navy both. And when they ask, 'Who started this, boys?' that fuckin' cowboy fingers me—"

"What you expect, Lou," said Vico trying to calm him down, "in Texas buddying up with a goddam shine?"

"You son-of-a-bitch!" Lou's fist shot up and caught Vico under the jaw. "Shine!"

Vico staggered back to avoid the full force of Lou's blow, then shouted in hurt amazement, "What the hell's wrong with you, guy? You got shellshock?"

Lou was surprised at himself the way his anger triggered off at Vico. Why did he let himself fly off the handle? It was because of Nina, basically. "Sorry, buddy," he said quietly. "It's not shellshock. But I got a hell of a big chip on my shoulder about Jesse Williams. He's the guy saved my life and you call him a goddam shine. You fuckin' around on easy street in your shiny new deluxe sports model back home. We're over there takin' the flak. And, yeh, I'll say it—you were over here layin' my best girl. That's the kind of buddy you are!"

"I know how you feel, Lou," said Vico still rubbing the pain out of his jaw. "You got the right to be pissed about that. But Chrisake man, Nina's ditched me. I offered her a ring—"

"Is that straight goods?"

"Yeh, we hadn't heard news from you so long we thought your number was called."

"You're not the marrying kind, Vico."

There was a long, long silence between them before Vico said, "OK, say it Lou. Gigolo. Say it if that's what you mean. Nina's the only one ever made a dent with me. But when you called her from San Antonio, she wanted her key back. And that was it. I guess you got what it takes. I'm missing a cylinder or something. You won the heat, so what we got to fight about? Congratulations! If you're joining Anselmo's outfit, we'll be seeing a lot of each other." Vico held out his hand, but Lou refused it.

"OK, if that's the way you want it," Vico shrugged and paused at the top of the stairs to add, "But to be honest, Lou, I don't think you and Gene are going to hit it off. You seem to think you're Jesus Christ or somebody." Lou watched Vico climb into his car, wave good-bye with his cigar and take off around the corner on two wheels.

"Luigi! Luigi!" his mother shouted at him to come downstairs. "Bad news,' she said with mischief. "Anselmo can't see you this morning."

"That's OK with me." Lou was still sorting out Vico's last comments. "If you're joining Anselmo's outfit—" Big IF!

"But you know what?" Kathryn went on with excitement. "It was Della. She wants you and Nina to come up to their place for cocktails. Wait till you see! Ten rooms on the Lake Shore. Anselmo says you use his season's tickets, take Nina to the ball game this afternoon. Ain't that the best ever?"

Lou's enthusiasm picked up. "Sure like to see the Cubs win for a change. But I promised pop I'd go up to Farmway and Nina's working."

"Call her," Kathryn commanded. "First see the building we're gonna buy." She seized him by the arm and ushered him faster than he wanted to go down Hemlock Street to 758.

Tony Ferrucini was just turning into the alley pushing his barbalucci wagon when he caught sight of Kathryn. "Kick us all out," he shouted, his voice booming like a cannon. Then he rushed in the side door and slammed it.

"You mean you're kicking Tony out, ma?"

"He's the only one left, stubborn donkey! All the rest moved to better places. Anselmo helped. He explains it."

The second and third floor windows where Fiuccis and Trombatores used to live stared like blind eyes out of an old face, while two pigeons, proud of their brown and white feathers, strutted up to the flat edge of the roof and curved their heads to eye Kathryn and Lou while exchanging little notes of warning.

"Ma, there're some things I don't like about this Anselmo deal. Kick old Tony out? How come?"

"Anselmo explains it all," she repeated pressing his arm persuasively. "You ask him."

#8

The Anselmos lived on top of the world in an enormous penthouse apartment. The city lay at their feet, north, west and south, sprawling out to smoky skylines. To the east over the trees of Lincoln Park, the lake rounded away to infinity.

Anselmo's living room was as large as a five room flat on Hemlock Street—with an acre of white carpet and slender Japanese style furniture reminding Lou of the Geisha houses in

Tokyo. The end wall was one great picture window opening on a roof garden where palm trees flickered in the sun and wind, and asters and gaillardias and chrysanthemums burned geometric shapes in an emerald lawn.

As the maid ushered Nina and Lou to the garden, Nina gasped, "How simply—" and was lost for words. She held closer to Lou's arm and Lou also gripped her hand more firmly, wishing himself back at the ballpark or anywhere else.

It had been home sweet home to Lou earlier that afternoon, the field and the players, the bleachers and the stands roaring and booing, the clean click of bat on ball, and the wallop of Chicago's home run king over the wall—even if the home team lost. And Nina was one of those rare girls who followed baseball. She knew most of the players who had been bought and sold while Lou was away and their approximate batting and pitching averages. She was radiant, too, in the life of that long afternoon, a center of attention. For the first time in his life at a major league game, his eyes were only half on the ball. He knew Nina was as happy to be with him as he to be with her. When they kissed it was like a promise for the future. And when the game was over, Lou suggested they skip the Anselmo deal and take a drive out to the lake or anywhere. "Just you and me, how about it, Nina?"

"Wonderful!" she exclaimed, hugging his arm to her. But she had never seen the Anselmos' apartment. She hesitated a moment, before asking, "Can't we do both?"

"OK, OK." Lou also remembered his promise to his mother. All the same, he had to drag his feet when the maid led them across the carpeted spaces. He was in no mood to talk Anselmo's kind of business.

Anselmo, himself, seemed in no mood to talk business. He was reclining on a chaise longue with his arm around Della. At Lou's greeting, "Hi, Gene, it's been a dog's age," Anselmo got to his feet and came down the roof garden path to meet them. His face was cocktail red mixed by sun and alcohol in the open air. He was wearing a yacht captain's tunic with gold insignia, a pair of featherweight wool pants, and white shoes.

"You're looking good, Lou." Anselmo's tone was full of simple affection as he put his hand on Lou's shoulder. "We're proud of him, eh Nina?"

Anselmo hadn't changed in three years, unless his hair had receded a fraction of an inch. But Della was like a stranger to Lou with her groomed beauty and her studied gestures. Artfully simple in a white linen dress with a wide gold belt, she seemed unapproachable like a statue. As she stood up to give Lou a homecoming kiss, he hesitated for a moment to put his arms around her. It was impossible to say the way he used to, "Hi, sis, how's it go?"

"It has been a long time," Della said with a smile, "and we've missed you, Lou." She circled Nina's waist with her arm. "You, too, Nina. It's wonderful to see you."

"Chrisake," said Anselmo pulling up two canvas chairs and handing Lou and Nina a highball, "while we've been going through the same old routine making dollars, you guys out there have been making history."

"Not like the history books," said Lou breaking through Anselmo's patronage. "In school we used to win all the battles."

"Let's not get technical. You held the beachhead," Anselmo insisted. "So they banged you up some?" He fired a dozen questions at Lou, hardly waiting for the answers, about how Lou got hurt, how the war was going, what was it like out at San Antonio. All the time, he was studying Lou intently, as if he'd once known a boy who was now sitting in front of him as a grown man. What he saw, he apparently liked. Lou's steady, deep-set eyes, his blunt nose, his firm mouth were all in his favor. Anselmo could understand why Lou was his mother's favorite, partly, too, because he had a clean cut straightforward look about him. Lou was stubborn, that Anselmo knew from the past. Yet stubbornness would be all to the good if Anselmo could turn it to account in his own business.

Lou was embarrassed by the examination. "What about this deal the ma's been telling me about?"

Anselmo filled his glass again. "You wanta make dough? Lots of it?" He winked at Nina at the same time. "Hand over fist?"

"That depends," Lou countered with a sceptical laugh.

"In ten easy lessons?" Anselmo was playing with him.

"Sure," said Lou matching his easy tone. "But if this deal's a job, like the ma said, I wanta know how much an hour. How many hours a week. Who's gonna be boss."

"You're OK, fellow," said Anselmo with a hearty laugh. He turned to size up Nina for a moment. "How's your old man?" he asked her abruptly.

Nina bent her head to right and left without much enthusiasm as if Papa Pagliani was the same as always and why did Anselmo have to bring him in.

With the same abruptness Anselmo turned around to Della. "How about barbecue supper?" Della was always agreeable to Anselmo's propositions.

Nina's eyes began to dance, but Lou shook his head. "I told my buddy to come over tonight." He explained to Anselmo he couldn't stand Jesse up the first time. Nina looked at him in the sheerest amazement.

"Call your buddy," Anselmo ordered. Once he had issued na invitation, he didn't accept a refusal. "Half an hour we eat, eh?" he said to Della. "And show Nina around the joint." He dismissed them with a wave of his hand.

As Della took Nina's arm again and sauntered across the garden, Anselmo poured Lou a third highball and filled his own glass. The gulls were wheeling overhead and the lake rolled off in a great circle to the horizon. What would it matter if Lou called Jesse and told him to come tomorrow? He didn't have any news for him about the job, anyway. It was too bad he hadn't made it up to Farmway like he'd promised his dad. But there were plenty of days ahead.

When they were alone, Lou called Anselmo's hand in his usual straightforward way. "So what's the deal, Gene?"

Anselmo began to pace the garden path with his hands relaxed behind his back, preparing his brief. Abruptly, he turned to face Lou. "OK, you want to be your own boss. That's it. OK, put in the time you want. No punching a clock, Lou. The first year you make ten grand if you're any good. Then twenty. Drive any car you want. Live anywhere you damn please. Sleep with any woman. Brother, there's no limit!" Anselmo was building up his case with sweeping gestures at the sky.

"'Now we got the pie down," Lou sliced through the generalities with a sarcastic laugh, "let's have the brass tacks, too."

"OK, in one syllable words," Anselmo sliced back. "Your ma

owns one building in Pioneer Street. She's remodelling another in Hemlock Street. You're back home from San Antonio. Fridays, you help her collect the rents. Next year, you buy two more buildings. The year after, eight. You know what geometric triplession is? That's the way it goes. Put in a few partitions, triple the rent. Colored people have it tough finding a place to live. You provide a service. Somebody's going to get their dough. Might as well be you." Anselmo leaned over in great good spirits to box Lou on the arm. "Comprende?"

"You didn't say nothing about moving the old folks like Tony Ferrucini—" Lou was blunter than Anselmo liked.

"Time all our people moved out of the slum," he had just enough patience to explain. "Besides, Tony's a goddam mule. We arranged a better place for him. He wouldn't take it."

"Sounds like a racket all the same," Lou persisted.

"Everything's a racket," Anselmo countered. "Can you come up with a better one?" He motioned Lou to join him at the railing. "Look! It's a city of rackets in a world of rackets, big ones and little ones." Together they gazed across at the Loop buildings which rose on the southern skyline like interlocking mountain ranges. Highest of all, the Board of Trade Building raised the statue of Ceres like a finger of authority above the city. "You have your office on top of the world," Anselmo invited Lou to smile with him, "or—" he gestured with a downward motion of his hand to the west where gasworks and factory chimneys stood up black against the sunset "—you slave in a factory. You've got to choose up, Lou, either you pick a good racket or a bad racket."

"That ain't what you said, Gene, that time they nabbed Vico and me for running hot stuff when we were kids." Lou could see Anselmo, a champion, standing up in a court to defend two teenagers that morning years ago when it seemed the world was about to close in on them. "These are not bad boys, your honor. A misdemeanor—" Anselmo had a strength and a determination as he appealed to the judge not to condemn them to the reformatory which he'd called a school to graduate criminals. "I will take personal responsibility for these boys, judge, to see that from now on they stick to the straight and narrow."

"Remember, Gene," Lou went on, "you gave us a lecture coming home from juvenile about sticking to the straight and narrow?"

"Sure, you were only kids then and you got caught. Sixteen?" Anselmo laughed as if that made all the difference in the world. "In America, it's what you can get away with that counts. That's what my dad used to say. He was only a poor immigrant from Sicily settling in Hemlock Street like your pa. But he decided to make money—"

"Yeh, I remember when they bumped him off."

Anselmo's tone was less friendly when he countered, "But pop raked in the dough, even if he was unlucky in the end." Anselmo went on staring over the city thinking about the fortune his father had pile up. "When pop picked up his lucky dice and came to America, he got here kind of late. Most of the good games were played already. Most of the big games were won. So pop had to horn in on the little ones at first, the little side alley rackets, selling fruit, driving a cab. And sometimes he landed in jail, just like you and Vico, when he didn't play it smart. But we aren't any more criminals than the Irish or the Swedes or the Germans. We came a little later, that's all. We had it tougher muscling in on the big money.

"We didn't have offices on La Salle Street then. We took the chances." As Anselmo added, "And pop paid the penalty," he was twisting his glass on the rail with a sudden nervousness. It slipped from his hand and went out in an arc, shining for a moment, then plunging twenty stories down. There was a faint tinkle of broken glass in the dark street below. Anselmo tried to conceal his agitation from Lou with a bluffness. "So we learned the hard way, through pop's experience. He was a pioneer, understand? Some of us went to the big schools and began to get into the bigger rackets. Then we stopped getting caught and we would make speeches about law and order and honesty. We had it tougher than the McCormicks and the Fields and the Armours—but where there is enough money, one makes one's own laws. That's the way things are in America, Lou, everything's a racket."

Anselmo's enthusiasm grew as he directed Lou's attention to the neighborhood of Hemlock Street. "That's where we came in, brother. Raised in the same slum!" Thousands of old brick and frame houses merged in a quilt of sombre colors. And beyond, warehouses and factory chimneys and railyards stretched away to infinity. "And here's where we are now—on top of the world!"

Anselmo shook his head with a philosophical smile. "Wouldn't pop be proud of us if he could only see us up here?" Only a remote whisper of traffic came up to these altitudes, and the evening light which slanted like an undersea haze into the depths still bathed the windows of Anselmo's penthouse with liquid gold.

"So that's about the picture," said Anselmo as he heard Della's and Nina's voices again. With a mysterious smile, he went on, "Maybe I'll have a little more to say about it at the homecoming. When do you get your broken-winged duck?"

"Monday, I go up to Fort Sheridan to get my discharge papers," said Lou full of questions he had no chance to ask Anselmo now. "It'll take a couple of days."

Nina was shouting across the garden in a voice jumping with excitement and envy, "You should see the breakfast nook, Lou. It's just like a ship's cabin."

"When you get back from Fort Sheridan, come up to the office," Anselmo concluded dryly, "and we'll get down to the brass tacks."

#9

Kathryn put down the receiver with an immense satisfaction. She had hardly dared hope Anselmo would open the door for Lou into his own home—and for Nina, too—right at the beginning. Della had told her about their barbecue suppers on the roof garden. Once tasting that life, could Lou ever think of going back to work in a factory?

Nina was a very smart and beautiful girl, the kind Kathryn herself would want to be if she was twenty again. The kind of woman Lou needed, too, because he was overgenerous and easy going. She would keep him hustling. And Nina, thank God, was one of their own kind, raised in the same street.

When they got married—Kathryn's dreams mushroomed like a cloud in moonlight—Nina and Lou could come live upstairs. Naturally, they would want to build later out in the suburbs. By that time, Lou would already be driving around in a red Cadillac, larger than Vico's, and she, herself, would be living in an apartment somewhere up by Lincoln Park, not as splendid as Anselmo's, of course, but a thousand times better than the house in Hemlock Street.

Quick as a hope she rushed to the top of the stairs, darted into this room and that and calculated how she would decorate, put in plumbing, furniture, and all the little nicknacks a young bride would want. It wouldn't be money wasted even if they moved after a few months, because the house would sell at a much higher price if it was a modernized two-flat building.

Lou's room was already in perfect condition. She darted in, as she had done a thousand times before he came home, to admire the cool combination of green and autumn blonde. But that stubborn Pete! There was Lou's old toolbox still sitting on his bureau where Pete had placed it deliberately. Its shiny fence green was enough to turn her stomach. In anger, she decided to push it into the darkest corner of the closet until Lou forgot he'd ever worked in a factory. It came sliding easily toward her as she pulled, but it suddenly overbalanced. As she jumped aside, it came crashing to the floor with a weight to shake the whole frame of the house. Her heart beat savagely as she kicked and shoved the toolbox past shoes under hanging clothes to the dark back corner.

To compose herself, Kathryn went to the crucifix which glittered between the windows and thanked the Holy Mother that her prayers in the darker days and her hopes for her boy were now being fulfilled. When she heard the usual sound of Pete's boots in the kitchen, she could hardly fly down the stairs fast enough to pour out her good news.

"For barbecue supper in the roof garden, Pete! Imagine, for our Luigi! Ain't it the best ever?"

All supper time Pete brooded. "The boy didn't come. He promised me."

"But, Pete, it was important—" Kathryn was sure one day Pete would get over that peasant stubbornness and rejoice with her. But he only shrugged with a disappointment that weighted down his shoulders as he set out for his usual nightcap at Pagliani's. With his boy home he should be happy. But his heart was filled with bitter juice.

As Pete started down the alley, he remembered Jesse Williams was going to stop by. "But that Jesse—" he called back. His words were like a protest.

"If he comes," said Kathryn in an offhand way, "I'll worry. Luigi left a message at his place."

So Pete went on. But Kathryn didn't tell him that she expected Jesse all the same. Lou had called her because he hadn't been able to reach Jesse and he wanted her to keep trying. "You see ma," he'd said to her on the phone, "I can't stand the guy up the first time I asked him over. Keep calling him, will you?"

But Kathryn figured, even while she was still talking to Lou, better she should see Jesse alone. There was a danger if Jesse was really desperate for a place to live, Lou might try to force her hand about the upstairs rooms. It was unthinkable that a Negro family should live in the same house. It was a puzzler to Kathryn, even after he'd told her all about Jesse, how Lou could have formed such a friendship. A man should mix with his own the way God had made the world. But since Lou didn't seem to want to understand these things, she would have to be very careful.

The best would be to arrange for Jesse to share Mrs. Osborne's flat down at 1250 for a few months. Later, Kathryn could give Jesse and his wife first choice at the new place in Hemlock Street when the remodelling was finished. That would put an end to Lou's worrying about Tony Ferrucini.

As Kathryn planned for the future, Jesse was no longer a frightening cloud on the horizon. She began to believe God had arranged his friendship with Lou to benefit them all. In the long run, when the Bianchis had moved out of the neighborhood, maybe Jesse would be the one to look after their interests at 758. She could make it worth his while by reducing his rent.

When Kathryn had finished the dishes, she went up front to poke up the canary. "Come on, sing for mama!" She held her finger through the wires of the cage and bird hopped over from his perch. He ruffled his wings a little and winked his eyes sleepily. He was too old to sing any more. "What do we feed you for, grasshopper?"

Kathryn sat down at her desk and took out her little black book to gloat over the figures she had set down in her round, clear handwriting. The figures in red were very small, though the largest, which was payoff to the building inspector for not reporting violations of the code, was enough to make her sigh with resignation. But on the credit side was a balance of more than nine thousand dollars. Not bad for an old lady in three years—after paying for the house and all. In her savings account was still more, almost two grand she and Pete had put aside through a lifetime of meager spending. When she heard the door bell ring, she was happy because she was ready to do business with her son's friend.

Lou had described Jesse well enough, a tall man with a dark skin rising head and shoulders above her as she opened the door. He was handsome, too, with a neat moustache, firm cheeks and chin, and large, steady eyes behind the glint of his glasses. Was he thirty-eight like Lou said? He looked younger as he smiled down at her. "You Mrs. Bianchi, Lou's mother?"

"Come right in, Jesse." She called him by his first name as if she'd known him for years. There was charity but friendliness in her tone as she explained why Lou was away. "First things first," she laughed.

"He told me he had a girl back home." Jesse looked around the house as if he'd been there before. "Nice boy you got, Mrs. Bianchi." He was wearing his stripes and battle stars, and as he saw Kathryn examining them he said, "Last time before my wife puts them into the cedar chest. I been house hunting—" He laughed as if the uniform might have made some difference, but didn't. "Last woman just closed the door in my face." He seemed to be examining Kathryn in his own way, looking and not looking at her, all the time his eyes wearing an impenetrable smile. "Seems like there ain't no places, you have three kids." But his tone of voice told her it wasn't only the kids.

"Well now, you don't need to worry any more, Jesse." Kathryn was kneeling down to open the cabinet in her desk. "I know Luigi would want me to give you a drink." She was determined to entertain him correctly, but with a reserve he apparently understood well enough. He sat down on the edge of the sofa, his attitude at attention. "My son and I are very grateful for what you did."

"That was nothing, Mrs. Bianchi. Lou helped me out of a tight spot, too."

"You were hurt bad?"

"Little bit in the leg and shoulder, kidney damage, but they mended us up good out there in San Antonio. We were the lucky ones." As Kathryn filled his glass again, he said, "Hits the spot."

A man who was so polite, on his dignity was easy to entertain, and Kathryn could almost forget his color—except when she thought of the flat upstairs. It was a pity Jesse wasn't white. Then there wouldn't be a problem. He was handsome, vigorous, large, full of an inner self-confidence, wearing his battle ribbons proudly. He had a splendid pair of shoulders and a pleasant deep voice that occasionally went high up in the scale when he laughed. Still, it couldn't be, it just couldn't be. Everybody should live with his own people, not mix up. That was what the great God intended when he made white white and black black.

"I'm gonna help you get a place, Jesse," she said with a sigh. "I bought a new building—right down the street. Remodel first—then two, three months you can take your pick. My son tells me your wife is in the beauty parlor business. How about first floor front?"

"That would be OK, but they gonna tear our old place down next week."

"I know, Luigi told me. Ain't it a shame!" Kathryn explained how she owned another building a few blocks away across the park. One of her tenants, Mrs. Osborne, wanted to sublet part of her flat. "She's a nice old colored lady. You and her would hit it off good—and your wife, of course." Kathryn was less certain about Mrs. Osborne and the three kids. Still, if she needed the extra money bad enough she'd have to put up with them.

"How much rent?" Jesse asked.

Kathryn resented his direct question when she was doing him a favor. "Only twenty dollars."

"A month?"

"Where have you been?" She laughed as if he must be joking. "A week, of course!"

"It's too much." Jesse was polite and firm at the same time.

"Maybe Mrs. Osborne will cut it to fifteen," she said without enthusiasm. It was pity Jesse had to drive a sharp bargain when everything was so friendly before.

"I'll be frank with you, Mrs. Bianchi, my old lady wants to buy when we got enough laid aside. She don't spend a penny she don't have to."

"Naturally," said Kathryn warming to Jesse again as she thought maybe the Williams would want to buy in Hemlock Street. "We're gonna be moving up by Lincoln Park one of these days." She watched Jesse's eyes travel around the room and up the stairs. "We got four nice rooms on the second floor. You couldn't beat it. Maybe you'd like to look around?"

"I'll tell Mrs. Williams," said Jesse.

"Drop by any time you feel like," said Kathryn effusively.

"OK. Now I got to be pushing along, Mrs. Bianchi. That was a good brand of whiskey."

"Glad you liked it. Now, you stop in at the corner tavern, Jesse, and find Mr. Bianchi. He'll take you down to 1250 and introduce you to Mrs. Osborne."

"Thanks a million." Jesse's massive hand swallowed Kathryn's bony little hand in a friendly good-bye.

When he was gone, Kathryn was very well pleased with herself. She could understand why Lou had made friends with Jesse now. She had never met a colored man like him. He seemed one in a million, a prince of a man. Firm, of course, but she was sure they could do business.

#10

As Jesse glanced through the window of Club Pagliani, he could see a crowd of older men gathered around a couple of tables as if they were holding a meeting. Several of them were waving excitedly and even in the street Jesse could hear their throaty voices. He wondered which of the old fellows was Lou's pop.

The bartender was resting his elbows on the bar and his two-ton chin on his knuckles while he gazed vacantly at the old guys. But the moment Jesse stepped in, an electric shock seemed to jolt Pagliani's enormous bulk. "We're closing," he grunted. Behind the tavern keeper's back, row on row of bottles rose to the ceiling. The tap at the bar dripped beer, overflowing with a smell of malt. Pagliani's offensive made Jesse want a drink in the worst way—and in his own right, not as a friend of Lou Bianchi.

"Make it a Schenley's and small beer." As Jesse placed his order, he clinked down a handful of change.

"We got a club here." a flush of anger began to redden upward through Pagliani's cheeks. His eyes were thrusting at Jesse like enemy bayonets. "You ain't a member."

"I been in Korea," said Jesse leaning toward Pagliani. His easy smile was hardening. "And I ain't had time to join no clubs."

"Hey, Boatman!" From the explosion in Pagliani's voice that gave commands like a bazooka, Jesse wasn't surprised to find that Boatman was one of his own people. A heavy set Negro about Jesse's age, he came edging up behind the bar from the back room. He wore an apron and held a broom defensively in both hands.

Over his shoulder, Jesse could hear cries of "Kick him out!" He wondered for an instant if they meant him. As he glanced around, he could see a man with dark hair and large, popping eyes, shaking his fists at another man across the table with pure white hair and shouting, "He ain't no better than the old lady. It's a shame to St. Joseph. Kick him out, kick him out!"

Jesse turned back to stare at Pagliani. "You don't serve me

that shot," he said quietly, "I'll break every bottle in the outfit."

Pagliani drew back as if Jesse had said every bone in his body. He made a sign to Boatman to throw him out and retired to the back end of the bar.

"So you're Mr. Boatman!" Jesse mocked, as if it was an honor to be introduced. Boatman seemed to Jesse like a two hundred fifty pounder with the build of a prizefighter gone soggy. His brown skin was pitted with black spots and there was a greyness around his eyes. "Throw me out, you got man enough in you."

Boatman's eyes were bloodshot. Peering at Jesse through a mist, he hesitated whether to bully or handle the soldier with gloves. His eyes settled on the overseas stripe.

"You know judo?" Jesse went on with a laugh. "Maybe I can teach you a few tricks I learnt out in Japan." As he spoke he was looking down the bar, issuing the challenge to Pagliani himself. "You gonna get me that shot?"

Pagliani raised his eyes like pistols at Boatman, commanding him to earn his pay. But Boatman's hands went limp on the broom handle. "You been out in Korea," he said with a show of respect. "Back home things ain't changed none." Boatman's hand rubbed the back of his neck as if to smooth out some painful irritation.

"You lick the same fat boots, you mean?"

"Man, that's dangerous talk." Boatman glanced sharply sideways and breathed heavily with relief to see that Pagliani had already gone into the back room. Then his whole manner changed. "Soldier, I'm gonna tell you straight," he began to talk like one buddy to another, "the boss is calling the bulls on you, you don't beat it."

"You think there's nothin' worse'n jail?"

Boatman's eyes closed for a moment and he squeezed the bar with his hands until his fingers paled from the pressure. "I ain't heard tell about it yet."

He looked around to see if Pagliani was coming back, then quick poured Jesse a shot. His hand was so shaky he overfilled the glass. The whiskey rounded out in a pool on the bar and spilled over the back edge. "Now drink up, soldier, and beat it."

"Thanks, buddy," said Jesse, friendly for the first time to Boatman, "but I ain't in no hurry."

"You ain't gonna be done with trouble nohow, soldier. You cain't change things the way they is set up, not by pushing no uniform around. You ain't no special person to the white folks. You're just a nigger like me."

"You lonesome for company?" Jesse clinked his glass on the bar for a refill. But Boatman put the bottle back on the shelf.

"Take my advice—"

"I don't want no part of your advice," Jesse interrupted. "Slice it any way you like, thick or thin, I'm choosy."

There was a sharp crack in Boatman's voice as he lashed back, "They're gonna get you and whip your ass good, you don't beat it." With his head down he was looking up at Jesse, his eyes defensively opened wide, as if he'd found out the hard way for himself. "You ain't got a chance with the bulls. They'll take your wallet, beat you up with rubber hose—"

A voice louder than Boatman's shut out what he was saying.

"Who wears the pants in your house, Pete Bianchi?"

"Why don't you shut up about me?" yelled Pete back to Tony. "Be friends like the old days."

"Kick him out," roared Tony hoarsely, "kick him out!"

"You been my oldest friend in America," Pete protested.

"Nobody's gonna kick nobody out of St. Joseph's," said Sam Vincenti laying down the law. "Thirty-five years already we been together. That's the way we gonna be. Next week, march in the parade. Joe, Pete, Tony, me. Understand? Put on the blue cap. Coat with gold braid. Band plays. It's nice every year for St. Joseph." Then he put one great hand on Tony's shoulder and the other on Pete's, and drew their heads together. "Now you shake hands!"

"So that's Lou's father," Jesse muttered.

"Soldier—" Boatman grabbed him by the arm. The lights of a squad car were spinning in front of the tavern. When Jesse refused to budge, Boatman withdrew down the bar into the back room, a great prizefighting hulk of a man, just as two cops came muscling in through the front entrance.

"What's all the trouble here, soldier?" The white cop opened up at Jesse while the Negro cop stepped around behind him. "You getting too big for your uniform?" he sneered.

Jesse's lips clamped together. His eyes turned on the very

slight smile of insolence he reserved for army officers and officers of the law when opening his mouth would be suicide.

"Trouble?" shouted Tony. Without knowing what he was doing, he was pumping Pete's hand up and down angrily across the table. "Goddam cops are the trouble."

"You don't shut your mouth, somebody's going to shut it for you." The white cop pointed his nightstick like a warning finger at Tony.

"Big fool!" Tony went on shouting as he saw Pagliani come venturing out of the back room.

"What's your name, soldier?" the Negro cop demanded.

"Jesse Williams."

"Declare your business." He gave him an official prod with his club.

"Jesse Williams!" Pete shouted. "That's my boy's buddy from Korea. What the hell's wrong around here?" He looked angrily at Pagliani as Jesse explained why he was looking for Pete Bianchi.

"OK, OK, OK," said the white cop nodding at Pagliani. "There must have been some mistake, then."

Pagliani wobbled his head with bewilderment as if he had no idea what the disturbance could be all about. "So what are you drinking, officer?"

"Make it a Jim Beam," said the cop. But he still had to wrap a threat in a wink at Jesse as he said, "When you get the uniform off, boy, take it easy. Be healthier for you."

And the Negro cop echoed, as Pagliani handed him a drink, too, "Be healthier for you, soldier."

#11

It was twilight when Pete and Jesse entered Pioneer Street. Flies buzzed up in a sleepy swirl from garbage cans and settled again as they passed. A brown rat moved like a shadow up the side of a barrel and vanished in the refuse inside.

The sounds and smells reminded Jesse of his own neighborhood. The street was densely populated. Cars were parked bumper to bumper. Garbage cans were lined up in platoons. And people filled the benches in front of the tenements, made bleachers out of front steps, and leaned out the windows like an overflow crowd.

Everywhere people were fanning hats and newspapers to stir up the air which weighed oppressively upon the street. Everywhere was the pulse of life and the sound of music. Jive and blues competed through the open windows. The kids were skipping around on the sidewalk. Teenagers were playing cards on a packing box under the street lights. Young men and women had their heads and arms locked together in the cars. And the old folks were laughing and joking because work was finished for the day and it was time for some fun.

"So you're Jesse Williams!" Happy as a child, Pete kept grabbing Jesse on the arm as if he couldn't believe this was actually the buddy Lou had told them about. "Find you a place to live, that's good."

"OK, Mr. Bianchi, OK," said Jesse as he followed Pete up the stairs.

Mrs. Osborne had never had two words to say to Pete nor he to her in days past when he was still doing repairs at 1250. Since then, her husband had died, and she sat hunched in her chair with her upward piercing eyes fixed on Pete as if grief itself were staring at him. In her faded purple dress with white lace at the neck, she looked saintlike and at the same time a little ghoulish. Maybe Pete had seen a bird watching him like that from cover when he was a boy out hunting. Maybe some animal.

As he introduced Jesse and explained why they had come, her eyes kept stabbing out at him while the rest of her face was set like a stone saint's in the church. Was she deaf or something? Pete came to a dead stop.

But Mrs. Osborne heard him alright. "Did Miss Kathryn say how much she's going to cut my rent?" Her skeptical inflection made Pete back away to the door. At the same time he was thinking Kathryn had laid a clever trap to involve him in the rent business again.

"We talked about it," said Jesse casually. "But it's up to you, Mrs. Osborne. It's your place."

"You gonna work it out." Pete was relieved and went backing out of the room.

"Thanks a million, Mr. Bianchi," said Jesse.

The moment Pete closed the door, Mrs. Osborne sat up straight in her chair and smiled at Jesse, as vigorous an old lady as he'd ever met. "What you done for that old Bianchi woman, Mr. Williams? She don't favor no man where she don't fix the price."

The transformation in Mrs. Osborne was too abrupt for Jesse to take with a straight face. "Me and her son buddied up in Korea. Happen we did each other a good turn out there."

"You and him?" Mrs. Osborne sighed. She could believe it because Jesse spoke simply, but her experience weighed heavily in the opposite direction. "I don't know nothing about the young one, but if he's his mother's son, Mr. Williams, you must have done him more than one good turn. I know the woman I'm talking about and there ain't nothing you can tell me." That closed the subject for the time being. "How many children you got, Mr. Jesse?"

"We got a girl who's twelve and two boys. One's about grown, big as me, but on the thin side. The other's a little runt with a big chip on his shoulder. He's ten years old already and won't cause you a lot of trouble."

"But some. That's the way little boys are, I know. Well, I ain't used to children, but I'll get used. You can have the rooms because I like the looks of you—and because I can't pay the rent all by myself. You can use the kitchen and make yourself at home. Since my husband—you remind me of him—" She raised her chin to point at a large oval framed portrait of Mr. Osborne. The curved glass reflected the light in such a way that Jesse could only guess at his features. "He wasn't a bad man, Mr. Jesse, and," she chuckled, "he wasn't a good man, not for long at a time." Her hands began to clench the lace arm covers of the chair she sat in. "But he was a *man*. She seemed to be remembering a hundred different experiences at the same time, all clearly sorted out in her mind. Her hands slacked into her lap as she summed up their life together, "Him and I was good for each other."

Finally, she had to face up to Jesse's problem. "So you want to move in next week?" She glanced around her neat sitting room as if for the last time. She stroked the lace coverings on the arms of her chair which she had crocheted when her husband was still living. She looked up at the oval portrait, again seeming to forget Jesse was in the room.

Through one door Jesse could see the kitchen. Through another and at the front was a room with two windows and moonlight flecking patterns on a great mahogany bed. And through the windows he could see rooftops and smokestacks and cooling tanks of factories against a bank of clouds, and down under in the distance, a range of skyscrapers shining with a million yellow lights.

"I'll have to bring the bed in here." Mrs. Osborne's complaint brought Jesse down from the clouds. It was fine to see the whole shining city from the front windows, but what mattered most was how Lil would take to Mrs. Osborne. If she didn't, a couple of months would be a long time, view or no view.

"I can help you move the bed," Jesse offered, "next week."

"You too much in a hurry right now?" Jesse could see by her smile she was teasing him. "Today, tomorrow—there ain't much difference to an old lady." Mrs. Osborne sighed like she meant it. "But you got time for one question, Mr. Williams. I'm wanting to ask you, and you can tell me the truth. How can a black man be friends to a white man—after all they done to our race of people?"

"You call that one question?" It was Jesse's turn to tease Mrs. Osborne. "That's a whole quiz program."

"Now tell me truth, soldier. Was things so different in Korea?

They treated you different? They made generals out of colored boys? They dressed you in big uniforms? You marched side by side with the whites? And *you* gave *them* the orders?" She held up her finger to warn him that she wanted nothing but the truth.

"Ma'am, we wasn't born yesterday," said Jesse.

"But they be shooting and raping and whipping?"

"It's war—"

"But war against the colored race of people. You see any white Korea folk?"

She was standing now, clutching up at Jesse's tunic. "Make friends with a rat or ol' rattlesnake, boy. But make friends with white folks? Next you'll be killing your own kin." Her eyes glittered with excitement. "Did Moses make friends in Egypt lan'?" Then she patted his battle stars like an affectionate grandmother and sank back into her chair.

"Fact remains," said Jesse, "that him and me did buddy up when the chips were down. How it's gonna be back home—that's the sixty-four dollar question. But you didn't ask me that one, Mrs. Osborne. Now I must be cutting."

"You think the Lord sent you like a mercy angel from heaven to change the leopard's spots?" She waved her finger at him and gave him a sarcastic wink. Jesse laughed, then Mrs. Osborne began to laugh louder till she was almost convulsed. When she could control her voice again she said, "But the Lord ain't done pulling your leg, boy. He's just got off to a start. He's got some mighty big shocks coming down in his ol' lightning for you. And the biggest is that woman sent you here."

Jesse put his hand affectionately on Mrs. Osborne's shoulder. "You sure pulled the wool thick over that woman's eyes. But I can see you's a she-devil when you cuts loose." Then Jesse and Mrs. Osborne shook and shouted with laughter.

"You're pulling my leg now, soldier." Finally she stopped laughing and with an old fashioned dignity said, "You tell the missus and the kids they can come in anytime you want to bring them. But they gotta take this nice old lady the good with the bad."

"You gettin' the worst of this bargain—" Jesse began.

"You won't say that, Mr. Williams, when you get to moving that bed. You can save your breath for that solid mahogany. And you'd best bring that army with you."

"There ain't no bed in this world, Mrs. Osborne, my oldest and I can't move with one hand tied. You think Jesse Williams is a cripple?"

"He's nobody's fool."

At the bottom of the stairs, Jesse heard a scream from the basement. "You blew that fuse a-purpose. Folks can't even do their laundry around here without some blatherass mixing in." A woman's face loomed in the basement stairwell. Her eyes and teeth gleamed with fierce whiteness as she shouted up, "You go whine back to Miss Kathryn and slobber her shoes up good, Mr. Boatman."

Jesse yelled down in protest, "You got the wrong Mr. Boatman."

But Anna Mae didn't hear him because she was already shouting, "Don't you go poking your nose down in this basement no more. We don't need no caretaker down in this hole. Tell old Money Bags to send us down a good ratcatcher. That's what we need."

When the shouting was over, there was something about Anna Mae's insolence that made him offer his services. "I ain't no kind of ratcatcher. But I know about fuses. Let me oblige."

"You razzin' me now," she said with a softening of tone and a laugh at herself. "But you just the size of a beat up old prizefightin' man name of Boatman. Who you be?"

"You ain't pullin' no compliments, sister—"

"I'm Anna Mae Green."

"OK and I'm Jesse Williams. Gonna rent half Mrs. Osborne's flat."

"Then we gonna be downstairs-upstairs neighbors," said Anna Mae.

"OK, but nobody gonna call me Boatman. Had the pleasure already of meeting up with that individual over at Club Pagliani. The boss wanted him to bounce me out of there bad, but between the two of them there wasn't man enough to do it."

"He only talks big mouth with the women," sneered Anna Mae. "When my sister's husband ain't home like tonight, that's the time Mr. Boatman gonna be pullin' out fuses, turnin' off the gas and the likes of that, crackin' the white folks' whip over the backs of his own race of people. He's a no-good nigger." It sounded to Jesse like Anna Mae would go on cussing at Boatman all night. It was a pity a woman of her spirit had to live down in a basement with the damp and toilet smells so thick a person could hardly breathe. Still and all, Jesse didn't want to spend any more time than he had to in that hell hole. "You got a substitute fuse?"

Anna Mae led him into the Roberts' flat where the gas stove gave a glimmer of blue light. It was a cave down there, out of this world it seemed to Jesse. A candle wavered and smoked.

"This is my sister," Anna Mae introduced Geneva as she fumbled in the table drawer for a box of odds and ends. "That Boatman ain't bothered us for two, three months now," she said. "Fuse maybe blew its own self. But contrariwise, maybe he heard us talking, sister, what we was gonna do to old Biomchi."

"You can't never tell," said Geneva staring at Jesse as if she wouldn't know who to trust.

But Anna Mae never wavered once she summed up a person. And when Jesse told about Boatman in the tavern, that was enough to satisfy her. "That old white witch wanta throw us out in the snow. But we got a lawyer told us to pay our rent with money orders for a few months and keep the receipts. You heard tell of Mr. Jefferson Wilkes, soldier?"

"Not that I can remember." With the help of his lighter Jesse located the right kind of fuse and asked Anna Mae to show him the fuse box.

"We gonna fix that old Biomchi," Anna Mae went on. "You know about triple damages?" Jesse shook his head as he took out the old fuse, so Anna Mae explained it to him. At the end she laughed with a kind of bitter exulting, "She gonna get her court notice come next week. Then she gonna pay back three times all that overcharged money."

The lights went on in the Roberts' flat. Darkness went back to crouch in the corners.

"Now, soldier, before you go back to that old army, you gonna sit down and rest your uniform." There was a style and sharpness about Anna Mae which began to grow on Jesse. And her sister, who was a quieter type, was a woman he could rest his eyes on. The room was full of kids, a baby on the bed, two older girls, and a boy of two or three. They were all smiling up at him as if he'd come down from a happier planet bringing light with him. He picked up Little Brother and set him on his lap. The boy put his finger on his overseas ribbon. "What that?"

"You don't wanta know about that, Little Brother," said Jesse. "Lots of time on up ahead when the Man gonna make you know."

"That's so right," said Anna Mae. "The Man gonna teach Little Brother plenty more before he's through. But the Woman been busy this winter, too, Mr. Jesse. She ain't been foolin'. Her old hound dog Boatman been shettin' off our gas if it's been cold. And I mean cold." Anna Mae hugged herself in a fit of the shivers just to think about it. "She ain't been happy yet, old Biomchi, when the pipes are froze and the toilet flooding out the basement, she still be figuring ways to fear Little Brother some more and all the folks live in this house."

Jesse drank his coffee in silence. It was a shame his people had to live in such a foxhole with a battle going on all the time. And Anna Mae Green was up in the front lines. "I thank you, Ma'am, for the coffee." He got up and set Little Brother down in his mother's lap. "And I'm proud I met up with you folks. Like you say Mrs. Green, we're gonna be upstairs-downstairs neighbors. And if your fuse blows after Monday, you just holler up the stairs and let me oblige."

Jesse went slowly up and out into the street. It was a restless, hot night. Somewhere blocks away, fire crackers were sputtering and booming, and he could hear a merry-go-round at a street carnival pumping out mechanical melody. As he looked up at the moon, he thought of Lil and his own kids. And then of Lou and the girl friend up with the rich sister and brother-in-law—the first time Jesse ever came to his house. He thought of Pete and his warm, trembling handshake, and he thought of Kathryn kneeling at her desk cabinet to get out her expensive whiskey for him; a little old woman with glasses who loved her boy, but drove a hard bargain with Jesse and his folks. He wondered if any woman could be so completely no good as Mrs. Osborne and Anna Mae made her out to be.

On up ahead one day, he would find out for himself.

#12

From the Anselmo's top of the world penthouse the night honey-comb of buildings was the substance of dream. The sun had gone down over the city and the moon had come out of a grey haze where sky and lake melted together. Time and space ran out to infinity.

"My God, fellows—" Anselmo called the shots on his Olympus. He shook his watch hard close to his ear and gave Della a wide-eyed warning. "That clam-bake!"

So it was time for Lou and Nina to go after a last look over the city. Down there in the neighborhood of Hemlock Street was a flare of unusual light and the banging of firecrackers, like cannon over behind mountains. It was fiesta time, and for a moment Anselmo reminisced about the old days when he used to set off three inchers in neighbor's garbage cans. "Poor old pop," he shook his head with a sad smile. "But that's gone." It was hard for Lou to remember that Anselmo was raised in the same street. "Things change, eh Della?" Anselmo went on. She responded with a nod, but her eyes were buried away in the slum heart of the city as if places she could abandon but not memories.

Nina hated to leave the barbecue pit where they'd broiled steaks and toasted rolls. It was hard to know with the Anselmos if she'd ever get an invitation back. But Lou was anxious to leave. More than anything else, he wanted to be alone with Nina. In the garden and the moonlight, Anselmo was welcome to the statuesque beauty of Della. Lou wanted the fire and warmth of a woman before the life was frozen out of her. Life in the army and at the hospital was slow death to love. A man petered out in casual encounters with a dead-end feeling and cynicism about women. But Nina—the expression of her eyes, the tone of her voice, the touch of her skin—excited him in a new way. She was beautiful, and every word she said was music quickening his pulse and warming the center of his existence. He could forget about Vico.

"It's gorgeous, Lou." Nina's enthusiasm hit the top of the scale, as the elevator sank to the ground level. "When we—" she hesitated.

"Say it," he encouraged her. "When we get our own place—" He hesitated too. Her dream was one thing, but reality was something different again. "—maybe it won't be so grand," he concluded.

"In that breakfast nook, Lou, honest to God, makes you feel like you're swimming around in an aquarium."

Lou winked at the elevator operator as if a guy had to keep his feet on the ground when a woman got her head up in the clouds. Then arm in arm they made their way between marble columns and palm trees in enormous brass urns out into the street.

"Did you get it all settled with Anselmo about the job?" Nina asked the moment they reached the walk.

"Not yet," said Lou as if there were some things about the job he wasn't sure he liked.

"But he offered you a job, didn't he?" Nina sounded as if the bottom of things was falling away.

"Not exactly. Sounded more like basic training." Lou put the palm of his hand on her forehead to smooth out a frown. "He said to come up to the office when I get my discharge."

"Well, then, it sounds like—"

"Nina, last night we said we've got to be honest with each other. Well, there are some things about this deal I ain't a hundred per cent sure about. Anselmo can pour all the oil he wants, still it's rough on the old folks. I heard Tony yelling again at ma this morning."

Nina flipped her chin to say that Tony was always yelling at somebody.

"Well, OK, they never been the best of neighbors," Lou went on, "but this was something different. So bitter, Nina, like he wanted to kill my ma. And pop told me Tony's cutting up pretty rough against him, too. Old pop's miserable. Anybody could see that with a glass eye."

"That's from the worry about you, Lou." Nina brushed off his worries with a smile. "I never seen pop so happy as last night when you stepped out of that plane."

Lou was still so thoughtful, Nina had to remind him where they'd parked her car.

"There's no use hiding it, Nina. It don't sound so good, the ma carrying a rod around in her purse. That's dangerous."

"Did Anselmo tell you that?" Nina was incredulous.

"Sure, while you and Della were barbecuing steaks. And he says he had to get your pa's handy man to go around with her Fridays for protection when she collects the rent."

"Well, Lou, we got to face it. Things are changing around Hemlock Street. It isn't safe for a woman to go across the park at night any more—"

"When was it ever safe?" He interrupted. "I remember—"

"But now there are dope peddlers, prostitutes," Nina went on. "Your ma needs the protection."

"So we went through prohibition days and gun-toting when I was a kid. I thought we'd done with all that. Like I told you last night, I had a bellyful of shooting and killing. And I don't like my own ma to be toting a gun around in her purse, that's all."

When Lou stepped on the starter, it was hard enough to make the car jump. But as he drove through Lincoln Park with the trees arching over the roadway, he wondered why he'd started lecturing Nina. "What you wanta do, kid?" He brushed her face with his hand and then with a sudden movement of his arm drew her close to him.

"It's all the same to me," she said not resisting when he kissed her, but not returning the pressure of his lips, either. He parked down by the lakefront where the sand was white against the water and dark groups of people were huddle together in beach parties. An accordion was tearing the silence apart with a polka and the moon minnowed the waters with silver wherever the breeze touched.

"Maybe he'll offer me the job at the homecoming," Lou said. "It's like him to wanta make a show. He was hinting around—"

"Why didn't you—"

Lou closed out her question with a kiss. And Nina who was starting to reproach him, ended by putting her head on his shoulder. "You see, Nina, at the bottom of it, I ain't sure I want a guy like Anselmo to run our lives for us. Look what he's done to

Della. She's down on her knees to the guy, worshipping him like God Almighty. She don't let a peep out of her no more that don't echo the wheel. All the same, when we was leaving, she had that funny look like she was trying to crawl back somewhere into herself. You know what I mean, like she's got no place to go—I don't know how to say it—"

"Nonsense!" Nina had to laugh at that. "Why, she's the queen! If you'd seen all her dresses—" Nina sighed with envy.

"But if she ain't got the real thing—"

"Who you trying to kid, Lou? She's got everything!"

"Nina, now honest to God, if we was to get married, what you want first is dresses, live in an aquarium—?"

"Lou, you're getting too serious. Let's go to the carnival. How about sausage and a big bun like the night you told me, 'You gotta wait for me, kid,' before you went overseas. Remember? And the merry-go-round and the ferris wheel?"

"OK, ferris wheel. But doctor's orders, no merry-go-round. But first you gotta answer me. You wanta marry a man or a mink coat?"

"If I worry about the right man, I won't have to worry about the coat."

"And suppose the man is Lou Bianchi. Supposing he don't go to law school and have an office in the Board of Trade Building—"

"If it's Lou Bianchi, I'm going to keep him guessing. Men are all the same. They want to get what they want from a girl—not what she wants anyway."

"How come you're talking different from last night? I wanta know what you want right now. You wanta marry me?"

"I'll be thinking about it," she said lightly.

"You had three years already."

"Yes, but it could be for life, marriage."

"That's what I'm talking about," said Lou. "For always."

"That's a long, long time."

"But I mean it."

"Don't rush me, Lou. There are some things—"

"What things? You're not still worried about Jesse?"

"No-o-o," said Nina hesitating.

"Then let's bury some things. If the war messed us up—"

Nina closed her lips on the back of his hand and drew his arm tighter around her. "I think I want the things you do, but I've got to be sure."

Festival flags fluttered over their heads. The band beat up an old tune which Lou and Nina had heard since they were babies— a march from the Italian opera, *Norma*. Sausages sizzling in hot grease and green peppers and yellow roasted almonds and red nuts stirred a kid's hunger deep inside him. Lou remembered the time he had won his first money throwing dice on the green beige and how he confessed to Father Guidarello as if it was a sin against the Holy Father. But the priest had explained to him how God looked favorably on fiestas because they helped support the church.

Kids were climbing up the legs of the bandstand, black and white together. And the street was full of traps and money making devices and barkers calling to everyone alike, "Try your luck!" Money had no color at the carnival.

"See how it is, Nina," said Lou with mellow excitement. "Everybody happy."

The enormous moon stood watch while dice rattled, the band played, and the weight guesser put his hand around the lady's ankle.

In five minutes, Nina was sorry they'd left the obscurity of the park and the lakefront to stroll into the bright lights where everybody knew Lou and had to welcome him back home and find out all about it over there, backslap, and swap stories and set up a glass of wine. She was as proud of him as a girl could be, but there was no privacy at the fiesta. It was an hour before she could get him as far as the ferris wheel, by which time he was punch drunk with the happiness of being home and seeing all his old buddies and girl friends and the old folks besides. The world came up and down around them. They were gazing off at the far skyline of the city at one moment, the next their feet were in the faces of couples in line waiting for the wheel to stop.

Nina had to shout like she was a kid before she settled down in his arm. "Always—always—always!" he whispered slaphappily crushing her against his chest. The heat of her body drew his pulse to her. Theirs was a passion like nothing else on earth, bringing oblivion and bliss. "I love you, Nina. Promise me, for always?"

"I love you, too, even if I'm a fool to tell you," she said dreamily, "but I can't help myself. Everything could be OK with a guy like you, the way you make me feel. But you got to promise me, too."

"It's a promise."

The world rolled up and down and around them. And every time the wheel stopped, automatically Lou handed out the quarters. Until finally they were still riding in each other's arms when the grand basket of fireworks threw its bouquet to the sky and the lights began to go out and the band players sheathed their horns and flutes.

The moon was on the down swing to dawn when Lou and Nina came home. Their happiness was too big to hold in secret between them. It burst the bodies of their old separate lives, exploding to fill the world.

Lou thrust open the door and shouted, "Hey, ma! Pop! She's gonna have me, come hell or high water."

#13

A fist of pain was closing around Pete's heart. He could hardly go through the routine of the day's work, his eyes were so blurred.

He reached up mechanically to turn the fuses in the transmission box. Area after area in the machine shop began to flicker and light up. The shadows of many shaped machines thrown in grotesque layers along the walls by the night lights went out and suddenly the machines stood up like an army in battle formation.

Punch presses began to bang away. Air hoses whistled like rockets. With the persistence of machine guns, bolt tighteners began to rattle. Overhead, the screech of castings at the cutting edge sounded like falling mortars.

It was a battle Lou would never come back to, Pete was sure of it now, the tough-fisted battle in the shop. Lou would be keeping company with the big shots in the private offices with his feet up on the glass top. No more punch the clock for Lou, but banker's hours—going home in the middle of the afternoon to easy street. Homemade wine was no good for him now, only cocktails at Anselmo's.

Even the engagement to Nina was arranged in the shadow of Anselmo and Della, and all Nina could talk about, after Lou said she was going to have him, come hell or high water, was Della's dresses and the breakfast nook like an aquarium. Nina would never be content to settle down in Hemlock Street now. That little pipe dream was finished, to have his own grandchildren raised in the room upstairs in the old house he had worked most of his life to buy.

Pete tried to whistle his favorite tune, Little Donkey of My Heart, but the sounds wouldn't come. Like a brass drum, a punch press began to beat close to his ear.

Boom-boom-boom. Scotty was bending forward on the job, his pliers moving with the speed of a cat's paw. The stamped parts fell with a clang into the basket. Wrinkles corroded Scotty's face, but his hair was still fiercely black and plastered firmly over his bald spot. At sixty, after a life time at the punch press, he still had all his fingers and thumbs.

"When's Lou coming back on the job?" Scotty seemed to have eyes in the side of his head for Pete.

"Maybe he don't come back," said Pete with a grimace that made Scotty take his foot off the pedal.

"He got banged up that bad?" Not waiting for an answer, Scotty went right ahead to say, "Well, ain't that a bloody shame! Never mind, Pete, he's gonna get lots of compensation, don't you worry your head. It's a bit of all right Lou's home all in one piece." Scotty kicked the pedal and his machine started to boom again. He had to bang away at top speed to make a dime above his day rate.

As usual, the orders to fill were laid out for Pete on the superintendant's desk. Typewritten words and the numbers on the order forms blurred together. Pete's hands were trembling as he set them down on his own bench. He shoved stickers, tabs, pencils to the back, kicked a package out of his way, and knocked a couple of milking machines off a truck by accident.

At the clatter of metal on the floor, the superintendent appeared at the glass partition of his office. With a twist and a writhe he slung his suit coat over the back of his chair and loose-jointedly plunged out into the shop. "Jesus Christ, Pete, we're a week off schedule." He rasped his voice like a file and jerked his eyes this way and that way, as if he was afraid the workers were goofing off all over the shop. "Listen, get Lynn, Lucille, Frances, Carrie, and that new girl. Keep 'em busy, Pete. We got the papers for that boxcar a whole week ago and that shipment ain't even half ready. We gotta seal that car down by four thirty tonight at the latest, or they'll cancel the order."

"OK, OK, OK," said Pete. It was the same business every day, rush-rush-rush. If it wasn't a boxcar, it was a truck. He watched Clarence leap up the steps three at a time to get to the tool room a second ahead of himself. Always wearing those rubber-soled shoes, sounding off at a fellow's elbow before he could hear him coming. Rush-rush-rush! One day he'd drop dead.

As Pete went down through the machine shop, Lou's special buddy, Phil, shouted, "Hey, pop, what the hell happened to our hero-boy? He's getting too swelled head or something?

Next to Phil's was the lathe Lou used to work. It stood idle, a great grey battleship of a machine, derelict without an operator.

"I dunno," Pete answered angrily.

Phil looked at him with a sharp flick of his blue eyes and a toss of his hair which came blinding down over his face the next moment. He had given Lou his basic training in the machine shop from the day he quit school and came to work.

"What the hell, he gotta have some vacation." Pete began to cover over his anger.

Down the aisle there was no time to exchange more than a wink or a nod with the operators. Their muscles were tense, their eyes fixed on the cutting edge of tools, their hands gripping and turning and shaping. The machines whirred and the chips flew.

Near the stairs, Andy the Kid, the age Lou was when he first came to work at Farmway, was hanging his weight on a drill press, all muscle and tenseness on a piecework job. Brass chips flaked up and covered the dial he was drilling with a glittering mound.

"What d'ya say, Andy?" Pete went on to crack his usual joke with the kid. "Hey, you know what we used to do in Italy when it rained hard when I was a boy?"

"Joke?" asked Andy, used to Pete's riddles.

"We let it rain," said Pete, ducking his head behind his hand.

"You didn't have not'in' better to do in Italy?" Andy flicked the dial he was drilling in Pete's direction.

As Pete reached the top of the stairs, a little pneumatic drill rising sharp above the din tatooed his ear drums. Then he left the racket of the machines overhead and came down the stairs to the packing and assembly room.

"What happened, Pete?" Lynn shouted above the other women's voices that rose to greet him.

He frowned at her and made a sign with his hands that she had ears tall as a donkey's and shouldn't ask so many foolish questions.

"When *is* Lou coming?" she persisted.

"You know about the monkey who had his tail chopped off?" Pete asked innocently.

The women had heard this one a thousand times and groaned in chorus, "It won't be long now!"

"That's the right answer." Pete's good humor was welling back now.

"I can hardly wait to see that boy." Lynn was such a small woman she had to stamp her foot a little to attract attention. She was hardly five feet tall and thin as the stem of a cornflower. As she lowered her forehead to look over her safety glasses at Pete, her eyes kept flashing. They were blue the color of a summer sky.

For the first time Pete wished it was Lynn instead of Nina Lou was going to marry. "Too late." His mouth clamped shut and his eyes went wide in a tragic expression.

"You mean he's gone and married one of those Jap-women?"

"Happy-go-lucky, that boy," sighed Lucille. She had two teenaged boys herself and was hoping the war would be over before they reached draft age. She was a large woman with sandy colored hair and a voice rich with sympathy. "He don't change, Lou?"

Pete nodded. "He changed. He got sober." Abruptly he added, "We gotta stop the monkey chatter. Clarence, he's burning me up about that boxcar."

At their benches the women were filling, assembling, packing, their hands moving like levers and gears. Only Frances stood motionless at her bench with her hands resting on the can of cleaning powder she was packing.

She was only a shade taller than Lynn, with a round face, black hair, and deep brown shining eyes. As Pete came over to her, automatically her hands began to move. Bend the cardboard, slip the can into place, push into the cube, press, gum down the wrapper. Repeat-repeat-repeat.

"What's the matter, honey—?" Pete saw that her eyes were wet in the corners and she was trying to keep from crying. "You ain't heard from him yet?"

Frances shook her head and went on gumming down the wrapper.

"Pete—" Lynn was calling him sharply.

"Coming, sweetheart, coming," he shouted. But quietly, so that only Frances could hear, he said, "War, it's a son-of-a-bitch."

Lynn was filling oil cans from a large drum. The handle was stuck, or she pretended it was. Pete reversed it with a jerk and the oil began to flow again. "Tell me, Pete—" she was beginning to ask him when suddenly she let out a yell and darted across the room to fling herself into the arms of a man in uniform.

It was Lou.

In a moment, most of the women in the department were shouting and demanding their homecoming kiss, while Pete watched with a joy that had no limits.

#14

It was his father's expression the night before that had brought Lou to Farmway in the morning. At the happiest moment of his life, with Nina radiant in his arms and his ma crying out thanks to the Holy Mother that her boy would marry a Sicilian, Lou saw his father turn aside his face to hide his hopelessness.

But now Pete was happy as he went upstairs with Lou into the machine shop. "How do you like it, son, back home?"

"OK, pop. Coming up the tracks, I was thinking of the first time, remember, when I quit school—"

"Ya, ya," said Pete delightedly.

Nothing had changed around the machine shop since Lou went overseas. Scotty was still banging away at the punch press. Phil was still bending over the same lathe. His blonde hair was falling into his eyes and he was still twisting his head back like a perpetual motion machine. And Mike, facing Phil on the grinder, still wore his green cap perched over his left ear and scowled as he checked the shaft he was grinding with his micrometer. All the old timers were around and a few new faces.

When the men saw Lou, they stopped their machines and came over to the aisle. They warmed his hand and slapped him on the back. "How's the old block buster? Rough on you out there, eh?" They were all laughing and talking at the same time in a demonstration that brought Clarence out of his glass office on the run.

"All you guys gone nuts or something—" he was yelling when his eyes grabbed on to Lou. "Well, Jesus Christ, fellow, it's good to see you all in one piece." At the same time he was motioning Pete back to the assembly room. "That boxcar," he complained. Then he seized hold of Lou's arm and guided him into the office so that the men could get back to work. He shook hands with Lou all over again and waved him to a chair.

"How was it out there, Lou-boy?" he asked as he sat down in his own swivel seat and began to fidget with the time cards on his desk. But before Lou had a chance to answer, Clarence was already asking him with his mind on the boxcar and government contracts, "Now what's it going to be?"

Clarence hadn't changed in three years, still wore the same rubber soled shoes. "I dunno yet—" Lou began.

"We could use a good lathe hand," Clarence interrupted. All the time he was sizing Lou up, estimating what his disability amounted to, and wondering would he be a liability or an asset.

"I gotta get my discharge first." Lou didn't intend to commit himself, but he didn't want to close the door either. "After next week—"

"We got a couple of rush orders, defense contracts," Clarence explained.

"I wanted to ask you, maybe you could use a buddy of mine. We was driving mates out there, got banged up together. A top flight mechanic, he was in Redball in the other war."

"If he's a good man, send him along."

"Damn good. Maybe need a little training on the job." With a casual flick of his hands, Lou added, "He's a colored fellow."

Clarence shot him a look of surprise, then began to shuffle the time cards and rock back and forth in his chair. "What we really need," he began to explain, "is a topnotch lathe hand, Lou. Outside of those government order, things are kind of slow."

"What you mean—"

"Let's face it, Lou. I ain't prejudiced myself." Still, Clarence was looking at the cards instead of facing Lou. "But suppose I put this fellow on today. How many of the guys are going to show up for work tomorrow morning? And the women? I got to think of those things."

"They won't quit." Lou was confident that the men and women he'd worked with for nearly six years weren't that narrow minded. "This Jesse Williams I'm telling you about was good enough for—"

"We might just possibly put him on as a helper," Clarence interrupted.

"He wants machinist work," Lou persisted.

"We gotta go slow on these things." Clarence shook his head skeptically as if Lou had been living out of this world for a long time.

"My way of thinking," said Lou stubbornly, "we oughta give everybody the same chance."

"I know what you mean," Clarence almost shouted. "Feel the same way myself." He looked around cautiously before he went on to say, "Had one of them in my own house last week, colored fellow—on business, of course—a salesman from the South. We're trying to broaden out our market. The farmers aren't buying dairy equipment the way you'd expect. They don't seem to have the same kind of dough as last war—for some reason."

Lou was burned up at getting the brush off, though it was what he had half expected. Year in year out, Clarence rocked in that cockeyed swivel chair while guys like Jesse risked blood and bones. Even in the army the orders to integrate had come through and in the veterans' hospitals—even in the South. Why not on the job?

As Lou thought about it, he could hear Jesse telling him what it was like to be a helper in a coalyard. "Takes brains to drive a truck, operate those cranes. Me, I'm the guy with the hand shovel. I'm down in one of the bins where the steam shovel don't reach. Or I'm driving out with the white guy, his face black as mine with that coal dust. Ain't no respecter of persons. All the same, he's white underneath, understand? So it's me settin' up the chute when we get there and it's him sittin' in the cab smokin' the cigar." When Lou had asked him, didn't he have a union, Jesse had only laughed. "OK, but he's the steward. So you get mean. It jams up inside you. You wanta lam out with that shovel. Goddam it, Lou, you'd kill that guy yourself he called you 'boy' again."

Jesse had pulled out the stops for the first time on that last trip down from the Yalu. He'd really told Lou what he thought. "Shovelling, sweep up. We get the ass end of the world. A guy better hold his head down—or he gotta bust right out when he see the whole world full of machines, engines, and cranes and all the like of that." His voice was deep-chested with contempt as he lumped Lou together with all white guys. "And you tell me I gotta sweep up chips all my life, while you run the machines?"

And Lou had said very quietly, "I thought it was bad enough bein' a goddam dago. But I never listened in on what you guys have to put up with." And then he had promised Jesse he would try to get him a job at Farmway when they got back home.

Jesse had laughed at that. "You gonna get yourself up mountains of trouble, fellow. You'd as easy get back up to the Yalu River."

As Lou sat watching Clarence turn over the time cards, his fists clenched with an anger that was swelling out of control. "Maybe you'll have a talk with him," Lou insisted. "He's an OK guy."

"Sure, I don't mind having a talk with him," said Clarence dismissing Lou with a casual smile. "Send him along and maybe we can work out something."

Abruptly, Lou got up and walked out of the office. "That horse's ass!" he exploded to Phil. "How can a guy be so goddam stupid?" Lou stepped up to his old machine and moved the turret back and forth with an angry spin of the wheel. Should he blow his top to Phil with all the conflict busting out of him, or try to hold it in?"

Across the shop, he could see his pa pushing a truck load of cartons toward the elevator. He could even hear that high pitched tune his father whistled when he was happy—high over the roar of machines."

"Hey, Phil, I wanta get my buddy on in the machine shop."

As Lou sat watching Clarence turn over the time cards, his fists clenched with an anger that was swelling out of control. "Maybe you'll have a talk with him," Lou insisted. "He's an OK guy."

"Sure, I don't mind having a talk with him," said Clarence dismissing Lou with a casual smile. "Send him along and maybe we can work out something."

Abruptly, Lou got up and walked out of the office. "That horse's ass!" he exploded to Phil. "How can a guy be so goddam stupid?" Lou stepped up to his old machine and moved the turret back and forth with an angry spin of the wheel. Should he blow his top to Phil with all the conflict busting out of him, or try to hold it in?

Across the shop, he could see his pa pushing a truck load of cartons toward the elevator. He could even hear that high pitched tune his father whistled when he was happy—high over the roar of machines.

"Hey, Phil, I wanta get my buddy on in the machine shop." Lou tried to be casual as he told Phil about Jesse. He had to shout and he saw Mike turn off his machine to listen.

Phil shook the hair back out of his eyes and stared in a sweat as if Lou had gone off his rocker. "A colored guy? Lou, let's face it—"

"For Chrisake, you talk like Clarence!"

Phil looked at Lou with a new kind of concern. "You got shell shock?"

Mike motioned Lou to come over. "About this buddy of yours," he boomed, "things ain't changed none since you been away."

"You ain't changed none, you son-of-a-bitch," Lou boomed back at him.

"Can't you get him a job somewhere else?" Phil began to be helpful with a friendly smile. "Down the tracks, maybe at Anderson's Coalyard—"

Mike and Lou had never been buddies, but he expected a whole lot more from Phil. "Aw, forget it," Lou growled. The bell was ringing insistently two long and three short for maintenance. "Jerry still with the outfit?"

"Sure," said Phil. He could see Lou was ready to pull a haymaker at somebody, so he humorously imitated Jerry's southern accent to draw off the heat. "Next time that elevator goes on the blink, I'm gonna damn well quit."

More than a bell was ringing in Lou's memory. As he thought of Jerry, a short stocky man with a flushed complexion, reddish hair and freckles, short arms and big hands, raised on an Arkansas farm, he remembered the stories he used to tell about the South. Lou found him at the top of the elevator shaft walking the plank to inspect the motor. Even up there, Jerry moved in an easygoing way with the walk of a man who'd never worn shoes till he was twenty.

"Lou Bianchi!" Jerry shuffled back to grip Lou by the hand and almost pulled him off the ladder. "I been thinkin' about you, fellow, ever since your pa said you was back—" Jerry motioned to Lou to make himself at home on the cat walk and, while he talked, began systematically to tear down the motor. "I was wondering how you'd like to take the committeeman job back and see all the little books get out to the union hall. Everybody's been delinquent around here because we never did fill your place."

"I'll have to think about that when I get my discharge," said Lou, "I'm still on vacation."

"Besides, I'm gonna damn well quit one of these days," Jerry went right on, "if Thompson don't loosen the goddam purse strings and put a down payment on a new elevator."

"You still quittin'?" Lou laughed at him. "Bet you said that every day since I been away."

"This time I mean it." In the same breath Jerry said, "Boss been tellin' me you wanta get your buddy on—"

"News sure travels," said Lou bluntly.

"Out there, I guess them things don't amount to—"

"I dunno," said Lou skeptically. "We had a sergeant from Texas—"

"Bad state," Jerry shook his head, "though it borders on the Arkansas line. But Arkansas, that's a good state. Only thing wrong with it—" Jerry sat back on the cat walk to fill his pipe "—folks are mighty damn poor." His legs swung beneath him as if he was a kid sitting up in a tree. "Far's that's concerned, I didn't buy me a pair of shoes till I went to town and got me my first job. It was a stinkin' hole, too, you ever worked in a tannery. Next to coal minin', that's it! I wasn't hardly there more'n six months when we hit the street for one goddam cent. That was a lot of money all the same, you figure we was makin' only fifteen cents an hour depression times. So we walked and we walked till our shoe leather wore mighty thin. And on top of that, we never got our jobs back. They ran the scabs in with the state police and all the like of that. We was all white guys, the scabs colored. We began to wise up when it was already too late."

"So you—?" It began to dawn on Lou what Jerry meant.

"Yeh, it would have been good job insurance to have some colored guys workin' along with us that time." Jerry motioned to Lou to stand clear. "This goddam motor's gonna turn over or bust. If it busts again, old man Thompson'll be out lookin' for a new maintenance man, because I'm gonna damn well quit."

The motor turned over and purred like a tame tiger cat. Jerry filled his pipe again. "We got government contracts now, Lou.

They're supposed to hire everybody."

"So you think there's a good chance we can get him on in the machine shop?" Lou smiled up at Jerry as he stood on the cat walk cradling his pipe.

"We could try," said Jerry as if harder things had been done before, "when you come back on the job."

Sunlight poured through the trap door above the elevator shaft and Jerry's head seemed to take fire up against the sky.

"When you come back on the job," Lou repeated to himself as he went down the stairs and out into the street. Behind the bricks and the grated windows of the factory, his father was pushing a handtruck loaded with milking machines. Scotty was booming away at the punch press. In the basement, Baldy, the caretaker, was selling a stale bun and pouring Jerry a mug of coffee out of the old enamel pot. They all wanted him back except Mike. He was their guy, not Anselmo's. His lathe stood idle waiting for him.

Homesickness for the old job closed like a fist around his stomach.

#15

Lou had something to tell Jesse, even if it was only about the possibility of a job. But he wanted to see him for other reasons.

A miracle had happened the night before. His ma had invited Jesse into their front room and served him with her most expensive whiskey, Anselmo's brand. She had told Lou over breakfast what a fine man Jesse was, so polite and well-spoken. And she had told him—and this was the hardest to believe—that she had invited Jesse to drop by again and invite his wife.

If his mother was that much impressed, why not invite him to the homecoming? The idea was taking shape in Lou's mind as he drove to the Southside. He remembered one time Jesse had said to him out in Korea, "We gotta push on up ahead, Lou, or we gone—all they way down."

As Lou turned in from the Outer Drive, the skeleton structures of buildings rose against the blue like a bombed out city. And as he drove down Jesse's street, the area reminded him of Korea with its vast fields of rubble and its foundation diggings yawning like bomb craters. The last building still standing was the house Jesse lived in. It bore the structural marks of its neighbor which had already been torn down, the floors and chimneys and the holes where the rafters had rested for several generations. A barrier marked the end of the street which plunged away into an excavation. A steam shovel blew in the hot air and grunted with its enormous mouth spewing bricks and caked mud into a truck. Cranes erected and swung their loads in the distance. There was a smell of old things torn down and of dead rats incinerated in refuse.

At the end of the street in front of the barrier, two children were fighting for control of the driver's wheel and the horn of an old jalopy while an older boy was cleaning carburetor parts in gasoline and laying them out on a level fragment of sidewalk. "You lean off that horn, Junior, Ernestine," he shouted. "Pop's gonna beat your butt, you run all the juice out of that battery."

The faces of the kids suddenly came alive out of a photograph Jesse had shown Lou a long time ago on the road down from the Yalu.

"Your dad around?" Lou shouted over the roar of the steam shovel.

The older boy spun on his heels. At the sight of Lou's uniform, he snapped to his full height, his eyes staring down at Lou's quartermaster badge and at the same time losing their suspicion of him. Charles was tall like his dad, but thin with a knife blade of a face that reminded Lou of Jesse. But it was Jesse's face reflected in a concave mirror with hollow cheeks squeezed together.

In a moment Jesse himself leaned out the second floor window. "How you, partner?" he shouted as if he'd seen Lou the day before. "These are my kids I told you about." As Jesse waved at them with an offhand pride, Charles nodded seriously and Ernestine and Junior laid off the horn long enough to stare at Lou. Ernestine had long braids with red ribbons flying like butterflies. Her face was round with solemn brown eyes in flight like a pair of swallows. Junior was the runt of the family with a thin face like his brother and a sharp impertinent smile.

When Jesse came down to the car, he apologized, "Ain't worth inviting you up. Everything's in an uproar." He waved across the street at the rubble as if their flat was in the same condition. "We shaking the dust for good. Neighbors and friends picked up and gone. Won't ever come back. Gonna be high rent places." Jesse had a way of opening his hands in an all over gesture as if there was nothing more to be expected. "Over and above that, they gonna be too rich for our blood. We lucky your old lady got us a place to live."

"It ain't much, I know," said Lou. "But wait till she's got the other place—" He stopped in the middle of what he was saying because he thought of Tony on the eviction list and of all the trouble in the neighborhood.

"Gotta move or get beat over the head with that eight ton ball," Jesse laughed as he watched the wrecking crew demolishing a building down the street and a crane operator bouncing the heavy steel ball on the sidewalk which crumbled like thin ice. Jesse pointed diagonally across the street. "Where my pa and ma raised us," he explained to Lou. There was nothing but a gaping hole to mark the spot.

"Your folks still living?" Lou asked.

"Naw," said Jesse. "She passed when we was over in Korea. And pa before her. That foundry work dries a man out like an old stick. And burns what it don't dry." Lou could tell from Jesse's tone he was in no happy frame of mind about the whole business of moving. There was no choice in it.

"I stood you up last night," Lou apologized. He could see by the way Jesse laughed that it had made some difference.

"OK, so you have a girl friend. First things first like your ma said."

"She said that?" Lou asked, then quickly went on, "She wants you and the wife to come over some time."

"I told Lil," said Jesse. "But she wanta buy a new place, way out, understand. So what can you do?"

So his ma had invited Jesse and his wife to stop by and have a look at the house, not to visit! The thought came to Lou with a shock. Still, he had come to his own decision. "Come over and see us anyway," he insisted. "How about tomorrow night? We're having some folks in, a kind of homecoming round up. Everybody invited."

It was a casual enough invitation to make Jesse study Lou to see if he really meant it. Lou insisted again, "I'm really serious." Jesse went thoughtful. The car radio had suddenly shifted from a downbeat rhythm to a recruiting speech.

"See the world. Learn a trade."

"Sure, sure," Jesse muttered. "Climb up on the ladder, boy, five-star waitin' on you up top. Who they kiddin', Lou?"

With all the bitter undertones, it was like the old Jesse: the man who walked in and demanded his beer at the PX, the man who bumped his head up against the brick wall on purpose and whose head was so hard the wall crumbled.

"When you dipping that pen," Jesse went on with a dry laugh, "then they put the frosting on. Wanta see your kids everyday? OK, OK. This is the peacetime army. Live at home if you want, corporal, like any old job. Sit right up in the driver's seat. Pay's regular. Grab a pension when you're fifty. Sign right here!" Jesse drowned out the last of the recruiting talk on the radio.

"All them promises," said Lou remembering how Jesse had told him, after he signed up for the peacetime army, they shipped him out to Japan.

"No sir, man," Jesse went on. "All the same, when you finished your three years, they carry you across the Japan Sea. Geisha girls ain't no medicine for that. Kidney's choppin' at your back bone like butcher knives—you do all that bumpin' around drinkin' rice whiskey. You in Korea, boy. Too far to swim back."

Hearing Jesse talk in the old familiar way reminded Lou of the long hauls on the road up and down from Seoul and that last trip down from the Yalu River as he listened to Jesse mutter, "That bad old temper busting out on me," as if that explained his signing up in the first place. "I told you about that job at the coalyard, the white guy always sitting in the driver's seat smoking the cigars and me workin' my head off. So one thing goes to another till I beat that guy over the ass end with my shovel. After that it was hard gettin' a job, even sweep up.

"You got to thinkin' about the other war, Lou, those Frenchies, the way they opened the door. Come right in, mon ami. They only had one bottle of wine, still and all half of it was yours. You wasn't black or white, just human."

For a while they sat listening to the music bumping and bopping and the steam shovels roaring through the hot afternoon. Then Jesse went on thinking aloud the way he used to on those long night drives.

"You keep takin' dough out of the savings every week. Don't look so good for that new house the old lady set her heart on. Kids don't stop eatin' 'cause you're sittin' around the house all day. Feet don't stop growin' through the kids' shoes. Ain't no good Friday when the rent man's bangin' louder every week.

"Lil's dead set against it, but two months of the like of that and she comes around. 'OK, go ahead, you wanta be a double time fool'."

Then Jesse was quiet, resting his hands in his lap, but twisting his fingers and squeezing them together as he remembered things he had never told Lou, the way he used to shout around the house after he was fired from the coalyard until the kids wouldn't look him in the eye any more, all the time thinking himself a no goddam good son of a bitch, while Lil looked what she thought but kept quiet. He'd seen her many a night bring herself a magazine home from the beauty parlor where she worked to forget the mess they lived in together. Then he'd make for the tavern, come home only when they'd all gone to bed. But the kids coughed half the night like they were going to cough their lungs out and yelled and started up in their sleep. Half the time from too much drink and lack of food Jesse puked in the sink before he crawled into bed. And Lil had her face turned against him to the wall. He wouldn't know if she was awake or asleep. And he wouldn't find out, either, he had that kind of shame eating out his heart like a bat from hell. There were some experiences locked so deep with bitterness that he couldn't talk about them to anybody. But when he thought about Korea, he could never forget them, either . . . .

"About that job, Jesse—" Lou's voice startled him out of his blue mood. "I was up there this morning. It has possibilities."

Jesse listened with sharp interest as Lou explained. "They got government contracts. So go up and put your application in. See what happens."

"Fill out all that paper?" Jesse shook his head moodily. "When you going back to work, Lou?"

It was a hard question to answer. The night before Lou had almost made up his mind to go along with the Anselmo deal, but after the morning at Farmway, he wasn't so sure. The life as a machinist had got into his bones again. It was a tough but familiar way of life. If he went back to Farmway, he would be with the guys he knew best. The sound of his father's whistle that morning was something to consider. If he went back, he was almost certain he could get Jesse a job. In the Anselmo world, how was he going to take bearings? From Vico's Cadillac or Tony's scream at his mother? And Nina—if the Anselmo deal fell through—would that make so much difference, as long as they were together? Would she measure their happiness by the number of dresses in her closet and the number of rooms in their apartment—if she loved him the way he loved her?

So Lou only said, "I don't know yet. Maybe next week after I get my discharge. How long did it take you up at Fort Sheridan?"

"Couple of days," said Jesse absentmindedly. "Well, Lou, you got yourself up mountains of trouble on up ahead!" Then he began to laugh with an overwhelming kind of heartiness. "Didn't I warn you?" He called out to Charles to get a couple of cans of beer from the refrigerator.

Over their beer, they reminisced about the PX and Jesse told Lou what happened at Pagliani's the previous evening. They talked about all the fellows they knew and all the things that happened on the Yalu Road. They shouted about the shovel of gravel Jimmy put into the sergeant's sleeping bag, and they called him Snakeface and String-'em-up.

At last, it was time for Lou to take off if he was going to pick up Nina downtown. He was suddenly reminded to tell Jesse the car they were sitting in belonged to Nina. Lou told him she was nothing like the old man, but took after her mother who was dead. And Jesse told him he could believe it.

"We're gonna announce our engagement at the party tomorrow night, fellow, so be sure to come and bring Mrs. Williams," said Lou gripping Jesse's hand with a pressure that meant nothing anybody else did or thought was going to interfere with their friendship.

And Jesse returned Lou's grip with the same solid pressure. "OK, buddy, you can count me in."

#16

By the end of the afternoon the cooking and baking for the homecoming were finished, and Kathryn's neighbors, Frances Angelino and the youngest Gagliano girl, went home to cook for their own families. Kathryn wondered why Lou hadn't come home. He went out after breakfast without saying where he was going. He must have gone up to Farmway!

Anxiety needled Kathryn's heart as she spread white linen on a long improvised table in the front room. In the center she placed the Madonna and Child, white and blue porcelain figures on a pallet of straw. Beside them she set Saint Joseph with his hand resting on the neck of his donkey and the Three Wise Men on their knees offering gifts with one hand and in the other holding staffs crowned with gold stars. She scattered ears of wheat and grains of corn around the Holy Family as in the shrine of a Sicilian village at harvest time. She spared no pains to create an atmosphere of worship and sacrifice and thanksgiving to celebrate her son's safe return from battle and to carry out the vows she had made to the Holy Mother.

While she was loading the table with wheaten cakes shaped like lambs and stars, *cannoli* or little cannon cookies, *crostate di fichi*— the fig tarts that were Lou's favorites—and a dozen other delicacies, it was a relief to hear steps on the porch. She rushed to the door. Nina was with her son. What a beautiful girl with the proud head and the keenest brown eyes in the world full of love for Lou! And Lou himself was as happy as Nina. The deep set grooves in his cheeks and the melancholy expression in his eyes had cleared away. He seemed relaxed and glad to share his love in a great open-faced smile and with a hug to squeeze the breath out between his mother's ribs. And with one arm around her and the other around Nina, he swept them both into the house.

"Oh, Kathryn!" Nina breathed with a hushed delight as she saw the festival board. "Isn't it beautiful, Lou?"

But Lou only said, "You promised me, ma, no fuss and bother—"

"That's no bother, what I promised the Holy Mother," she said crossing herself with pride. "She heard my prayers, Luigi. Ain't it the best ever? Tonight, Father Guidarello will say the thanksgiving—and Father Antonelli. He's young, about your age, Luigi, and handsome, eh Nina?"

Pete was waiting for them at the kitchen table with a bottle of Bianchi special. His hair was combed down and his cheeks were shining from soap and water. His smile of happiness went out to Lou and Nina, to the four corners of the house and the world. Between him and Lou a new understanding had grown up that day.

"Well, pop, it looks like big times ahead," said Lou expansively. While his mother and Nina were serving the meal, he started telling his dad about Jesse and the job.

So that was where Lou had been, up at Farmway. A needle of anxiety began to dig at Kathryn's heart again. Her hands trembled. "But that's all over for you, Luigi!" she said as if he had promised her to shut the door forever on the racket and grease of the factory.

Lou went silent. He watched his mother dish up the spaghetti into her Florentine bowl and pour on her famous sauce which took two days to prepare.

"So did your Jesse tell you when he was coming by to look at the house?"

"Sure, ma," said Lou, "he's coming over tonight."

"Not tonight, Luigi!" she reproached him as if he had lost the biggest part of his memory. "It's the homecoming."

"What's the difference, ma?"

"You mean you invited *him*—?" The precious Florentine bowl slipped from Kathryn's fingers and landed on the edge of Lou's plate. Onions, cut up green peppers and tomato sauce splashed over the table. Lou righted the bowl in time to save half the contents. But his own plate was split in two and spaghetti was worming its way across the table cloth.

Kathryn stood for a moment bewildered, wiping her hands on her apron. "Two days to cook," she rasped in a voice of misery.

"It's OK, ma. We saved most of it," said Lou as if nothing had happened.

"OK, OK, OK?" her voice rose madly. "You invited him?"

"But, ma, I don't get it. You invited him to come over yourself. You told me at breakfast."

Kathryn and Nina began to clean up the mess. "Not to the homecoming," Kathryn whispered fiercely as if she was talking to herself, "but see the house. Maybe buy." Her hands went out in a desperate gesture to show Lou what a terrible mistake he had made.

"We don't sell," said Pete quietly.

For a moment there was silence around the table and a tenseness of old conflicts never resolved between Pete and Kathryn.

"OK," said Lou, "what's done's done."

"But, Lou," Nina urged, "can't we call Jesse and tell him to come next week?"

Lou shook his head. "I told him, it was our engagement party." His eyes were reproving Nina for jumping in on his mother's side.

"What's Anselmo gonna think?" Kathryn began to moan. "And Della? And all our people? Fontanas, Sicilianos—" she named a dozen other families who had once lived in the neighborhood but who had moved to the far ends of the city and the suburbs. "Maybe even Nellie and Daniel De Rocco from Oak Lawn are gonna come. Please Luigi!" Her arms were around Lou's neck pleading and coaxing. "Call him like Nina says."

"But, ma," Lou insisted stubbornly, "I invited him. If he comes he comes!"

"What we gonna say?" Kathryn lamented.

"Tell 'em the truth." The talk with Jesse in the afternoon had made Lou feel even closer to him than to his own family. "Tell 'em he was my buddy out there. They ain't that narrow-minded. The guy saved my life, for Chrisake!"

"I don't know, son—" Kathryn was plagued with worry. She seemed to have no mind of her own, but only fear for what Anselmo would think.

"We got nice place here." Pete appealed to Lou as if he should stop his mother talking about selling the house. "Why we wanta move?"

Nina got up to clear the table. Her face was flushed with confusion because she had tried to head off a family quarrel and failed. And now Lou was staring down at the table, avoiding her. She didn't see why he had to be so stubborn, when his mother had done all the planning and work for the homecoming. Why force this Jesse on everybody? It just didn't make sense.

"Nice place!" Kathryn was throwing Pete's words back at him as if a child would know better. "We fixed it up nice inside. But what can you do outside? All garbage and rats!" She was warning Pete not to reopen all the old arguments they'd had before Lou came home. Then she turned to her son to justify herself. "Things have changed around here since you been in Korea. Our people are moving out. Soon colored are going to be in our block. And the way the Lord made things, everybody should live with his own kind."

"Ain't everybody wants to move," Pete persisted. "Angelinos, Gaglianos, Ferrucinis—"

Ferrucinis? You talk about them?" Kathryn was glad to have something to shout about. "That Tony's gonna land in jail next week, he don't move. Anselmo promised me."

"Thirty-five years—" Pete was beginning to answer her back when a knock at the door announced Boatman.

"What you want?" asked Kathryn distracted.

"Ma'am, it's rent night."

"My God, so it is!" Kathryn exclaimed as if she had forgotten all about collecting the rent for once. "Never mind tonight. It's the homecoming" She dismissed Boatman with a wave of her hand. "My son will go with me tomorrow." She looked at Lou in such a way as to leave him no choice.

"Ma'am," said Boatman with his eyes lowered, "Roberts and

Anna Mae Green gonna push that triple damages along next week."

"They dare!" Kathryn shouted.

Boatman nodded all the same as if he knew Anna Mae would dare. "That's what they say they gonna do."

When Boatman was gone, Kathryn appealed to Lou with a wide gesture of her hands. "You see what they're like, Luigi. Cause a lot of trouble." She didn't mention Jesse by name, but it was obvious from her tone of reproach she was meaning him as well as Roberts and Anna Mae Green. Impulsively she put her hands on Lou's shoulders and bent to whisper so that only he would hear, "If your Jesse don't come, eh? That would be the best."

She waited for him to say something. His shoulders felt like rock under her anxious fingers. In the silence the old clock began to beat in her ear. "My God, look at the time!" she screamed out. "They'll all be here before we get dressed." She turned and ran out of the room. Nina followed her.

For a long time Lou and his father sat at the table, uneasy in each other's company, until Kathryn came back in her party dress. A deep ruby wine color, it was frilled at the neck to cover up her shoulders. Her hair was brushed tight to her head and gleamed smartly. Her earrings glistened and she wore the kind of gold bracelet he had seen on Della's wrist. Her face was fully rouged and powdered and her eyes glittered with a smile as if she was determined to forget the arguments between them and to avoid any more.

"You ain't dressed yet?" she scolded in her mildest voice. "Come on now, Pete, Luigi. Hurry up before all the folks start coming."

#17

The homecoming was a triumph for Kathryn. As her house filled with the people she admired and loved best in the world, Anna Mae Green and the Ferrucinis and all her worries were gradually forgotten. Even the fear that Jesse would come faded out as the evening advanced. Surely, he had sense enough to know that it was a family party.

Everybody Kathryn invited, even Nellie De Rocco who had only said perhaps, came to celebrate Lou's safe return from the war. They also came because once or twice a year they enjoyed a sentimental pilgrimage back to Hemlock Street. It was where they were born or brought up. It was where the old folks had died. It was where the poor cousins, aunts, and uncles still lived out their less fortunate lives. They came from the suburbs and the four corners of the city back to Little Italy to measure their success in life—where they had arrived against where they once had been. And finally they came because they knew the most successful among them, the most feared and hated and respected would be there—Generoso Anselmo.

At first the neighborhood friends came in, the people Kathryn saw every day. They were tremendously pleased to welcome Lou home, the men with a strong embrace and the women with a kiss on both cheeks.

The Angelinos were the first to arrive. They only had to step across the alley. With Frances, a large-waisted woman with coal black hair looped back over her ears, came old Joe crated up in his Sunday best suit with his great construction worker's hands hanging from his sleeves and the white collar squeezing his neck. With them came their oldest son Santo, a truck driver for Fontana Brothers. When Lou asked about his wife, Santo explained she had another bambino in the oven and was big as a barrage balloon for the fifth time.

Pete and Joe began to bombard each other with riddles as usual. "I'm asking you for the last time," Pete insisted, "what goes up but don't never come back down?"

"They ain't changed none since you been away," Santo laughed. He was a lean-faced, sun-bitten worker, tough and muscular and quiet voiced, different from his brother Vico who was soft in the muscle and tough in the head. Santo glanced around for a third at poker.

"Old age!" Pete answered his own riddle because nobody had guessed. He poked his elbow into Joe's chest. "We ain't getting no younger, how about it?"

The Vitales and Gaglianos came in whole families and while they were all greeting Lou and drinking a glass of Bianchi special in his honor, Nina appeared at the front door to claim her festival kiss. Her hair was afire. Midnight blue shaded her eyes and made them shine at mysterious depths. Like a sheath revealing the fullness of her breasts, her gown narrowed at the waist only to spread out in a cloud of blue mist.

"Hey, kid you're a knockout," Lou whispered as he took her into his arms. The tenseness and irritation at the supper table were forgotten.

"How about a hand of poker, Lou?" Santo finally cut in with a wink.

The Gagliano girls and the rest of the women withdrew to the kitchen. But Nina stepped over to the card table and started to deal three hands. "Come on, Lou-boy, Santo," she commanded. She played boldly and won.

While she was dealing the cards again, Lou's oldest brother, Carlo, stopped in long enough to shake his hand. He left his wife and young son, Peter to enjoy the celebrations while he went back to his cab grumbling that these parties were always planned on his busy nights.

Old Pete poured out the wine freely, while Nina's hands moved back and forth across the table between the glasses. When Santo was sorting his cards, she glanced up at Lou to lock eyes. Soon Lou was not looking at his cards either and Santo muttered, "Suits me. I'm gonna sit this one out, too."

Outside, it was one of those nights with great thunderheads and the moon pouring between. The temptation to step out with Nina was overpowering. Arm in arm they crossed the street to find the privacy of moon shadows and the trees. But they had scarcely reached the park railings when Kathryn was calling after them, "Luigi, it's Fontanas!"

Headlights flashed out and a massive Cadillac pulled in at the curb. The Sicilianos arrived minutes later. From every part of town, from Cicero on the west and Evanston and Gary north and south, old time buddies at school and distant cousins Lou knew only by name crowded into the Bianchi house to welcome him back home. The fatted calf was roasting and the wine barrel was pouring out a stream of plenty.

Now everything seemed to be happening at once. Mrs. Siciliano was telling Lou how lucky his ma was and pressing his hand as if it belonged to her son who was still out in Korea. Lou was telling her, "They ain't gonna catch Jasper off base," while old Siciliano was asking, "What's chances of winning out there?" Even the florist business followed the ups and downs of the war.

Everybody had a friend or brother or son out there. They wanted to know if Lou had bumped into them. Would they be home by next Christmas? Was it as bad as the newspapers said?

"Ain't no picnic," said Lou privately to Mrs. Fontana whose boy was draft age. "Beats me how we got into it in the first place."

"Your mother looks so happy," she said with a tragic expression. She wore simple but expensive jewelry and a dress that was imported by Saks from a Parisian dressmaker. It was hard to believe that she had gone to school with his brother Carlo and used to flirt around with him in the Bianchi kitchen when Lou was young Peter's age.

"I forgot to congratulate you, boy," said Fontana with a second hearty handshake, "on the new job. If you ever get tired of real estate," he said playfully handing Lou his card, "there's always plenty of work in our line for the right guy."

Lou remembered how the Fontana brothers had built up their construction business down the street in the vacant lot by their house. The kids used to play cowboys and gangsters after dark among the piles of lumber. Now the Fontanas had moved up into the suburbs and it took Santo an hour to drive to work.

"Anyway, good luck, fellow." Bruno Fontana was still shaking Lou by the hand as if there were a lot of things he could say about Lou's new job if he ever got started. His hand was soft on the surface. He wore a flashy ring. And his skin was pink and white. But at the core of his hand Lou felt muscle and bone that had shaped up the hard way. Bruno had worked on a street laying crew—with a shovel. That was a long time ago.

"When you wanta build, let me know—one of these days." He winked at Lou as if he knew what he was talking about. A man who was young, good looking, and a go-getter didn't go on living in his ma's house for long. "Or when the folks move—"

Sudden quiet made Bruno stop in the middle of what he was saying. Father Guidarello stood in the doorway blinking to get his bearings. Then he crossed the room to greet Lou and to introduce young Father Antonelli who had followed him in. "I've heard about you from your mother," said the young priest. "We are all very happy to welcome you home."

Lou wondered what all his mother had told him and flushed a little as he shook hands.

"She's ambitious for you." Father Antonelli examined him with keen eyes ready to smile. His hand gripped Lou's as if he understood what he'd been through and could help him in the battles ahead.

"I know what you mean," said Lou returning his smile.

Vico came jaunting in at that moment to slap Lou on the back and claim his attention as if they were the best buddies in the world and always would be. And finally, as the fashionable end of the evening had arrived, Anselmo's sister Nellie De Rocco put in an appearance with her husband Daniel, the funeral director. She explained in a loud voice to Kathryn how they had just dropped by for a few minutes on their way home from another affair lest anybody should think the Bianchis were important enough to rate a visit from Oak Lawn. She shook hands with Lou and with a great hearty voice told him how wonderful it was to see him home again. She reminded him what a bambino he was when the Anselmo family had moved away forever from the slum of Hemlock Street. And she congratulated him for getting in on the ground floor with her brother. She also winked in Nina's direction. "You could do worse, Lou. She looks like an expensive article."

Lou wondered how Della could get along with Nellie. Chances were she couldn't—that much hot air. Anyway, she was a good sidekick for a man in the funeral business. Nothing pleased her and she could hollow out her voice and smile sadly at a moment's notice.

Old De Rocco himself was as calm as an old Roman statue. His head was bald as Caesar's with a fringe reminder of his youth. He had a large, immobile face. There was no need for expression when already he had made his money and everybody knew it. To him, Anselmo was a young upstart.

"I want to warn you, boy," he said to Lou when his wife was out of earshot, "don't let Anselmo call all the shots. It's a good opportunity for a young fellow—" De Rocco shrugged at the furnishings of the Bianchi home as if Lou couldn't help the poverty of his surroundings. "You won't want to live in Hemlock Street all your life." Daniel waved his cigar in a wide arc. "Colored are pushing in around here."

Lou was wondering why Jesse hadn't shown up as he muttered, "Far's I'm concerned, it don't matter where I live."

But Daniel didn't hear what Lou said in the confusion as Kathryn came up and put her arm in the arm of her distinguished visitor. "You got a fine boy," he flattered her.

A compliment from De Rocco made Kathryn's brain swim with delight. Nonetheless, she was listening to the sounds in the street. What if something had happened to Anselmo?

There was a rumble of thunder over the city and the curtains began to blow inward in a blast of cold air.

#18

The moment Anselmo and Della arrived, the homecoming for Lou was transformed into a welcome back to Hemlock Street for the Anslemos.

"Hey! hey!" At the front door was pushing and shoving and jockeying among the guests to make way. People crowded the stairway and the hall and jammed the front room. A whisper grew to a shout: "Anselmos!"

"They've come!" Kathryn screamed above the rest. There was no room in her cup of happiness for a drop more.

The next moment Della was embracing her mother while Anselmo was waving both hands to the crowd like candidate at an election rally. It was only when Della gave Lou a public kiss and said, "Welcome home, brother," he remembered the party was still in his honor.

"Jesus God!" Lou muttered with admiration. And for a moment everybody was quiet to admire. Even Nina faded out of the picture.

Della had come with the thunder and lightning at her shoulder and a sparkle or two of the first rain on her hair. Her gown was alive with a million invisible mirrors. It gave back the ruby of the central chandelier and the yellow and green of the other lights in the room with carnival gaiety. It radiated a mist of light with an inner brilliance like the phosphorescence of Hawaiian nights.

In this new creation of Anselmo's, Lou had difficulty recognizing his sister, the office worker who had gone about her own modest business while living at the Bianchi's like a boarder. Now her face was sculpted by an inner pride in her beauty and a sense of superiority that gave lift to her chin and a startling elevation to her eyebrows. The jewels at her wrists and throat burned with a cold blue fire. Around her hair which was smooth and burnished, a diadem of jewelled flowers from the workshop of a Tuscan goldsmith crowned her queen of the homecoming.

And Anselmo was still waving his hands over Della's head, now like a magician who had summoned a costly beauty into the world at the touch of his golden wand. Abracadabra! See! Let everybody admire, but with their eyes only. She belonged to him. She was the symbol of his money in the bank, his stocks and bonds, his hundred and one houses. She was the seal of perfection on his success in life.

When everybody had had an opportunity to admire his wife, Anselmo stepped forward to ask Lou in his great hearty voice, "How's your health, brother?" His hands dropped with a show of affection on Lou's shoulders as if he knew what it was to be wounded in battle. "We're proud to butcher the golden calf for you, fellow."

Lou was Anselmo's excuse for claiming the center of attention as Della melted into the crowd. Smart and jaunty in spite of his heavy waistline and florid complexion, Anselmo wore a feather-light tropical suit of an unusual deep marine blue shade, a sport of a hand painted tie, and a unique pair of shoes surfaced with Anaconda skin from the Amazon jungles.

Anselmo was not a handsome man. His nose was blunt and shapeless like an ex-prizefighter's and twisted a little to one side. His complexion was uneven. But his eyes were large and spirited. They pierced, they caressed, they grew warm and cold, subtle, naive, all in the same instant. Every move and gesture of his showed an immense fund of self-confidence and physical energy.

"Now you're home, brother, we're going to go places." There was no doubt in Anselmo's mind that Lou would join his staff of assistants. He rested his hand possessively on Lou's shoulder as if the deal was already settled.

Then he winked at Lou as he pivoted around the room to shake hands and backslap and exchange jokes. With the Vitales and Gaglianos and other local people he was hearty and patronizing. He remembered their children and grandchildren by name and wished them a happy life. "Don't forget when you move," he said, "I'll make you the best deal." To Santo, without the slightest hesitation, he said, "I hear it's going to be a boy this time. Good deal."

With the Sicilianos and Fontanas, Anselmo's exchange of greetings was on a different level. They understood each other. They had grown up together on Hemlock Street, gone to the same school, made good in the business world and moved out to fashionable neighborhoods. Fontana and Siciliano admired Anselmo because he was top man in the game they were all playing. When Anselmo laid out money, it multiplied like rabbits. When he invested in slum property and rented to Negro families, his income went up like a Texas gusher. He always seemed to hit the jackpot.

Fontana and Siciliano not only admired Anselmo. They respected him—because he was an educated man. At college, he had learned the difference between the letter and the spirit of the law and in court had applied his knowledge in a practical way by twisting both to his own advantage. His countrymen respected him as one of the sharpest lawyers in town and one of the ablest realtors. Big wheels in politics and the professions consulted him on their property investments and through the years he had become their front man. Through Anselmo, they held slum property in trust so that the real ownership could never become public information. Building and fire inspectors never entered their tenements. When tenants lost their lives in fires, no unfavorable publicity was ever pinned on Anselmo and his friends. It was the agent or henchman who had to take the occasional rap. But Anselmo got plenty of publicity when he wanted it, when he won a difficult case in court, or when he went to a $500 a plate charity dinner or attended a fashionable wedding. The part of his life he wished the public to see, he revealed. The rest he knew how to submerge like the undersea ten-elevenths of an iceberg.

On the road to success, Anselmo had long outdistanced his countrymen and former neighbors like Fontana and Siciliano. Aldermen and judges feared him. Assemblymen and state senators bowed to him. He took part in the inner political discussions which shaped municipal campaigns, state and national elections. And all because, in the areas where he owned or held property in trust, he knew how to deliver the vote.

Anselmo was smart. Even Daniel De Rocco shook his head with some pride that the son of a Sicilian could mix with the big shots at the stock exchange and join the exclusive clubs on Michigan Avenue. All the same, Anselmo should be put in his place a little, so Daniel tried to pull him down a rung or two by using the first name he knew Anselmo hated, "Well, Generoso, how's the boy?"

Anselmo only smiled. "How's business, Dan, in the heat wave?" Anselmo was poking fun at the funeral business.

"Good, good!" De Rocco said dryly. Anselmo was brash like all the Americans. He lacked the old-fashioned dignity of Anselmo Senior who had been a Sicilian born. Why should Daniel expect somebody born in America to show any politeness? But there was no one in the room who would understand what Daniel felt, so he shrugged his shoulders with private contempt for his brother-in-law. Money wasn't everything, even if Anselmo did have a foot in every door. And his shoes—why snakeskin?

Daniel went on thinking about Anselmo as he watched Father Guidarello step up to the long table to bless the food and deliver a prayer of thanksgiving. The old priest called upon Kathryn and Pete and Luigi to kneel as he blessed them. Then young Father Antonelli congratulated the family and all present that a man who was brave and devoted to his country had returned safe from a foreign battlefield. He shook Lou warmly by the hand, then embraced him. "May God bless you!"

When the religious ceremony was over and Anselmo got up on the stairs to speak, Daniel was not the only person to find his way to the kitchen. Pete had already made his way out. And Anselmo who saw everything noted their exit. But opposition was a part of life he enjoyed.

"Friends, neighbors, and countrymen!" He turned to shake his fist playfully at the youngsters on the stairs behind him who were shouting, "Speech, speech!"

"We got no time for speeches. We all want a hunk of that jumbo cake. Come on up here, Lou fellow, and we'll get it over with."

It was like Anselmo to get down to business.

"Lou-boy, it's all yours." He handed down an official looking scroll bound in heavy gold ribbon. "It was your mother's idea. I won't say I didn't whisper in her ear. How about a hand for Lou's mother?" Anselmo began to clap in Kathryn's direction till everybody joined in. "A man's ma deserves most of the credit." Bending toward Lou, he whispered, "While you're giving that document the short arm inspection, I'm going to say a few words. OK?"

As Lou opened the scroll his ears were filled with Anselmo's praises and his face reddened with embarrassment.

"Here's our boy safe home. Lou was in the advance guard. Risked everything—his life. And we're proud of him. It was rough out there, folks, holding the beachhead—" Anselmo was interrupted by a triple crack of thunder in the immediate sky. Rain came down with a trampling sound in the street. "You see what I mean, folks. It was like that out there—" Thunder and lightning roared and blared. It sounded like a vast battle for the heavens had just opened up with artillery booming, antiaircraft guns barking, and dog fights of enormous proportions. "Sounds worse'n Korea, how about it?" Anselmo joked with Lou.

But Lou's mother was nudging him to read the scroll. "It's all yours—758 Hemlock Street," she whispered excitedly. "Everything I did—it's yours, Luigi, yours! No more break your back. It's easy street. Next we buy up in Lincoln Park, I promise you."

"We gotta beat them down to their knees," Lou could hear Anselmo shouting above the thunder and his mother's voice. "We gotta drive them back over the Yalu and then some. We're going to keep this a white man's world, how about it? We're proud of Lou for what he did out there. Give our hero-boy a great big hand!"

The title to 758 rolled up in Lou's hands as he listened. Kathryn saved it from falling to the floor. Was Anselmo talking about Korea, Lou wondered, as he heard them clapping for him.

"Speech, speech!" the youngsters shouted from the top steps. Everybody in the room took up the chorus.

Lou who had drifted with the stream all evening was suddenly standing back on his heels. Anselmo could tell *him* all about the war over there!

"Speaking for myself," Lou protested, "I ain't the hero he makes out. We got chased like dogs, that's the plain truth of it—"

Anselmo stepped down to drop his hand on Lou's shoulder. "Attaboy, I know how you feel," he soothed as if Lou was suffering from battle fatigue. "But we're going to chase them back again—like dogs. We've got to win, Lou."

"I ain't so sure about that—" Lou began.

Anselmo waved the scroll above his head to rule out more talk about the war. "Open it up, Lou, you're in business."

Lou hesitated. It was only a piece of paper. But if he accepted it, was he going to drag Tony Ferrucini to jail next week for refusing to vacate the house he'd lived in for thirty-five years?

Impatient, Anselmo seized the scroll back from Lou's hands and began to flourish it over his head again. "This is only the beginning, brother. Shall we call it basic training for a lieutenancy with Anselmo & Associates? With lots of room on up ahead,

Lou, till you make the five-star!" He surrounded Lou with his arm to welcome him into a brand new life of opportunity, while everybody in the room let go with broadsides of congratulations loud enough to drown out the thunder. Kathryn seized hold of Lou and Nina came running to him to flood him with kisses.

"It's the happiest day of my life," said Kathryn. She even flung herself at Anselmo, hugged him, and gave him a kiss.

But Anselmo was staring over his mother-in-law's head. "Look!" he warned.

Kathryn turned to see Jesse at the door with the lightning framing his huge shoulders against the storm. "Holy Mother!" she said. But Lou stepped quickly across the room to welcome his friend.

"It's raining doggone cats and dogs," said Jesse to Lou in the enormous silence as he wiped the rain from his glasses.

"I'm glad you came," said Lou heartily. "Where's Mrs. Williams?"

"It's her busy night." Jesse spoke quietly but he could be heard all over the house.

"Speech, speech!" The youngsters on the stairs were the first to cut loose.

"Folks, I want you to meet my buddy from over there," said Lou. "We drove in the same outfit and got banged up together."

Then everybody started talking at once to cover up their surprise while Lou introduced Jesse to Anselmo and Della. "I'd be pushing up the daisies if it wasn't for this guy," said Lou. "You'd be celebrating my homecoming with a De Rocco Special." Everybody was quiet again to hear what Lou was saying.

"Same here," said Jesse. "We had to pull together out there, or go all the way down."

"Speech, speech!" The yells from the stairs began to build up again. But Anselmo held up his hand for silence. "Time for chow, how about it? That jumbo cake!" He grabbed Lou by the hand and reached over for Nina's hand, then dragged them through the crowd to the table where a great white cake rose up layer on layer to pinnacles and gold stars.

As Lou and Nina crossed hands to hold the great silver knife, there was complete silence again. Nina's hair gleamed brilliantly and her dress caught up the light like a summer cloud. She glanced at Lou as if she might have something to say in private about his choice of buddies. Then she smiled at him as if she had forgotten anybody else was in the room.

"I want to let you in on an open secret," Anselmo announced. "The lady said yes."

Lou surrounded Nina's hand with his and the knife sank into the cake while friends and relatives began to shout congratulations.

#19

Kathryn was happy and terrified at the same time. Anselmo was so calm about announcing the engagement, maybe he didn't really mind about Jesse. Her eyes blurred with happiness for Lou and Nina, but she held her cake in one hand without being able to raise it to her mouth. And in the other she was twisting and crushing the title to 758 between her fingers.

When she saw Daniel De Rocco hold out his hand to Jesse, then she was sure everything would be all right. But a few minutes later, Anselmo's hand closed around her elbow and he whispered he had something important to tell her.

In her room, watching Anselmo close the door, she began to feel like bird in a cage. She wanted to scream and fly past him and put her arms around Lou and Nina and laugh and shout with happiness. But Anselmo closed her in.

"Mama, something serious—" he began with his back to the door. "Too bad to have to tell you tonight, but business is business. I just heard this afternoon those tenants in the basement at 1250 are going through with that triple damage suit. You'll get a notice to appear in court next week."

"I know, Boatman told me," said Kathryn with a profound feeling of relief. Anselmo's serious business wasn't about Jesse after all.

"You don't seem to understand." Anselmo was surprised at her casual tone. "These people are getting organized. And it's in Federal Court, too, where it's harder for us to get cooperation."

"So what am I gonna do?" asked Kathryn almost cheerfully.

"First, see this Green woman and offer to lower their rent like you want to meet them halfway. That'll take the wind out of that old kite. If she doesn't fall for that, we'll have her arrested on charges of disorderly conduct. We can't go on fooling with her any more. Get that Boatman and a couple of his buddies to go witness she's keeping a house of prostitution. Then we'll get her out. You'll have to make it worth their while, of course."

"But Anselmo—" she was wondering what Lou would think about a proposal like this. "That ain't—"

"Mama, we got to be prepared to settle this right away. Because if the court serves notice on that triple damage suit first, it's going to be awfully hard to get them out. One way or another, let me know at the latest by Monday morning."

Kathryn sank down on her bed with her head bowed almost to her knees. She had never thought of framing Anna Mae before, however much she hated her.

"This woman's a saint?" Anselmo needled her.

"It ain't that, but Luigi—"

"Yes, mama, Luigi is the problem. But for a day or two he'll be out of the way getting his discharge." Laughter and music came through the door, but Anselmo was staring at her with the eye of a prosecutor. "Mama, who invited *him* here?" His eyes, grilling her, left her no chance to evade an answer.

Kathryn knew now why he had cornered her. If she told him the truth, his anger would strike out against Lou. He would take back his offer of a job. "There was a mistake," Kathryn whispered, her voice scarcely rising to sound.

"Some mistake! How many times haven't I told you, mama, you can't make friends and money out of the same people?"

"I wanted to sell him the house, Anselmo." She took the blame on herself. "I invited him to come over any time."

"Tonight?" Anselmo didn't believe a word.

"Is it my fault if he came tonight?"

"You don't seem to understand what it means, mama, to be called a nigger-lover. You put me and Della, all of us, on a tough spot. People will use these things against us." Anselmo shook his head angrily. "And Lou don't seem to understand, either."

"It wasn't his fault," Kathryn insisted. But Anselmo went on shaking his head as if he knew why she was lying. He opened the door cautiously to look out, then stepped back into the crowd.

"Ma, what's wrong?" Lou had come to look for her. "Folks are beginning to leave."

Kathryn longed to tell him everything, pour out all her troubles and be done with them. But she couldn't. It would make Lou turn against Anselmo. "Nothing," she said tapping her head with her finger tips. "All the excitement."

"Dr. Thomasello's right here—"

"No doctor," she ordered. "It's OK now." She stood up with an effort and put her arms around her son's neck. "Oh, Luigi—" she sighed. Tears were in her eyes. "I'm so happy for you and Nina." Then she went back into the room supporting herself on his arm.

PART THREE

#1

The homecoming was over. Daylight filtered through the curtains. On the improvised table in the front room the little porcelain figures still stood where Kathryn had placed them the previous day. It was hard for her to remember with what hope she had scattered grains of corn and ears of wheat around the Madonna and Child, Saint Joseph, and the Three Wise Men to celebrate the safe return of her son from the war.

All night, sleep had hovered like a vulture ready to pick the bones of her dreams. She envied Lou his step of confidence as he went upstairs to bed when the morning light was already squaring the window. She envied Pete his quiet sleep with his lips parted in a smile. But hour after hour she could only lie awake remembering that Anselmo had gone away angry and that Della's lips were hard as rock when she kissed her good-bye. The jewels at her wrist and neck were burning with a cold fire and the gleam of her dress was like the reflection from a million splinters of metal as she went out the front door. And Anselmo had smiled good-bye at everybody, excepting only Kathryn.

When sleep swooped down for an instant, nightmare figures assumed the enormous proportions of Kathryn's fears. Anselmo was forcing her down a lightless corridor. He had wings like an eagle's, beady eyes, and sharp claws. Kathryn woke with a scream and jumped out of bed. But Pete went on sleeping as if he could sleep forever.

She rushed into the front room to tear aside the curtains. If only Anselmo had a little more heart— If only Lou had never set eyes on Jesse— If only Anna Mae could be wiped out of existence— If only Kathryn herself could pray! She turned to the holy figures on the empty expanse of linen, but all she could say was, "Holy Mother of God!" Her life was a bitter vessel filled with hopes that had suddenly turned sour.

Slowly Kathryn wrapped the porcelain figures in soft tissue. She folded the white linen and laid it away in the bottom drawer of her cabinet. For a long time she stood staring at the bare boards wondering if Anselmo would ever give Lou the job now.

Finally, when she heard Pete stirring, she prepared his breakfast and served it to him in silence. Whistling his favorite tune, Pete went off to bowl with his old friends in the corner of the park behind the ball diamond. From the kitchen, Kathryn could hear the shouts of the boys playing ball. Everybody else seemed happy.

With the routine work of the day, gradually Kathryn's hopes came seeping back. It was just possible Anna Mae would listen to sense. Then, even if Lou didn't get the job with Anselmo, the rent from two buildings would be a start for him. The sooner they went down to see the Robertses, the better. The best would be if Anna Mae was at the hospital. Geneva and Charles Roberts were more reasonable people to deal with.

She prepared breakfast for Lou and took it up to his bedroom. "Sleepy head!" she scolded him lightly. She was glad he had a clean bright room to wake up in. The noon sun was beating down on the floor. Better she had the love of her son than of all the Anselmos in the world. She bent to stroke his forehead and kiss him on the cheek. "Wake up, Luigi."

As they crossed the park together, mother and son, Lou wanted to watch the ball game and stop by the bowling corner, but Kathryn urged him on. "We gotta get the rent before they spend all the money." She laughed a little and squeezed his arm closer to hers.

"That was some round up last night, ma," said Lou. "Seemed to go off OK."

When his mother didn't say anything, Lou went on, "Funny, how old Daniel took a liking to Jesse. Remember how he said so everybody could hear, 'Stick to your guns, boys.' And Nellie, too, that was the big surprise. I guess it was because she got remembering about Salvatore being killed in the other war when Jesse was telling her he'd been over there in Redball."

Still, Kathryn didn't say anything. It was Anselmo, not Daniel De Rocco, who had offered Lou a job. They were walking down the last block to 1250 when Lou went on, "And Father Antonelli invited Jesse to come to mass. He said it was time for us all to live like Christians."

Kathryn lowered her head. She remembered how Father Antonelli had held Jesse's hand for a long time while he talked to him. Anselmo and Della and Father Guidarello had already gone. "I won't say nothing more about it, Luigi," she muttered. "Maybe I got old fashioned ideas."

Kathryn began collecting the rent on the third floor and worked down. She was proud to introduce Lou to her tenants. They seemed to show him a kind of respect which even Boatman didn't command. "My boy you made the quilt for," she introduced him on the top floor to Mrs. Osborne. The old lady in the purple dress fixed her eyes on Lou and inclined her head slightly.

"I know," said Lou, "my buddy's gonna bunk in here for a while." He wondered how Jesse would get along with this old woman whose eyes seemed frozen out with grief or hostility, or both.

The flats downstairs were filled with children. Two or three families shared kitchen privileges and the whole floor used one toilet. Still, it was a place to live, Kathryn explained to Lou. "People can't be choosy these days with a war on." As the rent money accumulated in her purse, Kathryn's feeling of depression began to lift. She stepped down the stairs to the first floor with more confidence than she'd had all day. In the front flat, she introduced Lou to her best tenants, a retired post office worker and his wife who had their own furniture and kept their place looking like a hotel room. Mr. Martin was a handsome old man with keen frosty hair, sharp black complexion, and a sociable smile. His wife, recovering slowly from a broken hip, was always glad to have company. She liked to hand the money over personally to Kathryn.

"You see, Luigi, there's nothing to it," Kathryn said in the hall as she smoothed down two more ten dollar bills and slipped them into her bulging hand bag. "They know who's the boss around here. And they know they're lucky to have a nice place." As she saw Lou staring at the blackened walls in the corridor with plaster chipped and covered with crayon marks, she smiled as if the tenants were ignorant, dirty people. "It ain't like downtown, eh?"

As they descended into the basement, she told Lou he'd better hold his nose. Boatman cleaned up the place once a week, she explained, but five minutes later it was worse than before. "But upstairs it's nice, eh, by Mrs. Osborne's?"

After collecting the rent from the front two flats in the basement, Kathryn had to debate with herself before knocking on the Roberts' door. "These people have caused me a lot of trouble," she explained to Lou. "All the same, Anselmo wants me to cut the rent so they will have to drop triple damages."

"What does that mean?"

"Didn't Anselmo explain it?"

"He told me about getting this Boatman to go around with you."

"They wanta ruin us, Lou. That's what it means. But the judge won't listen to them if we cut down their rent. Then later we'll get 'em out and rent to somebody else, save a lot of trouble."

The air was fetid with garbage and toilet smells. How could anybody stand it, Lou wondered. But he was shocked out of pity the next moment by the harsh voice of Anna Mae Green and her belligerent attitude to his mother. "What do you want, Miss Biomchi?" She didn't even take the trouble to get their name straight, and she stood with her fists squared on her hips blocking the doorway as if she was facing thieves in the night.

"This is my son, Mr. Bianchi," Kathryn said in a tone that was forebearing and menacing at the same time.

Lou was surprised by the absolute hostility in Anna Mae's eyes as she examined his uniform from head to foot. He'd never even seen the woman before and yet she was glaring at him like a panther ready to spring.

"I'm gonna tell you something, Mae Green—" Kathryn's voice crackled with anger and shame. "You think you're smart getting your sister all tied up in court." It was impossible for Kathryn to soften her tone because Anna Mae was putting her to shame in front of Lou with the kind of insolent smile no tenant had the right to turn on her landlady, least of all a black woman. "You're all gonna get beat to the ground, 'less you stop it right now." Kathryn wanted to be calm, and yet she was threatening Anna Mae instead of reasoning with her. She tried desperately to smile. "Now I ain't a hard person to get along with—"

Kathryn could see the gleam of Anna Mae's teeth in a sarcastic smile. Behind her, Geneva was staring like a dark madonna protecting her children from evil spirits. Only the baby on the bed was oblivious to the tensions. For him the basement room was a world of joy because his belly was full of his mother's milk and his fingers had found his toes.

"That's the truth, Anna Mae," Kathryn urged.

"There may be some folks—" Anna Mae began. But Geneva put her hand on her sister's shoulder to restrain her.

"What you want with us, Miss Kathryn?" she asked in a neutral tone fixing her large eyes on Lou as she spoke to his mother.

"You got a good head on your shoulders, Mrs. Roberts." Kathryn spoke to Geneva in a manner calculated to draw her away from her sister's influence. "I wanta tell you something. You'd be a lot better off to keep out of the courts." Kathryn stepped closer to Geneva in a confidential way. "Like my papa used to say, poor folks ain't got a chance with the law. And the law makes poor folk out of rich folk. Who wins?" She appealed to Geneva, with a glance at Lou at the same time to be sure he appreciated how she was bending over backward to reach an agreement. "You or me? Or the lawyers and judges?"

"We wasn't the first to mess around with the law—" Mae interrupted.

"What you got on your mind?" Geneva persisted as if she was at least prepared to hear Kathryn to the end.

"So forget what's under the bridge," said Kathryn in her friendliest manner. "My son here and I both wanta meet you folks halfway. We'll cut down the rent to fifteen dollars a week if you drop this triple damages." She shrugged a little as she looked sideways at Lou. What more could she do to be obliging?

"Six bucks is ceiling on this mean little old piece of rat hole," said Mae flatly. "I seen it in writing with my own eyes down at the rent office."

"That's nonsense," Kathryn retorted. "They had no right to show you any papers. This is private between me and you. I'll come down to twelve bucks. But that's final understand?"

"My sister speaks truth," said Geneva. "Ceiling is six dollars."

"I'm warning you—" Kathryn began to shout. These idiots couldn't recognize a bargain even when she dished it up on a gold platter. She was offering them a reduction of eight dollars a week. "It's my last word—twelve bucks."

Mae and Geneva both shook their heads.

"I can make it tough for you!" Kathryn threatened.

"You ain't made it tough?" Mae's head went back with a roar of laughter. "You got a nose for smells, Miss Biomchi? You send that Boatman down here to mess around with the gas, blow out the fuses, knock the shit out of the toilet pipes with a sledge hammer—" Mae was looking straight at Lou as if it was time he knew the kind of landlady his mother was, if he didn't know already.

"Lies, lies, lies!" shouted Kathryn.

Lou put his hand on his mother's arm to restrain her. "Mrs. Green, if you don't like the way my mother runs her business," he said quietly, "wouldn't it be better you should move?"

"That's what I've told her." Encouraged by the support Lou gave her, Kathryn went on shouting louder than before, "And I'm warning you, Anna Mae, I ain't complained yet about the men coming down to your bed room two, three every night." She could believe anything of Anna Mae now if she only shouted loud enough. When Lou gripped her arm to warn her she should get her temper back under control, she shook herself free to yell, "You gonna land in jail one of these days."

"I never heard you holler about them women up front with their two, three men every night," Anna Mae countered. "Charge 'em double and take your cut. Wink both your eyes, you and the police, when they sell reefers to the kids. Fifty cents to ruin a kid. That's OK by you." Her scorn was cold and blighting and she spoke to Kathryn as no colored person had ever spoken before.

"You ought to be shamed of the shit you're standing in."

Kathryn raised her hand to strike Anna Mae. Her handbag slipped from under her arm. She tried to grab it in midair, but it fell with a thud to the floor, bursting open. Change scattered lightly under the bed and stove, and fives and tens spread out fanlike on the cracked linoleum. A little twenty-two rolled over a couple of times and lay shining in the middle of the floor.

In a flash Kathryn was down on her knees with both hands grabbing the bills. Mae stopped in the same instant to pick up the gun before Lou could reach it. Then with a steady smile, she offered it to Kathryn muzzle first.

"It's loaded," Kathryn screamed, seizing the gun.

"Take it easy, ma, for Christ sake," said Lou with his eyes hugging the weapon. He was steadying his mother at the same time with his hand on her arm.

"You seen her," said Kathryn excitedly. "She pointed the gun at me!"

Lou would never forget Anna Mae's smile at that moment or the metal hardness of her tone. "We keep our own protection, too, Miss Kathryn." Her eyes glanced sideways at the shelf above the bed, then sharpened like steel points against his mother. A tigress of a woman, ready to spring at her throat.

Lou steered his mother back out of the room while Geneva ordered the kids to hand up the change from the floor.

Kathryn went hysterical as she climbed the stairs into the alley and abused Anna Mae at the top of her voice. Lou gripped her arm and walked up the street with her and across the park while she went on saying what she was going to do to Anna Mae.

"Holy Mother," she screamed, "you try to help them and they kick you in the teeth!"

"Ma, Anselmo told me about Boatman," said Lou with a calmness to make his mother listen, "and all about you carrying a rod around in your purse."

"You can see how it is, Luigi. I have to."

"Yeh, but ma, she keeps a gun, too. I seen her eyes go up to the shelf over the bed when she talked about protection. You gotta keep away from her, understand?"

"But it's my house, Luigi!"

"Sure, and it's your life—"

"That's why I need your help, Luigi, in the worst way." She held her arm tight in his as if she would never let him go.

#2

All afternoon, Kathryn cherished her anger against Anna Mae. Even if Lou had been sharp about the gun, all the same he had told the woman to get out if she didn't like the way his mother ran her business. He could see what a rough customer she was. Nonetheless, Kathryn hesitated until Lou had gone off to a dance with Nina, before she phoned Pagliani to send Boatman over.

If Boatman would swear Anna Mae was a prostitute, they could have her arrested Monday and thrown in jail while Lou was away getting his discharge. That would be the end of the triple damage law suit and when Lou came back the future would open up the way Kathryn had dreamed. Anselmo wouldn't stay angry if she followed his advice. After his public announcement at the homecoming, he would have to carry out his promise and give Lou the job.

By the time Boatman stood on her kitchen doorstep, Kathryn had half persuaded herself that Anna Mae was in fact a prostitute. Even if Kathryn hadn't actually seen men going into her room, all the same, she was the kind of woman who would sell herself cheap. And after all the grief she had caused, why should Kathryn spare her?

With eyes lowered and shoulders rounded, Boatman listened to all she had to say. But when she was finished, he told her quietly, "Anna Mae don't have no men down in her room."

Kathryn was astonished at Boatman's stubbornness. "But you told me yourself—"

"Ma'am," Boatman interrupted, "since her man was killed down south—"

"Are you gonna do what I ask you to?" Kathryn was furious to have Boatman resist her plans. "She's a no-good woman and you know it." Maybe Boatman himself had fallen under Anna Mae's influence. He was a weak man for all his body strength, licked boots, Kathryn's and Pagliani's—a man with a scar from mouth to ear and a criminal record in the South. "I'll pay you for your trouble." With a gesture of contempt, she held out two ten dollar bills.

Boatman's eyes were suddenly meeting hers with a kind of insolence that was frightening. She kept holding out the money. His hands hung at his sides. "Take it!" she commanded. "If you don't, I'm gonna tell Pagliani. I know about down South."

Slowly, Boatman raised his hand to take the bills. "I'll double this," she promised. "And twenty bucks apiece for two men to stand up with you."

When Boatman was gone, Kathryn spent the evening justifying herself to herself. Anselmo was right. If she didn't get rid of Mae, Mae would get rid of her. If Mae won a triple damage suit, the other tenants would follow her example. Instead of twelve thousand dollars income, Kathryn would have to pay out at least double that in triple damages to pay the fine—or go to jail the rest of her life. The court would take 1250 and 758 away from her, the two thousand dollars she and Pete had saved in a lifetime, the house they lived in—everything.

All night the arguments kept rolling around in Kathryn's head like sharp pointed stones. Fitfully, she dreamed about Anna Mae and Anselmo as they took on gigantic shapes to frighten her into wakefulness. And she also dreamed about Lou—a melancholy face reproving her with those deep set eyes of Christ on the cross.

All day Sunday Kathryn waited anxiously for Boatman to appear. Evening passed and still no word. Lou and Nina had gone out to Round Lake for an all-day picnic and hadn't come back yet. Pete had already gone to bed when Boatman finally showed up at the back door with two men standing behind him like a double shadow.

"These are the men." His voice was very deep and low and his eyes were full of pain as if somebody was twisting a knife between his shoulder blades.

The time had come for Kathryn to take on herself the responsibility for swearing false witness against an innocent woman. She had never travelled this road before and she stood at the brink of darkness hearing Lou call her back as if he were standing in the room beside her, "Don't do it, ma." But before she could close the door in the faces of the three men, Anselmo's smile was filling the darkness with promise of money and success. "The woman's a saint?" She could hear him laugh.

So Kathryn hesitated only a moment before she said to the three who stood outside, "You will make a complaint with me down at police court?" Anselmo had become her conscience.

They nodded, but said nothing. The two whom she didn't know rocked a little forward and a little backward as they accepted the money she offered. They were both unsteady on their feet. But Boatman stood staring at her sullenly. His massive shoulders and thickset neck made her afraid of what he might do if he ever lost his fear of her and Pagliani. She handed him twenty more of the sixty she had promised. The bills stuck to the sweat on the palms of her hands.

It was a tremendous relief for her to close the door on the bargain she had driven and shut out the three men and the night that enveloped them. Thank God, she could breathe again.

All too soon she heard Lou's step in the alley. He must have met the men in the street. If he ever finds out, she muttered to herself. She could not bear even to think of her life without her son's respect. It was a terrible risk.

"What's the deal, ma?" he asked after giving her a hearty hug and kiss. His mother was trembling in his arms. "What's wrong, ma?"

"Nothing wrong. I'm tired, that's all."

"But Boatman and those two other guys, I seen them come out the alley—"

"They wander all over the place, those colored people—"

"You mean you didn't see 'em?"

Kathryn shook her head. But Lou wasn't satisfied. "Ma, there are some things about this whole rent business I been thinking about. This Boatman, did he really turn off the gas and all that sort of thing?"

"My God, Luigi, you didn't believe all her lies?"

"Well no, but—"

"Luigi, you gotta get up early, go get your discharge. So we go to bed now."

"OK, ma, we'll talk about it when I get back. But you gotta promise me to stay away from that basement and quit carrying a rod around in your purse—while I'm gone."

"I promise," she said tonelessly. "How's Nina?"

"Hundred per cent," Lou answered. "We got everything fixed up."

"When's it gonna be?"

"Next month. We're gonna live upstairs till we get our own place, if that's OK with you and pop." Again Lou hugged his mother. His step was full of life on the stairs as he went up to bed and she could hear him drop his shoes on the floor carelessly like the old days.

But Kathryn was afraid to go to bed, afraid of the nightmares that would come down upon her the moment she closed her eyes in sleep.

In the kitchen, all was bright and shiny. The canary bounced around his cage. The plants in the window box glistened with life. But deep in Kathryn's heart fear was swelling like fungus in the dark.

#3

Monday morning, the iron ball was already cracking up the pavement by Jesse's house. That very day the walls would come crumbling down.

"I can't say I'm sorry," said Lil. Breaking up house was a pleasure she had looked forward to for a long time. Lil was watching Jesse pack the last of their clothes in the car he'd borrowed from her brother. "I'm tired to death of these mean old flats. Cold water. No bathtub."

Lil's eyes were full of resentment as she thought of the years with and without Jesse she'd spent in the flat upstairs. "Everybody messing up the toilet. Jesse, we gonna begin to live human—soon."

"Tell me about it," he said absent mindedly. He was hoping Lil would like Mrs. Osborne. Or perhaps it was more important Mrs. Osborne should take to Lil. They were both blunt, opinionated people and if they crossed each other—three months could be next to a lifetime.

"You'll like Mrs. Osborne," Jesse said hopefully. He put his arms around Lil and held her tight to him. "It won't be long, hon, before we move to the other house and have the front room for Lil's Beauty Salon."

Lil laughed scornfully and drew away from him. Jesse hadn't even asked what the rent would be in the Hemlock Street building. Desperately, she wanted a house of their own where they could make all the decisions. But Jesse was so impractical. If he'd stayed on the job four years ago, instead of letting his temper get the best of him, he never would have lost his job at the coal yard. With his earnings and hers, they would have had enough to make the down payment by this time. Now, it would take them two more years. We got the lot bought anyhow, she thought with some satisfaction.

Lil was a smart looking woman with a lean face and large, sharp eyes, a mouth that was set in a determined line. She hardly ever smiled. Raising three kids for three years without Jesse's help and working at the beauty salon on 47th Street near the el every afternoon and evening and late Fridays and Saturdays had worn away her youth and made her tense like a steel spring.

"Anyways, I don't want none of Mrs. Bianchi's leavings," she snapped. "We're gonna build a new house, Jesse."

"Lou's ain't a bad house," he insisted, "with a park across the street for the kids to play."

But Lil had settled the question once and for all and she was giving the truck ahead a final glance of inspection. "Junior!" she called sharply as she saw their younger boy stretched out on the sofa bed in the back of the truck with a comic book held up against the sky. "You sit up with Ernestine."

"You ain't ready *yet*?" Ernestine was so excited she leaned her head out the cab window till the ribbons in her hair fluttered like butterflies.

Charles pounded the horn of the jalopy at the head of the calvacade. The steam shovels grunted and the great ball kept pounding a few feet away, demolishing the street where the kids had played baseball and skipped rope.

"All clear!" Jesse waved at Charles. The jalopy took off and the truck wheels began to turn. Jesse stared a moment at the excavation across the street. In a way he was glad his ma and pa hadn't lived to see this day. "That's it," he said with a forced smile at Lil.

"Thank the Lord." She cut off further sentiment. As she stepped into the car, their dog Jeep came bouncing off the back of the truck. He was long, and he had round fat legs.

"Oh Jesus Christ, Lil!" Jesse had a bad moment. "I forgot to tell Mrs. Osborne about Jeep."

"Mrs. Osborne will like Jeep!" She mocked his hopeful tone of a moment before when he said she'd like Mrs. Osborne. Then she gave him a kiss for forgetting. "You won't ever change, Jess."

"He won't be able to get his teeth in that mahogany bed," said Jesse, "any way!'

"Better keep him down in the car for a while," Lil decided.

Her tactics were wise. For, even without the dog, Mrs. Osborne gave them a stiff reception, only staring when Jesse introduced all three kids, one after another. With her immobile face and sullen eyes, she made them all feel like intruders who had no business depriving her of her privacy and half the space she lived in, even if they were paying rent. She looked haggard and pouchy round the eyes as if she'd stayed awake all night.

But after she had supervised the moving of the mahogany bed, she relented toward Jesse and Charles. And she made Lil welcome in the kitchen they would have to share.

"She looks like a cross old bitch," said Charles to his dad. He had a confidence in his own opinion which made him speak out louder than was tactful.

"Mind your language, Poke," Jesse warned.

"I didn't mean nothing by it," Charles defended himself. He wasn't taking orders from anybody if he could help it, not even his old man.

In a moment Mrs. Osborne brought them both a cup of coffee. "You moved the bed." It was an achievement in her eyes worth a reward.

"See?" said Jesse as they went downstairs to bring up the last of the clothes from the car. "She's an old widow woman thinking a tornado's hit her, but she ain't mean."

As they reached the alley level, Jesse could see the head and shoulders of somebody large waiting at the bottom of the basement steps. There was a flicker of white from the eyes, then the face was lowered. From the size of the face and the set of the shoulders Jesse guessed it was Boatman. "Don't blow no fuses, man," he called down. The face withdrew completely into the shadows.

As Jesse and Charles stepped out into the street, the drone of a flying boxcar came puttering down from the sky. It was still a novel experience for Jesse to hear the motor of a plane without getting ready to dive for the nearest ditch.

"Dad, how long's it gonna last over there, anyway?"

"You think your dad's the prophet Isaiah?" Jesse's eyes were drilling up into the sky. "That's some old crate, Poke."

"You think it's gonna last a year, two years?"

"Well, to be honest, boy, I thought the war was over when I seen our men lay down the rubber pontoons across the air strip at Hamhung. They piled up the C-rations and all the trucks and tanks they couldn't load on to an L.S.T. Then they took the stoppers out of some of them fifty gallon drums and started 'em rolling and splashing gasoline all the way down the field. When I seen 'em light a match to those mountains of junk—it's a fact, Poke, I thought we might's well call it quits."

"Me too." In another year and a half Charles expected to be drafted. Jesse could tell from the sound of his voice, even if he wouldn't admit it out loud, that he didn't want to be sent over to Korea.

"You got some sense, boy." Jesse exchanged a look of complete understanding with Charles. "That's my last war."

As he was speaking Jesse lowered his voice because a police car swung around them and parked in front of 1250. First a Negro cop jumped out. The white cop who was doing the driving followed him down the alley at a slower pace. They were the same cops had come at Pagliani's call the previous week to bounce Jesse out of the tavern. But this time they paid no attention to him. They disappeared in the side entrance and he could hear the fall of their boots on the basement steps.

"Damn bulls," Jesse muttered. As he banged the car door, Jeep set up a homeless howl. "Take a chance now and let him come up?" Jesse asked Charles' advice.

"We're in, ain't we, dad?" asked the boy realistically.

Jeep bounded up the two flights of stairs, encouraging them to follow with a toss of his head over his shoulder. He met Mrs. Osborne with a yap full of joy, then dived past her to jump up on his favorite Ernestine.

"He's just an old lazy dog," Jesse explained with a show of calm he didn't feel. "Don't bite or chew. Keeps the cats and rats away, Mrs. Osborne."

"And I put the flea powder on him last night," said Ernestine. "You almost stopped scratching, ain't you Jeep, old boy?"

The shock was too much for Mrs. Osborne. She sat down in her great chair and clutched the lace along the arms with unsteady fingers. "I told you, Mr. Williams, I'd have to get used to the children. But a dog!" She spoke as if Jeep was man's worst enemy.

"I can tell you, Mrs. Osborne," said Lil quietly as a confidence shared between two women, "Jesse honestly did forget to tell you about the dog. But that's the way he is."

"That's the way they all are, praise the Lord!" said Mrs. Osborne with a resigned look at her husband's picture. At least she and Lil had something in common.

Jesse and Jeep and the boys had all vanished between the curtains that divided Mrs. Osborne's rooms from theirs.

"The kids had to have a pet to take it out on so they wouldn't get me down," Lil went on to explain. "I can tell you it was lonely without their dad. For me too."

"Please, Mrs. Osborne," begged Ernestine when she saw a favorable opening.

But Lil looked out the window and quickly changed the subject. "This is some improvement, Mrs. Osborne. For years it seems like, we've been hearing nothing but that old steam shovel. We won't miss that, will we Ernestine?"

"Or the rats, ma."

"Rats, child?" Mrs. Osborne asked. "You know any part of town where there ain't rats? Cause if you do that's just where I wanta move."

"We didn't have any rats after we got Jeep, did we, ma," said Ernestine as if now there would be no further question about Jeep's right to stay.

"What's that thing you got there?" Mrs. Osborne, too, felt that she had lost the battle against Jeep. "Where's the doll's head, girl?"

"It's what my dad brought me from the war." Ernestine's voice was hushed out of respect for the dead Korean girl who had once played with the doll. Then she said proudly, "You believe it, this doll saved my father's life. When he was fetching her down in the ditch, his truck got all shot up. Ain't that right, ma?"

Lil nodded. There was enough for her to do without sitting talking to Mrs. Osborne all day about dolls. And her schedule called for her to start work at the beauty parlor at two o'clock that afternoon.

"That ain't nothing!" Junior, who'd been listening from the other side of the curtain, butted his way through with Jesse's helmet down over his eyes. "My dad didn't wear this helmet, they'd of shot his head off a million times." As far as Junior was concerned, the Korean war was a wild Western in which his father had played the lead part in that helmet.

"Pull the curtains back, boy," Mrs. Osborne ordered, "so I can visit with your ma."

Mrs. Osborne had resigned herself at last to the invasion and had decided to make the best of it. What the further punishment would be, she didn't know. But Lil was fortunately a self-sufficient woman, motherly and sensible. Her voice was in her favor. And she talked in an educated way with a lot of different inflections. She was no ignorant fool, which was a blessing, Mrs. Osborne thought, because she personally had great admiration for an educated woman.

As for the children, Mrs. Osborne had already made up her mind. She liked the girl because she was a sharp-witted child. Mrs. Osborne was pleased the way Ernestine had carried on her crusade to keep the dog. There was no baby nonsense about her.

And she liked her round face, full lips, and her large eyes flying around the room like a pair of birds. Wild birds, too.

But Mrs. Osborne had a different opinion about Charles or "Poke" as Jesse called him. He was tall as his dad, broad shouldered, and thin as a lamppost. With his deep-set solemn eyes, dusky complexion, full lips and sideburns, he was as handsome a boy of sixteen as Mrs. Osborne had ever seen. He acted the real gentleman. But if he was as much the son of the pa as he looked, he was sure to have a lot of devil in him. She wondered what cross old bitch she had overheard him talking about when she was making the coffee. It would pay her to keep on her guard.

"You've got a man-sized boy there, Mr. Jesse," she said warily.

"Yeh, and a grown son's an expensive article," he answered. Charles was already wearing his army shirt with stripes and insignia. While Jesse was in the army, Charles had grown into his civilian clothes in height if not in breadth. The dark blue suit and the light summer suit which he expected to step back into when he put his uniform in mothballs were frayed at cuffs and sleeves and bagged out at the knees. And Charles had worn out Jesse's shoes and thrown them away. It was the same with his shirts, ties, pyjamas, everything. "I'm just waiting on the day, Mrs. Osborne, when Poke'll be too overgrown to wear my clothes."

In the little corner room the boys had already set up their double-decker bed and fitted in their table and chest of drawers. In the main room Jesse had rigged up two wires, crossing in the center, from the tops of windows and door frames. He had shut of a quarter of the room with curtains to provide Ernestine with a semiprivate cubicle. The bed sofa, Lil's dressing table, and four straight-backed chairs filled what space was left.

"Looks like a second hand store," Mrs. Osborne sighed at what they had done to her rooms. "It's a change, anyway."

Jeep was lying asleep on the floor curled in a shaft of sunlight. Ernestine's ribbons were fluttering. The boy's voices filled the rooms that had been still since the death of Mr. Osborne.

To Jesse's surprise, Mrs. Osborne called them all in to have lunch with her in the kitchen. She served ham sandwiches, beer, coffee, and milk.

"What are you going to be when you grow up?" she challenged Junior right after the blessing, as if the best way to handle him was to keep him on his mettle. "Railroad engineer," he answered her back.

"You seen any colored railroad engineers? There never was any, boy!"

"You sound like Lil," Jesse complained as he grabbed Junior by the shoulder. "Never mind that there wasn't. It's what's gonna be that counts in the long run."

Mrs. Osborne looked at Jesse as if he was joking. As she turned her attention to Charles, her eyes fixed on his can of beer. "What *you* gonna be?" In her opinion he was too young to be drinking.

"Dunno yet," he said with a wink at his dad as if he'd agreed not to tangle with Mrs. Osborne. He set his empty beer can down on the table with a clink.

"You do know, Poke," said Lil. "Don't be bashful. He wants to be a printer," she explained to Mrs. Osborne. "That's why he's going to the tech. For my own part, I wanted the boys to go to college."

"To college?" Mrs. Osborne was impressed. "You got enough brains, boy?" she teased Junior.

"My wife went to college for a year, Mrs. Osborne." It was Jesse's turn to explain. "If you ain't heard all about it yet, don't worry, you will." Jesse spoke humorously, but Mrs. Osborne could see it was a touchy subject with Lil.

"You ought to be ashamed running down education," she scolded. She was just going to give him the kind of lecture she thought he deserved, when the kitchen door rattled open.

When Randy and Charlene and their little brother came crowding in, Mrs. Osborne started shouting, "You children can see I got company. Now shoo, shoo!"

But Charlene stood her ground. "My ma wants to know can we stay with you. She has to go down to police station to get my Auntie Mae out of jail. The polices took her away."

"Well ain't that a morning's work!" Mrs. Osborne closed the door behind the kids. "Ernestine, look like you need some company. Show the Roberts kids your dolls, honey, and keep 'em out of the kitchen, you don't want me to go through the roof."

When the kids went to play in Ernestine's little cubicle, Mrs. Osborne said with the satisfaction of a person who had known all along what would happen to Anna Mae Green if she started messing round with triple damage suits, "She can't win 'gainst the white folks. She might's well quit and get on with the nursin'. That was my advice to her, take it or leave it. But some folks don't take to advice. Would you believe it, she tried to get me to sign that triple damage paper? I'd get me a thousand dollars back after the lawyer took his cut. That's what she say. Oh no, not old Osborne," she blew out her breath, "I heard the like of that before. Why, if I'd messed in on that, I'd get me in the police wagon alongside of Anna Mae, that's where I'd get me."

But Mrs. Osborne was angrier at Mrs. Bianchi than she was at Anna Mae. "What'd I tell you, Mr. Jesse? You think ol' Pharoah in Egypt Lan's gonna have mercy on our race of people?"

"I know I seen Boatman down in the basement," said Jesse. His chin doubled up like a fist. "Wish I'd beat the daylights out of him," he muttered through tight lips. "Next time I'll do it. That Mrs. Green had a bad deal from Boatman and Mrs. Bianchi."

"You know everybody around here already?" Lil was surprised and anxious.

"Sure, their lights were out the day I was over seein' Mrs. Osborne. Blown a fuse."

"Jess, you won't get mixed in on this?" Lil's hand was on his shoulder to steady him down. "And who's this Boatman?"

"He's your old Uncle Tom," Jesse grumbled.

"*My* old Uncle Tom?" Then Lil realized what he meant. "Don't be bitter, hon."

Jesse stared back at her steadily as if there were some things she never would understand about him. "Ain't you gettin' yourself late for work, Lil?" After his bitter words, Jesse was soft spoken with his wife. "You said you had to be on the job by two o'clock."

#4

It was the middle of the afternoon before Geneva came upstairs to collect the children. The baby was asleep in her arms. Wherever she went, it was home to him. When he was hungry she fed him. And when he was full he went to sleep. But life was not so simple for Geneva.

"You got Auntie Mae out of jail?" Charlene called out. She had the headless doll in her arms and was laying her down to sleep on Ernestine's bed.

From where Jesse lay dozing on the sofa bed, he could hear Geneva talking to Mrs. Osborne. "It weren't no good, no good at all." There was no lift in Geneva's voice. She sounded dead beat. And Jesse wondered why Mrs. Osborne stayed so quiet.

"You know how much bail the Man wants? Five hundred dollars! It's too big for a mint of poor folks, leave alone only us," Geneva complained. "So she gonna hang us good this time, old Bianchi. Come on, Randy and Charlene, bring Little Brother. We bothered Mrs. Osborne long enough."

"When do she come before the judge?" Mrs. Osborne asked.

"Tomorrow morning."

"I told Anna Mae not to mess in with her. Bianchi's got the judges, the police, everybody on her side. Who's Anna Mae got?"

Geneva was quiet a moment. Then she whispered, "Come on, babies."

Mrs. Osborne wasn't expecting an answer. She fired another question at Geneva. "What they laying at her door?"

"Bad morals."

"You'd best get the lawyer, Geneva. Anna Mae's gonna get whipped anyway. But she'll get a worse whipping you don't."

"She ain't never done nothing bad."

"Where she get all the sass in her?" Mrs. Osborne asked.

"She was born that way," said Geneva. "Wouldn't take nobody's leavings. They called her crazy back home. Everybody stands up for herself they call crazy," said Geneva angrily. "Anna Mae won't get down on her knees to nobody. Won't lick nobody's boots."

"Where's it gonna get her?" Mrs. Osborne's tone was heavy with pessimism.

"You think she's scared about that? Back home she and her old man Jack kept all the white folks in our county out of our lane when we didn't want 'em in. Nobody gonna put the fear up Anna Mae." Suddenly, Geneva was laughing. "Mrs. Osborne, you gone crazy too?"

"Now you get the lawyer like I say. But don't go telling Bianchi old Osborne mixed in."

Mrs. Osborne must have given Geneva some money, a sizable amount, Jesse figured, if it was enough to pay a lawyer.

""Yes, I'll take the baby for this once," Mrs. Osborne went on, "but don't you never ask me again. Mr. Jesse, Mr. Jesse!" she called out. "Here's a woman needs a big favor. You think your brother-in-law's little old piece of car can carry Mrs. Roberts down to the lawyer's office?"

Jesse was already putting his shoes on when he answered, "OK, Mrs. Osborne." In spite of Lil's warning, he was getting involved in the struggle between Mae and Kathryn. And Mrs. Osborne of all people—and after all she had said—was the one to get him involved. As Jesse slipped on his jacket, he couldn't help remembering the way Lou's mother had treated him at the homecoming party. She couldn't bring herself to shake hands with him—even when he was leaving.

"Your sister's a woman of spirit," Jesse said to Geneva as he followed her out the side entrance. "And that Boatman's got the sin of Judas on him, selling his own folks down the river."

"Why he have to put the finger on her for that old white witch?" Geneva was almost crying with anger. "If Mr. Roberts was home, instead of working, I won't say what he wouldn't have done when they took Anna Mae. You seen her, Mr. Jesse. She ain't done nothing bad."

Geneva was proud of her sister. On the drive to the Southside, she told him how Anna Mae had stood up for them all on their tenant farm. And when her husband was shot dead, she'd come to Chicago and started work in a laundry. She'd saved enough in two months to pay Geneva's ticket north. Later, when Geneva got married and had the kids, Anna Mae helped raise them. "I don't know what I wouldn't do without sister."

"When she start to nursin'?" Jesse asked.

"About two years ago, she went to school and learnt it all," said Geneva proudly. "And she at her age. How old you think, Mr. Jesse, she'll be?"

When Jesse showed with his hands he was no judge of a woman's age, Geneva said, "Fifty," as if it was an achievement to live that long. "And she ain't had it easy like some folks, I can tell you that."

A lot more she told him before they reached the lawyer's address on South Park. It seemed to relieve her mind to talk about Anna Mae. But she was nervous when she got out of the car, stumbled and almost fell over a wire guarding the boulevard lawn. Jesse offered his arm and had to support her up to the front door and into the lawyer's waiting room. She sat with her eyes fixed on the floor for an hour until the lawyer stepped out of his private office. Only once in that time did she look up to say, "If you only knew my sister, Mr. Jesse, Anna Mae never messed around."

When Mr. Jefferson Wilkes came out to talk to her, he was already preparing to go home.

"Well, Mrs. Roberts," he said assuming that Geneva had come about the triple damage suit. "By the end of this week, Mrs. Bianchi will get her notice to appear in federal court." As he spoke, he was gesturing to his secretary to put some document into his briefcase. Except for her hair, she looked more like a white than a Negro to Jesse. "Too bad you haven't been able to get any of the other tenants to file suit with you. With three or four families we could build up a much stronger case in court." Mr. Wilkes was so sure he knew why Geneva had come that he was making excuses and explanations all in one to save himself time.

"It ain't what my business is about this time." Jesse was impressed with the simple blunt way Geneva spoke. As she went on to explain, Wilkes remained standing with his chin resting against his hand and his arm propped on the swinging barrier. He was very light complexioned in contrast to Geneva. Back and forth he moved, but he couldn't hurry Geneva. And then he began to listen intently to her story. It was an old, old story to him, but one that aroused his irritation. Before she was through, he was pacing the floor and snapping his fingers quietly and frowning, as if all the world's troubles rested on his shoulders.

"So they stacked the cards, Mrs. Roberts." His deep set eyes stared for a moment to learn from her face if she was holding back any information. Then he offered his advice. "We should call for a jury trial. But that would cost a lot of money, a lot of money. Particularly if they should win the case. And that's something we have to consider likely. I guess we'll have to leave it in the women's court. But that costs some money, too. I would like to offer my services free. But I wouldn't be in business long, now would I, Mrs. Roberts? So that wouldn't help."

"Here's twenty-five dollars, Mr. Wilkes, a friend lent me," said Geneva. "It was all I could get." Jesse knew now how much Mrs. Osborne was prepared to risk.

"I'm sorry, it's not enough. You see I'll be on the phone half the night talking to the police, checking the charge and so on. Then it's a whole morning in court—and there may be complications. My fee will have to be fifty at the least."

A whole morning! In Geneva's face a protest was rising, particularly when she saw how he held on to the twenty-five dollars. He seemed to expect her to produce twenty-five more without too much difficulty. "Can't you bide till Friday for the rest?"

Geneva's eyes went straight to his conscience. It took her husband four and a half days to earn fifty dollars. But he stood and smiled back with pained sympathy. "Sorry, I'd be in the poorhouse, Mrs. Roberts."

"In that triple damage suit, you was agreeable to waiting till things was settled before you got your cut."

Wilkes was annoyed to hear Geneva call his fee a cut. "That's different all the way around. In the first place, it's a sure thing—"

"This is a sure thing, too," Geneva insisted. "My husband gets his pay Fridays."

It was a deadlock. Geneva and Wilkes stared, both waiting for the other to make the next concession. But Jesse couldn't remain a bystander. He had fifty dollars of his severance pay left after the moving. His hand closed on the little roll of bills in his pocket. His palm was sweating as he thought what Lil would say when he told her. But there were some things a man had to do.

He pulled his fist and the bills out of his pocket in a clumsy gesture and began to count out five fives. "You can pay me back any time, Mrs. Roberts."

Geneva hesitated to take his money. Wilkes studied Jesse for a moment. His eyes said that he could easily understand a man's interest in a woman like Geneva.But there was no man-to-man understanding in Jesse's eyes as he looked down at the bills and handed them to Wilkes. "Take them," he said roughly.

The lawyer nodded pleasantly as if he would expect a man like Jesse to be crude. "By the way, Mrs. Roberts, what's the bail?"

"Five hundred dollars."

"That's high," he muttered, meaning that Anna Mae would have to spend the night in jail. "I'll get up to see Mrs. Green first thing in the morning before the case is called. Can you bring any of the tenants in the building to testify to her good character? As he looked thoughtfully at Jesse, he added, "Preferably women or old folks."

"I'll try," said Geneva dubiously.

"Keep your spirits up, Mrs. Roberts. What can be done we'll do. And on that triple damage suit, Mrs. Bianchi's going to have her turn in court. I was just reading the decision this morning in one of those cases where the tenants got back three and a half grand. Not bad, eh?"

Then he shook hands with Geneva. "See you tomorrow. We'll do what we can."

#5

Something had to be done about Anna Mae Green, the thought was nagging Jesse when he got up as usual at six in the morning before the rest of the family was stirring.

He stood at the window yawning himself awake. The sun was gold-plating the factory chimneys and burnishing the huge tank at the gas works with a brightness to make him rub his eyes. The air was still clean over the city. To the east the tall buildings along the lake front squared up to the morning sky. Jesse watched a gull wheel at a great height and circle back toward the lake. Its under wings were gold in the sun.

"The day's coming," he muttered, "when we all gonna live human." Anna Mae was sure going to take a beating unless some of the tenants went down to court and stood up for her like the lawyer said.

The previous evening, Mrs. Osborne had refused. Perhaps Geneva had jumped her too bluntly. But the loan of twenty-five dollars had raised a reasonable hope. When Mrs. Osborne said, "Ain't there other folks know Anna Mae?" Geneva answered, "The Martins, but they won't go 'less you go. It was hard for Geneva to control her disappointment and, rather than show the tears that boiled into her eyes, she turned and went back downstairs. Right after that Mrs. Osborne said she had a terrible headache and went to bed.

When Lil came home from work later in the evening, Jesse told her about the visit to Jefferson Wilkes, omitting only that he had advanced twenty-five dollars from his severance pay to help Geneva out of a tight spot. "Lil, we ought to do something for that Mrs. Green."

"People have a way of solving their own problems," she said crisply as if they had been all over this ground before. "We got plenty of our own." After she had finished eating her supper she sat down on the sofa to glance through a magazine while Jesse completed a wiring job he was doing to give her a good light to read by.

"I hate the guts of that Boatman putting the finger on her," Jesse complained.

"Jess, why you want to mix in?"

"We should help her," Jesse insisted.

"What you mean?" Lil's voice began to rise. "That sounds simple enough," she said as if she'd have to let him in on some of the facts of life. "But that means sticking our neck out to help her against Mrs. Bianchi. And how do you know this Mrs. Green isn't just one of these ignorant women off the plantations?" Lil put such contempt in her voice the fight sounded hopeless.

"I ain't studying Mrs. Bianchi no more," Jesse countered bluntly. "She's all the landladies we ever had in one package."

"But she's *his* mother," said Lil. "I thought he was going to get you that job you want and you were going to be buddies?" There was a skepticism about Lil's analysis that brought out a battling smile on Jesse's face.

"You want me to buddy up with *her*?" Jesse was smiling at the impossible. "He can't help who his mother was."

"Like mother like son," said Lil with the inflection of a preacher.

"I hang on to thinking that Mrs. Green's got what it takes," said Jesse refusing to be side tracked."She's from the South, and she's no ignorant woman."

"Tell me, Jess, you haven't got enough to stick up for with me and the kids?" From many angles Lil had surrounded him with the same reproach. She had not forgiven him for leaving his family to sign up. For the second time, too.

"You never will get it, Lil, why I have to jump in on a fight. I can't master it. It masters me, that's all."

"But you said you should never have messed in with Korea. It was a white man's war from the beginning Why did you have to go and sign up? I'm asking you again, where did it get you?"

"That ain't the fight I was talking about. It's a white man's world right here. And I been fighting all my life to get a better job. That's what I meant. You gotta be fair. When I signed up it was peacetime. You rather have me shovel coal or drive a truck? The war caught me off base, that's all. You remember, Lil, they promised they never would ship me out of the country when I enlisted, a married man with three kids. So next year they shipped me out to Japan! And then when trouble starts in Korea, I get shipped out there. That's promises for you, Lil, and that's the army."

"I know, I know." Lil spoke very quietly now. "But, Jess, you can't change everything in five minutes. The world was made a long time before you and me."

Jesse knew Lil was right. But she was also wrong. When he woke up next morning he had no intention of following her advice. A plan began to shape up as he turned away from the window to pull his clothes on.

When Lil reminded him after breakfast to take her brother's car back, he said, "That's what I'm fixing to do." But his eyes didn't promise her the way his words did.

"I want to do some shopping," Lil told him. "You can drop me off downtown." But when Jesse had dropped Lil off, he swung back north through the Loop.

Mrs. Osborne was just finishing her breakfast when he arrived home again. The kids had gone to school. "That car has wings, Mr. Jesse!" She was amazed to see him back so soon.

"My ma used to say—she was a preacher in her own way, Mrs. Osborne—you gotta do the thing you put off doing when your conscience got you round the neck. Now you said yourself that Anna Mae's gonna take a beating somebody don't go down to court and stand up for her."

Mrs. Osborne listened to him as if he was a stubborn fool she was going to have to tell to mind his own business. But Jesse wouldn't let her interrupt till he said, "And there's a woman needs a big favor."

"You think these old bones can stand up front of a judge?" she asked Jesse fiercely as if he was expecting her to give up her life. "Why don't you go talk to *her* boy? He's your buddy."

"I'll make you a bargain," said Jesse ignoring her taunt. "I'll drive you down in my brother-in-law's little old piece of car—"

"You mean you ain't took it back to him yet?" She couldn't resist the impulse to scold. "Ooh, when Miss Lil finds out you ain't done as she said—"

"And who's gonna tell her?" Jesse challenged Mrs. Osborne with a smile.

"You don't know what you're asking an old lady." Mrs.

Osborne was weakening.

"After all, you got twenty-five bucks tied up in that case already, same as me."

"You found out?"

"Them curtains have big ears."

"You borrowed her twenty-five dollars, too?"

"The lawyer's fee was fifty."

"Greedy hog," she snorted. "But I'll tell you one thing you don't know, Mr. Jesse. You ain't as big a fool as you think you are. I'm gonna tell you why. I borrowed Geneva forty dollars once before to keep Bianchi from throwing them all out on the street, and Anna Mae paid me back." She sighed deeply. "Tell me, you think she has a chance now, Jesse?"

It was the first time she'd left off the mister. "Why not?" he asked. "You must have thought she had a twenty-five dollar chance yourself yesterday."

That decided her. "Well, I'm three times twenty-one and old enough to know better. But I'll go along with you. If Miss Kathryn throws us all out on the street, we'll have good company. Now I'll get my Sunday dress on while you step down and tell the Martin's I'm gonna stand up for Mrs. Green." She was now putting the heat on him. "Mrs. Martin's half crippled up because she broke her hip three years ago and her old man's got the arthritis bad. His fingers are all knotted up like tree roots. We gonna travel like an old folks' home, Mr. Jesse, so best we get started." She was now taking full charge.

In five minutes she was downstairs, helping Mrs. Martin get her shawl tied over her head and a moment later holding the baby for Geneva in the front seat of the car.

But in the court, Mrs. Osborne's fighting spirit took a tailspin when she saw Mrs. Bianchi sitting up in the front row. She clutched Jesse's arm as if she wished herself any place in the world except in the women's court. He had to give most of his attention to Mrs. Martin who was a stout woman and had only regained limited use of her legs after her accident. She breathed heavily and dragged herself along on his arm and her husband's. "Oh Lord!" she exclaimed when she caught sight of Mrs. Bianchi. "Osborne, you gone and dragged me into something."

"Shame the way you talk," said Mr. Martin, "after the way

Anna Mae helped you these three years." He winked at Jesse as he scolded his wife.

"You was always sweet on the womenfolks," she answered him back when they were all seated. "If I didn't keep my eye on you, Mr. Martin, you'd be smilin' at that Miss Kathryn herself."

"Now you gone too far." The snap and twinkle disappeared from his eyes as he reproached her.

The worst moment was when Kathryn turned to look around. At first her face sweetened in a spontaneous smile for the two elderly women, but when she saw them sitting next to Geneva, her smile froze. She looked back again. She couldn't believe Jesse was in their company. A crazed look of hate and fear swept her face. He was close enough to hear her mutter, "Dirty double-crosser." Then she turned and faced the bench as if her head and shoulders had frozen solid.

While they all waited for Anna Mae Green to be called, half a dozen cases were brought before the judge. The first was handled in such whispers, Jesse could hardly hear a word though he gathered it was about some indecent sex act. The only case that held his attention was of a Negro woman accused of keeping a house of prostitution. The judge rocked back and forth in his chair like a mechanical man, needling the defendant with a superior little smile. He called her "mama" and handed down a verdict in two minutes. Jesse's fist tensed at the insult to his people. The judge had treated the white women with more respect.

"But judge, how can I pay five hundred dollars?" the woman screamed at him in a high voice.

The judge motioned to the police women to do their duty and went on rocking in his chair.

While the clerk was calling the next case, Anselmo came swaggering into court in a loose travelling coat as if he had just stepped out of an open sports car. He nodded and winked at Kathryn and walked straight up to the bench. Though he spoke quietly, still Jesse could hear him say, "How's your health today, judge?"

The judge turned to the clerk. "Call Anna Mae Green next."

Anselmo took off his coat and laid it with a flourish over the back of the seat beside Kathryn.

"Witnesses," the judge called. Then Anna Mae Green appeared in the company of a policewoman. Behind her followed Jefferson Wilkes whose eyes jumped from the coat to Anselmo waiting with Kathryn at the other side of the bench. Behind them stood three Negro men, one very heavy set, bullnecked, staring across at Anna Mae, the other two with their eyes on the floor.

Anna Mae was dressed surprisingly for court. As the cops had arrested her just as she was setting out to work, she was still wearing a navy blue cape lined with crimson, a white dress and white stockings and shoes.

In the daylight she seemed almost a different woman to Jesse from the Anna Mae who had scratched through a box of odds and ends to locate a fuse by candle light. Her complexion was covered with freckles. Her hands, grown large and rough from hoeing and pulling cotton, were clenched with a purpose. Her eyes, large and lemon brown, raced everywhere and examined everything in an instant. She attacked Kathryn with a wide offensive smile, but she turned to Mrs. Osborne and the Martins with an expression of surprise and affection. All in the first moment, she was making little signs to the baby in Geneva's arms and nodding at Jesse as if she was proud he was keeping them company.

Jesse was sure Geneva was right when she said her sister hadn't done anything bad. But her sister was not the kind to bow to anybody. She seemed a woman of great spirit and fearless.

Even when things went bad for Anna Mae, her hard breezy smile blew through her cheeks as if nothing anybody could do to her would take away the certainty that she was right and they were wrong.

After a few technical queries, the judge rocked back in his chair and let Anselmo take over. Question by question, Anselmo built up an elaborate case against Anna Mae. Through Kathryn's answers he showed the court that she was a woman of bad temper, drank heavily, and threatened people with guns.

It was more than Mae could bear to keep silent any longer. "About that gun, tell him it was the one you carry around in your own purse, Miss Biomchi. I only picked it up when you dropped it on the floor."

"Steady," Wilkes whispered, while the judge scowled and

told her she could speak when it was her turn.

It was time for Anselmo to clinch the case. "Mr. Boatman, have you ever been alone with Mrs. Green in the room which serves as her bedroom?"

"Yes." Boatman's eyes were bent away lest he meet Mae's stare of judgment.

"Any length of time?" Anselmo seemed to be prompting, rather than questioning him.

"Best part of the night," he answered.

Jesse wondered how much Kathryn had paid Boatman to dirty his soul. And while Boatman stared at the floor, Mae and Geneva were staring at him with loathing, withering him down to smaller than man's size.

Anselmo held his palms up as if the verdict was already rendered. But then with a shrug, meaning that justice would be done without any shadow of doubt, he repeated his questions to the other two witnesses and they gave similar answers.

"Dirty liars," Anna Mae whispered loud enough for everybody in the court room to hear.

"Do you have anything to say for yourself?" The judge turned to her bluntly.

"Your honor—" Jefferson Wilkes interposed.

The judge allowed him with a show of reluctance to question his witnesses. The judge's frown showed that he hadn't expected Anna Mae would have a lawyer and that he was impatient to hand down the verdict.

"Mrs. Roberts, have you ever seen the second and third witnesses?" Wilkes asked.

"Those men with Boatman?" Geneva shook her head with disgust.

"Yes or no," Wilkes insisted.

"No."

"You live next door to your sister?"

"Next door? Why there ain't nothing but a piece of cardboard wall between us. I can hear every sound goes on in her room and there ain't nothing the like of what they said. That Boatman's—"

Wilkes interrupted Geneva to get a character testimonial from Mr. and Mrs. Martin. "You see, judge, how crippled up I be," said Mrs. Martin after her husband had testified. "Yet I would drag these legs around the whole world to say that Anna Mae Green is an OK angel."

When it came her turn, Mrs. Osborne spoke to the judge with old fashioned dignity, straightening the lace at the neck of her dress. "Your honor, Anna Mae Green is the strictest morals woman I ever was blest to know. She don't spend a penny on herself. It all goes for the babies. And you can't tell me—" she was shaking her head at Kathryn's witnesses "—there's room in that coal hole for two grown folks at one and the same time."

Mrs. Osborne's testimony was a shock to Kathryn. Jesse remembered how she had called her a nice old colored woman. It was a bad shock, because once stirred to anger Old Mrs. Osborne spoke with a bluntness that made the judge sit at attention.

Then Wilkes took a necessary chance. He began to question Anna Mae about how long she had occupied the little room and how much rent she paid.

Anselmo banged the fleshy side of his fist on the bench and shouted, "Out of order, your honor!" His hand painted tie flashed red and angry beneath his red and angry face. "This is ridiculous!"

Wilkes persisted. Anna Mae told how Boatman had taken a sledge hammer to the toilet plumbing. In the middle of winter he had turned off their gas. Every day or two he pulled their fuse or cut their wires.

"I can't listen to this all day," said the judge banging his gavel down on the bench.

"One more question, your honor," Wilkes insisted. "Mrs. Green, are you bringing suit for triple damages against Mrs. Bianchi for overcharges prohibited by the Rent Control Act?"

"You said it. She charges more'n three times—"

"Judge, this is out of order," Anselmo shouted.

"I'm only trying to tell you, judge," said Anna Mae, "why she wants to get me out. And if you want the truth, why don't you ask old lady Biomchi why she carries a gun in her purse?"

"Out of order," shouted the judge himself this time.

Mae's lawyer tried to restrain her, but she went on at the top of her voice. "And I wanta ask her what all the men go in her alley for when Mr. Biomchi's gone to work."

Mae's words registered above the confusion of Anselmo yelling, "Out of order!" and the judge banging his gavel and bawling, "Do you want me to declare you in contempt of court?"

"Your honor—" Wilkes tried to interpose, but the judge banged his gavel down for silence.

"Now," he said angrily to Anna Mae, "do you want to go to jail or get out in twenty-four hours?"

The judge didn't dare sentence Anna Mae to jail, it was such a frame. But he was tearing her away from her family and putting her out into the street.

After conferring with Anna Mae for a moment, Wilkes said, "She will vacate."

Anger swelled the muscles in Jesse's fists as he watched the judge, swaying back and forth again like part of a perpetual motion machine, call the next case.

In the moment that followed, Kathryn glared triumphantly at Anna Mae Green. She had got rid of her at last. Then she stared with contempt at Mrs. Osborne as if she meant nothing to her any more. But as Kathryn glanced at Jesse, hatred and fear flushed the triumph from her cheeks and eyes and out of her heart.

She clutched Anselmo's sleeve and almost stumbled down the aisle as she left the court.

#6

It was a half hour drive from the women's court to Pioneer Street. The folks started home with Jesse in silence, Anna Mae and Geneva in the front seat and Mrs. Osborne and the Martins behind.

In the little daily acts on the street at the store on the job every second of every minute of all their lives they had experienced the kind of justice meted out to Anna Mae, the

Man's justice. And when she had spoken out against the landlady, thrown the stacked cards with contempt back into her face, Anna Mae had said only what they all thought—but she had spoken aloud in a public place.

"Mae, where you get all that spunk?" Mrs. Osborne's eyes filled with pride and her fear died away. The real victory was Anna Mae's.

"She ain't never gonna trample us into the ground," Anna Mae answered fiercely, gripping her sister by the arm. "Eh Genny? We gonna show Biomchi, wait see." The next minute she was laughing. "Spunk! Remember old man Wilson and his bullwhip?"

"Spunk," laughed Geneva. "You got more'n your share, sister."

"Old preacher Samuels, he had more'n any man's share," Anna Mae came back. "Preachin' how Jesus was a cropper himself in the Holy Lan'. Remember, Genny?"

"And when you saw that old white fool layin' it on to that man of God, sister, you grabbed hold on that hoe—"

"But the ants was the worst when we was lyin' down in that ditch with the guns." Anna Mae and Geneva roared with laughter as they pretended to scratch the ants out from under their arms. "Old man Wilson and that posse never did come up our lane. You talkin' about spunk, Osborne. That was the time when my Jack was still with us."

Geneva put her arm in Anna Mae's and they started down the walk together. Jesse could hear Anna Mae telling her sister that when they got all that money back in court on those triple damages, she was going to buy a piece of Mississippi land and go back home. "Ain't gonna be no white folks bossin' me what to do."

Mrs. Osborne watched the two sisters disappear into the side entrance. She could hear them laughing as they went down the basement steps together. "You so right," she said to Mrs. Martin as Jesse helped her step out of the car, "that Anna Mae is an OK angel." Quietly but fiercely she added, as she remembered the way Kathryn had stared at her after the verdict, "Old lady Bianchi ain't gonna fool around with us no more. We don't throw her, she's gonna throw us. I about decided to sign up on that triple damages."

Mrs. Martin was looking sideways at her husband as she said, "We're all the way with you." It was a big step for a retired government worker, but after a moment's testing over the idea the old man inclined his head in agreement.

"A man can't croak but once, 'less he been dead all his life." Mr. Martin's bald head with its white rim of hair was tipping the scales against Kathryn Bianchi.

"To my way of thinking, we're gonna win," said Mrs. Osborne as Jesse helped deliver Mrs. Martin back to her armchair.

"Yay," sighed Mrs. Martin, "with your soldier-boy—"

"Miss Kathryn ain't gonna never hear the last of this day's work," Mrs. Osborne interrupted. "Now, young Jesse," she went on as if Mrs. Martin had reminded her to tell him, "you'd best get that little old piece of car back to the wife's brother, or—" She didn't finish the threat as she was reserving the rest of her breath for the stairs ahead.

"OK, Mrs. Osborne. If Lil's home already, tell her I've been and gone." As Jesse climbed back into the driver's seat, he repeated to himself with a laugh, "Soldier boy! They think I'm a young punk." But underneath was a feeling of satisfaction that old Osborne was right when she said Kathryn would never hear the last of this day's work.

But the brother-in-law would have to wait a little longer for his car. Before Jesse saw Lil again and explained about the lawyer's fee, he wanted to be able to tell her he'd landed him a job. His hand went to the tiny roll of bills left in his pocket, no larger than a pencil twisting between his fingers. One thing he was determined about, no matter how hard up he might be, he would never take back the twenty-five dollars from Geneva or Anna Mae.

At the government employment service, Jesse had to wait a long time for the veteran's counsellor to get back from lunch. There was no use thinking about the Farmway job any more. When Lou got to hear that Jesse had stood up on Anna Mae's side in court against his mother, it would cause him a lot of grief. He had given Jesse a hearty welcome at the homecoming, but now he would probably be less friendly. Chances were memories of Korea would gradually fade out. His family and friends would put the heat on, his fiancee, and in the long run Lou himself, would have to side with his mother—or give up the idea altogether of working for Anselmo. So what was the use, Jesse figured, of going over to Farmway and wasting his time filling out all that paper?

When the veteran's counsellor finally returned from lunch, he came swaggering in, like Anselmo in the court room, as if he owned the place and everybody around him was so much furniture. He took all the time in the world with the two white vets waiting ahead of Jesse, convincing them that his own outfit in World War II was better than any outfit in the Korean War. His outfit wouldn't have beat it down in the first place from the Yalu River. They would have chased the enemy across the river and followed them into their own territory.

When the time came at long last, he glanced at Jesse's discharge papers. "So you're thirty eight years old." The way he said it was enough to bury Jesse's hope of a job. "What are you looking for?"

"Machinist work," said Jesse.

"Experienced?"

"Thirty-eight years," Jesse snapped back. Nobody was going to bury his confidence that he could do the kind of work he wanted. "I learned dishwashing, coalhandling. I handled all kinds of stock in all kinds of plants. I operated a crane. I drove a truck in Redball, and there ain't a part of a car or truck I couldn't repair in my sleep."

The counsellor laughed at that. Jesse was forcing him to lower the color bar and treat him human, but it was a battle. Even the counsellor's laugh was tolerant rather than hearty the way he'd laughed with the two white vets. "OK, sergeant," he said breezily, "my advice to you off the cuff is to borrow $10,000 on a G.I. loan, set yourself up in your own garage or anywhere as an auto mechanic. Work in your sleep if you want. That way you'll make a lot of dough."

Jesse rubbed his brow and shook his head. He wasn't going to be put off with his own joke. "Can't I get it into your head, man, I wanta be a machinist, not a mechanic?"

The counsellor was getting tired of the discussion. "That's a skilled trade," he said tonelessly. "You'd have to go to trade school for four years to begin with." He was rocking back and forth in his chair like the judge at the police court. They all liked handing down decisions, these officials, Jesse thought bitterly. Don't wanta find out, just wanta judge.

"Listen!" Jesse demanded the counsellor's attention. "I been to school for thirty-eight years. The best practical school in the whole world—hard work. I don't need no more schooling. What I need's a job to make use of what I learned already."

"Mechanic or machinist, does it make all that difference?" The counsellor was sorting the papers on his desk preparing to close out the interview.

"It does to me," Jesse retorted. "Is it your job to help me get located, or to try to get me down?"

The counsellor stared at Jesse as if he was a stubborn, unreasonable guy. Then he shrugged a little and began writing on his card.

"How come," Jesse asked, "in a free country you can do anything except what you want?"

The counsellor handed him his card and referred him downstairs to the public office. "Next," he said curtly as if he had no time for gripes.

Downstairs, Jesse explained briefly the kind of job he wanted, this time to a Negro consultant. "I might as well tell you," he started out on the offensive, "I don't wanta work in a foundry, moving around packages at the post office, or—"

"No, I get it. You want machine work. First try at Ford's. It's a long way out from where you live, but maybe your neighbor works there too."

"They take on everybody?" Jesse asked.

"Sure. Defense contract. They are compelled to by law. If for any reason it don't work out for you there—" the consultant wrote out four referral cards for him "—try these other places. Some are partial to Korean vets. Come back if you don't get what you want. And good luck all the way, Mr. Williams."

It took Jesse an hour to drive out to the far southwest. But when he got to Ford's, they told him at the employment office to come back in a couple of months. There were some changes in government specifications that required retooling. Jesse didn't even bother to fill out an application form.

He followed three more referral cards across the length and

breadth of the city, ending up on the Northside not far from Anderson's Coalyard. At the fourth plant, the employment manager told him, "Quite frankly, I like your record. But we haven't anything for you in the machinist line. You wouldn't consider stock handling or janitor service?"

Was he so frank, Jesse wondered as he stepped back into the street. If so, why did they put in a request for machinists at the employment office?

For the hell of it, he decided to stop in at the coalyard and see if any of the old work gang were still around.

When Jesse reached home late that evening after finally returning the brother-in-law's car, Lil was already back from the beauty salon. "I got me a job," he announced.

"Well, that's good news," said Lil happily.

"Yeh, at Anderson's coalyard," Jesse went on tonelessly. "Lucky thing that old foreman passed while I was out in Korea. So they didn't remember how I beat that guy with my shovel."

"Lucky!" Lil muttered as if she hated to believe Jesse was going back to the old job. "What happened to this job your friend was going to get you?" she asked suspiciously.

"I'll tell you about it when I've had my supper," he said wearily. "Yeh, it's great to be back home again."

#7

Jesse was dead beat after his first day back at the coalyard. It was lucky the boy came up to meet him in the old jalopy. "How you like it back at work, pa?"

"Same difference, Poke." Jesse shrugged as if nothing had changed from before the Korean War. "It's a job."

Ernestine met them in front of the house with news she could hardly wait to deliver. "He's waitin' on you, pa. He's been here a long time."

Jesse raised his hand to pinch her cheek, but she drew back from him. His face was powdered with coal dust streaked with sweat. "Who you talkin' about, honey?"

"The white soldier."

"What he want?" Jesse asked himself out loud, not expecting an answer from the girl. His joints felt old joints as he climbed the stairs, his legs were heavy and tired deep into the bone. He had to force a smile to greet Lou.

It was the first time Jesse had seen him in civilian clothes. He looked a different guy in his light pants and large patterned shirt, his hair slicked down. He didn't hold out his hand as he said, "I had to see you, Jesse." He stared grimly at Jesse's old pair of overalls, black from the day's work.

"You got your discharge, OK?" Jesse nodded to the sofa. "Rest yourself—" He wanted to say "buddy" but the word petered out behind his teeth. "Poke!" he called out, "Get Mr. Bianchi a can of beer. I'll be with you in a minute, Lou."

"Jesse, for Crisake, don't start sharpin' up for me. You gone back to work?"

"Yeh, Anderson's Coalyard."

"Tough lines." Lou took the can of beer from Charles and held it between his fists.

"Ran out of dough," said Jesse simply, "moving and everything."

"You didn't try Farmway?"

Jesse shook his head. It was too complicated to explain.

"Maybe later, eh?"

"I can always change my job."

Lou's fingers played nervously on his beer can. "You been a straight guy to me, Jesse," he finally said. "One of the best. We been buddies out there. Back home, hell, you seem closer to me than my own folks."

"Same here. I know what you mean."

They let it rest at that while they drank their beer. Lou offered Jesse a cigarette. Jesse's eyes came very close to his, asking him what the score was, as he held out his lighter. "You know what you're doing," Lou went on jerkily. "You always figured the shots. But Jesse, the ma says you stood up in court against her—" Lou's eyes were full of accusation and for the first time Jesse caught a glint of hostility. "She's all broken up about it. I can't figure it myself." Then Lou probed as if there must be some mistake. "After she got you the place to live—" He glanced around the room crowded with furniture. "I know it ain't much," he muttered.

After a long hesitation, Jesse said, "Since we got on to these things, best we say 'em out and be done with 'em. But first I want to know why you think your ma was in the right?"

"That Mrs. Green is a pretty rough customer," Lou answered. "I seen it myself when my ma offered to lower her rent. She practically kicked my ma in the teeth. And she's caused a lot more trouble besides. I know my ma ain't an angel. Still, this Mrs. Green kicked up such a big row Sunday night all the neighbors started to complain. She don't seem too particular about the men she shacks up with—"

"What your ma don't like," Jesse interrupted, "Anna Mae Green's the kind stands up for herself. She won't take a whippin' from nobody. Her and the old man was growin' cotton in the South. They wouldn't bow down on their knees back then and she won't now. She wants to weigh out her share no more nor no less than what's hers by rights."

"I understand all that—" Lou began.

But Jesse cut in on him again, "Most times I don't mess in with other folks' business. But when I see the cops drag off a woman to the Bridewell, then face her up in court with two men she never seen before—"

"You believe it was a frame-up?" Lou was dazed as if Jesse had clubbed him over the head.

"Too bad you wasn't in court. You could have seen for yourself." Jesse's eyes, too, were raising a barrier of hostility for the first time. "Those two witnesses were slinging green money around at the tavern last night. Most times they ain't got two nickels for a glass of beer."

"Jesus Christ, it ain't like my ma." Lou banged his beer can down on the floor and stood up. "She couldn't do it, Jesse, she couldn't do it."

"I ain't saying as your ma was the one," said Jesse coolly. "That Anselmo handled things in court like he was calling the shots. Still and all, Lou, if you gonna work for him—" Jesse held out his hands as if there was nothing more he could say.

"Anselmo?" Lou's expression changed. The anger paled out of his face. He stood looking down at Jesse thoughtfully. "I wish to God I wasn't away getting my discharge when all this happened."

"Maybe the brother-in-law planned it that way. Seems like he's a shrewd operator." Jesse studied Lou's face. It was hard to tell if Lou believed him. He wanted to find out one way or another and had come straight over to see Jesse. He obviously hadn't been able to believe his mother's story a hundred per cent. All the same, he couldn't believe anything bad about her, either. She was the best ma a guy could want, he had told Jesse a dozen times out in Korea when he was opening up packages from home and sharing them with the other fellows in the outfit.

"The ma couldn't have known about it," Lou almost shouted, "if there was anything like a frame-up." But he couldn't help remembering how Boatman had come out of the alley Sunday night with two men and his mother had acted strange when he asked her about them. In uncertainty and to himself, he muttered, "I'll have to see Anselmo." He held Jesse's hand in his for a long time, but his eyes were lowered as he said, "And I thought our troubles were all gonna be over—back home!"

"It's a long row to hoe—" Jesse gripped Lou's hand as if to encourage him to face up to Anselmo "—but we already come quite a piece together."

#8

Supposing Jesse was lying to him? Lou was eaten up with doubts the next morning and soggy from a poor night's sleep as he walked the last block down La Salle Street. Massively, the Board of Trade Building shouldered out the sky at dizzy angles. He walked unsteadily like a man who'd lost his bearings.

In the elevator, two slick dressed men were negotiating a ten million dollar deal. Their day was just beginning. Lou grabbed the rail to steady himself. It was like riding a rocket out of this world.

But why would Jesse lie to him? He was a straight guy. If he said the woman was framed he believed it. He could be influenced by the fact she was one of his own people. And maybe he was prejudiced by the attitude of Lou's mother. She hadn"t given Jesse any kind of welcome at the homecoming and God only knew what she'd said to him the night she'd met him for the first time when Lou and Nina were up at the Anselmos. Lou found himself inventing suspicions and at the same time wondering what good it would be to see Anselmo—unless he asked him point blank: Did you frame the woman?

Lou had to wait a long time till Anselmo came breezing in with his briefcase clamped under his arm. He was wearing an expensive looking blue suit and a hand painted tie. Already his face was red from morning drinking.

"Brother!" exclaimed Anselmo cordially after a flicker of surprise.

"You told me to drop up—" Lou began.

"Sure, come in." Anselmo led the way into his inner office. "You got your broken-winged duck?" he asked without too much interest as he glanced through his mail.

Lou's eyes travelled across the autumn blonde carpet, the natural wood finish desk with the glass top, the leather lounge chairs, the chartreuse walls, the porous soundproofed ceiling, the enormous spread tiger's pelt that covered half a wall, and finally settled on Anselmo. Here's the big shot the ma and Nina want me to be, Lou was thinking, sitting on top of the world with his hands on all its strings. The man who played God Almighty to his people in Hemlock Street. The man with all the money.

Anselmo's smile suddenly flashed on Lou. "You look like you need a pick-me-up. What'll it be?" His finger hit a button and presto! the side of his desk was transformed into a bar. "Bourbon?" All the time he was observing Lou like an eagle from the stratosphere.

"I got some questions," said Lou. He toyed with the glass of bourbon on the arm of his chair, while Anselmo tossed off his glass and waited.

"Look, Gene, I ain't a guy for beatin' around the bush—"

"Me neither," Anselmo cut in, "and I have some questions, too. Some very serious questions." For a moment he and Lou stared at each other like wrestlers in the ring each waiting for his opponent to make the first move.

"Why did you have this woman arrested while I was gone?" Lou's question bristled with a hundred other questions.

Abruptly Anselmo's manner changed from tense to amiable as if Lou had asked the most natural question in the world. "She kicked up a big fuss Sunday night. The tenants complained. So your ma called the police Monday morning." His smile was intended to overwhelm Lou. "Didn't she explain it?"

"She explained it all right," Lou retorted. "But she didn't explain why Boatman and two colored fellows came out of our alley Sunday night. I seen them myself. And I didn't ask her to explain why these same guys were slinging around the dough at the tavern after they'd been to court—"

"Oh, I see. You're asking *me* that?"

"That's about the size of it."

Anselmo's manner crisped. "Wouldn't it be better if you went home and asked your mother?"

"I know who's calling the shots."

"I see," said Anselmo. From looking at Lou he got up and walked over to the window, began to clasp and unclasp his hands behind his back as he looked out over the city. "You're making a big mistake, Lou. You got to take the world the way it is—or break your head on the stars. Look, it's a big world, too. A wonderful world if it don't throw you. Come over here, Lou, I want to—"

"I heard it all before, Anselmo," said Lou keeping his seat, "about picking up our lucky dice and coming to America. Everything's a racket!"

Anselmo turned away from Lou to gaze down into the canyon. "You don't know what a big mistake you're making, fellow. You'd better stop and count ten."

"If you mean—"

Anselmo swung to face Lou with the smile of a prosecuting attorney wheedling a difficult witness. "You want a Cadillac to go places? A home that's more than a cold water flat? You want to marry Nina who's an expensive article?" He gave Lou a chance to change his mind, but Lou faced him with a steady examining eye.

The guy was stubborn. Still, it was worth a battle to Anselmo to win Lou over. The stubborn ones went furthest once they got to know the score. That blunt nose, those thoughtful eyes, the set of Lou's mouth were worth dollars and cents to the real estate business. Lou was a man's man, but the women would go for that deep set, melancholy expression and the spread of his shoulders. And Lou's battle record alone was worth a million to drape Anselmo's latest deals with the flag of patriotism.

"You got to make choices." Anselmo drew up a chair and dropped his leg informally over the arm to talk to Lou in a relaxed way. He poured them both another tall one. "It's like this, if you go back to work in the factory—" Anselmo's hands showed what a dope Lou would be. "Sure, the rent business is a racket. I told you that before, but can you show me an easier one?"

"Did my ma know you framed her?" Lou asked abruptly.

"What words you use!" Anselmo tried to laugh him off. "You'd better go home and ask her." He went back to his desk and began to thumb over his correspondence.

"I'm gonna give her the benefit of the doubt," said Lou pushing himself to his feet. "When I went overseas, she was the best ma a guy could ever want."

"OK, Lou," said Anselmo with a pleasant smile. "You're a straight guy, don't let anybody tell you different. Go back and work in the factory if you want to. You got the brains for it."

"A guy has to live with himself, too."

"He has to do the best for himself."

"Does that mean framing people?"

"People, Lou?" Anselmo stood up and began to pace the carpet again. His shoes sank into the deep pile, but the moment he passed there was no trace left of his footsteps.

"I said *people*," Lou insisted.

"OK, call your buddies people if you want to. But it's a law of life to look after your own first. That's the way the world was made. Now, take this Green woman. First of all she's dangerous like a rattlesnake. She keeps a gun. In the second place she's a threat to all your ma wants. Before she started this triple damage suit, we didn't have any trouble in that building. Now, if the other tenants should join her, your ma would go bankrupt. The court would take over everything, even the house you live in. So we had to get rid of her." Anselmo filled his glass again and stared at the amber liquor waiting for Lou to get out. "She didn't leave us any choice."

PART FOUR

#1

The plunge from Anselmo's world was final. Lou's fingers tensed into fists as the elevator sank under him. The loss of solid footing was like the first leap into the blue in parachute training at Fort Bragg. He felt the same bottomless stomach and wondered where in hell he would land. What his mother would say, he knew already. He must get to Nina.

As he rushed up La Salle Street, he turned to look back over his shoulder. The Board of Trade Building rose like an immense cliff of stone and glass. Near the top was the window from which Anselmo had surveyed his world. And higher still stood the statue of Ceres whose stone face without eyes or features dominated the city. Clouds hung like an ermine coat over her shoulders and only a few shafts of light penetrated to the floor of the canyon.

The sky up top was full of blue lakes and the light blinded. It was like that day, lifetimes ago out by the Fox River, when he first told Nina he loved her. Light was pouring the same way through open spaces in the clouds. Particles of dust climbed up and down as on a ladder. Like the voice of a million people a hum of traffic from the whole city filtered into the canyon and Lou could hear water pouring over a dam. All through the fields fellows and their girls were playing ball, laughing, or arm in arm strolling down the paths. Down by the dam they played at fishing. The roar of water made them shout and scream to be heard. From a mile down the river, Lou and Nina could still hear their voices.

The elevator up to Nina's office moved like a slow freight. When the door finally half-opened on her floor, Lou burst through to the information desk. "Nina—" Over the receptionist's head the immense office was a blur of machines, women operators, superintendents manning desks, private doors of important lawyers and executives. "Miss Pagliani," he corrected himself in a whisper as he read a name in gold on a brown panelled door: Mitchell Bardett, Chairman of the Board.

"She's busy right now." The receptionist was too busy herself at the switchboard to give him a second glance. The wait lengthened out. Easy chairs and lounge were not for Lou as he walked and fumed. Then he stared out the window at a great loop of Lake Michigan merging with the sky. Far out, sails marked the limit of a world. Lou remembered the way Anselmo looked in his yachting outfit with the blue cap and the gold braid. All that dog. It was the first day in Lou's life he'd thought of Anselmo with contempt. There was still the emptiness of anger in his stomach, but he was glad he'd taken the leap.

Nina came finally down the aisle with a coolness because he was disturbing the routine of her day. He wanted to leap the barrier and claim her. But he knew a hundred heads would raise and fix eyes on them. So he only stood and waited till she came to the bar. Her little gold crucifix swayed in the fold of her blouse and his pin was there.

"How about you take the afternoon off?" He whispered with embarrassment because she was not ready yet to break routine, even smile back at him.

"What did you find out from Anselmo?" Her voice was quiet like his, but businesslike.

"Jesse wasn't lying."

"Oh God!" Her face lengthened as though Lou had just told her somebody she loved was dead. "So what does it mean?" In the clean vast air-conditioned office, she reserved herself from him and made him feel like an alien.

"That's what we got to talk about." His grimness matched hers. Then he laughed in a way that had no joy in it. "The Anselmo deal's off. Can you punch out?"

Nina shook her head as if she didn't even want to. "We're loaded down today."

"But Nina, we gotta iron this thing out."

"You want me to lose my job?" What she didn't say but thought about Lou's announcement came out then in her sudden anger. "Did you tell your mother?"

He only shook his head.

"She'll be all broken up about it—"

"Nina, we can't talk about these things here."

"Pick me up at five, then." She handed him her car keys. Her voice was rough and he knew she was trying to keep from crying. What a pair of eyes she had, beautiful but full of pain. "Don't take it so hard, kid." He tried to put his arm around her shoulder, but she broke away from contact with him and started down the long aisle to her desk. He waited, but she didn't turn back. She seemed part again of a vast impersonal machine with which he had no business.

In the streets Lou stared at expensive furs behind steel grated windows. How nice Nina would look in black sable! For a long time he stood in front of a jeweler's window comparing prices on rings. If he went back to work at Farmway, where was the money coming from?

When he called his mother, he came to the point with an abruptness that made his voice sound dry and hard. "I wantcha to know, ma, the Anselmo deal's off. We can't get together on certain things—"

"I know, Anselmo phoned me already." His mother's tone was even grimmer than Nina's. "He thinks you gone nuts in the head." She dropped the receiver. He could picture her leaning forward at her desk, her shoulders rounded, bursting into tears of rage.

With all afternoon to kill, Lou was alone in a street filled with people coming and going. They all knew where, but he had no place to go. And yet they seemed to move in a vacuum. The same he'd known before he went overseas. The same faces in the street. He was the one who had changed. The Anselmo deal seemed something dreamed up by Nina and his mother. Reality lay back on the Yalu Road and in San Antonio. The men he knew were together at the hospital, Jesse and Tennessee Al and the rest of his buddies. He wished he was back playing pool in a wheel chair with Jesse.

Lou had told Anselmo he had to live with himself. Nina would have to understand that, too. The night he came back she'd said the job didn't make that much difference. It was him, Lou, she loved. The touch of his arm, his smile did things to her. It was the same way with him. The sight of his pin on her blouse, the feel of her shoulder under his hand. She was a girl with a sharpness and beauty, a spirit all her own. Memories of her had kept him alive. And she had matured when they were separated. She was disappointed now, but she would get over it.

All afternoon he waited for her. When he sat back in a half-empty theater, he was dreaming about her, holding her, teasing her, playing with her, loving her. Faces and bodies on the screen only caught his attention from time to time. When the feature film repeated, he still didn't know what it was all about, or care.

Lou wished time had stopped the afternoon he first made love to Nina. A mile away from the shouts and games of the other picnickers, they had found a spot in the woods near the river. Last year's grasses lay thick and dried. Nina pulled away from him then and tried to run. But she tripped and he caught her and they fell together on the ground. The river purred in their ears. The sun throbbed in their faces. The beat of passion was a delight created by the sun. He took her, reached for her deeply, till there was no reservation between them. Union drenched his body with satisfaction and melted down her independence from him. "I love you," she said, "only you." And his hands cupping her cheeks felt tears. Passion roused in him again to search her to the very heart of love. "I can't ever let you go, Nina," he whispered. His voice seemed to come from far away. "Understand? Never!" And he knew she was with him.

"I can't ever let you go, Nina!" The words repeated like an echo through the afternoon. In the candlelight that evening at Agostino's he held Nina's hand and told her how much he loved her, how he'd always loved her and always would.

"I know, Lou," she answered, returning the pressure of his hand. "It's the same with me." All afternoon she must have been thinking about him the way he was about her, job or no job.

"Remember the picnic, Nina, after your senior prom, the way it was, you and me?" He drew her closer. He could feel her breast against him. "Maybe you're thinking like me, next month's a long time to wait. How about we get married now, Nina?"

"On what?" she sighed. Her cheek withdrew from his. Her eyes had that melancholy slant of the late afternoon when the sun no longer throbbed on their faces, when he roused to find she was no longer in his arms, but sitting apart from him thinking her own thoughts and staring at the river. The water was smooth and reflective of the sky. Clouds moved below and above them with hugeness and fantasy. But the air had a chill in it and the closeness of her mouth and body was only a warmth to be remembered.

The orchestra began to beat out a tango. A couple rose from a nearby table and caught up the rhythm. Lou held Nina's hands in a grip to raise her to her feet, circled to meet her, and swung her out on the floor before she had time to refuse him. He put her through the routine but her heart and feet weren't in it. Her cheek didn't take fire from his. "How about next week?" he urged.

She withdrew from him as the orchestra played down and out behind the final crash of the drum. "I told you not to rush me, Lou." She withdrew further till the table came between them. "I don't know what else to say—"

The waiter filled their glasses and set their dessert. Spumoni was green and crimson and full of candlelight and coffee steamed in spirals. "I just can't get away from it—" Her eyes were searching his as if to find the cause of all that troubled her. "It's like you wanta throw your whole life away—and mine with it. Gene made you an offer—"

"You want to marry a frame-up artist?" He might as well say it all out and be done with it. Then he would know where he was with her. "You want me to call the bailiff on Tony and kick him out? You want I carry a rod around, collect rents way above what the law says, so you and me can barbecue steaks on our roof garden?"

"I just don't figure what you're going to do—" Nina spoke in a monotone as if she hadn't listened to what he was saying. "It was all so wonderful that night at Della's—with the steaks. I could see you and me, Lou—not so grand of course—but different from Hemlock Street. You could go to law school. You wouldn't have to work for Anselmo. Set up on your own. I can go on working. We'll make out—"

Lou put his hand roughly over her cheek and hair and tried to draw her close to him. "I don't know about the law school business. But sure, everything's gonna work out the way you and me want it."

"You don't seem to have any ambition, Lou." For a while she was very quiet and then as if thinking out loud went on to say, "I don't know, I just don't know. It's all so mixed up with this Jesse business."

"So that's what's been eating you all along!" Lou snapped as if Nina was being completely unreasonable.

"I know you'll think I'm prejudiced, but it isn't true. Honest to God, Lou. It's just the way you forced him on everybody, at the homecoming—"

"Think what you're saying!"

"I know what I'm saying."

"Father Antonelli, Daniel De Rocco, even Nellie—"

"But your ma, Della, Anselmo—"

"To hell with Anselmo. He's the only one you and the ma ever think about. You can't say what you want or do what you think's right without Anselmo breathing down your necks. You're afraid of him—like he's God Almighty. Well, you wanta know something? The guy's afraid himself, the big shot, scared like a lousy little rabbit. That night he offered me the job, we got to talkin' about his old man. The thought of old Anselmo gettin' bumped off made Gene's hand shake and he lost his grip on his glass. Maybe you heard it bust on the sidewalk." Lou brought his eyes close to her, appealing and accusing at the same time. "Look at it my way, Nina. I come home from hell and gone. I find my girl and my ma are making a god out of this guy. And he's turning the bunch of you into crooks and ninnies. That's what I know now since I talked to him this morning. I can see it plain as looking at you. You fell for it. Barbecue steaks! That's what you wanta make out of life? Well, make it. Marry Vico if you want. Ride around in a Cadillac deluxe!"

"Why do you talk to me like that, Lou?" Nina pulled away from him. "You sound like you just went up to Gene's office on purpose this morning to pick a fight with him."

"You changed a hell of a lot, you know?" Lou countered. "Beats me. You always wanted to live your own life, sure, the way you pleased. But you didn't seem to worry so much about the trimmings before I went overseas. It was you and me that counted most then, not Anselmo and Della. When I loved you in those days, remember how we used to talk about having kids of our own? We wanted a girl like you—and, sure, a boy like me. That's what I dreamed about out there when the going got rough. Life would go on—we would be somebody that way—not making a big splash in the papers, but loving each other like nobody's business—raising our kids and keeping them out of trouble and helping them grow up straight. We could say, that's you, that's me. Wasn't that what we wanted?"

"I understand all that," said Nina wearily. "I want the best for you and me now, and I did then. But you've changed. Oh I know this guy saved your life, Lou, and you feel you have to pay him back. But when we get married, the first guy you'll be inviting home—"

"When we get married, Nina," Lou interrupted, "Jesse and his family are gonna be welcome in our house. Not because he saved my life and I want to pay him off or any of that crap, but because he's an OK guy. He's my buddy, see?"

"You mean I'm not going to have anything to say about *our* house? You're going to treat me the way you treat your ma?"

Nina and Lou sat staring at each other across the table, a gap widening into a rift and broadening out between them.

The orchestra swung into a fast waltz. They had quarreled before and made up. Lou felt like taking her in his arms and dancing the feet off her. Then maybe she'd come down to earth. "How about we dance?" he said gruffly.

"Dance? Not the way I feel. Let's go home." She began to gather her purse and handkerchief. He reached out his hand to keep her in her chair. "Nina, I can't help but get the feeling you're holding out on me for some reason. Give, for Chrisake!"

"And I get the feeling Lou, you're different from the guy I used to love—" Her bitterness came through more and more as she went on, "Maybe we both changed. Maybe I do want different things from you—"

"Such as Vico?"

"I don't know why you bring him up—" She drew her compact out of her purse and toyed with her lipstick pencil. Her eyes didn't meet his. "I thought we got that settled once and for all!" Nina stood up wearily. "Shall we go now?"

There was no longer a choice in it for Lou. He followed her out of Agostino's with inches of space between them. He didn't try to take her arm and she didn't feel for his. They stared at the furs and dresses in the great show windows on State Street. A couple of mannequin children were playing in the floodlights on a green carpet at Marshall Field's.

Lou wanted Nina to see things his way. There would be no home to bring children into if she didn't. He wished with all the power of his brain that she would come round, but he was too proud to lay hand on her as they crossed the Loop to the parking area under Michigan Avenue. And Nina was sunk so deep in her own thoughts she seemed to walk alone.

They drove most of the way home in silence until she finally asked, "So this means you've decided to go back to your old job at Farmway?"

"What's wrong with that?"

"Where do I fit in?" Her laugh was like a cry. "Washing blue jeans in the basement, shouting at you the way your ma shouts at your pa—" Her voice went up hysterically as Lou parked her car in front of her father's tavern.

"A guy works with his hands ain't good enough for you," he said quietly.

"I don't want to marry a bum either," she said blowing out her anger at him.

"If that's the way you feel—" Lou spoke with a forced calm "—you better marry Vico." Then his voice went up beyond control. "See if I care when he ditches you for the first whore on Clark Street!"

"My God, Lou, how can you talk to me like that? You must be crazy!" She stared at him as if she thought he was, then grabbed the keys of her car. "Why do you talk to me like that?" she repeated in a desperate whisper.

He should reach out and grab her and force her to take him for what he was. But if he let her twist him around now, he would never know where he was with her. Suddenly she turned away from him and rushed into the alley. He followed her to the side door.

Aunt Maria was already calling from upstairs, "That you, Nina?" Her voice sounded like a death rattle.

"Don't you love me any more?" Lou put his hand around her shoulder to keep her from running upstairs.

"I don't know, Lou, I just don't know." She broke way from him. "Why don't you go your way?" she called down from the top of the stairs. "And let me go mine." Then she slammed her bedroom door.

As Lou turned and went back into the street, he argued with himself, "She'll come around." But the sight of Vico's car parked in front of Angelinos made his heart pound like a ball of steel in his chest. It was Vico who tried to persuade him to turn down the Anselmo deal. "You're not the type. You think you're Jesus Christ or somebody." He understood Nina, that boy! She wouldn't want to link up with a guy who only worked in a factory. Nina was the only one who had ever made a dent with Vico. He'd offered her a ring. Vico! Vico! Vico! If he'd stepped out of the Angelino house at that moment, Lou would have wrecked both fists on him. That handsome, smiling face! Lou turned to stare up at the light in Nina's window. He could imagine Vico sprawled out on her bed, waiting to take her in his arms. Lou saw Nina drawing the curtains. "Nina!" he called up, "Nina!" The last crack of light between her curtains blacked out.

Then Lou turned away and went home. For a long time he sat on the front porch staring into darkness. The moon was behind clouds. The wind played around in the trees. The leaves were crisp and rustled. It was an autumn wind with a chill in it.

#2

A different kind of sound than the wind began to register on Lou's blunted senses—a crackling. On the railings by the park a strange light was wavering and growing stronger. A smell of smoke bought Lou to his feet. In an instant he was across the street breaking the glass of the fire alarm with butt end of his lighter.

The fire was at 758, the flames already pouring out the basement windows. And in front of the house a man was standing unsteadily watching the fire and raising both fists and shouting, "That teaches her. Burn 'em up!" It was Tony Ferrucini. When he saw Lou, he turned like a spirit of wrath to pour curses on him. "You gonna be big shot like Anselmo?" He pointed to the house. "Oh no, Oh, no, Oh no! Your ma kick us out, Ok. Cops, OK, OK. Now, see!"

Tony gloated as he heard the fire engines clanging around the corner. "Burn 'em up," he shouted, "burn 'em up!"

Only when his mother was standing beside him in her slippers and nightrobe, her hair untidy about her head, did Lou realize the street had filled with people. "Holy Mother of God!" she was shrieking. "Ain't they gonna put it out? Luigi, Luigi!" In terror she watched the firemen break windows and doors with their picks to get at the fire with their hoses.

The hissing of the water and the sudden mushroom of steam enveloping the tenement relieved Kathryn's terror. "Thank God we got insurance." She leaned heavily on Lou's arm. "That stubborn old fool!"

Two policemen were prodding Tony into their wagon while he went on yelling, "Burn 'em up, burn 'em up!" and waving his fist at Pete and Kathryn. They could still hear Tony above the siren as the police car went around the corner.

"Take me home, Luigi!" Kathryn's strength seemed to melt away. When she went in, Lou waited for his pa on the front porch.

Across the park, the houses rose up in a wall of darkness. At the top of the city, the buildings of the Loop stood against the sky like far away mountains. Their battery of red warning lights winked on, winked off. Topmost was Anselmo's building with its finger of authority raised to the highest red light over the city. "Yeh, we were all raised in the same street," Lou muttered. He could hear the siren of the police wagon die out over by the station.

His father stumbled up the walk and Lou caught him in time from falling on the steps. Pete's eyes were large and shining and bitter. "My countryman," he muttered. "Now it's all over. Goddam to hell."

Inside, Kathryn was searching the pigeon holes of her desk and ransacking the drawers. Finally she laid her hands on the precious insurance papers. "So let him go to jail," she said with a bitter triumph. "That's what he asked for."

As she turned to Lou and Pete, her scorn collapsed like a balloon. The events of the day flooded back, all the anguish. "Oh Luigi! The Holy God must be punishing us today for all our sins." She sounded hysterical.

"Ma," he said in an even tone, "you didn't tell me Sunday night why Boatman and the other two men were here. It would have saved a lot of trouble." Lou tried to ease her down in a chair.

Faced up with her own lie, Kathryn began to shout, "Goddam it, leave me be."

"I only want to tell you, ma, if you know it or not—and I hope you don't—that Anna Mae Green was framed in court. I asked Anselmo about it and he good as admitted it. Then he told me to go back and work in the factory. I know she's a rough character and caused you a whole pack of worries. I seen how you tried to help her and the kind of thanks you got. All the same, ma, that don't excuse framing her."

"You told Anselmo that?" Without waiting for an answer she went on hysterically, "Oh God, Luigi, I didn't know I had a fool for a son. Can't you tell him you didn't mean it?" She held her hands beside her face in a gesture of despair. "And Nina—"

"I told her already," said Lou quietly. "You two seem to think it's the end of the world."

Then Kathryn understood that the Anselmo deal was finished. In hysterical rage she began to scream out all the things she'd ever done for Lou. When he tried to calm her, she shouted all the louder, "You listened to him, all his lies, your Jesse! You wouldn't believe your own mother! Lies! Lies!" Finally she broke down, cowered to the sofa, held her arms over her face, and sobbed with great body heaves, "It was the happiest day of my life when my son came home. It was gonna be easy street for my Luigi. No more break his back every day—"

"Ma!" Lou was kneeling on the floor beside her. She looked at him glassily. She seemed to be trying to remember who he was. Then she grabbed him by both arms and sank her nails into his flesh.

"You wanta be boss," she shrieked. "Kick your ma around like dirt in the street. Goddam it, tell me who to have in my house. It ain't my house no more. Holy Mother of God, so listen to an old fool of a mother!"

Kathryn stood up, raised her fists and shook them at the ceiling. Her face was corpse pale. Her eyes glittered with hatred at her son. Hate and fear and ambition in the months Lou was away at the war and now a terrible disappointment had turned her blood to acid and eaten out her flesh from within.

"I won't have him in the house, your Jese," she shouted. "He double-crossed me. He's a dirty black bastard!"

She turned and ran into her bedroom. In her fury she slammed the door so hard the whole house trembled.

It seemed to Lou like his mother had gone out of her mind. "Should we call the doctor?"

Pete shook his head because her trouble was something no doctor could cure. "She hates colored."

Lou was deeply shaken. "Did you see her, how she looked at me?" He rubbed his arm where his mother's nails had opened up the flesh in three long scratches.

"It's terrible," said Pete. "What can we do?"

"Get her away from Anselmo. She never used to be like this. She was the best ma a fellow could want."

In the chapel tower at the end of the park, Lou could hear three little bells chime out. Then the big bell clanged twelve times for midnight and the beginning of a new day.

#3

In the morning it was so quiet in the house when Lou stood on the backstairs landing for a moment he could hear the Valone clock measuring out the seconds with monotonous beat as if nothing had changed since he was a kid. His pa was eating breakfast at the table the way it used to be, while his ma was packing the lunch box. It was hard for Lou to remember he had ever been out to Korea or spent six months on his back in San Antonio. He could even believe that the terrible conflict the night before was only a nightmare.

As he came down to the kitchen, however, his ma stared at his toolbox without looking up at him. Her face was sodden with grief and fatigue, her eyes black pits behind her glasses. He wondered if she had slept at all.

The sight of his toolbox was more than Kathryn could stand. As she watched him set it down by the kitchen door, she put her hand to her head. "I don't feel so good," she complained. "Go back to bed when I finished the dishes."

It was the first time in his life Lou had heard his ma say she was going back to bed. It was a sin, she'd always said, to lie in bed after six o'clock in the morning.

Lou rested his hand on her shoulder. "Sure, ma, put your feet up." He kissed her on the back of the neck. She made no sign of recognition. "You knocked yourself out running everything for everybody—" he went on with a nervous cheer pitching his voice high.

But his heartiness was empty, and his ma knew it. As she looked up at him for the first time, he couldn't help resenting the reproach in her eyes. He might as well say what he thought and be done with it. "Why don't you give up this rent business, ma? Take it easy. Pa's gonna get his security and I'll make enough dough to keep us going. Besides, I get my disability—"

"Never," she muttered.

"Think it over for Jesus Christ's sake!"

"Never, understand?" Her voice rose and her fist hit the table. "Never, never, never!" she screamed as if he was trying to take her life away. "Holy Mother, you had to punish me with a fool for a son!" She stared straight over his head as if she was praying in the church. Her voice was bitter and vinegar thin.

Pete made a motion toward the door and Lou followed him out.

"I dunno, pop, she's—" Lou began.

But Pete cut him off. "You come back to work—what the hell?" As they took the shortcut to work up the railroad tracks, he encouraged Lou with his slant-eyed smile to forget about his ma. "Everything's gonna be OK."

From habit, Lou crouched in on himself when the whistle up at Anderson's Coalyard earsplitted upward like a raid siren, then came down in a bellow. The cranes began to swing across the tracks. The steam shovel began to blow and scoop. From the hopper a waterfall of coal came pounding down into an empty truck, filled up and mounded over. A black chunk or two rattled down at the end. Then the truck moved forward, silting particles across the coalyard. The face behind the wheel was white. The driver's assistant was a Negro. The day's work had begun.

As Lou watched the giant cranes circling and shifting and blocking the sky up ahead, he looked around for Jesse. In the yard he saw two Negro workers cleaning out a bin with shovels. Even at a distance he could see the sweat gleaming on their faces. "Well, pa, what's chances of getting him on, you think?"

"Jesse?" Pete laughed as if anything was possible again and began to whistle his favorite tune.

When Pete turned the fuses in the transmission box, the lights began to flicker on all over the machine shop. At the click of a button, machines here, there, everywhere across the floor began to turn.

In the locker room the men had given Lou a new welcome, now he was one of them again. But the bell cut short the talk and ordered them to take their places in the shop. They were now bending over their machines, absorbed in the job of the day. Blueprints were clipped at their eye level. Cutting tools, entering steel and cast iron and brass, threw a spray of chips and filled the air with metal dust.

The rattle grew enormous with the heavy and light artillery of production: the boom-boom of punch presses, the scream of the air hose and the machine gun chatter of the pneumatic drills. It was like Korea all over again for Lou. A flare from the welder's booth hit the ceiling with violent light and smoke oozed out through holes in the curtain.

Clarence came rushing down the aisle to hand Lou a blueprint and say over his shoulder as he was already hopping past the next machine, "How does it feel to be back on the job?"

"OK," muttered Lou to himself as he studied the blueprint. There was an old familiarity about his machine and the feel of his tools. It was going to be a tough grind again. But it would have been a tougher grind, Lou figured, to have to knuckle under to Anselmo in that eagle's nest of his up at the top of the canyon. There were no chartreuse and autumn blonde trimmings around the machine shop or tiger's pelt spread on the walls, only grey and black. But once Lou had punched the time clock, he didn't have to worry about saying the wrong thing to Anselmo or what his ma wanted—or Nina. Or did he? At the thought of Nina, her face took shape between his eyes and the blueprint till lines and dimensions were blurred behind a head of red hair and brown eyes burning at him like flares. He had to shake the blueprint to snap his attention back to the job.

He was still sharpening his tool bits and setting up his turret when Mike stepped over from the grinding machine. "Well Lou, you old faker, still got them lucky dice Phil gave you?"

"Sure," said Lou. "I hope you're loaded today because I got a lucky streak on." He'd noticed Mike was five minutes late as usual, so went on to needle him, "I see you still keep banker's hours."

"I ain't changed none," Mike boasted, "how about yourself?" There was a challenge in Mike's tone like the opening shot in a battle Lou was expecting.

But Lou was looking at Mike's old green cap set low over his left ear. "You ain't changed none for sure. Still wear the same goddam old grease cup." Then Lou remembered Mike's boy was in the navy. "Say, how's the kid?"

"Missing," said Mike.

"That's a tough break."

"Some guys have all the luck." It wasn't hard for Lou to figure what Mike was driving at when he added, "Weren't no colored guys around to help pick up the pieces."

"That was tough," said Lou in a tone to match Mike's sarcasm.

For a moment, they stared at each other to take measurements for the days ahead. Then Mike winked at Lou and went back to his machine.

Phil came over the next minute, tossing his hair back and settling his hand on Lou's shoulder. "You ain't going through with that business?" His eye was blue and chalky, not hostile like Mike's, but wondering.

"Sure," said Lou. "They tell me we have defense orders. Old Thompson has to hire everybody. It's the law."

"You amaze me, Lou!" Phil looked at him as if he was a man from a new planet. "Honest to God!"

"I amaze myself sometimes, too," muttered Lou as he bent over his work again. "But I don't let it go to my head."

#4

At the coffee break, the machines in the basement were all quiet at the same time. Already, as Lou pulled the strap to open the elevator door, he could hear Mike shouting, "I don't care whose buddy, we don't want no niggers in this outfit. We got enough dynos around here already."

"Ain't you the broad-minded son-of-a-bitch," Scotty shouted back. "Being as it was your buddy, you'd be hollering bloody murder."

The fellows were huddled around Mike and Scotty at the bench where Baldy, a midget of a man crippled up with a twisted shoulder, brewed coffee and chickory and sold stale buns at a nickel apiece. "Why don't you shut up?" Baldy screamed at Mike and Scotty both when he caught sight of Lou stepping out of the elevator. They turned and the argument dropped dead. There was a silence like eleven o'clock on Armistice Day.

In the middle of the aisle, Baldy's cats were tearing raw liver into bloody pieces. The kittens were playing at it, but the ma meant business. She growled like a tiger when Lou's boot came close to one of her babies.

"Baldy!" Mike boomed with a great humorless laugh. "Ain't you gonna pour your buddy a cup of that cat's piss?"

Jack and a couple of the other old timers working in the basement stepped up to shake hands with Lou. Then Jack rinsed out a cup at the sink for him and Baldy filled it, overflowing the cup in his nervousness to please.

"We was just talking about Moano," said Jack. "You remember him, don't you, Lou? Used to work down here in the pump department." Moano was usually good for a laugh in a tight situation. He was the old timer, dead now, who couldn't stand the sight of food.

"His blood ran one hundred proof, remember, Lou?" Scotty picked up the ancient history. "Mind, a snort first thing in the morning, two shots for lunch and a fifth for supper and a night cap. 'Sandwiches?' Remember how he used to say it? 'That'll be the death of you boys yet.'"

Moano wasn't going across as usual with the fellows, even with Scotty's big push.

"Sure, I remember him," said Lou pulling out a box from under the bench and sitting down to drink his coffee.

"So it was tough out there, Lou?" Jack asked after a general silence. He was already bouncing his right knee up and down because he could hardly wait to get back to work.

Lou glanced up at Jack moodily. The old guy was whiter in the face, more bloodless than Lou remembered. Jack coughed and coughed again. One of these years, the cast iron dust in the basement was going to finish him off.

"Korea? It was like this goddam basement." Lou had to blow his top with all the tension built up. "By God, you ain't even got a blower yet to pump the shit out." Lou was glad to find something to hit out at—knowing the fellows would be with him. "You forget when you're around here every day. But, honest to God, it's a hell hole. Baldy, you got one of them stale buns?" Lou plunked a nickel down on the bench.

"Attaboy, Lou, give it to 'em hot and smoking!" said Scotty. "It's like old times again, eh Jack?"

"We ought to make Thompson move the pump department upstairs, for Chrisake," Lou went on.

"You and who?" Mike asked sarcastically when he saw Lou grabbing the limelight.

"We talked about that a million times," said Jack wearily. "But Art would never do anything about it."

"We got Jerry now for steward, ain't we?" Lou countered. "And I'm gonna be around again."

"You was on the committee with Art," said Mike with a big laugh. "Nothing happened—zero!"

Jack didn't like arguments. He went back across the basement to a set-up job on one of the big grinders. He looked small and white and ghostly beside the huge machine.

"Jack don't look so good," Lou muttered.

"You ask me, he ain't long for this world." Scotty's voice sounded like a funeral. "No sir, he don't look at all good. That piecework kills a man, eh Lou?"

The coffee break was over at the long clatter of the bell. The fellows were already drifting away in different directions. Baldy was rolling a refuse can toward the boiler room.

"Take it easy, Lou," said Mike. It was a warning, the way he said it. The fellows turned around to stare at Mike and Lou as if all along they had been expecting something to blow out into the open.

"OK, guy," Lou bluffed along.

"Well, I'm gonna come right out with what all the guys are thinking. We like the way things are around this dump. It's a white man's outfit and that's the way we intend to keep it. No hard feelings, Lou." Mike smiled as if the fellows were a hundred per cent with him. "You're a great guy, kid, don't let anybody tell you different."

"You dumb son-of-a-bitch," Lou muttered. Out there a guy like Jesse was up front. Back home, why should he take a back seat? "Goddam it, Mike," Lou exploded, "your boy's out there. A guy's stood up to all that punishment got the right to choose up on jobs. Let him work where he wants. I'll stick out on that. Same with my friend, Jesse Williams."

Lou felt the quiet pressure of Phil's hand on his shoulder. "Give him the works, boy." From Phil this was suddenly something different again from his four-thirty whistle. The best Lou had hoped was to make him sit on the fence, but now the guy was coming over to his side.

"What the hell, Mike," Lou went on with a rising challenge, "you think we can tell the world, boys, here we come, hotstuff for freedom. And all the time, narrow-minded sons-of-bitches like you are holding up the stop light back home? Step down, for Chrisake. You ain't God Almighty. Or have things changed around here since I been away?"

"God Almighty!" Scotty directed his pipe stem at Mike. "That's 'im, all right."

Walter who was standing over by the shaper yelled across, "Wise up, Lou," when he saw that Mike was getting the worst of it. "They'll steal the shirt off your back. I worked with 'em. The day Thompson hires a shine around here, I'm getting my ass the hell out of this joint."

"That's what I been telling you," yelled Mike to drown out Lou and Scotty. He had lost his smile of confidence that the fellows were a hundred per cent with him and bullheaded anger flushed his cheeks. "Goddam it, Lou, why don't you get a job where they hire jigs? Ask Dougherty. He'll fix you up fine and dandy, you and your buddy both." Mike dashed the dregs of his coffee to the floor. "That is, if you don't want a lynching around here."

After laying down his ultimatum on the line, Mike tramped back to the elevator and pulled the doors together with such a bang that the whole basement roared with the repercussion.

"His ma didn't bring him up right, that boy," said Scotty. "He ain't got no manners." The rest of the men went back to work.

The pounding of the shaper and the zizz of the boring machines dinned in Lou's ears like the sounds of a major battle. The air was full of casting dust and the smell of cats. Lou sat on his box muttering, "I'll fix that son-of-a-bitch." But he still didn't know how he was going to do it.

The door on the inner side of the basement leading from the stock room suddenly filled. A chunky man with short legs came along the aisle with an easy walk. He put his feet down with care and took his time. He padded along as if his feet were bare, responsive to every crack or scrap of metal in his way.

"Hi-ya, fellow?" Jerry's face was sunburned and crowded with freckles. "You look blue. What's a matter?"

"Well, you don't look blue, fellow," Lou answered him. "What you do, take the kids fishing over the weekend?"

Jerry nodded and poured himself a first cup. The coffee was getting low, so he put in some more water and set the pot back on the gas ring. "Baldy still makes the same old coffee, one bean to the gallon," Jerry started to beef. Before he could settle down on a box beside Lou, the bell rang two long and three short. "Same old elevator," said Jerry as if that explained everything that was wrong with the world. "I'm gonna damn well quit if Thompson don't shell out for a new one."

"You missed the fireworks," said Lou.

Jerry nodded as if he could guess. "What do you expect?" He was needling Lou with a funny kind of smile. "You want to change everything in five minutes?"

"Ignorant bastards," Lou muttered.

"Sure," said Jerry. He poured himself and Lou a cup of thin coffee. The call bell rang again. "That Clarence," said Jerry absent mindedly with a gesture of brushing a fly off his nose. "All the same, Lou, the guys think you're OK. You put up a fight on contract and conditions when Art and Dougherty were selling us down the river. They don't forget that easy."

"What happened to Art?"

"The prick got himself a gravy job somewhere. Then the fellows elected me, I dunno why. We never did fill your position. Say the word if you want it back. We're having a meeting on the new contract tonight over at Bill's Tavern."

"If the fellows and gals want me—" Lou hesistated.

"We'll reinstate you. That's settled."

"But look here, Jerry, I wanta get my buddy a job like I explained it to you last week. How about coming up to see Thompson with me? It's no use talking to Clarence again."

Jerry shook the coffee pot. It was empty at last. "We'll put the bite on Jack," he muttered as if he had no intention of answering Lou's question.

Jack looked small and white faced beside the dark bulk of the grinder he was setting up. As he bent forward with a wrench, his head and shoulders were swallowed up by the machine.

"Hey, Jack!" At the sound of Jerry's voice, Jack turned his head sideways to listen. "Lou wants to get his buddy on here," Jerry went on in his easy bluff way, putting his foot up on the base of the grinder and leaning his head and shoulders forward to speak a few inches from Jack's ear. "Machine work. He's a colored fellow, you know that."

"I guess Lou knows what he's doing," said Jack trying to head off the talk. He gestured impatiently with his wrench to let Jerry know he was holding up production.

"Will you take him on?" Jerry persisted. "Show him the works, if Thompson hires him?"

Jack withdrew head and shoulders from the jaws of the machine to face up to Jerry and Lou. His cheeks were flushed a little from bending over. He looked almost healthy for a change. "OK, Jerry, if Thompson hires him I'll have to," he said with a dubious glance at Lou. "It ain't my funeral."

"That's all I wanted to hear," said Jerry patting Jack on the back. "Ain't gonna be nobody's funeral—'less we don't get your pump department upstairs."

"Walt will quit," said Jack pessimistically.

"OK, give his job to the new man," said Jerry not allowing him an inch to wriggle out. "Be a damn good thing if Mike walked out with Walt. But he's got too much mule in him."

"What if the fellows hit the street?" Jack was hard up to find a way out.

"That's easy," Jerry laughed, "then we'll have to shoo 'em back in."

#5

In the shipping room at lunch time, the papers were hardly off the sandwiches before the men were down on the floor, their mouths stuffed with food and their hands reaching for their money. Lou tossed his lucky dice into the ring with a challenge, "Mike, I'm gonna take the shirt off your back."

Mike picked up the dice and bounced them suspiciously on the flat of his hand.

"Bite 'em," said Lou.

A smile came out on the faces in the circle. "Could've loaded 'em since," Mike growled.

"Sure," said Lou, "for bear."

The guys grinned while Mike concentrated on twirling the dice between his palms. "Fade you," somebody muttered as the dice hit the floor.

It was Thursday and the men who had run out of dough for the week sat on the packing cases at the back shooting the bull and watching the contest between Mike and Lou.

Lou's luck was out. He lost steadily, dollar by dollar, until the pile of bills in front of Mike was high enough to begin to wobble. Twenty-five bucks, Lou figured. It was Mike's turn to throw. He laid down a fin. Lou matched him with his last five. He had to win.

Mike made a great business of cupping the dice, breathing his orders to them, and with a circular motion of his hands sweeping them down to dance on the floor. As the dice steadied at one and two, he grunted, "Hell!" and flipped Lou the fin. Another five went down. Mike tried to magnetize the dice with the friction of his hands. He threw a five and a three.

The side bets went down. The third throw was a seven. Lou reached for Mike's five. "Not so fast," Mike grumbled but handed it over. Reluctantly, he tossed the dice in Lou's direction. Mike was still cocky about winning, but Lou was beginning to make it hard for him. The fellows on the packing cases had interrupted their bull session to concentrate all their attention on the dice.

Lou threw a double six and the money passed back to Mike who began to crow, "All or nothing." He challenged Lou to shoot for a ten. Lou put down all his money and won.

"Goddam, what'd I tell you," Mike began to shout, "them are loaded dice!"

The fellows were laughing at him. His face reddened up as he pulled out all the money in his pocket. When he saw Lou put down a five, he laughed contemptuously. "Chicken, eh?" He counted out thirty dollars. "All or nothing, how about it?"

Lou had to borrow a five from his pa. The men had come over from the packing cases to ring the contestants with a triple row of faces. The circle narrowed. Lou couldn't afford to lose now. Everybody knew the stakes were more than the money on the floor.

"OK, Mike, if that's the way you want it." Lou rattled the dice in one fist and threw a long roll. The first showed a five while the other went on spinning like a top.

"Come eleven," Lou muttered in the silence. It wobbled down by his foot and steadied. It was a six.

"Must have kicked the bastard." Mike stood up in a rage glaring at Lou and stamping his feet on the bills he'd lost. "I told you them dice were loaded."

"Now, how about your shirt, Mike?" Lou asked him with a cool grin. But the twelve-thirty bell rang out the end of the lunch period.

"We'll even up the score," Mike boomed as he shouldered his way out of the shipping room. All afternoon, he was caucussing up and down the shop, avoiding so much as a glance in Lou's direction. It seemed like he was afraid he'd lost more than a game of dice.

After work, the drinks were free at Bill's Tavern. The busines agent of the union set them up. Charles Dougherty was a large, comfortably built man in his late fifties. His face bulged over his jaw bone and settled on his collar. His grey fedora with its narrow band contrasted with the caps and shock heads of the workers. Under his grey hat his grey eyes flicking here, there, and everywhere at once caught every expression on their faces as they came into the tavern.

"A little warm-up, ladies" When Dougherty caught sight of

Lynn, he said in a sweet voice, "Say, step up. A shot? A coke? A beer? What do you say?"

"He can throw our money around, that Dougherty," grumbled Pete. "But he can't get us a raise." Lou was following his dad through the swing door into the billiard room when the business agent pivoted on his stool.

"Well if it ain't Lou! Long time no see, fellow." He crossed the room with a beaming smile and his hand went flabby in Lou's for an instant. "Step up, boy. For old times." The heartiness was all on the surface. Dougherty was studying Lou with an eye that had no warmth in it. "Well you old block buster, what's it going to be?"

It was a poor moment, as far as Lou was concerned, for Lynn to start griping. He was thinking of the time he'd been on the negotiating committee with Art and stuck out against Dougherty in front of Thompson for what the fellows wanted. But Lynn insisted on registering her complaint about Lou's buddy in front of the business agent, Lou had to answer her, "What's the problem? If we can die together, OK for Chrisake, we can work together." Lou glanced at Dougherty but his face was a blank. "Blood's the same color, out there anyway."

Then Lucille joined in. "My old man don't like it." There was a frightened kind of complaint in her voice like a little kid's, surprising from a woman her size and age. "We never had colored working here."

"But Lucille, you're not narrow-minded yourself?" Frances asked wearily as if the argument had been going on all day.

"No-o-o—" Lucille answered slowly.

"Well then, your old man don't work at Farmway." Frances turned quickly to Dougherty as if that settled it.

The business agent sat sipping his glass of beer with a deadpan expression as if these little difference of opinion were outside his jurisdiction. He began to ask Lou questions about Korea and the war out there. "Looks like we may have to settle," he said grimly pointing at the headlines in the evening paper. Then he folded his paper and slapped it on the bar. "Drink up, ladies. Time we got this meeting over with." He gave Lynn a special wink and put his arm around her shoulder.

"The women didn't even get the nickel last fall," Frances

complained to Lou as he held the swing door back for her. Then he crossed the room to sit by his father. His legs gave way under him as he reached back to steady himself against a chair. The first day on his feet had taken it out of him. The calves of his legs ached and his whole body felt stiff and numb. The throb in his spine reminded him of the first days at San Antonio.

"Dougherty ain't got thinner since last meeting," John leaned around Pete's shoulders to tell Lou. "No sir, he ain't got the least bit thinner." John had worked at Farmway longer than any of the other workers, had a habit of repeating everything he said because he himself was a little deaf. "Wouldn't hurt Dougherty to take a hand loading a boxcar, eh Pete? Then he'd be skinny and hollering for a raise like the rest of us."

They watched Dougherty take up his position behind the billiard table with Jerry. His complexion was red and bright above the green table. He didn't bother sitting down because, as usual, he intended doing all the talking.

"We got this contract," said Jerry by way of opening the meeting. "But first I wanta say we're glad to have one of our brothers back—with his lucky dice." There was a general smile on the faces of the fifty men at the meeting, though it didn't register with the women. "Lou was comitteeman around here and we never filled up his job. Must have known he'd be back with us again. A lot of us are delinquent around here, so I guess Brother Dougherty will be glad Lou's back to handle the little books again. Come on up, Lou."

"Objection!" Mike was on his feet.

"Any other objections?" Jerry asked.

Nobody got up to support Mike except Walt. "Sit down, why don't you?" John shouted. And a mutter went round the room, "Sit down, sit down."

Dougherty was playing with his fingers nervously on the green beige as Lou took his place beside Jerry. "Now we got that settled," he said, impatiently taking over the meeting from Jerry, "Brothers and sisters—"

More than half the Farmway workers had come across to the meeting. They sat shoulder to shoulder, leaning forward in their chairs, determined to make the most out of their bargaining power. But in Dougherty's voice was a curious kind of drone as if someone was letting the air slowly out of a balloon. "I'm going to lay the cards down on the table first," he said spreading his hands out flat. He began to explain in one syllable words why it was impossible to get a raise this year. The nickel they got the previous September brought them up to the wage stabilization ceiling. "Remember," he emphasized, "there's a war on."

There was a deadpan expression on the faces looking up at him. There was no leaning forward now. The workers slumped back in their seats.

"As contracts go, it ain't a bad contract," Dougherty's tone was cheerful now. They'd all have to make the best of a complicated situation. "I'd advise you to sign it." He paused, not wishing to pressure the workers too much, at the same time hoping for a motion to accept the contract. "You get paid holidays after thirty days," he added earnestly, "and ten percent night differential."

"How many of the guys work nights?' Pete's aside to John was heard all over the room.

'We've all been around more than thirty days, Dougherty," John raised his voice indignantly, "and nobody's worked nights since the second World War. You ain't got us nothing."

"You're getting it as good as the next guy," Dougherty countered. "No worse than most of our shops. As long as we got this wage freeze, we got to buckle down. That's about the size of it. It ain't the fault of the union." If he only went on talking long enough they'd all quiet down and want to get the meeting over with so they could go home. Dougherty knew they were all tired and hungry. "You can take my word for it," he went on slowly, it ain't anybody's fault personally, you know that. But there's still a war going on in Korea. They call it police action, of course, but we all know it's a sizable war. Lou Bianchi here can tell you all about that."

"Don't sign it," said Phil standing up to challenge Dougherty. "We can do better than that with one hand tied behind our back."

"Damn right I'll sign it, just to get it over with," said Mike rising up from his side of the room. "The union's nothing but a joke. You want a raise you go see Thompson. Everybody knows that. If you wear down a deep enough path to his door, maybe you stand a chance of getting one, too."

"That's right," said Walt who was sitting next to Mike. "Who's kiddin' who?"

"What's got you fellows eat up?" asked Dougherty as if he was stepping in among them to stop a fight. "A lot of you fellows are making good money on the lathes and the drill presses."

"He ain't said nothing about women," Lucille complained with her finger pointing at Dougherty.

The business agent smiled. "Everybody at once! Let's get the pie down from the sky!"

"We didn't get the nickel you were talking about, either," said Frances ignoring his joke. "We want more than a free glass of beer at the bar this time."

"Well, this contract don't exactly favor the women," Dougherty admitted. He looked straight down at the billiard table for a moment.

"Or the older workers," grumbled John.

"That's right," said Pete. "We ain't favored. A nickel in two years ain't even peanuts."

"Is there a guy who makes coffee all day?" countered Dougherty. "Well, Mr. Thompson don't aim to raise him." Baldy slouched down in his chair humiliated and effacing himself. "In fact, I may as well tell some of you older fellows that it's only the union—" Dougherty tactfully said the rest with an empty gesture of his hands. "There's another thing you fellows leave out of the picture—" He had completely forgotten the women by this time "—the layoffs in Detroit and also right here in Chicago. If you boys didn't have a union and a contract—"

"Nuts," said Walt.

"Remember," Dougherty warned, "Thompson may have to close down the plant if priorities don't ease off. I was telling him this afternoon how to get some government contracts, some new ones. That's where the union can help out. Then you fellows wouldn't need to worry about a layoff. Now it's up to you. Are you ready for the vote?"

"It's all what Thompson says," Pete grunted to John. "Why don't Dougherty ever come around and ask us what we think?"

"It's up to you, everybody," said Jerry. "Are you ready for the vote?" He motioned to Lou to help him pass around the ballots.

When the vote was counted, it was a landslide against the contract.

While Jerry read out the results with a favorable smile, Dougherty mopped his face. Then he picked up his fedora from the billard table and placed it back in exactly the same spot. His face doubly red from mopping and embarrassment as he said, "Of course, I'll have to go back and see Thompson, or anything you decide—"

"You and us both," Jerry interrupted with a wink to Lou. Dougherty didn't thank Jerry for the interruption, but gave him a sharp sideways glance which reminded Lou of Anselmo for some reason.

"It it's time for new business—" Mike's shoulders rose massively above the heads of the workers and his cap seemed to stand up against the ceiling "—there's some things been bothering most of us around here. So I wanta move that we restrict our membership to white only." Walt raised his hand right away to second the motion.

There was a long silence which none of the workers seemed ready to break. Dougherty went on playing with his fedora on the billard table. Finally, with a great show of reluctance, he said, "I'm afraid the brother's motion is out of order."

"That's right," Pete stood up and shouted at Mike. His anger was rising. It was no longer a wordless anger against Dougherty, Thompson, and Washington. It was savage anger against a man who was attacking what his son wanted. Pete was happy Lou had come back to work. In many ways, it had been the happiest day of his life. He was proud when Jerry called Lou up front. Now Mike was trying to spoil everything. "You keep your mouth shut," Pete shouted.

It was like a body blow to Mike. He couldn't believe anybody would talk to him like that and mean it. "You'd better hold in your horses, dago," he threatened.

"That's out of order, too," said Jerry. "We ain't dago's or nothing else in this outfit. We're all workers."

"Fellows!" There was kindness and patience in Dougherty's tone. "I want to explain to the brother about his motion. I'm telling you, brothers and sisters, we had our hands full this week at headquarters. You know our union board can't afford to support a strike with injunctions and million dollar fines hanging over our heads. So when the members at one of our plants walked off the job, we had a devil of a time getting 'em back. You know why they walked out?" A little smile began to spread outward and downward from his grey understanding eyes as he talked straight to Mike. "Most of us don't like it," he went on with a side glance at Lou, "but there's just one condition with these government contracts. That's about hiring colored. When a colored machinist and an apprentice in the tool and die shop were hired at this plant I was telling you about, the workers came out with a bang. They were like a bunch of bears stung by hornets. But it don't pay to act rash, even when you know you got a raw deal. We had to prevail on 'em to go back on the job. But I want to add a word of warning against forcing the issue." Now he was looking at Lou as if he'd placed them all in an embarrassing position. "This integration's gonna come sooner or later, so why cause a lot of hard feelings by rushing things? Do I hear a motion to adjourn?"

In the confusion of adjournment, Mike boomed out a question, "Hey, Dougherty, are those colored so-and-so's still working at that plant?"

"Far's I know." Dougherty picked up his hat and made for the door.

"That's a good place for Lou to work," Mike said in a loud voice to Walt, "with his buddy. What plant did you say that was, Dougherty?" But the business agent was already bolting through the tavern. "You'd better find out for Lou," Mike turned to sneer at Pete.

Pete's heart flared up and his hands closed tight. He could see Mike's eyes smiling down at him. Suddenly his fist went out of control, shot up and socked Mike under the chin.

Mike groaned with pain and surprise. It was such a powerful blow his head rocked back on his shoulders. "Well you—" he knuckled his fists together. But Phil and Scotty and John and half a dozen other fellows were closing in around him. "I'd knock your block off, if you wasn't an old man," he shouted at Pete. He wiped his hands in a contemptuous gesture. "Goddam dagos!" He stared at Lou as he thrust his way out of the room.

"Well, that dirty bastard!" Lou felt Jerry's hand on his

shoulder restraining him from going after Mike.

"Take it easy, for Chrisake, Lou. It's your first day back," said Jerry. "By the way, you asked me this morning would I go and see Thompson with you. How about some time tomorrow?"

#6

After the union meeting, Lou and Pete set out for home along the tracks. At Anderson's Coalyard the cranes hung idle and the workers had already gone home. "It looks good about the job, eh pop?" Lou was thinking about Jesse scraping a shovel all day long. "We'll clinch it tomorrow."

Loaded cars and buses, people on foot, everybody was moving on home from work. Even the clouds were on the move, low-flying down the tracks, speeding Lou and his pa home.

But they walked into an empty kitchen. There was no supper on the stove. The table wasn't even set. The clock made the only sound in the unusual silence.

Lou went up to the front of the house. "Ma!" he called. He opened the door into the bedroom.

His ma was lying on the bed with her eyes fixed on the ceiling. One hand was folded across her breast in a lifeless attitude. "Hi, ma!" he said with a terrible fear.

"It's what you wanted, Luigi." Her voice seemed to come from a different room. With a hand sagging to the carpet, she was pointing at scraps of torn paper which littered the floor. "It's what you wanted, ain't it?" She raised herself on her elbow to face him. "That's 1250!"

Lou knelt to pick up the title deed to the tenement on Pioneer Street. His mother had ripped it from top to bottom and from side to side. Another paper of some kind was torn into thousands of little pieces so small that it would have taken hours to piece them together.

"I'm gonna give up the whole goddam business," she screamed at him. "Everything!"

"That's good," he said in a normal tone, trying to calm her. But he wondered, as he set the tatters of the deed down on the dressing table, if his mother was going out of her mind. Only that morning she had said she would never give the business up. "Ma, you look done in," he soothed her, "better get some shuteye." He sat down on the edge of the bed and tried to smooth her hair and calm her to sleep.

"They wanta drag me into court. Get me on my hands and knees." Kathryn sat straight up in bed and her fists tightened. "That's your colored people. They wanta whip me like a dog!"

"Tell me about it tomorrow, ma. I don't understand what it's all about."

"*You* don't understand!" she exclaimed with contempt. "You been egging them on. That Jesse of yours—" In a burst of passion she began to scream about Jesse and Anna Mae and the court summons which she had torn into confetti in her first rage. "They wanta ruin us. Take away all my money! Our house! It ain't only 1250! The two grand we saved up in the bank, Pete and me! Worked all our lives! Everything, understand?" Lou tried to restrain her, but she yelled all the louder, "Every penny! And you tell me go sleep! I hate you!"

Kathryn got out of bed. "I go tell Pete." She began to cry and lean on Lou's arm as if she couldn't make it to the kitchen without his help. But she still had strength to kick out savagely at the tiny scraps of paper on the floor. "Goddam triple damages! I won't go to court. The nerve! I'll throw them out in the street. Wait and see!"

When she got out to the kitchen, she sank on a chair beside the table. Her face flopped over on her arms and she cried hysterically with all her pent up hate and fear and frustration until finally her hysteria ended in a prolonged sobbing.

Lou moved about the kitchen quietly to drop the spaghetti into the great pot of boiling water. He put a bunch of escarole down in front of his mother, a bowl, olives, pimentoes, an onion, a bottle of vinegar and jar of olive oil. "Ma, you make the salad."

In a moment her fingers were mechanically cutting up the greens. "Luigi," she complained, "you forgot the pepper."

"Ma," Lou urged in a quiet voice, "Anselmo's got you into this mess. Why don't you make him get you out?"

For a moment Kathryn didn't say anything. She was too busy stirring up the greens in the olive oil. Lou wondered if she had heard him.

"It *was* Anselmo," she finally sighed as if she couldn't remember until Lou mentioned the name.

"First, he got you to buy that joint," Lou went on. "Then he told you to jump the rents above the rent ceiling?"

Kathryn nodded hopelessly. What was the use of going over it all again?

"I remember," said Lou, "they used to pay about fifteen bucks down there when Bartuccis lived in that building. That was tops for a whole month. Then Anselmo told you to move our folks out, charge the colored people twenty bucks a week for one little room—"

Kathryn nodded again. She got up and began to set the table.

"But that's water under the bridge." Lou's voice was deep and soothing as if all her troubles were over now. "Let Anselmo worry. He's the guy makes all the dough out of these deals. Call him tonight, ma. Tell him we're through."

"That's what I say." Pete asserted himself at last. "Anselmo changed everything by you and me. We forget now. Go back. Remember? Back home." Pete's face was happy as a boy's as he remembered how he would come to the window at the back of her father's store and Kathryn would close down the old man's books. "It's hot and the flutes and the crickets—tze-tze-tze—remember how they sing?" He held her face between his hands and kissed her with his old time affection. "And the stars, Kathryn! Not like here, all covered with smoke."

"OK, OK," said Kathryn drawing away from him. All the same, she was moved. "But we come to America. Then everything was different."

"One day we go back home," Pete promised.

Slowly Kathryn's head went back and forth with the impossibility of ever going back home. "You wanta live like field rats again?" she asked with a terrible bitterness. "So we work like crazy. All sweat and sit up night. Then one day we buy our own house. It's nice. Get some money in the bank. It's old age now.

Wrinkles, white hair. But you won't help me, repairs at 1250, nothing. It's finished. Everything I do for you, Pete, and our Luigi. But what he say? Same old slave in the factory. Grease on his pants. What good is it all? Why we don't stay in Valone, sleep eight, ten in the family on straw bed on the floor?" She held her hands up in the air. "Easy street and the boy says no. Oh, God! I can't stand to think of it no more. Call him up tomorrow, Anselmo. Tell him—finished! Take his house back. Everything! Can I live with my boy hating me and my Pete looking at me like I'm gone nuts in the head?" She looked very old and tired and bitter to Lou—worn away to the bone. But she clenched her fists with a reserve of energy as she went on, "But colored in my house? Never, never, never! Say auntie to Anna Mae Green? Never, Luigi, understand?"

"Eat your supper, ma," said Lou quietly.

"Never, never, never! I ain't hungry. Help me back to bed, Pete. I got heart burn. It's gonna bust out on me. I never felt so terrible. I'm gonna die."

"Gonna be happy, Kathryn." Pete eased her back in her chair, "Now eat spaghetti the boy cooked for you. Luigi's back home—after all the nights we didn't sleep—remember?"

"Ma, call Anselmo tonight," Lou urged.

"Tomorrow," she promised wearily.

#7

Kathryn heard train bells ringing at her through a vast station. Hurry, hurry. While the great clock on the balcony stood still.

The harder the bells rang the harder it was to move her feet. A crowd of people rushed past her to the gates. Why wouldn't her feet move any more? Everybody else slipped and dissolved and melted away, left her standing in the great empty space with her feet frozen to the floor.

Even the clock went back and away and out of sight. And when she lost it, four children came into the empty space. She knew she had given birth to all of them at the same time. But there was no pain. She was glad to have company in the vast emptiness.

Now their blank faces began to show features. There was Carlo, her eldest son, a little fellow looking fresh and bright eyed. Another's face was hidden, but from the shape of his head she knew it must be Georgi. And the third, of course, was Luigi. Why were Carlo and Georgi fresh and young, but Luigi, her youngest, old and sad looking? He had the face of the Savior on the Cross. Then he began to smile at the fourth, a child whose face was growing darker and darker.

Had she given birth to him?

Her feet unstuck themselves from the floor. She gathered her three children around her and moved as fast as she could lead them. She moved faster, running. It was impossible to keep her own children close to her any more. And Luigi had turned back to put his arm around the shoulder of the Negro boy. The boy had a man's face. It was Jesse's.

"Holy Mother of God!" Kathryn was half-awake praying now. "Let me sleep." But she couldn't pray away her dream. It haunted her even when her eyes were wide open watching the light from outdoors falter on the ceiling.

It was daylight. There was no sound in the house. Pete must have gone to work already. It was the first time in her life she hadn't got up to prepare his breakfast. And there was no sound upstairs. Luigi must have gone, too. She was all alone.

Finally, when it was time for her to call Anselmo, she groped her way to the front room. "I'm gonna give up the whole business," she said so quietly over the telephone that Anselmo asked her, "Is that really you, mama?" There was no breath left in her lungs to answer him. "What's wrong, did they serve the court order?"

Kathryn only said, "I ain't gonna worry no more, Anselmo, with Pete hating me, and Luigi. They're all against me."

"Say, mama," Anselmo asked with a sympathetic inflection, "did Lou go back to his old job?"

Kathryn could hardly bear to tell him. "Yesterday."

"I'm worried about that boy, the way he's acting." Anselmo's voice was full of concern for Lou. "Like he had concussion or shellshock out there. Did he say?"

Kathryn couldn't remember him saying anything like that. Still, the suggestion that Lou was acting strange gave her an edge of hope. "He ain't been himself, that's the truth, Anselmo."

"We got to talk about this, mama. Can you come up to the office right away?"

She should tell him no. She'd made up her mind. She had promised Lou and Pete to give up the whole business and she would carry out her promise. But she would have to see Anselmo sooner or later to give him back all the papers, including the title to 1250 which she had ripped across and up and down in her first anger after the court summons was delivered.

"Are you still there?" Anselmo was impatient.

"OK, I'll come—" She still was hesitating when Anselmo dropped the receiver.

Kathryn walked slowly down the street to take the bus. She stopped in front of 758. The basement and first floor windows were boarded up after the fire, but the rest of the building looked the same as ever, dilapidated but sturdy. The pigeons had come back to nest in the gables. The male was strutting and cooing little notes of warning from the roof while curving his head to look down at Kathryn.

It would have been a wonderful investment. Even now, in a couple of months with the insurance money, she could put it in shape for renting. Regret lumped up in her throat.

Supposing Lou was really suffering from shellshock. That would explain why he looked so melancholy at times, why he put so much importance on his friendship with Jesse, why he turned down Anselmo's offer, and why he made her promise to give up the business she'd put her heart into so that they could all live on easy street. What had happened between him and Nina, she didn't even know. When she had stopped by the previous day, Pagliani told her the girl had gone to stay with her aunt for a few days. If Lou had concussion, maybe even his brain was affected. That would explain everything. Kathryn got on the bus with hope suffusing a new strength through her whole being.

When she was alone with Anselmo in his skyhigh office, the

tiger's pelt spread on the wall behind him and the autumn blonde and chartreuse harmony of colors made it impossible for her to put conviction into the words she had planned to say, "I've decided to give it all up. I'm through."

Anselmo looked at her curiously. "Mama, you look like you seen a ghost."

Kathryn was shocked at the reflection of her own face as she glanced at the mirror across the room. Anselmo was right. She was gaunt and green. She turned quickly away to watch him press the button and convert the end of his desk into a bar.

"Marsala, mama?" He poured himself a whiskey at the same time. "Now what's the trouble?"

It was hard for Kathryn to explain. So she only said, "The notice—about court Monday—I tore it up!"

"Let me ask you, was it the Roberts only, or some of those other tenants who testified in court for this Anna Mae Green?"

"It was them too," said Kathryn dispiritedly, "Roberts, Martins, old Mrs. Osborne—"

"They'll have a price," Anselmo laughed cynically. "There's no use going into a tailspin, mama. We'll have to see what we can do."

"But that ain't the only thing, Anselmo. Maybe it was a sin, taking her to court like that. Maybe the Holy Mother—"

"It's nerves, Kathryn. The Holy Mother never said we should let anybody walk all over us. That's what this Green woman was trying to do—till we caught her out. Anyway, she's out of the picture now."

But Anna Mae was not out of the picture for Kathryn. She could see the color of her eyes when she closed her own—light and fierce like the eyes of a tigress, still menacing her. "Not yet, Anselmo, until we get the Roberts out—"

"That'll be next," said Anselmo with profound assurance. She was no longer talking as if she meant to give up the whole business. "No mama, let's be frank with each other," he went on quickly. "It isn't the Green woman who's knocked the bottom out of your confidence. It's Lou. He's acting screwy, that's all we can say. He invites a colored fellow to our private family feast. He turns down a job with me when he's got it made. He has a bust up with Nina Pagliani the week after they get engaged—"

"How do you know about Nina?" Kathryn asked with a terrible breathlessness.

Anselmo parted his hands in a casual gesture as if he had ways and means of finding out everything.

"Nina." Kathryn muttered desperately.

"What's behind it all?" Anselmo went on reflecting aloud. "We got to ask ourselves." In a moment he went on to answer his own question. "It's war, Kathryn. The worst hell there is on earth." Anselmo was pacing the floor with his hands behind his back. He stopped at the window to gaze down into the Canyon. "But we have to fight or be licked. Now Lou took a beating out there. Remember what he said at the homecoming? 'We got chased like dogs.' That was a funny thing for a guy like Lou to say in front of everybody. He's no coward. Nobody would think that to look at him or talk to him." He turned around to face Kathryn. "But something's happened to him out there. That's why I asked you if he had concussion. If you don't know for sure, we should write out to San Antonio. It would explain the buddy business, too. He's trying to ram this Jesse fellow down everybody's throat. Now this integration's one thing in the army, but back home everybody knows it's different."

"Not for Luigi," Kathryn objected. The rest of what Anselmo said seemed to make sense. But Lou had always played around with the colored kids at school and in baseball leagues. "He had friends before—he took colored kids to the church bingo games—"

"You never told me." Anselmo was sharp with Kathryn. "And you didn't tell me, mama, you got this Jesse a place to live at 1250. You should discuss these things with me first."

"I wanted to tell you—" Kathryn began to defend herself.

"So much water under the bridge." Anselmo dismissed the whole subject as if he knew exactly what she would say and wan't interested. "The main point I'm making, mama, we gotta treat Lou like he's a sick person. We can't expect him to act natural after all he's been through. We've got to humor him along. Let him work in a factory for a while. He'll get tired of it. In the meantime, go right ahead with what you're doing. The report from the insurance patrol shows we can repair the situation at 758 in a month or two. Before the end of the year, the rent money will be pouring in. When Lou sees you making money hand over fist—"

"But I promised him!" Kathryn sighed with a deep regret. Everything seemed so simple when Anselmo explained it to her.

"Well, OK then," said Anselmo with a shrug. "Tell him it's going to take a couple of weeks to wind things up. You can't sell the building till this triple damage suit is settled. Another drink, mama?"

The wine was penetrating every tired nerve and corpuscle with little charges that filled her whole body with new hope. "If Luigi turns against me—" Her gesture showed that the whole business would be without meaning. "It's all for him." But there was a glint now in her eyes as Anselmo filled her glass again. And in the mirror across she saw a little color flushing into her cheeks.

"Don't worry, Lou thinks you're about the best ma a fellow could want," Anselmo reassured her. "Now I'll try to get a continuance on this triple damage suit. Maybe we can drag it out a few months. We'll go ahead with the repairs on 758." He picked up the pieces of the title to 1250 and smiled as he said, "We'll have to do a repair job on this, too." His buzzer and phone were both ringing at the same time. "Keep in touch with me, mama. I'm right here," he said patting the receiver before he raised it to his ear. "And keep cheerful!"

It was easy for Anselmo to keep cheerful in an office at the top of the world with only the sky up above and the whole city at his feet. But Kathryn's eyes blurred in a mist of chartreuse and autumn blonde and she walked unsteadily across a carpet that yielded deeply under her shoes and rose into place again as she passed away from Anselmo and the cheerful sound of his voice.

In the outer office, she stumbled into Vico who put his arm around her with an easy affection "You look like you're going places, mama." His tone was cheerful like Anselmo's. He was handsome, Vico, with his aquiline nose, his deep olive complexion, and his hair immaculately cut, curled and shaped. His eyes penetrated and caressed and his smile was already like Anselmo's.

Why was it Frances Angelino had this boy for a son who was all a mother could have hoped: handsome, successful, going up in the world? Till one day he would sit in Anselmo's office under the tiger skin. But Luigi—what was wrong with her own son?

When Vico asked, "What's this I hear about Lou going back to his old job?" Kathryn pretended she was in too big a rush to answer.

"Down, down!" she screamed as she closed the door in Vico's face. The elevator sank away beneath her. She clung to the rail as if the earth itself were sinking away and leaving her no solid footing.

Her head swayed and she saw a million dizzy spots as she stepped out into the canyon, plunged in the shadows of tall buildings.

#8

In the front reception room at Farmway, the goldfish made an easy living as they cruised around their aquarium under the eucalpytus tree in the green tub. But across the barrier, secretaries were on the hop from one private office to another, and a battery of typists, red-faced in spite of the air-conditioning, were clattering away under the eye of the office manager.

"You'll have to wait," the receptionist told Lou and Jerry. "Mr. Anderson's busy."

Typewriters and adding machines chattered like light artillery in comparison with the big machines in the shop. And here in the cool, most of the racket was sopped up by sound proofing on walls and ceilings.

Lou and Jerry had waited all morning and half the afternoon for a chance to see the top brass. Finally, it was the works manager, not Thompson himself, who agreed to see them for five minutes. "Anderson's the guy who runs the show, anyway, so relax, Lou," said Jerry sitting down at ease on company time under the eucalyptus tree. His eyes idled after the goldfish in slow circles, then shifted to the typists, his easy smile dropping a wink here and there.

But Lou couldn't help thinking about Nina as he watched the women at work in the office. After the big argument with his mother the previous evening, he'd gone over to the tavern. At first, Pagliani didn't know where she was. Then he said she was at her aunt's. But when Lou went back into the street, he was sure he saw the curtains in her bedroom move slightly, then close together again. "Nina!" he'd called up. "Nina, for Chrisake—"

Lou jumped when he saw Clarence come hopping out of Anderson's office like an aggressive jackrabbit. "Mr. Anderson will see you now," he said in a respectful whisper. "Remember, only five minutes, guys."

As Lou and Jerry came into his office, Anderson was still too busy to look up from his desk. Lou remembered the bargaining session more than three years before when he came in with Art and Dougherty to negotiate. The works manager, an ex-colonel from World War II, was a tough bird to handle. All they got out of him that time was a nickel raise and a couple of minor fringe benefits. That was before the wage freeze, too. It was Anderson, Lou rememberd, who handled negotiations, only calling Thompson in at the last to offer the nickel like some Santa Claus from the North Pole.

"You were at the Yalu?" Anderson flashed his public relations smile at Lou. He sat up at attention behind his desk as if he was stationed somewhere on the ground floor of the Pentagon.

"Yes, sir," said Lou automatically.

Anderson's head was balding. But his eyes behind his glasses were alert, far-seeing, and changing direction at every instant. Smiling and at the same time agressive, his expression reminded Lou of Anselmo. His cheeks and nose like Anselmo's were flushed a whiskey pink. "Active combat?" he asked.

"It sure seemed that way, sir, especially our last trip down from the Yalu." It was an encouraging beginning, though Lou was annoyed at himself for buttering up Anderson with "sir".

"Mr. Buffington—" Anderson nodded at Clarence "—tells me you made some new friends overseas."

"That's what I wanted to see you about." Lou began to focus the spotlight on Jesse, but Anderson was in a reminiscing mood.

"I was out there in the other war, in China," he said reflectively. "They haven't got the big guns. But they know how to fight. We talk about them being yellow—" Anderson shook his head. "We can't beat them by calling them names. What do you think, Bianchi?" he shot his question at Lou.

"Folks back home don't get the hang of it," said Lou cautiously, "that's for sure."

"Now, it looks like we'll have to settle—" Anderson gestured impatiently at the headlines of the morning paper on his desk. "We should have trained more native troops, starting back in forty-five. Then they could have carried the ball on the ground and our boys in the air. Instead, we got ourselves mired down." Anderson shook his head pessimistically. "Bad strategy. Now, about that friend of yours. Mr. Buffington tells me he's a colored boy."

"That's right," said Lou. "He's an OK—" Lou began, but Anderson vetoed the personal business. It looked like Lou wasn't going to get a chance to say any of the things he'd planned.

"What I want to know, is he qualified?"

"He was in Redball in the other war," Lou explained. "he had to learn everything you could get to know about a six-by. He's operated a crane—"

Anderson held up his hand again. "What's the problem, then?" He turned to Clarence. Evidently, they had already planned their strategy.

"The fellows may walk out, that's all," said Clarence.

"That's the only trouble," said Anderson putting the problem up to Jerry.

"If they walk out," said Jerry in his easy going way, "then we'll get 'em back in."

"We can't afford a walkout," said Clarence. "It's our busy season."

"You know what the law is, Mr. Anderson—" Jerry smiled at him easily "—with defense contracts, if you don't hire colored—"

"I know," Anderson interrupted. "They've been putting the heat on from downtown. But we always thought you fellows were against it." He was still trying to shift the load from his own shoulders.

Jerry was smiling at Anderson as if he was a hypocrite. "It would be tough if the government cancelled those orders."

Anderson flushed a little at Jerry's blunt warning. "I'm sure Mr. Thompson won't have any objection, if he knows there won't be any trouble."

"We can handle that," said Jerry.

"There wasn't any trouble at the hospital," said Lou. "One or two big mouths at first. Now they're gonna integrate the whole army."

"That's it," said the ex-colonel, glad to find a way to retreat and advance at the same time. "We can't show the rest of the world unless we take a few steps at home. It's the only way we'll win out there in the long run. No, I can't see anything against hiring one colored fellow, can you Clarence?"

"Whatever you say, Mr. Anderson." Clarence was pointing at this watch because the five minutes were up.

"All right, Bianchi, bring your friend in next week." Anderson's public relations smile flashed on and off as he turned back to his work.

"Say, how do you figure that bird?" Lou asked with a new respect for Jerry as they went back upstairs to the machine shop. If it hadn't been for Jerry, things might easily have gone the other way.

"Great armchair strategist, that's Anderson. When he sees we got the firepower lined up against him, he knows how to advance to the rear." Then Jerry laughed. "Get ready for the fireworks, Lou, Monday morning."

#9

As Lou waited for Jesse outside the coalyard, cranes were still arching over the tracks. Jets of steam burst and towered into the air and from the giant hoppers coal thundered down into trucks. At the five o'clock whistle, everything stopped at once. The men came crowding out into the yard, their eyes flashing in coal-blackened faces. At a distance Lou recognized Jesse from his height and shoulder spread, the long oval of his face and his glasses. But it was impossible to tell who was white and who was Negro among the workers as they came through the gate.

"Hey, partner!" Jesse shouted in surprise as Lou landed the flat of his hand between his shoulder blades.

"Good news, fellow," said Lou proudly, "We got it made for you. He's gonna put you on in the machine shop."

"You gone back to the old job?"

"Sure, me and Anselmo had some words. I told him I didn't want no part of his frame-up business."

"You told him that?" Jesse was amazed and delighted. Then he burst out into a roar of laughter. "So you got me the job!"

"It's no more'n what they have to do. They been holding out on us." Lou told Jesse what happened at the union meeting and about his interview with the works manager. "That Jerry about swung it. He thinks hiring colored's good job insurance for everybody."

"He ain't kiddin', neither," said Jesse. "Hey, I got a buddy of mine needs a job bad. Maybe we could fix him up, too. Most got his leg burnt off out at the steel mill last winter. They put him back on sweep up at half pay."

"He's a colored fellow?" Lou asked. It meant going back to Clarence, maybe to Anderson, starting a whole new struggle before the first was settled. Still, he had told Jesse it was good insurance. "OK, we'll talk about it Monday."

They were standing across the street from Pagliani's Tavern at the parting of their ways, Jesse's leading across the park and Lou's down Hemlock Street. A squad car came cruising by, nosing into Jesse's and Lou's business. When the cop in the driver's seat recognized Lou, he saluted him like an old time buddy.

"Those were the bulls I was telling you about," Jesse laughed, "the first time Mr. Pagliani put out the welcome sign."

"Nosey bastards," said Lou. "I went to school with that guy. Say, speaking about Pagliani's—" Lou made a drinking motion with his thumb.

"At Pagliani's?"

"Remember the PX?" Lou asked.

"He's OK," Jesse imitated Lou's voice the way he talked to the sergeant that night. "He's from Chicago."

"Old Snakeface got the worst of that," said Lou. "Come on, we'll say how-de-doo." Lou glanced up at Nina's window, but the blind and curtain were both drawn. He had a feeling, all the same, that somebody was watching them.

Lou steered Jesse to a table in the tavern, then came back to face old Pagliani at the cash counter. A couple of young fellows at the bar glanced at Jesse, then nodded to Lou as if he should know what he was doing. But Pagliani shook his head with a sour mouth-pucker. He was staring at Jesse's shirt and overalls, black from the day's work. "What the hell?" he muttered.

But Lou slapped his hand down flat on the bar. "Two shots."

For a moment, Pagliani opened his enormous eyes wider to stare Lou down. When that didn't work, he reached up to the whiskey shelf. His hand closed around the neck of a fifth of Black and White. Then he turned the label toward Lou as he poured. "Mixing drinks ain't good business. Lot of trouble! Lot of trouble! Your ma, boy, Nina—all broke up." He tapped his forehead. "Better get wise up here, eh?"

"Where's Nina?" Lou asked if Pagliani was shooting a lot of hot air. Still, he knew that his ma must have come by to complain to Nina about giving up the rent business.

"Lot of trouble!" Pagliani went on shaking his head. "Nina cry all night. She think you gone nuts in the head."

So Nina was upstairs all the time. Lou took the drinks and went over to the table. "Goddam liar, Pagliani!" He explained to Jesse how Nina had cut up rough on him when she heard he wasn't going to take the job with Anselmo. "But she'll come around. So, Jesse, here's luck on the new job." They clinked glasses. But Lou's heart wasn't in it.

Maybe Nina wouldn't come around. Maybe she and his ma had put their heads together. Goddam that Pagliani! "Hey, another shot," Lou shouted. "Make it Black and White."

There was a battle of eyes with Pagliani before he finally shouted, "Boatman!"

Boatman came up to their table on the defensive, his head lowered but his eyes on the alert. It was the first time Jesse had seen him at close quarters since the trial of Anna Mae Green. His fists were aching to bust out. "Judas!" he muttered between tight lips. All the same, his deeper anger went against Pagliani. "They trying to frame him on rape in South Caroline," he said to Lou. "They got him around the neck."

"I know," said Lou. The joy of celebration went down to the zero mark. In Jesse's eyes he could read anger against his ma, too, when he said "they." And Lou was wondering again if his ma had paid Boatman off to testify at Anna Mae's trial the night he'd seen him and two other men come out of the alley. But even if she had paid them, maybe she believed Anna Mae was a prostitute. It was hard to get anybody to testify in court without making it worth their while. Besides, Anselmo had held his ma pretty much under his thumb. She would have believed anything he told her. Thank God she had promised to give up the rent business, even if she had come complaining around to Pagliani. And the chances were she'd seen Nina, too.

Lou watched Boatman move back to the bar with the wariness of the professional boxer. It was a relief to know his ma would have no further need for the protection of a muscleman with a scar across his cheek, sullen eyes and massive pudginess.

"My ma's gonna give up the rent business," Lou explained as if Jesse had put him on the spot. "It's too tough on her at her age."

But there was no compromise in Jesse's eyes over Lou's mother. Anna Mae Green was already framed, tried and convicted. For a long time, they sat staring at their glasses in silence. Then Jesse wrenched his face into a smile. "I got an appointment with the old lady for some chow," he said lightly.

"I gotta get home, too." But Lou went on sitting at the table when Jesse got up. "See you Monday, guy."

"Keep your chin up," said Jesse. His hand closed over Lou's shoulder. "On up ahead, things gonna be OK, buddy." There was a sudden warmth of friendliness in Jesse's smile that went back to that rainy night in the PX.

The moment the door banged behind Jesse, Boatman came stepping over to the table on the balls of his feet. "Mr. Lou—"

What did Boatman want? Lou looked up into the mask of a face. "Miss Nina wants to see you—"

So what if he didn't want to see her? It wouldn't hurt to keep her waiting for a change.

"In the kitchen—" Boatman waited for his answer with an impassive expression.

"I seen you coming down our alley Sunday night," said Lou. Boatman went on waiting without changing expression. "It was you all right, with two other colored fellows."

This time, Boatman shook his head as if Lou must be mistaken.

"You don't tell me I'm a liar." Lou stood up. How much money would it take to make him tell the truth, Lou wondered cynically.

Boatman lowered his eyes away from Lou's and stood with his head bowed. Then Lou brushed past him. Pagliani watched him go behind the bar toward the kitchen. His mouth closed tight and a frown drew his features together.

Nina was standing on the back stairs halfway down from the landing. Lou couldn't believe she'd cried all night, because her eyes were fiery and her cheeks full of color and she was all dressed up. She was a proud girl, Nina, and even though she was calling off the walkout, she looked as if she was ready to call it back on at any moment. Lou hesitated to run up the stairs, seize her in his arms, and kiss away that accusing look. "You was around all the time," he accused back.

"That's my business." Her eyes went dull and stony. She drew her breath with a sudden rise and fall of her chest. "I have to tell you, Lou," she said as if carrying out an unpleasant duty, "your ma came by today. She's all broken up."

Nina was trying to get at him through his ma. She wouldn't see that he had made up his mind once and for all about the

Anselmo deal. "Nina, can't you see—?"

"Why are you making her do it? Can't *you* see, Lou, she's set her heart on it?"

"That's my business," Lou flung back at her. He wasn't going to let her go on needling him about his ma.

"She thinks you got concussion or shellshock. Oh Lou, why didn't you tell us if it's true? We could help you deal with it."

"Nuts!" he said. So that was what Anselmo had told his ma, the dirty bastard. "Nina, I'm surprised at you falling for that."

They stared at each other. He noticed for the first time that she was wearing the blue dress she had worn at his homecoming party. "Who you stepping out with?" he asked with sudden anger.

"Supposing I want to go places?" The hardness of her voice broke. She couldn't admit to Lou that she'd dressed up for him especially when she saw him come into the tavern with Jesse.

"Who's the lucky man?" Lou sneered.

Nina didn't answer him. She was crying, but she didn't want him to see. "You fool, there's no lucky man. Why do you have to treat me like this?" She turned and ran up the back stairs.

Lou walked off home hardly seeing where he was going, angry at Nina and his ma at the same time, angry at himself and Jesse. He turned once to see Vico's red Cadillac draw up in front of the tavern. So she's going out with that gigolo, Lou thought with a bitterness without bounds. Things were finished between him and Nina. Let her shack up with Vico. She was about his type, anyway.

But memories of the night he asked her to marry him came back on the music of the carnival, the ferris wheel turning the city up and down. And Nina with her hair blowing in the wind. It was a dream, the happiest of Lou's life. Why couldn't she take him the way he was?

#10

When Lou sat down at the kitchen table, he put his face between his fists. He was dead beat. Nina's words kept dinning an accusation into his ears, "She's all broken up." It was true. His ma had been crying. Her eyes were inflamed. She set his supper in front of him with a meager greeting and went back to washing up the dishes. She held her head down over her work.

She must have had words with Pete. His father was sitting back with his hands gripping the arms of his chair. He hadn't even looked up when Lou came in.

Lou pushed his plate back after a couple of mouthfuls. His stomach knotted up.

"I'll heat it for you, Luigi," his mother offered. Her tone was a complaint.

"Don't bother, ma, I ain't hungry." He sat watching her as she rinsed out the dishpan and cleaned the sink. Then she took his plate from the table and dumped his supper into the garbage can.

"Ma, why did you tell Nina I had concussion?"

Kathryn stood wiping her hands on her apron, then went back to work as if she hadn't understood what he said. She got down the dish cloth and began to scour the sink all over again.

"I'm a hundred percent OK. That's what they told me before I left San Antonio. Same thing up at Fort Sheridan when I got my discharge." His words were a bitter accusation. "I got disability in my back only."

His ma went on fussing without seeming to hear him. But her shoulders went down, her whole body seemed to droop.

Wearily Lou got up and put his arms around her shoulders while she sobbed. He helped her over to a chair, got out a bottle of wine and filled a glass for her. "Bianchi special, ma." He poured a glass for his pa and one for himself. But his ma sat bleakly staring down at the table.

There was a rap at the door. Pete went to open. Kathryn's eyes jumped up to watch Boatman come in. "Holy Mother, I forgot. Rent night!"

"But ma, you promised to call Anselmo, give up the whole goddam business." Lou's voice rose to a shout. "You didn't call him?"

"You didn't believe me, Luigi, when I promised?"

Boatman stood waiting in the doorway.

"Jesus Christ, ma, you been crying on Nina's shoulder like you wasn't planning—"

"Anselmo says I'll have to go to court first," she interrupted him. "Then he can settle." She couldn't resist adding, "He thinks you gone nuts!"

"Concussion, eh?" Lou snapped. "Everything was OK around here until Anselmo put his big nose in. My way of thinking, everybody went nuts while I was out there in Korea, except pop."

"You go down with me, Luigi, just once more to collect the rent," she began to plead with him as if even now he might still change his mind.

Boatman waited like a great shadow in the doorway.

"Forget about it, ma. Let Anselmo handle it from here on out." Lou put his arms around his mother and held her tight. "Now, maybe we work things out again, you me and pop—without all the shouting."

But she hesitated only a moment before slipping out of his arms. "I gotta go, Luigi. They owe me the money."

"Forget it," he said. But she reached up for her shawl and followed Boatman into the alley.

After they were gone, Boatman's face burned in Lou's mind. On the surface, his face said, I wanta play ball with you folks. But behind the mask, what was Boatman really thinking?

"Goddam it, pop," Lou exploded. "That Boatman, you trust him?"

Pete sat in his chair with his face buried away in his hands. Things were too confused now for him to begin to understand. All he wanted was for his son to be happy. "That Anselmo," he said in a voice that was a growl, "if he tell her, 'Go to hell,' then she wanta go" He shook his head back and forth as if he'd lost control.

"God Almighty, pop, I should have gone with her!" Lou walked up and down the floor creaking under him. "Explain it to me, why everybody's gone nuts—me, too."

He went up to his room. The chartreuse and autumn blonde walls closed in on him—like Anselmo's office. The big shot had taken over the house, his mother, everything—even Lou's own room.

Finally, eaten up with worry, Lou went down the front stairs and out into the street.

#11

In the basement flat, Jesse found the Roberts sharped out in their best clothes. Geneva was wearing a white starched dress with a red belt and buckle and a sparkle of red stones at her ears and throat. Her eyes were keen and large as she smiled at Jesse.

"Steppin' out with the young lady," said Charles proud of his wife's beauty. "She puttin' up with me ten years. Gonna celebrate."

"Young married folks gotta have their fun," said Jesse like somebody's grandfather. "So I'll see you tomorrow."

"Out with it now, man you got something to say."

"I got me the job."

"Yeh, he gone and got you on in the machine shop?"

"Biomchi's boy?" Anna Mae wasn't going to believe it.

"I'm telling you," Jesse insisted.

Charlene and Randy looked up at Jesse as if they knew something special had happened. "I talked to my buddy about gettin' you on up there, too."

"Sweep up?" Charles asked cynically.

"No, machine work," Jesse insisted. "That's on the level."

Anna Mae was still shaking her head. "He looked mean as a yard dog, Biomchi's boy, in his soldier's uniform."

"I don't get the hang on it, nowise," Charles muttered.

"OK, OK, we'll talk about it tomorrow," said Jesse.

"Better be tomorrow," Anna Mae warned bluntly. "After Monday her boy won't be helping no Charles Roberts get no job. When we get old Biomchi down to court on triple damages, we gonna take hold on her like stewin' chicken waitin' on the boilin' pot. She gonna cut-cut-cutockit like she laid her last bad old rotten egg. We gonna show her who's bad morals!"

"You better kind of lay on easy, Sister Mae," Charles lectured her. "I wonder you want what's comin' to you by rights more'n you want a good fight anyhow."

"That's Anna Mae Gree," she said proudly beating on her chest.

The moment Charles and Geneva left the basement room and their kids and worries behind, Charlene began to take up a battle she'd already lost.

"Wouldn't let me go. Never want me and Randy to have no fun." Charlene was as stubborn a child at the age of nine as Anna Mae must have been herself and she deliberately imitated her auntie's expression because she had an audience in Jesse. "You the meanest auntie ever in the whole world." Then she ducked away from the flat of Anna Mae's hand that came swooping to stop her mouth.

"You get too sassy one day, girl, I'm gonna think you mean it. Then you watch out."

In an entirely different tone, Anna Mae went on to show her surprise at Jesse. "You mean you asked her boy to help get Charles a job? Jesse, what you thinking?"

"I'm thinking—" Jesse hesitated. Anna Mae was making him out the worst fool in the world. But he'd be a worse fool yet not to see she was admiring what he did. "When you got a lucky streak, gotta push harder, eh? But one thing's got me guessing, Anna Mae, I'll be frank with you. He said she's gonna give up the rent business."

Anna Mae studied Jesse for a moment. "You believe that?" she asked. "You think she's that beat up and afraid because she gonna take a whuppin' in court?" As Anna Mae puzzled over it, her sarcastic smile began to shape up again. "Biomchi?" She shook her head decisively. "No, Jesse, the Friday she don't come round reachin' out her hand for the rent money, that's the Friday she's gonna be dead."

Jesse shrugged and started for the door. Then he turned back to ask, "What's Anna Mae gonna do with all that dough, Monday, if she gets triple damages?"

"You ask me?" She seemed surprised Jesse came out with such a foolish question, after she'd told him and everybody else a hundred times already. "I'm gonna get me a piece of Mississippi land. You know, where there ain't no white folks bossin' me around. You believe it, I wanta pick me some cotton with these two old hands again? A basement flat ain't a decent place for no rat to live in. Look at the babies, Jesse—"

Three kids were lying in a single bed. The eyes of Randy and Charlene gleamed over the sheet alert to what their aunt was saying about Mississippi and picking cotton. At the other end of the bed, their little brother was asleep and the baby was kicking on his mother's bed, turning over and sitting up in the excitement of his new won powers and staring at Anna Mae and Jesse with happy eyes that saw something new and amusing every minute. But the damp walls were sweating in the September heat and the air was heavy with toilet smells.

"And *we* gonna go this time, Auntie Mae," Charlene said confidently.

"Ain't nobody gonna say no, Charlene."

"And you gonna take me too, Auntie Mae, and little Brother and the baby?" Randy asked anxiously.

"Ain't nobody said no, Randy."

"And we gonna fry some good old chicken. That's what I like," said Charlene.

"That's right, baby," said Anna Mae. "Gonna be heaven so fast, you better start growin' them angel wings—right tonight." She winked at Jesse. "And we gonna get ourselves a little old piece of house no police and no old lady Biomchi's gonna stick their big nose in."

"After Monday, eh, Anna Mae?" Jesse laughed as he started up the basement stairs.

#12

The laughter of children followed Jesse up the stairs. He could hear Anna Mae promising them again, "And that's the way it's gonna be."

Up on the first floor, a sharper voice cut into Jesse's mood of happiness, "I never thought you was going to double-cross me." Kathryn Bianchi was threatening old Mrs. Martin and pleading with her at the same time. "Before you sign up for that triple damages, why you didn't talk to me first about the rent? After all I done for you! You better drop that triple damages now, or I'm gonna—"

Kathryn changed her mind in the middle of what she was saying when she saw Jesse come up through the basement door. "I'm gonna cut the rent down. Can't you get that into your head?" While she spoke, she was looking at Jesse the way she did after the frame-up trial of Anna Mae Green—with a desperate fear and hate.

"Evening." Jesse nodded to Kathryn and Mr. Martin who stood holding the door half way closed as if to protect his wife. It didn't sound to Jesse like Kathryn had given up the rent business. What was Lou trying to tell him?

Mr. Martin inclined his head slightly in Jesse's direction. His mouth was firmly set against Kathryn in a maddening silence, while his wife began to answer her back. "Never cut it down yet, only raised it," she complained. "We gonna have to let the judge decide now."

Kathryn thought she could see a smile shaping up in Jesse's eyes as Mrs. Martin publicly defied her. She saw Jesse deliberately force Boatman to step out of his way as he turned his back and went upstairs. Even her own hired muscleman cringed away from Jesse as if the house belonged to him. He was the one who had made her authority crumble away to nothing.

And egging Jesse on was her own son. That was the bitterest thought of all. It made Kathryn raise her fists beside her cheeks and tremble without being able to strike at the cause of her rage. Lou had elevated this black man above his own mother.

Kathryn could no longer face the Martins. While Mrs. Martin was shouting at her husband, "And don't you pay her no rent, 'less she gives you a receipt like the lawyer say," Kathryn pushed the door shut in the old man's face. It had been the same upstairs with Mrs. Osborne. They were all joining with the Roberts in triple damage suits to ruin her.

"You gonna have to get out of my house," Kathryn shouted through the door. Then she turned her fury on Boatman. "You, you goddam coward!" she raged beating her fists against his chest. "You let that Jesse push you around like junk. What the hell do I pay you for?"

But there was no satisfaction in beating away at Boatman when it was Jesse she wanted to whip, and Anna Mae—and her own son.

Lou wouldn't do what she asked him, begged him. After all she'd done for him. All his life. He had forced her to make promises she could never carry out. He had destroyed everything: her hopes, ambitions, and her dreams.

Kathryn put her fists up to her forehead. "Holy Mother of God," she moaned, "better my boy had never come back from Korea!"

As if everybody had stopped what they were doing to listen to her cry, there was no sound in the many rooms of that house, only a great restless silence—until from the basement a fountain of children's laughter burst up the stairway and flooded the house.

Then an unmistakable voice rose up the basement stairwell, "Ain't tellin' you no lies, babies."

"Anna Mae!" Kathryn whispered. Hate throttled her voice. "How dare she?"

Boatman filled the basement door, deliberately barring her way. "Ma'am, take it easy," he warned, trying to restrain her with his hands.

Even Boatman was pushing her around. It was the final humiliation for Kathryn. "You goddam black bastard!" she screamed as she fumbled in her purse for her gun. "Get the hell out of my way."

At the sight of the gun, Boatman started moving backward down the stairs. Kathryn pushed and struggled past him. "I'll kill that woman!" she threatened. "How dare she show her face around here again after all she done!"

Boatman followed her down the steps into the darkness. "Miss Kathryn," he urged, "Miss Kathryn!"

But Kathryn hesitated at the bottom of the stairs only long enough to steady the gun in her hands before rushing into the Robert's flat.

The laughter was finished. The children's faces blanched grey. Randy hid behind her Auntie Mae and Charlene grabbed her arm for protection.

Kathryn waved her pistol in their faces and shouted at Anna Mae, "How dare you come into my house again? How dare you? Get out, goddam you, get out!"

But Anna Mae stood firm in the middle of the little room. And her eyes said to Kathryn defiantly there was nothing anybody could do or say would move her out of that basement flat while she had charge of her sister's children.

In the silence, the baby began to whimper and then to cry with a thin catlike wail. Kathryn's hand was shaking and the muzzle of the gun danced around out of her control. "You think I'm afraid to shoot?"

"Miss Kathryn—" Behind her, Boatman's eyes peered out of the darkness as he kept repeating, "Miss Kathryn, Miss Kathryn!"

Finally Anna Mae said in the professional tone she used for dealing with mental patients, "You'd best put that back in your hand bag, Miss Biomchi."

But her calmness made Kathryn lash herself into a new frenzy and yell out a string of insults, "You started all the trouble, you whore. You got to sass everybody around. You got to be the boss. You turned my own son against me. All the things I wanted—finished! The Lord's gonna punish you, Anna Mae Green—"

In the same calm voice Anna Mae repeated, "You best put that gun away, Miss Biomchi, before something terrible happens."

"I got the law on my side," Kathryn shouted on the defensive. The louder she shouted, the less strength she felt. In a moment the gun would slip from her fingers. Her knees were weak. She would fall to the floor at the feet of Anna Mae Green.

"You won't get out?" she pleaded desperately. Her heart was pounding at the walls of her chest. She closed her eyes and pulled the trigger.

The shot passed over Anna Mae's head through the basement window. The glass came tinkling down on the stove.

Anna Mae was still standing in the middle of the room unhurt. "Don't let her fear you none," she said to Charlene. "Now, Miss Biomchi, you gonna leave me mind the babies till my sister comes home."

"Never," said Kathryn drawing back as if Anna Mae might spring on her. "Never!" She tried to steady her gun again.

In an instant, Anna Mae shoved the kids to the floor and herself leaped up on the bed where she stood reaching up to the top shelf.

Now Kathryn was terrified to death. She knew Anna Mae kept her own protection on the shelf above the bed. It was her or Anna Mae now. Kathryn tried to steady her hand to aim. But the gun raced round in circles.

She shot and shot again and shot and shot until there were no bullets left. She saw Anna Mae grab her shoulder and wheel around on the bed with a gun in her hand.

At the same instant a final shot burst in Kathryn's ears and in her heart and in her whole body. She felt as if somebody had kicked her in the belly. There was no strength left in her knees. She pitched forward on the floor still pressing her finger on the trigger of her empty gun.

"Luigi," she sobbed out in terror. "Oh, my son!"

#13

Upstairs, Lil and Mrs. Osborne were joking with Jesse about how Bianchi was going to cut down the rent. When they heard the first shot, Jesse's shoulders drew together. From habit he was ready to hit the floor. "Car backfiring?" he shrugged.

Mrs. Osborne went on with what she was saying, "She'll cut down the rent when that old judge tell her to—not before. Then you gonna hear some hollerin'."

"Sure looks that way," said Jesse, "for all that her boy said she was through with the rent business."

"We'll know Monday, if she don't evict the lot of us first," said Lil dismissing the whole question. "Now, Ernestine, you get your pa his supper before the man starves to death. And Jess, come on, tell us about the job."

"He got me the job," said Jesse simply. "That's about it."

"Bianchi's boy?" Like Anna Mae, Mrs. Osborne couldn't believe it. "There's an old rat in it somewhere."

Doors were opening in the corridors. There was a stir and shuffle of feet below.

"Seems like what the old lady do," Jesse muttered as he opened the door to listen, "don't always set right with Lou. He got a mind of his own, that man."

A racket of gunshots roared up the stairway. Then a final shot, louder than the rest, reverberated through the house.

Jesse hit the stairs on the run. Tenants were crowding the doors on the second and first floors as he plunged down. He caught blurred sight of Mr. Martin's white hair and anxious face. On the basement steps he met Boatman coming up. They blocked each other for an instant.

"Tell me, man, what's the score?" Jesse grabbed Boatman by the shoulder. "You done something bad?"

Boatman looked at Jesse with eyes large and full of terror in the darkness. "For Christ's sake, soldier—" Then he twisted out of Jesse's grip, doubled back down the stairs and, battering the door open with his shoulder, broke into one of the front rooms.

Jesse heard a window crash and a woman scream out as Boatman made his getaway.

In the Roberts' flat, the children were crying hysterically. Jesse could hear Charlene above the rest, "Auntie Mae, Auntie Mae!" People were pressing down the stairs as he rushed into the room.

Lou's mother was lying on the floor, face down, moaning. She was still holding a revolver in her outstretched hand. Anna Mae was sitting on the bed holding her shoulder. Her gun was resting in her lap.

"She started the shootin'?" Jesse shouted.

"You ask?" Anna Mae was wild with indignation and pain. "Get a doctor, Jesse. I'm hurtin' bad and I'm afraid she's done for. For Jesus' sake—"

Jesse stepped over Kathryn to reach the door. A trickle of blood was gathering into a pool near her breast. She was heaving and groaning with pain. He could hear her breath drawn in agony as she moaned, "Where's my Luigi? Get my boy."

Jesse pushed his way upstairs through the crowd to the Martin's flat. "Call the doctor, any doctor. Anna Mae's hit bad. I got to tell Bianchi it looks like his ma's washed up."

Boatman had disappeared by the time Jesse ran out into the street. It was only then Jesse thought of the seriousness for Anna Mae. If Kathryn passed, Anna Mae could burn for it. Why the hell hadn't he kept hold of Boatman, the only witness beside the children?

Jesse drove only a block up the street before he met Lou who was already on the way to meet his mother. "Lou, you gotta come quick. Your ma's been hurt bad."

"How bad?"

"I dunno yet."

"I should have gone with her when she asked me," Lou muttered as if he'd been afraid something terrible would happen.

"Anna Mae was only defending herself," Jesse tried to explain. It was clear as day to him that Kathryn shot first. In a world which was always dishing out trouble to a person whose color was black, Anna Mae wasn't going to take the first step. Besides, her gun was on the shelf above the bed. And Kathryn's was handy in her purse. But once Kathryn started shooting, Anna Mae wasn't the type to stand around for a free target.

"You seen what happened?" Lou asked.

Jesse shook his head. "Mrs. Green told me."

As they approached the house, Jesse sensed a great change in his friend. Lou's eyes avoided him, but they were beady and hostile. "By God, if anything's happened to my ma—" Lou's jaw set with a terrible firmness.

Jesse led the way down into the basement.

Lou's heart began to burn like a lump of hot lead on the floor of his chest. He dropped down on his knees beside his mother. With a sudden movement, he tried to take her in his arms.

"Best leave her be," Jesse warned. "We called the doctor."

The groaning of his mother and the pool of blood at her breast unnerved Lou. He turned savagely toward Anna Mae. In his eyes was a lynch hatred. Then he looked up at Jesse accusingly. "Defending herself!" he spat out.

In the first instant, Jesse was surprised at Lou the way he turned on Anna Mae blinded to what really happened. "For God's sake, Anna Mae didn't do it!" Jesse's anger rose almost beyond his control. "Lou, you got to understand."

Two cops came on the double down the basement stairs. "Nobody leaves," the white cop ordered. The Negro cop grabbed Jesse's arm as if he was trying to run out. Then he recognized him. "Not so fast, soldier-boy!"

Dr. Thomasello and two detectives from the homicide squad arrived a moment later. The doctor bent over Kathryn to begin his examination. Then Pete pushed his way through the crowd into the basement room.

One of the detectives confronted Anna Mae Green. "Tell us exactly what happened."

"Anything you say they can hold against you," Jesse warned.

"You shut up till you're asked." The detective motioned to the cops to pull Jesse back in the corner.

"What you bothering that man for?" Anna Mae's voice went up indignantly. "He ain't had no part in it."

"We'll make the decisions around here." The detectives moved closer to Anna Mae, his face and shoulders looming over her. He had chalk-blue, sarcastic eyes, a battering ram of a forehead. "Now listen, sister, talk." His voice banged like a hammer.

Anna Mae sat up proudly, even if the pain was great. "I ain't got nothing to hide," she said. Her face was grey and drained of blood. "But I need the doctor, too." She looked down at the hand with which she was holding her shoulder. Blood was seeping between her fingers. She told the detective how Kathryn had come to the door with a gun and ordered her to leave the place. But she couldn't leave because she was minding the babies for her sister and brother. "I got my own protection, too. It ain't no world for a black woman 'less she knows—"

"Never mind the philosophy," the detective hammered at her. "Who started the shooting?"

"My gun was up on the shelf, inside that magazine. Who do you think?"

"Answer my question."

Anna Mae wasn't going to let him browbeat her. "Miss Biomchi," she said after a deliberate pause. "Ask her the questions."

The detective grabbed the gun from Anna Mae's lap. "You shot her with this?" He waved the pistol threateningly a few inches from her face.

"When I felt the pain in my shoulder—" Anna Mae began to explain what happened, but he cut her off.

"Got any witnesses?"

"The babies."

"I mean grown."

"Boatman." Anna Mae explained who he was. "He ran out of here like a scairt rabbit." And then she began to complain, "You want me to bleed to death?"

It was only then with Jesse shouting, "Get her a doctor, get her to the hospital, for the Lord's sake," that one of the policemen began to help Anna Mae up out of the basement.

"California Street," he heard the detective order. They didn't believe Anna Mae's story that she was innocent. And they would drive her all across town to the jail hospital before they would begin to treat her—if she didn't die on the way.

In the meantime Dr. Thomasello had put a compress on Kathryn's wound and had her raised to the bed. She was too badly hurt to be moved from the basement flat. The doctor indicated to the detective with a gesture under his heart that she had an internal hemorrhage.

With a sudden snap at his wrist, Jesse found the plainclothesman had handcuffed him to his own wrist. "Come on, you," he said roughly.

"What you putting the wrist bands on me for, officer?"

"You seem to know all about it. Now come along." The detectives took Jesse and the children out with them, pushed the crowd back and closed the door. A baby's wail filled the corridor.

When the room was cleared, Lou and Pete sat by the bedside while Dr. Thomasello stood looking at Kathryn with his hands behind his back.

It was a poor place to die in, with the bed crowded against the kitchen stove and the walls sweating with damp heat and the smells of the toilet deadening the air they breathed.

"We gotta get her out of here," said Lou.

The doctor shook his head. "Not safe to move her." He stared at Kathryn with a flicker of a smile, a strange fatalistic grimace without humor. "If she pulls through the next twenty-four-hours, then—" The doctor shrugged. He couldn't put belief in his own words. "In the meantime, I'll get a trained nurse. But on no account move her."

He went out promising to be right back. His steps haunted the basement stairway with a whispering echo.

It was terrible in that place of all places. It was hell on earth for his mother. She deserved something better if she had to die. The agony of Lou's own nights of torture came back to him, the fever and the nightmares after his accident on the road down from the Yalu River. He took his mother's hand quietly and gripped it as if he would never let her go.

Her face was flushed now with fever that brought a little blood to her cheeks. Green and haunted and deep, her eyesockets were like cavities in a skull and the flesh of her face so eaten away from within by greed and fear that there was nothing but yellow wrinkled skin drawn over her bones. Oh God, why hadn't he come with her when she asked him? Why had he been so bullheaded? His mother had worn out her life slaving for him and the family. Now there was nothing left of her but this terribly brittle frame of skin and bone struggling in a last agony.

When she opened her eyes finally, it was to stare at Lou and cry out in terror, "Holy Mother of God! Take him away! He wants to kill his own mother!"

And as she turned to Pete, she screamed with an equal terror, "No more children! Can't you understand? It's enough!" Then she began to mutter hoarsely to herself, "Carlo's a no-good. Georgi went away. Luigi came back from the wars, but it wasn't my Luigi any more." Then she whispered with a little hope, "Where's Della?"

"I go call her," said Pete slipping out quietly. He couldn't bear to listen to her ravings.

"My head's blowing up like a firecracker," Kathryn moaned. "My heart's busting out—" She began to cry. "Take me out of here. It's dark. It stinks like a toilet." Lou glanced wildly around the room at the sweating walls and the stain of his mother's blood on the floor.

"Luigi, Luigi! Why did you leave me all alone so that black bastard—" Kathryn began to rave about Anna Mae in a hoarse whisper. "She'll burn for it!" There was a terrible glee in her eyes as she gloated. "Promise me?"

"Ma!" was all he could say at first. Why should anybody die? "Ma, you're gonna be all right."

"Oh, Luigi! Everything I did was for you." She was shaking her head feebly. "Now it's finished."

"Try to sleep, ma." he said quietly.

"I couldn't help myself," she whispered as if his face was blurring away from her and she was staring into space. "Holy Mother of God, forgive me what I done!"

At last Pete came back. "Della be right over," he said aloud, but he whispered to Lou very quietly, "She's gonna call the priest."

Kathryn smiled a little at Pete. "My Pete—we go back home to Valone—one day—" There was nothing left of her voice but a terrible hoarseness in her throat. "Back home—" What she tried to say then was stifled. Her lips only went on moving. She choked, clutched at her throat, struggled to draw another breath, but the stubborn life went out of her and her hand lay quiet in her son's hand.

PART FIVE

#1

The empty house was filled with the sound of Pete's grieving. "She wanta go home, back to the old country—" the old man was crying with his fists screwed into his eyes.

In the last moment of her life, Kathryn had forgotten the things that had divided her from Pete. "You understand, son? She said she wanta go back home. To hell with Anselmo! That's what she meant."

"I know, I know, pa," Lou whispered hoarsely. He had never heard his father cry before.

"Too late." Pete nodded mechanically with the chime of the clock striking twelve. His eyes went up to the face of Saint Joseph on the yellow parchment which he and Kathryn had brought with them from Valone. It was a long time ago.

"I can't tell you, boy, how she talk. Valone, sleep on the floor. That's for rats and dogs." He imitated her scolding tone with an angry shake of his head. "When we can go back home, she don't want. 'We stay in Chicago, you old fool! Live on easy street like Anselmo. Feed the ducks by Lincoln Park, eh?' There ain't no ducks back home?"

"Pa—" But there was no stopping the rush of his father's grief.

"For two coats, can you believe it? Hates colored, your ma, Luigi. All bawl out, get mad—" Pete spoke as if Kathryn were still alive and hating. He rocked back and forth in agony because of the quarrels that had flared up between them.

"She listen to Anselmo, your ma, son." Pete stood up to shake his fists hysterically at the ceiling. "All hate and shoot," he yelled. "Gonna pay the rent or throw you out. Anselmo says carry gun in her purse!" Anselmo had become the boss of Pete's house. Anselmo had divided husband from wife with his big shot ideas.

Anselmo had brought down their life in ruins. "All Anselmo—" Pete held his hands out helplessly and sank back in his chair.

"But, pa, before she went over the hill—" Lou began.

"Too late now," Pete cut him off. "What the hell? Too late, Luigi. Never go back home now."

In the emptiness of the house, a terrible vaccum sucked at Lou's heart and brain. Only a few hours before, his mother was setting his supper out on the table for him. She hardly greeted him. Her eyes were red from crying. She bent her head over her work in an attitude of despair. And then she asked him with a kind of desperation to go with her. But he wouldn't listen.

"If I'd only gone with her, pa—" Lou's clenched hands beat on the kitchen table with anger at himself. He had let his ma slip away from him, take her shawl down from the hook, and follow Boatman into the alley without doing anything to stop her. When he saw her next, she was lying face down at the feet of Anna Mae Green. The woman was sitting on the bed with the pistol in her lap. She stared up at Lou defiantly. She didn't seem sorry for what she'd done. She had a grim look of satisfaction as if she'd taken her revenge and was glad. And all the time, Lou's mother lay at her feet on the floor, dying.

Could Jesse actually believe that Anna Mae was only defending herself?

"She's gonna pay for it, pop," said Lou. But Pete was buried too deep in his own grief for thoughts of revenge. "Anselmo told me they're booking her for murder."

As soon as he arrived with Della, Anselmo had wasted no time in drawing Lou out into the basement corridor. Della was moaning at her mother's bedside while Father Antonelli consoled her, "There is no cause to grieve. Your mother will be a saint in heaven." The coroner's physician was just beginning his examination.

"Lou-boy, I know it's a great shock—" Anselmo's voice was soothing at first like the priest's "—but you got to pull yourself together for your ma's sake." Anselmo's tone grew harsh and explosive. "The detective says it's murder." Anselmo's cigar burned fiercely in the dark. It filled the basement with an expensive incense. "Do you think your Jesse Williams was in any way involved? He tried to resist arrest!"

"Jesse?" Lou shied away from the question. "He came right up to get me. How could he?"

"Things aren't always the way they seem," Anselmo insinuated.

"Why did they nab him?" Lou asked.

"What exactly did he tell you?" Anselmo countered.

"That Mrs. Green was only defending herself."

"Very clever," Anselmo sneered. "That's all I want to know." He put his arm around Lou's shoulder. "You take Della and your pa home, fellow. And I'll go over to the police station. We'll make the guilty ones pay for this, don't you worry." He handed Lou the keys to his car.

"But Anselmo," Lou insisted, "I know Jesse didn't have nothing to do with it."

"That's up to the police now. They've taken it out of our hands."

At the vindictiveness in Anselmo's tone, Lou began to have all kinds of doubts. He even wondered how Anselmo could be so sure of what had happened. His ma's words came back to disturb his own certainty.

"They're sure this Mrs. Green started it?"

"Lou, get hold of yourself." Anselmo gripped him by the shoulder and shook him. "You couldn't believe your ma would shoot first. This woman's a savage!"

"But right at the end my ma said, 'Holy Mother of God, forgive me what I done.' "

"Of course, of course. Can't you understand? That's our religion. Nobody wants to kick the bucket without having their sins forgiven first."

Lou wanted to be convinced, though he had no trust in Anselmo. When he remembered how his ma had said, "She'll burn for it. Promise me?" then his doubts died away.

"Besides, Lou," Anselmo went on in a tone respectful of the dead, "your mother was very human. She hated to hurt anybody, you know that. But she had to defend herself."

When the coroner's physician finished his examination, the ambulance men came out of the basement room bearing a shrouded stretcher. Anselmo helped Della up the stairs and Lou followed with his father.

It seemed to Lou the old tenement was a wall of faces, his mother's tenants staring from every window and doorway. The cops had to push back the crowd in the street to make room for the stretcher bearers. There was neither grief nor happiness on the faces of the people who saw the ambulance door close, only silent wonder at the passing of Kathryn Bianchi.

The siren rasped with a little whirl of warning as the ambulance turned into the main thoroughfare and its taillight winked out beyond the corner store.

"I want to go with her," Della cried. "Gene, let me go with my mother."

But Anselmo lifted her into the front seat of his car. "Quick, Lou!" he ordered. "I'll be over soon."

Lou helped his father into Anselmo's car and slammed the door. They should let his ma go for the last time without all the staring. He glanced up angrily at the faces looking down from the windows. On the third floor he recognized Mrs. Osborne and the boy Jesse called Poke. And his anger began to die away.

There was no reason to blame them all for his mother's death. Anna Mae Green was the one. Even if she had been framed before, even if his ma knew Anselmo was framing her, that was no justification for shooting his ma down in cold blood.

But the cops had no business arresting Jesse. He was a straight guy. If he said the woman was only defending herself, he believed it even though he was making a terrible mistake. Lou was beginning to regret the way he'd lashed out at Jesse.

All the same, Anselmo had raised a suspicion of Jesse in Lou's mind. The guy wouldn't lie to him to save Anna Mae's neck. Or would he? Had Jesse seen the shooting and was trying to cover up for one of his own people?

At last the phone rang and Anselmo's voice was saying, "They haven't located that boy Boatman yet. But they're on his trail. Don't worry, Lou, we'll make the guilty ones pay for this. How's Della taking it?"

"Sleeping, I think," Lou told him. "Took some of the ma's sleeping pills."

"Be right over."

Lou pushed the telephone back on his ma's desk. One of her handkerchiefs, lying on the blotter where she'd left it, filled the air with the scent of summer flowers.

An official paper blurred white on the desk in front of Lou, a fragment of the summons ordering his ma to appear Monday in a triple damage suit in federal court. Lou remembered the thousand tiny pieces of paper his mother had torn up and scattered across her bedroom rug the day she promised to give up the rent business. It was only yesterday! He crumpled what was left of the summons in his fist and hurled it into the basket.

When Anselmo walked in as if the house belonged to him, he was already shaking his head at Lou. "Your Jesse, he's a bad actor."

Lou resented Anselmo's swagger and his arrogant tone as if Lou had committed a crime in the first place for buddying up with Jesse.

"He's a goddam stubborn son-of-a-bitch," Anselmo went on. "They questioned him for an hour. Still sticks to the same story."

"Maybe he believes it's the truth," Lou shot out at Anselmo who was pacing the room with his hands behind his back.

"Now let's get things straight around here—" Anselmo came over to where Lou was sitting at his mother's desk and grabbed him on the shoulder. But Lou twisted out of his grip and stood up to face him. "Before your ma got a place for your Jesse out of sympathy because he did you a good turn anybody else would have done, we didn't have trouble at 1250. These people generally don't dare stick up for themselves—till some troublemaker starts stirring them up. Maybe you don't know, but your Jesse drove the sister down to court to testify against your ma and he actually drove this Green woman home! After your ma got him a place to live and everything, still he double-crossed her. More I think of it, more I'm sure he's somewhere at the bottom of this." Anselmo pointed his finger at Lou as if he'd committed the sin of his life to make friends with Jesse.

"Now let me tell you something you know already, Gene," said Lou in a cold rage. "If you hadn't framed this Mrs. Green, my ma would be alive right now."

"Framed!" repeated Anselmo as if Lou had gone out of his mind. "Is that what your Jesse told you?"

"It ain't what Jesse told me, you goddam hypocrite. It's what you said yourself. That spiel about rackets and how the woman left us no choice!"

"Good God, Lou, how you twist things around!" Anselmo held his hands wide in a gesture of innocence. Then with deep concern he asked, "In that accident out there, Lou, did you have concussion?"

"Well, you son-of-a-bitch!" Lou stared at Anselmo as if he could kill him. "What I'm telling you is you framed the woman, so she took revenge on my ma."

"The only sense I make out of what you're saying," Anselmo sneered, "this savage was justified in murdering your mother." For a moment they stood staring at each other with blazing eyes. Anselmo was the first to speak. "She hated your ma, Lou. She's a vicious, vicious woman. Just figure it, a woman so bloodthirsty, so filled with spite, she laid a trap. Then shot your mother down in cold blood. It's one of the worst murders ever happened in this town. Read what the papers say!" Anselmo flung some clippings down on the sofa for Lou to read, then went over to Kathryn's desk as if it was his own and began to search through the drawers. "You should have heard the officer who went out to the Bridewell, Lou," Anselmo spoke over his shoulder. "All the things that woman said against your ma. I wouldn't repeat them. All a bunch of dirty, filthy lies, of course!" Anselmo was leafing through the papers now and making rapid calculations with a pencil on a pad. "It's hard to believe sometimes these people are human."

Slowly Lou bent to pick up the clippings. The papers had already built up a case against Anna Mae. The words danced before his eyes as he read about his mother's death. He remembered how Anna Mae had treated his ma the day she offered to lower the rent. He remembered the way her eyes went up to the shelf where she kept her gun.

"I wasn't defending the woman," Lou said quietly. "But Jesse's an OK guy. And you won't make him change his story if he believes what he says is true. You better let him go."

"You're too generous, Lou," said Anselmo. "You think everybody's like you. But the world's full of crooks and liars."

"I can believe that from you."

Anselmo appeared too busy with his figures to hear what Lou was saying. When he had finished calculating, he turned around to hand him a complicated series of additions and subtractions. "I just want you to see what the score is with the property. She borrowed ten grand to buy 1250. After interest and installments—well, you can see for yourself. I'll cancel the loan on 758 Hemlock Street, OK?"

The figures were meaningless to Lou. He handed the paper back wondering how Anselmo could be so much concerned about the money at a time like that. He hadn't even gone into the bedroom to find out how Della was taking it.

"Figure it out, Lou. With the balance we'll have Dan De Rocco arrange a funeral for your ma nobody in town will ever forget."

Then Anselmo opened the bedroom door. Della was lying on her mother's bed with her shoes on, dressed for dinner, with her diamonds at her throat and wrists. Her coral dress was crumpled about her like the feathers of a flamingo dead in a heap. The paleness of her face was shocking in the frame of her hair, still shining black and immaculate.

"She took it hard, poor kid!" Even Anselmo was moved to speak softly. "She thought the world of her ma."

He lifted her from the bed and carried her sideways through the front door. "Lou," he said in a brotherly way, "I was going to tell you I still have a job waiting for you any time you want to change your mind." Anselmo was already propping Della's arm and head over the front seat of his car when he called back, "But the way you talk makes it hard."

"I wouldn't take a job with you—" Lou began to shout. But Anselmo took off like a pilot at the controls of a jet bomber.

Step by step, Lou groped his way upstairs in the dark to his own room, haunted by the picture of Anselmo going through his mother's papers, the money hungry bastard, before she was decently buried. In the darkness and emptiness of his room, Lou could see his ma laid out in a casket at the funeral home as plainly as if he were standing by her side.

#2

There was no sleep for Lou that night or the night that followed. Sunday morning when the church bells began to ring over the city, he got up and went to early mass because he thought it was what his mother would want him to do.

Father Antonelli's voice, rising and falling with the intonations he had mastered in an eastern seminary, reminded Lou how his ma had wanted him to be a priest. She had hoped he would be a bishop, perhaps even a cardinal one day. Her ambition for him had been without bounds. But Lou had gone out to play ball and neglected his Latin.

The sun streamed down through the stained glass windows, through the body of Jesus on the Cross, and lit up the figure of Mary who was cradling her Child in the holy garden. A thousand memories of his mother and his own childhood came back to Lou, how she brought him to mass on a Sunday morning and to the bingo games in the church basement on a Wednesday night. He remembered how much she had enjoyed the home fiestas, the annual band parades honoring the saints, and the carnivals in the streets. He thought of his ma the way she was when he was a child with her dark hair and alert brown eyes, and he began to curse Anselmo and pray that God would punish him as well as Anna Mae Green.

The bells began to ring, and Lou was surprised to find himself almost alone in the church. Father Antonelli was coming down the aisle to greet him. "You are a man of courage, Lou Bianchi." The young priest gripped his hand. "I am sure the tragic death of your mother will not embitter but only strengthen you in friendship for your neighbor and love for your fellowman."

Father Antonelli held Lou's hand in his for a moment, then turned and walked slowly back toward the vestry. The bells reverberated through the empty church. Lou's step quickened. The sun was streaming in through the great door.

In the afternoon Nina came to his house. "I wanted to know if there was anything I could do to help you and pop." Lou was staring at her simple black dress as if she was a stranger. Her flaming hair was now a sober brown again. She hesitated to cross the doorstep. When Lou kept silent, she went on quickly to say, "I saw you at mass this morning. You didn't even look at me, Lou. I wanted to tell you how I felt about your ma. But you don't give me a chance—"

"What do you feel about her, Nina?" Lou asked in a very low voice.

"She was like a ma to me, my own ma, not only yours. She stood up for herself. Not like my ma letting the old man beat her up all the time. I guess I am just as stubborn as she was—or you. Don't want to get down on my knees." There was a cool distance between them. Lou's hands hung limp at his sides.

"What about Friday night?" he asked, a vacuum still sucking at his heart. "I seen Vico's car was parked out front under your window."

"You don't want to understand, Lou. You know he's in the bookie business with the old man—"

"You mean you weren't stepping out with him—"

"I wasn't stepping out with nobody! I put my best dress on for you when I saw you come into the tavern."

Lou could believe her the way she looked at him with her eyes full of spirit. "Come in, Nina," he finally said, opening the door wide for her.

"I can't live without you, Lou." She flung her arms around his neck, then began to cry. "My aunt's been telling me I should take the vows. All men are the same. But they're not. When I saw you this morning—"

Lou began to smile, "You, a nun?" and hugged her closer. "It don't make much sense, does it? I guess we both got a lot to learn."

#3

Two nights and a day dragged out endlessly for Jesse with his back a mass of bruises. But the worst torture was thinking about Anna Mae Green, how the Man was drawing the noose tight around her neck. Every time Jesse heard the bells of St. Joseph boom across the city and through the high grill into the lockup, it was a reminder that time was running out for her. If only he could bust out and find Boatman, things would be different.

The best Jesse could hope for now was that Boatman had made a clean getaway. If they caught up with him, he'd never stand up to their third degree. He'd already helped to frame on Anna Mae once. In a case like this he'd sign all the confessions they wanted, let them only raise their hose to his back or threaten to hang him from the plumbing in the basement. He was wanted in Carolina. They had him bound and gagged, half lynched already.

Besides, Boatman had no protection on the outside like Jesse. Jesse knew he couldn't win by force when two plainclothesmen had rolled up their sleeves and begun beating him over the back with rubber hose. They had him bound and handcuffed. But they'd picked the wrong guy to break down. "You better quit that," he yelled. "I'm gonna get my lawyer down here." The third man in the room who was in charge of forcing a confession began to show concern at the mention of a lawyer and raised his chin outward in a cease-fire order. He was a thin man, with close-set eyes and close-cropped hair and a smile that seemed to come and go beyond his control. Jesse had seen him in a huddle in the corridor with Anselmo. "My lawyer's name is Jefferson Wilkes. I'm asking you to call him." Jesse gave Wilkes' telephone number and address. "That's my right."

Jesse didn't put much stock in his legal rights, but he was sure Lil and Mrs. Osborne would put their heads together and call the lawyer. Or Geneva Roberts would think of it. One thing Jesse knew, they wouldn't rest till they got him out of jail.

After asking Jesse a few more questions, the thin man disappeared for a few minutes. When he came down into the basement again his nervous smile flashed on and off as he made a no-go sign with his hands to the two plaintlothesmen. Anselmo must have told them to lay off. Then they took Jesse upstairs again to the lockup. He thought he heard the thin man whisper, "We'll have to hold him till we get that other guy."

The pain in Jesse's back was like barbed wire pulling across his flesh and fire burning at the same time. Hour by hour was measured out in vast intervals by the bells at St. Joseph's. Finally, the second night paled out at the square window and the everlasting flies began to drone in and out through the high bars. It was Sunday morning and the church bells began to ring over the city.

And at long last, when the day was already like a hundred days in one, a sergeant unlocked the door and took off the handcuffs. "Get your ass out of here, fellow," he ordered, "on the double!"

Lil was downstairs waiting for him, and with her was Jefferson Wilkes, thin in the face and sad-eyed as if he had more problems than he could work out in a week of Sundays.

"Seems like they didn't want to let you go, soldier," he said in his dry sarcastic voice. "I'll drive you home." In the car Wilkes could tell Jesse the whole story. "They wanted to keep you in jail till after the inquest."

In the back seat of the car, Lil who was not much of a crying woman had to hide her face on Jesse's shoulder. "Thank God!" Jesse winced away from her hand on his back. "They beaten you? That's what I was afraid of, Jess. Those scum!"

"That's the Man for you, while he got the hose. Kids OK?"

"Waiting for you, Jess. We all been waiting a long time." In the mirror Wilkes was studying Jesse, how he drew away from Lil when she put her arm around him. "Third degree, eh?" he muttered.

"They roughed me up some." Jesse tried to laugh it off. "Wanted to change my mind about things. They wanted me to say Anna Mae pulled her gun first. How's she doing?"

"Doing fine," said Wilkes, "considering it was a nasty wound and the fact they took her across town to the Bridewell before patching her up." Wilkes got out a dry kind of bitterness when he wanted to scrape the bottom of the barrel.

"They caught up with that boy, Boatman?"

"Yes, that's just the trouble. They brought him in this morning. Now about this inquest tomorrow—" Wilkes was a man to get down to essentials without wasting time on details. Besides, it was his Sunday off and he wanted to spend part of it with his own family. "Boatman will say what they want. The police charge is murder. The press have cooperated by throwing all the blame on Mrs. Green. That Anselmo wants to make an example of her. Remember, he owns a lot of property around this neighborhood. He'll fight like a tiger to get a conviction tomorrow from the coroner's jury. He'll throw some money around—"

"But how can they prove she did it?" Lil objected.

"Proof and evidence are two different things," said the lawyer drily. He went on to explain how the mechanics of the inquest would work against Anna Mae. And even though she herself would get a chance to speak, her testimony would carry very little weight with the jury. The children would not be allowed to testify. The jury would come to a decision, therefore, almost entirely on Boatman's testimony. And the jury would be all white.

It was a gloomy picture. Jesse cursed himself for letting Boatman slip through his fingers.

"But Mr. Wilkes, what happens then?" Lil asked.

"If the coroner's jury brings in a verdict of murder, then the case goes to the states attorney, grand jury, and finally criminal court." Lil sighed deeply, "It don't seem she has a chance." She was overwhelmed at the prospect of all the legal machinery grinding out an inevitable verdict against Anna Mae.

"What you gonna do, Mr. Wilkes?" Jesse was putting him on the spot in a belligerent way. Lil's fatalism didn't go down with him.

"Fight it all the way." Wilkes smiled the first time since Jesse's release from the police station. "You're going to help me, Mr. Williams."

"How?" asked Jesse simply.

"First, you better get Mrs. Williams to put some salve on that back of yours. Then, how about talking to young Bianchi?"

Jesse shook his head slowly. "You know that lynch look, Mr.

Wilkes. That's the way he looked at Anna Mae, then at me, when he seen his ma lyin' on the floor."

"Still, it's our best bet." Wilkes went on to tell Jesse how, after the cops took him to the station, Mrs. Martin heard Lou talking with his mother before she passed. The chances were she must have told her son what happened.

"Won't do no harm, Jess." Lil followed what Wilkes was saying with a little hope growing up again for Anna Mae.

"I understand from Mrs. Williams that this Lou Bianchi is not a prejudiced type. You buddied up overseas. He helped you get a job in a plant where none of our people are employed. But the most unusual thing I get from Mrs. Williams—let's not play it short—is that he wanted his mother to rent you the flat upstairs in his own home. He told you that down in San Antonio?" Jesse nodded. "Well, Mr. Williams, considering the type she was, the boy has some guts."

Jesse nodded again. "I'll be thinking about it." Wilkes was already turning into Pioneer Street when Jesse went on to ask him, "With all these things stacked up, how you work it to get me out of the lockup?"

"They wanted to keep you in bad." Wilkes winked at Jesse in the mirror. "But yesterday after your wife called me, I found out from the neighbors which way they took you. At the station, they'd never heard tell of Jesse Williams. But I had a pretty good hunch to tell the captain I was counsel for the NAACP. When they know folks on the outside are likely to start hollering, especially when we got a few whites with us—to cut a long story short, the captain managed to locate you this morning exactly where you'd been all the time since Friday night."

Jesse and Lil stepped out into a welcoming crowd. "You'll call me if you get to see the boy?" Wilkes shouted as he drove off. "And bring all the folks to the inquest tomorrow."

Friends and neighbors and his own kids surrounded Jesse. He was more a hero coming back from the police station a mile away than from Korea the other side of the world.

"Hey, Jesse, they beaten you?" Charles Roberts was asking. Everybody was talking excitedly at the same time. "Take your wallet?" "What they done to Boatman?" "They tryin' to burn that Anna Mae?"

"You wanta help *her*," Jesse said, "you better come on along to the inquest tomorrow." He made his way through the crowd, a big man with a serious smile. "We gotta take off from work, and we all gonna go out there together."

#4

The dust rose like a cloud across the low sun as Jesse crossed the park. On a Sunday afternoon, ball teams were playing on both diamonds. The shouting and cheering went skyhigh. And in the corner of the park behind the railings, Joe and William and the rest of the old timers from Sicily were playing boche ball.

But Jesse's thoughts were grim and his eyes fixed ahead. He had to drag his feet across the park toward the Bianchi's. For two days and nights, Lou couldn't have raised a finger to get him out of the lockup. Lou must have known the cops would beat him up to try to get a confession. He'd been raised in the neighborhod and knew the score by this time, Jesse was sure, Boatman had signed the testimony they wanted. The Man was drawing the noose tighter around the neck of Anna Mae. Wilkes was right, the only hope left was for Jesse to see Lou and try to talk some sense into him before the inquest.

Lou's girl opened the door, her eyes leaping with suspicion as she recognized Jesse. "I gotta see Lou," he said.

Nina narrowed the door. "He's busy right now."

In the hostile silence Jesse could hear Lou at the phone. He could see him bent like a shadow over his mother's desk. "I'll wait," said Jesse.

"Why don't you leave him alone?" Nina whispered with a hatred that left Jesse in no doubt. She believed he was an accomplice. Anselmo must have won Lou over too.

"Miss Pagliani, you don't want somebody innocent—?"

Jesse's tone was quiet but insistent.

"Who are you talking about?" she interrupted him.

"Mrs. Green."

"Innocent?" Nina raised her voice in a cry of pain. "She shot Lou's ma."

"But she was defending herself."

"It was a terrible thing to do."

"It's a terrible thing to burn a woman in the electric chair for a crime she ain't committed."

"But this Boatman seen it all. Anselmo just told me on the phone. They caught up with him and he admitted everything."

"You believe a man they beaten?" Jesse raised his voice loud enough for Lou to hear.

"Why don't you leave him alone?" Nina shouted back. She heard the receiver click and the floorboards creak behind her. "Tell him to go away, Lou. The nerve!"

But Lou came to the door. His face was pasty white. He looked more gone than that night on the Yalu Road when Jesse and the other fellows dragged him out of the wreckage of the six-by. "Ain't no use, Jesse." Lou's hand clutched and unclutched the doorknob. "This Boatman's told the whole story."

"I ain't gonna let you duck out on me now," Jesse said, "after the long piece of road we come together." Jesse put his hand on Lou's shoulder and roughed him up in a friendly way. "And I ain't duckin' out on you, neither." Lou stepped back and Jesse came into the front room. "Why you figure they put the cufflinks on me, taken the rubber hose—"

"They beat you up?"

Jesse nodded. "Lou, honest, tell me the truth. Do you think I was mixed in on this?"

"I ain't blaming you for no part of it," said Lou.

"But the way you looked at me—down in the basement. Like you'd soon as not put a rope around my neck—"

"I was mad at her, not you." And then Lou began to get excited. "Jesus Christ, she's gonna hafta pay—"

But Jesse interrupted him. "You wouldn't believe me when I told you what happened. Now you believe this Boatman when you know they taken the back off him and he framed on her before."

"If she's innocent like you say," Lou's voice sliced thin and accusing, "why did she shoot to kill when my ma only hit her in the shoulder?"

"Did you see where that bullet clipped Mrs. Green?" Jesse insisted.

Lou didn't know. He put his hand over his temple as if he didn't want to think about it.

"In the back of the shoulder, Lou."

"You want me to believe my own ma was a killer?" Again Lou's face was full of anger and hate the way he'd looked at Anna Mae when he first saw his mother sprawled at her feet.

"You know the difference between the sound of a twenty-two and a thirty-two—" Jesse began.

"What the hell's that got to do with it?" Lou cut him off.

"Plenty. I heard six shots from a twenty-two. Then one from a thirty-two—that was Anna Mae's gun. Your ma shot first."

"But you didn't see the shootin'?"

"I heard it. I was right upstairs. And I saw the rods. So did you."

Lou looked at Jesse as if he couldn't believe he was telling the truth, but only trying to shield Anna Mae Green from the punishment she had coming to her. As though dazed, his eyes wavered away from Jesse's.

"Why don't you go now?" Nina, who had been standing grim and white faced behind him, stepped forward to blaze at Jesse. "Can't you see what you're doing to him? It was his own mother, for Christ's sake!"

"I ain't got nothing more to say." Lou turned away from Jesse and started groping his way up the stairs, as though in a daze. "If she did it, they gotta give her the works. If she didn't, it'll all come out at the inquest tomorrow."

"We ain't babies yet," Jesse shouted fiercely up after him. And when Lou turned back surprised, Jesse's temper let go on him. "I thought you had more sense'n that. You know what happens to my people. Out there you told sergeant Snakeface where the hell to get off. And you yourself, remember what you said that last night, 'I thought it was bad enough bein' a goddam, dago. But I never listened in on what you guys have to put up with.' And when we got back home you invited me to your homecoming party and you put up an argument like nobody's business to get me a job as machinist. You can't go all the way back down the hill on me now. A guy gotta stand up for the things he knows even when he's hurtin'. You know that. That's the kind of guy you always been."

"But my ma wouldn't do a thing like that," Lou said in a mechanical way as if he couldn't rightly listen to what Jesse was saying.

"Why you think they slap the cufflinks on Anna Mae and drag her off to the Bridewell? Why they talk in the papers already like she done it? She's black, that's why. That's her crime, Lou."

"It ain't she's colored," Lou came back at Jesse like he was way off the beam. "It's because she done a crime."

"You believe that, then?" Jesse shook his head as if there was no further use talking. "My race of people's guilty," he muttered "till they prove theirselves innocent. That's the Man's law when you got a black skin. But I thought you was a guy could see it different."

Lou kept on shaking his head as if Jesse had him all wrong.

"Your brother-in-law got you gagged up and tied like he had your ma, Lou. He's got you one hundred percent right here." Jesse closed his fist angrily. "Why don't you open your eyes, man? He's stacked all the cards in the deck."

"I told you more than once he's a son-of-a-bitch," said Lou as angry as Jesse.

"And I'll tell you he's selling you and me down the river," Jesse shouted. "And Anna Mae. Because she sticks up for herself, he wants her out of the way. You think he worries about your ma?" Jesse shook his head. "He's number one, understand? He's the bossman. He pushed her into doing those things against Ana Mae. Then your ma got afraid, toted a gun around in her purse because she done crooked things. And when Anna Mae wouldn't get the hell out Friday night, your ma went crazy. She couldn't help herself—"

Lou was astonished to hear Jesse say the very words his ma had used. "I couldn't help myself." For an instant, Lou's face lit up with an expression of understanding. His eyes brightened. "That's what the ma said."

"Then you know—" said Jesse with a sudden burst of hope.

"I know what she said." Lou's eyes sank away from Jesse's again. "But I don't know what she meant. I don't know. I just don't know."

For a long time Lou sat on the landing of the stairs clasping and unclasping his hands in uncertainty.

"It's a woman's life, Lou!" Jesse urged. He could hear the old clock on the kitchen strike five times.

"But she hated my ma, Jesse. Can't you get that into your head? She shot to kill."

Nina who had been waiting with her hand on the door knob directed Jesse to leave with a toss of her head. "What's the good going over and over it. Can't you see—"

"Ain't no good," Jesse muttered bitterly. Anselmo had twisted Lou around his little finger while he was dazed by his mother's death and suffering from the shock.

Jesse glanced back at the Bianchi house as he crossed the park. Lou's face, white and remote, was watching him from the upstairs window.

Then the roll of thunder made Jesse quicken his step in the opposite direction. Against the clouds to the south, skyscrapers rose up like a vast irregular roof. And highest of all on the skyline, Anselmo's building raised its finger of authority.

As Jesse stared up with anger in heart and fist against Anselmo and the pain of rubber hose on his back, he could see a thunder cloud rearing a mushroom of vapors over the city a thousand times larger than the Board of Trade Building.

"The Man gonna fall down on his face one day," Jesse muttered, "and nobody gonna help pick up the pieces."

#5

The pain of Lou's injuries in Korea was as nothing to the torture of the inquest.

The room was warm and heavy with an atmosphere that weighed on the lungs with a smell of disinfectant. The walls were bare of ornament and the stained woodwork was dark as a tomb. The oak seats with their vertical backs were like pews in an old church.

People moved soundlessly as in a dream. The friends and neighbors of Anna Mae Green filled one side of the room. Jesse was there and his wife and the two little Roberts girls with their red ribbons moving like butterflies and the Martins and Mrs. Osborne and a crowd more. Lou wondered if they all could believe Anna Mae was innocent.

On his own side of the room, across an aisle that divided like a chasm, Lou sat among his own folks: Nina on one side and his father on the other, Della next, and Carlo and his wife, Margaret. In the seat behind with old Pagliani sat Father Guidarello and Father Antonelli, also Mrs. Santiani and Nellie De Rocco, and behind them friends and neighbors from Hemlock Street.

When Lou nodded across the aisle, Jesse's eyes met his with the hardness of granite. The previous evening as Lou had watched Jesse cross the park, his uncertainty had grown enormous like the storm cloud mushrooming over the city. In the oppressive atmosphere he had heard the bells of St. Joseph's ring out a warning to his conscience. A woman's life rang in, rang out with the toll of the big bell.

And now this woman sat in the defendant's seat in the inquest room watching the old men of the jury take their place across from her under the windows, while over their heads carrion flies buzzed in and out on their eternal mission.

Time was running out for Anna Mae Green. If she was guilty—but she *was* guilty, Lou insisted to himself. Sitting there on the bed with the thirty-two caliber pistol in her lap. Arrogant. Proud of what she'd done. Lou's ma lying at her feet, bleeding to death.

But Jesse said she was shot in the back, she was innocent.

Through a mist Lou stared at three scratches on his arm. In an uncontrollable rage, his own ma had dug her nails into his flesh.

She couldn't help herself.

Lou's head sank down on his arm until the scratches blurred together.

Jesse said Anselmo had stacked all the cards in the deck. Lou wondered if it was true. In the corridor, Lou had heard Anselmo whisper to Vico that the coroner's deputy who would preside over the inquest was a college friend of his. Anselmo had laughed cynically. And when Anna Mae was escorted past them by a cop and a policewoman, Anselmo sneered, "See what a cruel bitch she is!"

Anselmo was confident of winning a verdict against her. He gloated when Boatman passed them into the inquest room. Only one thing had crossed him up. When he tried to draw Jefferson Wilkes aside for a private conversation, the Negro lawyer had brushed past him. Vico had laughed cynically this time and said to Lou, "One boy without a price tag."

"The inquest will come to order—" Lou raised his head at the sound of the deputy's voice. It was the voice of an educated man, mellow and bored with his job.

The coroner's deputy was a thinner man than Anselmo with more regular features and a milder manner. But he wore the same kind of ring on the same kind of hands. And his complexion was the same color of whiskey pink as if he too was a morning drinker. He wore the same kind of tailored blue suit and reserved grey tie. And his cufflinks, like Anselmo's, were the size of silver dollars.

The deputy called first for the report of the detective from the homicide squad and then for the statement signed by Boatman. With a terrible fascination, Lou watched the deputy examine the weapon which ended his mother's life.

If Lou had only gone with his ma when she asked him, he could have protected her. When Della began to cry, he had to squeeze his head between his fists. To think of it was the worst torture. After all his ma had done for him all his life, he had turned her down.

In the midst of his self-accusation, Lou was startled to hear Jesse whisper fiercely, "Why don't you tell the truth, man? You wanta hang Anna Mae?"

Jesse's words were intended for Boatman who sat directly ahead of him in the front row of seats between two cops. But like a slap in the face, they shocked Lou out of his morbid reflections.

He watched Boatman sag forward to take the witness stand. He heard him swear to tell the truth. And he cursed him out quietly for not protecting his mother. A man of Boatman's chest and arm development could have stopped a fight between two women if he'd wanted to.

"You are sure, absolutely sure, the defendant, Mrs. Green, was the first to shoot?" The deputy questioned Boatman with the smile of a father trying to get the truth out of a teenage son. "Remember," he waved his finger pleasantly enough, "her life may depend on your answer."

Boatman leaned forward in his chair to nurse his cheeks between his hands. Sullen and fearful, his eyes were fixed on Anselmo who sat almost directly across the table from him. Above him loomed the deputy's face and across from him beneath the windows sat the six white men of the coroner's jury. Over their heads, the flies buzzed in and out the windows.

Boatman hesitated a long time. There was a stir on Jesse's side of the room, a shifting of position, a general restlessness. Anselmo's head was moving up and down more and more insistently. Finally, Boatman answered in a voice nobody could hear.

"Speak louder," whispered Anselmo across the table to his prize witness.

"Speak up," the deputy ordered. "The jury wants to hear your answer." It was absurd for a man with such a barrel chest to speak in a voice that carried no meaning or conviction.

"Yes, sir," said Boatman.

"Mrs. Green shot first?" the deputy insisted as if any lingering doubt in anybody's mind must now be ended. As he rocked his head knowingly, his eyes fell by design on Jefferson Wilkes who sat facing him at the end of the table, then on Jesse and from one face to another of Anna Mae's friends and neighbors and finally on Anna Mae herself.

"Yes, sir," whispered Boatman in the terrible silence.

That settled the case, the deputy indicated with a wave of his hand to the jury.

Anselmo put a cigar between his teeth and began to play with his lighter as if the inquest was over and the verdict already in the bag.

Boatman shuffled back across the room like a sack of flour on legs. There was nothing left of the old prizefighter's bounce in his step or swing in his shoulders. His scar gleamed like an exposed vein.

As Lou watched him slump down between the two cops, then start forward from the back of the bench, he caught Jesse's eyes accusing him, "You can see for yourself the guy taken a beating. They made him say what they want."

If only the past could be unrolled again, if only Lou's ma could step back into life, if only Anna Mae had never raised that gun against her, if only his ma— Lou found himself wishing impossible things as he lowered his eyes away from Jesse's.

If only he and Jesse were at Farmway and this terrible thing had never happened. It was the coffee hour. If only they were eating one of Baldy's stale buns together!

"I must warn you," the deputy was speaking to Anna Mae now, "everything you say under oath will be entered as evidence." He explained how the state's attorney would review the evidence, then pass it on to grand jury investigation and eventual trial in criminal court. "Now is there anything you want to say?" He spoke as if he had lowered a rope over Anna Mae's shoulders.

"Yes." Anna Mae stood up. When a policewoman offered to assist her, she smiled and said, "I ain't no cripple, honey."

Lou watched her make her way alone to the head of the table, a woman without fear or self-pity. Her face was puckered up from the pain of movement, so bleached of color and grey that her freckles stood out in sharp black points. One arm hung in a sling and her shoulder was a lump of bandages.

Anna Mae swore to tell the truth, then sat down across the table from Anselmo. Her eyes sharpened against him with a meaning that was plain to Lou, "You gonna see for yourself can you boss the whole show." She stared at Anselmo as if he was a pygmy of a man.

Anselmo had called her a savage. But she seemed now in her own defence to have great dignity and strength, a different woman from the one who had faced Lou and his mother like a tigress the day they had gone down to the basement to offer to lower the Roberts' rent. Instinctively, Lou found himself looking at Anselmo with contempt the way Anna Mae did. And as Lou listened to the deputy's questions, he wondered if a white woman would get the same gruff handling. He couldn't help remembering what Jesse had said the previous afternoon, "She's black. That's her crime!"

"You say you're a nurse," the deputy harrassed her, "and yet you used this weapon to fire the fatal shot at the deceased?" He picked up the thirty-two caliber pistol from his desk, turned it over and around between his fingers, and shook his head as if he couldn't believe a woman whose job was to save lives could be so vicious as to take a life herself in cold blood.

"I had to defend myself," Anna Mae answered, staring back at the weapon.

She was either innocent or putting on a very clever act. "She'll have to pay for it," Lou muttered to Nina. But he had little feeling of anger left against her now. And as his eyes fell on her bandaged shoulder, he couldn't forget the pain he'd felt that night he battled for his life after his accident on the Yalu Road and for months afterwards in the hospital at San Antonio. And he couldn't help thinking of the way his ma had said, "Forgive me what I done," before she went over the hill.

"You had to defend yourself," the deputy repeated cynically as if all defendants said the same thing. "Now, Mrs. Green, to help the jury reach a decision, is there anything you could say—"

"That Boatman ain't told any part of the truth." Anna Mae wrenched her eyes from the gun to stare up at the deputy with a boldness that made him glance away. "Boatman's a damn liar," she shouted.

The deputy moved his hands outward in a gesture to the jury to mean that the case against the defendant had been hopeless enough before. Now, by shouting abusive names in a violent temper, she had sunk herself beyond all possible salvage.

All the same, the defendant's lawyer could ask her a few questions if he insisted. With a kind of gracious condescension, the deputy waved permission at Jefferson Wilkes with the gesture of a gloved hand holding a riding whip. "Counsel!"

Wilkes leaned forward in Anna Mae's defense, knotting and locking his fingers together. A mist of sweat came out across his forehead and the vertical grooves deepened between his eyes. But he spoke to Anna Mae quietly as if only two people were talking together trying to get at the real cause of what happened.

He asked her why she was in her sister's flat, and Anna Mae told him it was her sister's anniversary and she was minding her babies.

Anna Mae was breathing heavily as she watched the deputy continue to turn the gun over and around between his fingers.

"Were you wounded by the first shot?" Wilkes went on.

"The first shot bust out through the window over my head," Anna Mae answered. "I told Miss Biomchi, 'Go on home, or something terrible's gonna happen.' But she was waving that gun like crazy—"

"And the second time, she hit you?"

"While I was standin' on the bed, tryin' to reach for my own protection."

"I see. The shot entered your shoulder from behind?"

"That's right."

For an instant Wilkes glanced up at the deputy and across at the jurors to be sure the significance of Anna Mae's answer registered with them. And he studied Anselmo's expression and Lou's before he went on to his next question.

"Do you think Mrs. Bianchi came down with deliberate purpose—"

"To shoot?" Anna Mae shook her head. "She liked to throw her weight around, show who was boss around there. She figured, 'I'm gonna scare that Anna Mae Green till she never shows her face around here again.' But I don't scare that easy. When she couldn't make me go on out, that's when she went mad crazy."

"It's facts we want, not opinions," said the deputy.

"Why was she angry with you?" Wilkes went on in spite of the interruption.

"Down at the bottom of it, she was scared to lose her money. See, we was gonna drag her up to the judge on triple damages this morning, me and some of the folks." Anna Mae glanced down at Mrs. Martin and Mrs. Osborne as she went on, "Biomchi charged us all three times over and above the ceiling rent. She was scared we was gonna get it all back."

"Counsel," the deputy interrupted, "we can't spend all day on details."

"Did she say anything to you after what happened?" Wilkes persisted.

"Yes—" Anna Mae hesitated. She turned to glance around at Lou. Anselmo was watching her like a panther.

"Something must have come between her and her boy. When she was down on the floor, she was cryin', 'My son, oh my Luigi!' Like she'd done something terrible she never wanted him to know."

The only sound in the inquest room was the buzzing of the flies weaving in and out the windows over the heads of the jurors. In the words Anna Mae repeated, Lou could hear the very sound of his mother's voice as if she was blaming herself for what had happened. Anna Mae was staring at Lou, so were Jesse and all the people in the room, as the deputy gave the nod to Anselmo.

"What do you think, Lou?" asked Nina profoundly disturbed by Anna Mae's defense.

"I don't know what to think." Lou bowed his head and clasped his hands between his knees, while Anselmo fired his first question at Anna Mae.

"Now, Mrs. Green, tell me, did you or your sister, or both of you together, ever refuse to pay Mrs. Bianchi the rent when she called for it?" Anselmo leaned forward across the table to try to intimidate Anna Mae.

But she, too, thrust her head forward till her face was only a few inches from his and shouted, "Miss Biomchi wouldn't give no receipt."

"Answer his question," the deputy ordered.

Anna Mae looked up surprised at him. "I ain't answered his question?"

"Tell the deputy, Mrs. Green, and the jury—" Anselmo rapped his knuckles on the table "—why did you keep a gun on the shelf above the bed?" He banged out his question like an explosive.

"A black woman gotta have her own protection." Anna Mae

was looking down at Wilkes and behind Wilkes at her friends and neighbors. "You know why that is—"

"That's right," Mrs. Osborne and Mrs. Martin responded together.

"Mrs. Green," Anselmo demanded, "why did the court order you to vacate the premises at 1250 Pioneer Street?"

"It was a frame on me." Anna Mae slapped her words at Anselmo. "And you was giving her advice all the time. You told her to turn off the lights and gas when the babies was freezing, bust the plumbing—" Anna Mae shouted with indignation.

Instead of being cornered by Anselmo's questions, she was turning them back against him, hounding him off the very ground he had chosen for the kill.

"Answer my question, Mrs. Green. It was on conviction for disorderly conduct, because you had a number of men in your room—"

"The Lord's gonna punish them," Anna Mae cut him off. Then, in a quiet voice as if she understood he was trying to make her lose her temper by publicly shaming her, she went on, "And the Lord's gonna punish you, too, for all that you have the law on your side. Because you paid them yourself to make false witness."

Anselmo had to fight with himself to hold in his own temper now. "Since you won't answer my other questions, for reasons best known to yourself, maybe you'll oblige the deputy and jury by answering this one," he shouted in a cold rage. "Why, after the judge's order, did you return to 1250 last Friday and lay a trap for Mrs. Bianchi so that you could murder—"

"It's a goddam lie!" In Anna Mae's shout burned the anger of a lifetime against the injustices done to her and her people.

But Anselmo was quick to turn her violent outburst against her. "From Mrs. Green's behavior at this inquest, Mr. Deputy and Members of the Jury, I think you can get some idea of what the deceased had to put up with in the last moments of her life."

Anselmo had achieved his purpose and was once more confident of winning an indictment for murder and wiping Anna Mae out of existence. He glanced at Lou with a tragic smile as if any lingering doubt could now be washed clean out of mind. "What insolence!" he went on, "What hatred! What blasphemy!"

Anselmo's eyes travelled arrogantly from face to face of the friends and neighbors of Anna Mae Green. Let them beware of what would happen to them, too, and beyond them to the whole Negro community in the city if they should step out of line.

"She hasn't got a chance," Nina sighed. "But Lou, she don't sound—" her whisper trailed off in uncertainty.

Anna Mae was not beaten down the way Nina thought. She stood up and shouted over the heads of the reporters at Charlene and Randy, "You tell 'em, babies, who started the shootin'. You seen it."

Randy shrank to one side to clutch her mother's arm and bury her face away out of sight, but Charlene had eyes only for Anna Mae. "Miss Biomchi." Charlene's answer shot up in terror as she remembered how the landlady had opened fire on her Auntie Mae, the person next to her mother and father she loved best in the world. "She tooken her gun, bang, bang, bang!"

Everybody in the inquest room was staring at Charlene as she stood facing the deputy and the jury, a nine year old girl in a print dress and butterfly ribbons.

"At's telling 'em, baby," said Anna Mae proudly. "You gonna save my life."

The people around Charlene were stirring and muttering. "She speaks truth." "That's right!" "Let the girl tell about it." "The Lord put the words into her mouth."

"Lou—" Nina was pulling at his arm "—do you think they coached the child—"

"To scream like that?" Lou shook his head, ashamed now to look in Jesse's direction.

"Then you think Jesse was right when he said she was only defending herself?"

"Could be," he muttered lowering his head between his fists.

The procedure of the inquest itself was now on trial. Anna Mae had broken through the red tape to give the truth a chance to bust out free in the words of a child. In this unforeseen situation, the deputy examined the faces in the room below him, while he debated with himself what to do.

But Anselmo was in no doubt. "This is outrageous, deputy. I insist you compel the defendant to observe the rules of procedure."

"Sit down," said the deputy angrily to Anna Mae. He made a motion to the clerks and reporters that the interruption was off the record.

"In view of the circumstances, deputy, since Mrs. Green would not answer my questions and during the interrogating has shown the most barefaced contempt for these official proceedings, and also in view of these planned interruptions, I ask permission to make a statement to the jury which I am sure will assist them in reaching a verdict."

Anselmo didn't wait for the deputy's permission, but turned to face the old men by the window. "What was Mrs. Green doing at 1250 Pioneer Street last Friday evening?" he asked in a tone of prosecuting attorney schooled by years in the courtroom to insinuate, to bully, and to destroy. "Mrs. Green knew the deceased would collect the rents on Friday. Filled with hate and spite, Mrs. Green came there, I tell you, with deliberate purpose."

Anselmo wheeled and stood up at the same time to face the jury at closer quarters. He went on speaking as if the inquest had turned into a trial for murder. "Members of the jury it's time we put the record straight. Mrs. Green set a trap for Mrs. Bianchi with malice aforethought." Anselmo clenched and unclenched his fingers as if he could hardly restrain himself from tearing Anna Mae to pieces. In a hoarse whisper he said, "This woman murdered Mrs. Bianchi in cold blood!"

Over the objections of Wilkes and the uneasy rapping of the deputy's knuckles on the desk, Anselmo raised his voice to roar out in a frenzy of indignation, "She committed one of the most savage crimes in the annals of this city. If you were to exonerate this woman on the basis of a child's scream of fright because that child was coached to tell a lie, then no person's life would be safe and no person's property inviolate from this moment on. It would mean the end of law itself and human society."

Anselmo spoke as if he was now a hundred percent sure of winning a verdict of murder. "Only one course is open to you, members of the jury. That is: to commit the doer of this crime to eventual justice in criminal court."

The deputy and members of the jury nodded an amen as if Anselmo had now put the record straight.

#6

In the audience, a hum of protest began to swell and fill the inquest room. And it assumed a voice, "Your honor!"

Lou turned to see Jesse stand up pushing himself taller with his fists on the back of the bench in front.

"What is the purpose of this interruption?" the deputy asked in a tone to freeze Jesse out.

"That girl told you the truth. Mrs. Green didn't do no crime."

"What's your name?" the deputy asked with a weary gruffness.

"Jesse Williams." Jesse stood up tall and massive, ready to battle for the life of Anna Mae Green. The boom in his voice torpedoed Anselmo's smile of victory.

"I object to this man using this inquest as a sounding board for his personal opinions." Anselmo registered his objection with a blow on the table. Lou could see that Anselmo was deeply concerned as if Jesse was the one person he actually feared might swing the verdict.

"Isn't this the man who refused to make a statement to the police?" Anselmo shouted his question across the room at the detective from the homicide squad.

The detective raised his chin with a gesture of contempt. "That's him all right."

"I want to object." The dry, sharp voice of Wilkes spoke out for Jesse. "If Mr. Williams has any evidence which will help the jury arrive at a decision, then, as I understand it, it's not only his right but his duty to bring it forward. Is not that the case, Mr. Deputy?"

"Of course, of course," said the deputy impatient now with Wilkes for putting him on the spot and with Anselmo for letting the whole inquest get out of hand.

"Mr. Williams is a veteran of World War II and of the Korean conflict," Wilkes insisted, "a man with a distinguished service record."

"Were you an eyewitness of the occurrence?" the deputy asked Jesse.

"Your honor—" Jesse began.

"Don't elevate me," the deputy said sarcastically with a private smile for Anselmo. "Save that for the judge. I'm a deputy."

"OK then, deputy." Jesse wasn't going to be thrown by a little ridicule. "I was down in the basement with Mrs. Green and the kids just a few minutes before the shootin' started. They were talkin' all about the land they was gonna buy back home in Mississippi without anybody bossin' them around—"

"Now, Mr. Williams—" The deputy smiled at the jury as if they had to expect these irrelevant remarks from ignorant people. "Please answer my question."

But Jesse went right on. "They was gonna buy that land from the triple damages the landlady overcharged. Mrs. Green was one hundred percent sure she was gonna whip Mrs. Bianchi in court today. Mrs. Martin and Mrs. Osborne here were in on that deal with her too." He turned around to gesture at the two women.

"That's right," said Mrs. Martin.

"That's truth you're telling 'em, Jesse," said Mrs. Osborne.

"Now why would Mrs. Green wanta start the shootin'?" Jesse asked. "She didn't have no reason. She was gonna win, understand? A person only gonna pull a gun when she's whipped, specially a colored woman who knows she'd get the short end of things."

"But you didn't answer my question. Were you an eyewitness?" the deputy demanded.

"That's what I'm coming to," said Jesse. "I heard the shootin'. And I saw where the shots went through the window, the stove, and the wall behind Mrs. Green. There were six shots from one gun and only one from the other."

"You mean you could tell the difference?" The deputy shook his head with a sceptical smile.

"Sure. I been in the army, Mr. Deputy. If I couldn't tell the difference between a twenty-two and a thirty-two—"

"All right, all right. But you still didn't answer my question."

"All I'm telling you," Jesse insisted, "the thirty-two shot once at the end and that was Anna Mae Green's gun." There was general astonishment in the inquest room and a shifting of position in the momentary silence. Jesse turned to look squarely at Lou.

Anselmo jumped up and waved his fist at Jesse before he could beat down the anger inside him. "Mr. Deputy, I demand that we follow inquest procedure. This man is entirely out of order. He wasn't sworn in—"

The deputy nodded as if Anselmo was in the right. "I'll have to ask you to sit down." When Jesse stood his ground, the deputy's voice grew harsh. "Otherwise, I shall have to ask the officer to remove you from the room for creating a disturbance."

"Objection!" shouted Wilkes. But the deputy overruled him. At the same time, he made an erasing gesture to the clerks to indicate that since Jesse was not sworn in nothing he said should be entered in the record.

With a bitter smile at Lou, Jesse began to sit down. Gripping the back of the bench ahead, he rounded his knuckled fist into the middle of Boatman's back. Boatman started forward, groaning with pain. He began to cry and hide his eyes in his fists, a bulky prizefighter of a man, his humanity beaten to the ground.

In a voice loud enough for everybody in the room to hear, Jesse muttered, "Lou Bianchi can tell you which way Boatman is lying."

Vico leaned over to put a restraining arm on Lou's shoulder and whisper, "Don't let him provoke you, buddy. You know he's a goddam liar."

"Maybe he tells the truth," said Pete.

"They beat up Boatman," said Nina as if that made all the difference in the world. Then she asked sharply, "Lou, could you tell the difference between a twenty-two and a thirty-two?"

"Yeh," he nodded.

"Then the woman's innocent?" Nina asked as if she was hoping and fearing at the same time.

"I'm afraid she is." Lou's eyes were pits of misery.

Nina put her hand through his arm and squeezed close to him. "What are you going to do?" she whispered.

Lou turned his eyes up to the ceiling to steady himself. "I dunno." His head moved mechanically back and forth as if at last he had to believe his ma had shot first. "She must have gone off the deep end, Nina."

Anselmo must have framed Anna Mae Green for the second time. All his manoevers began to fit into one picture as Lou thought about them. Anselmo had made him believe in the first place his mother was murdered. At the very end she had said, "Holy Mother of God, forgive me what I done." Anselmo had insisted it was her religion and naturally she would ask forgiveness of her sins before she passed. But that didn't explain the agony of her expression in the last moment of her life—or the hope.

"Are you sure?" Nina was asking him like the voice of his conscience.

"Ma said she was sorry, Nina. That's what she must have meant. But Anselmo twisted everything around. And what did he care for her?"

"You gotta say something, Lou." Nina whispered.

Only a couple of hours after his mother was dead, Anselmo came swooping down on her papers like a vulture.

"I should have whammed straight into him," Lou muttered as he listened to the coroner's physician read the report on the physical causes of his mother's death. His anger towered against Anselmo. "She didn't need to die—if I'd only seen it straight. How far off the beam he took her. She couldn't help herself."

When the clerk sat down, the deputy began to instruct the jury: "In view of the numerous interruptions here this morning, I must point out to the members of the jury that only sworn testimony can be admitted as evidence. Furthermore, if there is the slightest suspicion that a crime caused or contributed to the death of the deceased it is your duty to record that suspicion in rendering your verdict." The deputy was pressing for an indictment for murder while Anselmo, at his right hand, nodded serenely with the assurance that a long battle had been won.

If Lou knuckled under to Anselmo now, he would never have enough respect left for himself to raise his eyes from the floor. He had to push himself up with his hands fiercely gripping the back of the seat ahead. His heart throbbed in his throat, and he felt the emptiness of fear in his chest, the way he had always felt in battle. He stood up to his full height and said, even if he could only get the words out in a whisper, "On a point of order, Mr. Deputy—"

As Lou spoke, he saw Anselmo's face in profile, his nose sharp as the beak of an eagle, turn savagely—his eyes angry and beady, the eyes of a bird who was afraid of missing his prey.

"You are the son of the deceased?" the deputy asked in confusion.

"Yes," said Lou. "I wanta testify because I don't think this Mrs. Green is guilty."

For an instant, Anselmo seemed surprised out of speech. Then he jumped up. "This is terrible for young Bianchi, you understand—" he appealed to the deputy with his finger at his own temple to indicate that Lou's mind was affected. "Wounded in Korea, six months on his back in hospital. Concussion!" Anselmo jerked his words out. "And now this terrible shock. I demand a continuance."

"My son, he ain't got nothing wrong with his head," Pete spoke out angrily as he stood up beside Lou. "He speaks the truth."

"Let him talk," Anna Mae shouted out.

"Let him speak," came from Wilkes and Jesse and Charles and Geneva Roberts and their friends and neighbors in a swelling protest.

The deputy steadied his forehead with one hand while trying to mop the sweat off his face with the other. His collar was wilted down around his neck.

When Anselmo saw the deputy was hesitating because the people had taken things into their own hands, he changed his request. "Mr. Deputy, a recess," he said in a voice that was low-pitched and tense with a kind of desperation. The moment before, he was confident of winning a conviction. Now, his only hope was to talk to Lou alone.

"Do you wish to take the witness stand?" the deputy asked wearily staring over Anselmo's head at Lou.

Lou nodded.

"All right, then." The deputy spoke as if he would never want to go through the proceedings of that day again. "But first," he said, standing up to assert his authority and give Anselmo a chance to bring Lou back to his senses, "I'll call a ten minute recess."

#7

Before Anselmo could reach Lou, Jesse had already stepped across the aisle to grip his hand. "You're OK," he said.

Then Anselmo was surrounding Lou's shoulder with his arm, brotherly again. "Step outside with me for a minute, Lou-boy. I got something important—"

"You got anything to say, say it and get it over with." Shaking Anselmo's arm from his shoulder, Lou stood facing him across the back of the bench, still gripping Jesse by the hand.

"But for Christ sake, fellow, it's about your own mother—"

"You wasn't ever worried about her, Anselmo. Or you wouldn't have started her doing crooked things. It's yourself, number one, that's all you think about," said Lou savagely. "You're a disgrace to our people!"

"Well, you goddam little son-of-a-bitch!" Anselmo blasted at Lou. "And I thought you were white!"

Anselmo's cheeks and eyes were flaming with anger as he went stamping back to his place at the end of the table. He began to shuffle through his papers and was stuffing them into his briefcase when the deputy called the inquest back to order.

"But Lou, think what you're doing to our mother's memory," Della whispered in a last indignant protest.

"He's going to put the record straight for her," said Nina in a flash of anger at Della. "Can't you understand, he doesn't want a woman who was only defending herself—"

"Defending herself!" Della scoffed and turned her back on Nina and Lou.

"Luigi Bianchi!" the clerk called out and summoned him to step up to the witness chair.

The deputy swore him in, then asked in a neutral tone, "You wish to give testimony?"

"Yes," Lou said in a firm voice. "I came here this morning because I believed a crime was committed against my ma. I wanted to see the guilty person get what was coming. But the guilty one is not Mrs. Green. Even if all the things said here this morning aren't legal evidence, all the same they tell the story. The only witness was beaten—"

The deputy rapped his gavel sharply.

"The kid here," Lou went on angrily, "well, you can't coach a child to scream like that. And anybody who's been out in Korea can tell the difference between a twenty-two and a thirty-two. But I'm not up here to talk about these things. Just to tell you what my ma said before she went over the hill. She said she was sorry for what she done. And it's clear as day to me now what she meant. It wasn't like her in the first place to carry a gun. But she came under the influence—" Lou stared straight across in Anselmo's face.

"Lou, for God's sake," Anselmo muttered, "think of what you're saying about your ma, that she was a killer!"

"She came under the influence of a big shot." Lou went on staring at Anselmo as if his words were meaningless. "He showed her how to do crooked things. She wanted what they'd get her—a big house up Lincoln Park. In the last days of her life, she didn't act like herself. My ma was the best ma a guy could ever want. But since I came home from Korea, she acted like she was afraid of somebody, like she didn't have a mind of her own no more. She was all skin and bones, eaten up with worry. But just before she passed, she seemed to be done with it all. She grabbed my hand like she wanted to set the record straight. She said she was sorry for what she done. She prayed to the Holy Mother to forgive her. She didn't want an innocent woman to burn in the electric chair."

Lou pressed his face between his fists.

He heard the deputy advise the jury to give due consideration to the additional evidence.

And then across a chasm of time, a moment or an age, he heard the chairman of the jury announce the verdict: Homicide in self-defense.

When Lou looked up, he saw Geneva Roberts embracing Anna Mae and crying with happiness while the red ribbons of Charlene and Randy were dancing in circles around them. She was a brave woman, Anna Mae Green, and free again.

Lou glanced toward the door, but Anselmo and Della had already gone. And Mrs. Santiano and Nellie De Rocco and Vico and most of Lou's other friends and relatives followed them. He saw Father Guidarello stalk out, but young Father Antonelli sat waiting. And Pete was waiting for him and Jesse. And Jesse's side of the room was still filled with friends and neighbors talking and smiling.

Down at the end of the room, old Pagliani was holding Nina by the arm and ordering her to the door. But nobody ordered Nina around without getting the worst of it. When Lou saw her wrench her arm away from her father, he smiled and went down the aisle to meet her.